THE
DARK
BEFORE
LIGHT

COPYRIGHT

THE DARK BEFORE LIGHT

L.M. HALLORAN

We only appreciate the dawn because of the night that precedes it, and we only survive the night because of the moon and stars.

— Kieran Hayes

For the queens
whose kings kneel
like good boys

PROLOGUE

TALIA

GALWAY, IRELAND

"Oi! You lost?"

The voice, close and unexpected in a place I thought I was utterly alone, causes me to gasp so hard I suck in rain and cough. My heart takes off, adrenaline streaking like lightning through my veins. I jump to my feet. Dizziness makes me sway, my hip knocking against waist-high stone.

Two identical young men scowl at me from ten feet away. Rough-looking sorts, standing so close they look like conjoined twins. They wear matching, hooded black sweatshirts, holey jeans with dirty cuffs, and scuffed, muddy black boots. Dark hair curls damply around their narrow, pale cheeks. Under straight black brows, their eyes are blue. Maybe gray—the fading daylight makes it hard to tell. They're extremely tall and slender, with that perpetually hungry look teenage boys have. They can't be much older than me.

I should be running but can't remember why. The more I stare at them, rapt and still swaying, the less dangerous they appear. Something about them makes me aware of every fast beat of my heart. I can almost hear my sister's excited, hormone-soaked whispers and wonder if I'm finally—for the first time in my fourteen years of life—experiencing sexual attraction.

As I mull on this revelation, the boys lift damp, hand-rolled cigarettes to their mouths, suck deeply, and exhale identical streams of chalky-blue smoke. Licking their full lower lips, they gather a bit of escaped tobacco on their tongues before spitting it to the side.

This must be some weird performance art.

"You look like a wet hummingbird," they say, but even though both of their mouths move, I only hear one voice. The same lilting tenor I heard before. Logic surfaces like a whale breaching in the sea of alcohol that is my brain.

Wait.

Oh.

I blink rapidly, squinting, and the two figures resolve into one. Not twins, after all. A giggle escapes me. Mortified, I slap a hand to my mouth, then wince as my braces grind against delicate flesh. The boy makes a face like he thinks I might be crazy and drops the dark stub of his cigarette to the ground.

Before I can stop myself, I say, "You shouldn't litter."

He grunts. "You shouldn't be hammered and wandering around a graveyard at dusk, Birdie, but here we are."

My thoughts hopscotch over his words, landing hard on the one making my face heat. "My name isn't Birdie."

He shrugs. "It is now. You'd better sit back down before you fall, *Birdie*."

My head swims and my knees weaken, depositing my ass on soggy grass. I slump against the gravestone at my back and close my eyes. My senses melt, softening and expanding. Raindrops tickle my face with a hundred tiny kisses.

Sudden pressure along my right side brings my eyes open a crack. At the sight of the boy so close, his shoulder and arm touching mine, shock ripples through me. But it's muffled by something brighter that feels like someone lit a New Year's Eve sparkler in my stomach. A sputtering, stubborn sensation I've never felt before. But I've also never been this close to a boy who looks like this one.

He gazes straight ahead, a tiny, knowing smirk on his face. He's aware I'm ogling him and is amused. I'm suddenly grateful for the shots my sister gave me. Finding my way back to the hotel in town and dealing with my parents—probably distraught by now since Olivia told them we were going for a short walk—is a problem for future me. Present, drunk-me is glad I don't care if this boy knows I think he's hot.

I can't stop staring at the sweep of long, sooty lashes as he blinks. The faint freckles on his nose and blade-like cheek-bones. The way a raindrop condenses at the tapered edge of one eyebrow, rolls downward, and is caught by a piece of dark hair on his cheek. There's an indent beneath his lower lip, almost like a dimple. A promise of facial hair shadows his jawline and chin.

He shifts a little, hooking one boot over the other, long legs crossed casually on the soaked grass like the objective misery of wet jeans can't touch him. The movement makes our arms press more firmly together. A familiar smell teases through the thick petrichor in the air. It takes me a few seconds to place the scent and where I've smelled it before—on my sister when she sneaks in late after partying with her friends.

He wasn't smoking a cigarette.

"Do you have another joint?" I try to mimic Olivia's flirtatious, confident voice, but the words are high-pitched and alarmingly slurred.

His head swivels to me, eyes bright with mirth. "Not a chance, Birdie."

I sway toward him, caught in the undertow of his eyes. Their color is as unique as the rest of him—shifting ocean currents with hints of gray. I barely notice their glassy sheen or bloodshot sclera.

"How old are you?" I ask, then wince. I hadn't given my mouth permission to say that.

His smirk returns. "Eighteen."

The same age as my sister. She'd *die* to sit next to this boy.

For a second, I feel guilty that I get to look at him up close and she doesn't. Then I remember why I'm lost and soaking wet in a graveyard in Galway, Ireland to begin with. Because my sister lives to humiliate and discard me.

"What brings a wee bird out of her nest to fly among the dead this fine evening?"

His voice is so dry I can't tell if he's making fun of me or not. I've never heard anyone talk like him. Then again, in the week my family has been touring Ireland by car, I haven't had a single one-on-one conversation with a local past generic, service-oriented pleasantries. Maybe they all converse in lines of satirical poetry.

Or maybe he's as high as I am drunk.

"Vacation," I mumble.

He chuckles, a manly sound that percolates sluggishly through my body, and taps his chin with a long, pale finger. His palms are big like he hasn't stopped growing yet. I've never noticed a boy's hands before.

"Let me guess where the bird flew from." He squints at me, taking in my baggy sweatshirt, the black joggers on my thick legs, and the tasseled ankle boots that are hand-me-downs from Olivia and years past trendy. He snaps his fingers suddenly. "California!"

My sullen silence makes a smile overtake his face. It's blinding but fades fast. An eclipse.

"Go on then, tell me."

I frown. "Tell you what?"

"Why your eyes are so angry and sad."

My heart jackknifes, slicing as it goes and spilling blood into my cheeks. "What?" I squeak.

His stare is heavy. Penetrating. Not exactly kind but not condemning, either, like he knows my problems are those of privilege but thinks they're still valid. This boy, with his tattered jeans and sweatshirt with too-short sleeves, wants me to unburden myself.

It occurs to me with syrupy certainty that this is the most terrifying, humbling, and exhilarating moment of my life.

"This is your villain origin story, Birdie," he says in a voice that's my new favorite song. "The moment you confront who you are and decide to be someone else. Tell me."

As the sky grows darker overhead and the rain keeps falling like a rippling veil between us and the rest of the world, I tell him everything. How my parents are getting divorced but this trip was already planned. How awful and awkward it's been with them trying so hard to act normal while they can barely stand to look at each other.

How over the last two years, my sister has become a pretentious, vain bitch who treats me like a pet or a slave depending on her mood. I tell him what happened tonight—how when she asked me to go for a walk, I was stupidly excited she wanted to spend time with me. How she dragged me into a pub and stowed me in a dark corner before ordering four shots of whiskey from the bar. How a group of boys flocked to our table—to *her*—and I fell for her act when she introduced me like I mattered, telling them I was the coolest sister in the world.

I wanted so badly for that to be true that when she shoved two of the shots at me, I drank them one after the other. But they were disgusting, so disgusting, and afterward I had to hold my hands to my mouth to keep from throwing up all over the table. My sister laughed, the boys laughed, they all laughed at the awkward, mousey girl who wasn't cool at all. Then Olivia did her own shots—easily, perfectly—and told the boys to take her somewhere better, leaving me without a glance or a goodbye. The bartender, noticing me alone at a table of empty shot glasses, panicked and shoved me outside. It took twenty minutes of stumbling back to the hotel for me to realize I was going the wrong direction. The graveyard called to me because no one here can laugh.

I tell him how I'm bullied at school and have no friends because I skipped two grades and am still at the top of my class. How I spend lunches alone, my head stuck in a book, and even the nerds won't talk to me because I'm too weird for them.

Sometimes I feel like there's a monster inside me trying to get out, clawing at my skin from beneath. And I don't feel like I fit anywhere in the world.

"I'll never fit anywhere," I finish in a cracked whisper.

My confessor is silent. The encroaching darkness obscures his expression, but I can tell his eyes are closed. For a second, I think he fell asleep, and the devastation I feel is so violent, so encompassing, that I make a small, wounded noise.

His head swivels in my direction, eyes like dark pits but alert. They suck the remains of daylight, shimmering. Stars on a midnight sea.

"Do you know how I know you'll be okay?"

I can barely speak over the relief clogging my throat. "How?"

A cold finger taps the end of my nose. "Because I was wrong. You're not a bird, after all. You're a lioness. A queen of the jungle still growing her claws. Hold fast, Birdie. Someday the world will kneel to you."

I stare at him until my vision blurs and I'm forced to blink. Tears or rain gather on my lower lashes. My throat aches as I ask, "Even you?"

He doesn't smile, but I feel his delight. "Maybe even me."

Wind stirs around us. All at once, my body screams with complaints. I'm soaking wet, freezing, tired, and hungry. A shiver wracks me. My teeth start chattering. My head pounds.

He climbs to his feet, pale palm outstretched between us. "Up you go. I'll walk you back to your hotel."

His hand swallows mine and he lifts me easily to my feet. I stumble and he laughs, catching me with his other hand on my shoulder before I face-plant into his chest.

"You'll start feelin' better once we walk a bit. What's the name of the place you're staying?"

I tell him, knowing it means the end of us but powerless

to stop it from happening. His fingers slip away from mine. I hate the way my hand feels without them. Small and pointless.

He turns and strides toward the entrance of the graveyard, skirting trees and gravestones like he has night vision. I totter after him, half-running to keep up with his long legs.

In no time at all—seconds, it feels like—we walk down a familiar cobbled street and halt outside a green awning. The rain has stopped. We're not alone anymore. It's too bright and loud. I want to go back to the graveyard. I want to ask him to tell me, *tell me everything, too*. Why he was there. What he dreams about.

But it's too late.

I don't feel like a lion or even a bird, each free in ways I can't imagine. I'm afraid to face him, to be exposed physically the way I'm already exposed emotionally. He's eighteen and beautiful. I'm fourteen and not. Maybe I looked okay in the half-light and shadows. But now he'll see my lank, wet bangs and frizzy hair. My mouth, puffy from the braces behind it. My too-thick eyebrows. The roll of fat beneath my chin my mom says I'll grow out of. The pimples that appeared on my face this morning, big and red.

The only thing that could make this moment worse would be my sister suddenly appearing in all her tanned, lithe, clear-skinned glory. But the universe must deem me worthy of pity because she's nowhere to be seen. It's just the two of us. Not alone anymore but still together, the last grains of us draining through the hourglass.

"Maybe I'll see you in California one day," he says softly.

I can't help looking at him. Unsurprisingly, he makes waterlogged look like a fashion choice, even with the frayed hem of his hood sitting askew on his forehead.

"California?" I echo.

"That's the plan," he says, smiling slightly. "I'm going to wake up to palm trees and beaches every day while I make my mark. Someday the world will kneel to me, too."

I believe him.

"Not you, though," he adds with a wink. "Equals don't kneel."

"I think they do," I whisper, my face flaming. "But only to each other."

He grins. "Guess we'll find out." Touching an imaginary hat, he tilts his head. "Enjoy your stay in Ireland. And maybe lay off the whiskey until your claws grow in."

He turns and walks away.

Panicked, I blurt, "Wait! What's your name?"

He swivels toward me but keeps walking, his backward steps preternaturally confident over the uneven cobblestones. People stream around him like water around a boulder. I wonder if he realizes the world already sees him—makes way for him—and that's why he knows they'll kneel.

"Kieran Hayes," he says, nearly shouting.

"I'm—"

"Birdie!" he interrupts with a grin. "Your name is Birdie." Then he turns a corner and disappears.

CHAPTER 1

TALIA

17 YEARS LATER

I'm about to take a bite of my favorite omelet in the world, courtesy of my favorite café in Santa Monica, when my phone buzzes on the table. It shimmies over the polished wood surface, heading toward the edge. Ignoring its impeding demise, I shove my fork in my mouth and flavors explode on my tongue.

I groan. "I'm convinced Rhubarb's kitchen runs on magic dust."

My breakfast date, Mia, laughs and snatches my phone before it can launch itself to the floor. Placing it safely on a napkin, she glances at the screen.

"Don't tell me who it is," I say quickly, but my mouth is

full again and the words come out garbled except for "tell" and "who."

"Gail Katz," Mia says helpfully.

I blink in surprise and swallow. "That's a name I haven't heard in a long time." I load up my fork with another piece of heaven and shrug. "She'll leave a voicemail."

The buzzing thankfully stops, though no voicemail arrives. Stuffing down my curiosity, I focus on catching up with Mia. I relish our standing monthly breakfasts, especially now that they have an expiration date—or at least an upcoming hiatus.

As Mia shifts in her chair and winces, I ask, "And how's the tiny terror treating his mama today?"

Her smile is radiant as she rubs a hand over her rounded belly. "Currently tap-dancing on my bladder."

I make a face. "That sounds awful—I mean, so happy for you."

She laughs, and my phone starts buzzing again. We look down at the same time to see the caller. *Gail Katz.*

"Weird," I mutter.

The phone stops buzzing. Once again, there's no voicemail.

Mia gives me a concerned look. "You should call her back. What if she can't leave a message or text for some reason?"

I sigh and grab the phone. Mia is a counselor at a middle school and her husband, Leo, is a gifted psychiatrist. Bleeding hearts, the both of them.

I scoot back my chair and stand. "Fine, but only because I can't say no to a pregnant woman. Be right back."

She waves me off. "I know the drill."

Stepping out of our secluded corner, beautifully screened by potted trees, I stride purposefully across the crowded restaurant toward the patio doors. Eyes follow me and whispers ripple in my wake, a recent development in my life and a giant hassle.

For the thousandth time in the last two weeks, I regret the charitable impulse that made me say yes to an interview with a tiny, online health blog. If I'd known the interviewer was going to warp my words for maximum shock value and pitch the resulting article to Buzzfeed, I never would have agreed.

Live and learn.

The patio is empty, the January temps keeping diners indoors. I take a deep breath of the ocean-scented breeze, then dial Gail. It rings twice before she answers.

"Talia, hi! I'm so sorry for calling twice. I should have left a voicemail or texted, but I panicked. Both times. Sorry."

I'm suddenly back in a cramped off-campus apartment at UCLA with the fastest talker I've ever met. It brings a smile to my face.

"Hey, Gail. How are you?"

"Um, good. I'm good." She giggles, a nervous burst of sound. "You're probably wondering why I called. Twice."

"A little, yeah. Not that it's not nice to hear from you."

"It is, isn't it? I mean, it's nice to hear your voice, too."

She hesitates, and I have a ten-year-old memory of her face flushing in embarrassment. "Sorry again. I'm not really sure how to say this."

"What's going on?" I ask gently.

"I need a favor. A big one." She takes a breath. "Long story short, my brother-in-law is in dire straits. His situation is unique, and, um—"

I frown as she falls silent. A few seconds later, I hear a door close.

"Gail?"

"Yes, sorry." She suddenly sounds like a different woman. Tired and stressed. "I heard my husband coming downstairs. He knows I'm calling someone who might be able to help, but it's a touchy subject. He's really worried about his brother."

I chew my lip, wishing I hadn't listened to Mia. "I'm really sorry about whatever's going on with your brother-in-law, but this isn't how I operate. If you want to pass along my information to him, feel free to do that. Full disclosure, though, I think my soonest appointment isn't until late March."

There's a long beat of silence, another indicator of maturity from a woman who rarely thought before she spoke.

"He can't wait that long," she says finally, her voice even softer. "I realize there's a risk I'm burning the bridge of our friendship, but I'm begging you, Talia. Help him. Please try."

My stomach sinks. Dropping my head back, I stare at the giant, spiky fronds of a nearby palm tree.

"My brother-in-law is Kieran Hayes. If you can see him today, we'll pay you triple your normal rate."

I barely register the second half of her statement. My ears ring, his name the reverberation of a mighty bell. Closing my eyes, I breathe past the sudden sensation of a free fall.

If it were anyone else...

Shit.

"Okay, Gail. I'll see him."

AFTER ENDING THE PHONE CALL—THAT went on long enough my fingers feel frozen and my hair damp—I return to the table to find Mia gone, the bill paid, and my leftovers packaged. I shoot her a text thanking her and apologizing, then head to the valet outside.

Fifteen minutes later, I unlock my front door and step inside my personal oasis. For the first time in memory, however, I don't feel any calming effects. The anxiousness that's been simmering since speaking with Gail spikes as I look at my watch.

I wasn't lying when I told her this isn't how I operate. I normally conduct two hour-long video calls with prospective clients prior to booking. An essential getting-to-know-you period. There are good reasons why, too. Only one out of three actually commit after they learn what I really do and what's required of them: complete surrender to the process.

But I don't have weeks or even hours to prep. I have fifty-six minutes until the man known as the King of Silicon Beach—Southern California's tech hub—arrives at my Marina Del Ray office.

The same man who, a lifetime ago, found a broken girl in a graveyard and told her someday the world would kneel to her.

Perching on the edge of my unmade bed with my phone, I open a browser and search his name for the first time in years. I scan various headlines before finally clicking on his Wikipedia page. My eyes linger on the included photos, even though they're the least important detail and I already know what he looks like. You'd have to be living under a rock not to.

All the mismatched beauty I saw in a scrawny boy has found its home on the face of a king. Tousled, longish dark hair, straight brows, and heavily-lashed, piercing blue eyes. Strong, defined jawline and blade-like cheekbones. Hawkish nose. Lips a touch too full and sensual for his face.

No one would call him classically handsome or something as mundane as attractive. But likewise, no one would deny he has that unquantifiable *something* that causes eyes to linger and makes cameras love him. Even in his professional uniform of custom suits, he looks unkempt and a little wild. Like a wolf wearing human skin. It's hard to stop staring at him, but I do.

I skim through his basic background, most of which I know. He's thirty-five. Born and raised in Galway, Ireland. One brother, Alistair, older by fifteen months. His father was a mechanical engineer, his mother a primary school teacher. Both are retired now. He received dual undergraduate degrees in Physics and Electrical Engineering from Oxford. Relocated to California at twenty-three to pursue a Master's in Microelectronics from Stanford.

At twenty-six, Kieran founded Lumitech with his brother. Nine years later, the cutting-edge microtechnology company has swallowed dozens of smaller startups and has a market cap of 150 billion dollars. They have contracts in automotive, aerospace, military, and industrial sectors, as well as a significant presence in mass-produced consumer electronics.

I open my Notes app and type:

- Highly intelligent and driven
- Strategist/analytical thinker
- Likely respects creative thinking
- Logic centered

I swipe back to Wikipedia. While Kieran's family, education, and professional history is significant in the sense it gives me basic insight into the way his mind works, it's not what I need. I find that under the section entitled Personal Life.

He met Elizabeth Foster, daughter of Hollywood producer Donovan Foster, seven years ago at a charity benefit. They dated for two months before marrying. Four years ago, she was tragically murdered in a carjacking ten minutes from their Beverly Hills home. There was an investigation but no arrests. The consensus of law enforcement was that she was in the wrong place at the wrong time, a victim of senseless violence.

I remember hearing about her death—it was all over the news for days—but I'd forgotten the circumstances. Another detail comes back to me, and a quick search confirms it: Elizabeth was two months pregnant when she died.

With a sympathetic grimace, I drop my phone to the bed and walk into the bathroom to shower. As I wash my hair, I think about what else Gail told me. What's not in his Wikipedia. That after his wife's death and a brief period of intense grieving, Kieran threw himself back into work and dating with shocking zeal. In the years since, he's maintained seventy-hour work weeks and an average of two to three "dates" a week. His productivity has been great for Lumitech's net worth, but his dating habits have given their PR team ulcers and generated enough NDAs to wallpaper a building.

Then, five weeks ago, he stopped... everything.

Stopped going to work. Stopped answering calls and emails. Leaving his house. Shaving and showering. And from Gail and Alistair's routine visits to his home, they suspect most of his meals are of the liquid variety.

The head of a massive, publicly traded tech company abruptly disappearing is not good for business. That the cause is a possible mental breakdown is immeasurably worse. So far, the company has managed to keep Kieran's absence on the down-low, but it's only a matter of time before the media catches wind. Alistair is desperate to help his brother and on the verge of a breakdown himself as he tries to fill Kieran's distinctive shoes at the helm of their company.

It's a rumbling mountaintop with the potential for an avalanche of multibillion-dollar proportions. And Gail believes I'm uniquely suited to stop it.

"I know you can get through to him, Talia. He's an out-of-the-box thinker, and there's no one more out-of-the-box than you."

Backhanded compliment or not, she's right. I'm firmly out-of-the-box. Sure, on paper I'm qualified to be his therapist. I have a PhD in Clinical Psychology from UCLA and have been a practicing psychologist for seven years. But to say I use my degree creatively is an understatement.

If it ever leaks that he's seeing *me* for therapy, we might as well ignite dynamite under the mountain ourselves.

CHAPTER 2

TALIA

Despite the ominous ticking of my internal clock, I dress with care. Slim black slacks, a black silk blouse, and bright red stilettos. My wet hair goes into a sleek bun. I keep my makeup understated with the exception of winged black eyeliner, mascara, and a touch of blush. No perfume, lipstick, or jewelry. The clothes are the real statement.

As I grab my purse and keys and head to my car, I'm aware I might be entirely off the mark. But there's no time for more research, no time to carefully craft my persona as I usually do for a new client. So I went with my instinct—that Kieran won't respond to someone who in any way resembles his late wife.

I already have height and hair color going for me. Elizabeth was blond. I'm a brunette. She was petite. I'm five-ten without heels. Most notably, however, I didn't find one picture of her in black. She was most often photographed in pastels, radiating an air of delicate femininity next to her tall, rakish husband.

The drive to my office is spent lost in nebulous thoughts, so much so that when I pull into the private lot behind the building, a disquieting feeling of not remembering the drive rolls over me. Following it is a flutter of nervousness I haven't felt in years.

"Why did I say yes to this?" I mutter.

I know the answer, of course. I just don't want to own it.

When I see the time on the dash, my momentary self-reflection is forgotten. I hustle to the back door of my home away from home, its boxy, pale stucco walls and red tile roof softened by lush greenery on all sides. Inside, late morning sunlight streams through the front windows and down the wide hallway, warming the oak floors and the doors to either side of me.

The entire downstairs is mine: a main office, two additional work rooms, and a full bath. I rent out three of the four upstairs offices to other therapists. Their clients come in the front door and use the stairway; mine arrive and leave through the back. A privacy screen normally separates my hallway from the lobby. Since it's Saturday, I leave the screen retracted. No one is here but me.

At least for the next four and a half minutes.

I stride to the door with my name mounted on a plaque,

unlock it, and slip inside. The first thing I do is pull aside the curtains behind my desk, flooding the room with natural light, then I crack a window for fresh air flow. Next I turn on an oil warmer hidden behind plants, allowing my personal cocktail of soothing scents to mist out. The furniture is thankfully already where I need it—two chairs facing each other in the center of the room. There's a couch, but he has to earn that.

On the small table beside my chair, I place a blank notepad and pen. I rarely take notes during sessions, preferring to compile my thoughts afterward, but it's an effective visual tool. An unspoken language, just like the color palette of the furniture and decor. One of my former clients, an interior designer and television personality, called my office the perfect balance of sophistication and whimsy. They also said I had too many plants, but that critique had more to do with their aversion to dirt—or rather, *dirtiness*—than anything else. Case in point: at the end of our time together, they brought me a parting gift of another plant.

With the final sixty seconds rapidly dwindling, I take a swig from my water bottle and pop a mint, chewing fast. I'm swallowing the last of it when the eleven o'clock hits and there's a knock on the door. I had a feeling he'd be prompt, mainly because I doubt he drove himself. A spike of adrenaline overwhelms my satisfaction at being right.

I let him wait three more seconds while I take a deep breath and center myself. Then I prop a hip against my desk and cross my arms over my chest.

"Come in," I call.

The doorknob turns. Wood swings inward.

He stands before me. A king like he said he'd be. A stranger with a familiar face.

Six-foot-four and perfectly proportioned for it, Kieran wears sweatpants, a T-shirt, and flip-flops. In one large hand, he holds a baseball hat and sunglasses. Unsurprisingly, all the items attached to his person are black. Surprisingly, he doesn't look like the broken man I was expecting.

He looks feral.

Even stalled on the threshold with only one foot inside the room, his presence permeates the space around me. I inhale subtly, catching a hint of expensive cologne. Something probably concocted exclusively for him based on his skin's pH level.

At least he showered.

As soon as I think it, though, I realize it would have been better for me if he hadn't. Scent is an effective weapon. I should have used a stronger oil in the warmer.

Time melts and stretches. It could be two seconds or two minutes that we blink at each other. My heart drums, fast then faster, before my head eventually confirms what my eyes can see: he doesn't recognize me. As much as I knew he wouldn't—he never knew my name, and I'm as different as he is the same—a small part of me had wondered if he would see through me to the shorter, chubby, braces-wearing teenager I was.

Reality snaps like a rubber band against my throat,

jolting me into the present. Into the body of who I am today. My relief—and the ache of illogical disappointment—fades.

"Welcome, Mr. Hayes. I'm Dr. Stirling."

He nods, and his cool, remote gaze finally leaves my face to flicker around the room. Free to study him, I notice what I didn't before. Details his natural charisma blurred. Shadows smudge the skin beneath dark eyelashes. A short beard—more scruff than anything refined—covers his jaw and makes the sensuality of his mouth even more pronounced. His hair is too long for its cut, and his eyebrows are drawn together like he isn't sure why he's here. Though the latter might be a projection on my part.

Despite all my training on micro-expressions and body language, I have no idea what he's thinking or feeling. Par for the course for someone of his position—I'm sure he's had his own training—but irritating nevertheless.

I'm already at a disadvantage as a woman. If I can't secure my authority now, I never will.

"Come in and close the door."

Please drips to the edge of my tongue. A light clench of my teeth holds it there.

When his eyes return to me, there's new life in them. Waves in a formerly placid cove. But I still can't decipher their depths. If eyes are a window to the soul, Kieran's soul is a footstep from the void. He's not broken yet. But he's close.

With smooth grace, he closes the door and turns. There's no hesitation in his movements as he strides forward and lowers his body to the chair I chose for him, placing his hat and sunglasses on the floor beside his feet.

I settle in the chair opposite his. A larger, more comfortable chair. I'm sure he registers the difference, maybe even realizes I manipulated him, but there's no outward indication.

Oh, he's good.

As I cross my legs, his gaze drops to my feet and pauses for an instant on my stilettos. No subtle flaring of his nostrils. No twitch of eyelids. Zero physical reaction, but it still feels like a victory.

His eyes lift back to my face. "Nice to meet you, Dr. Stirling."

Goose bumps unfurl like wings across my lower back. One wing his voice—deep and lilting, warm and a little bit rough—and the other the movement of his lips shaping the words. All familiar and not, distorted by time and memory and faded fantasy. An absolute mindfuck.

I've never been more thankful for my skill at masking emotion.

"You as well," I say with a brief nod. "Why don't you tell me why you're here?"

"I think we both know the answer to that," he says flatly.

"Indulge me."

The silence stretches, as does our eye contact. The urge to drop my gaze grows the longer he stares at me. In another life, I might laugh at his clear bid for superiority. After all, it's his fault I grew claws.

The sudden buzz of my phone on my desk ends our stalemate with no winner declared.

"Apologies," I murmur as I snag the device and put it on silent.

When I look at Kieran again, his eyes are roaming the framed degrees and certifications on the wall to my right. Depending on the client, I either display them or don't. If I'd had the time—or thought about them at all—I would have removed a few of them.

Nothing to be done about it now.

Kieran's gaze stalls, and I know exactly which frames have caught his attention. Another moment passes before his eyes return to me. The blue is frigid. The vast, underwater depths of an iceberg.

He finally deigns to answer my question. "My brother informed me this morning that he'd have me removed as CEO of the company I founded if I didn't present myself here." His gaze flickers back to the wall. "Though I suspect he was obeying the whims of my sister-in-law."

"And why do you think he felt it necessary to threaten you?"

He sighs, an ocean of annoyance conveyed in the sound despite little to no change in his expression. Color me unsurprised when he ignores the question and nods at the wall.

"That fancy degree from UCLA. Is it real?"

"According to the bank that acquired my student loans, yes."

"You look a little young for a PhD."

"I have one of those faces."

His eyes narrow. "Unlike my brother, I looked you up. Made a few inquiries."

I uncross and recross my legs, gratified when a muscle ticks in his cheek. "Don't keep me in suspense, Mr. Hayes."

His fingers drum on the arm of his chair. When he realizes what he's doing, he stops immediately. I almost smile.

"No one could tell me shit about what you actually do. They made you sound like the Wizard of Oz. Your website is vague, your social media presence almost nil. Besides that ridiculous Buzzfeed article, I have no idea if you're a legitimate professional."

"You're right—that article is ridiculous."

A moment's stillness betrays his surprise. Then something predatory flares in his eyes, warming them like an electric current. I do smile then. Just a little.

He opens his mouth, but I beat him to it.

"As you can see from my accreditations, Mr. Hayes, my skillset is rather unique. It allows me to customize different therapeutic approaches with each client. If you're willing to do the work, together we can change your life. If you're not..." I shrug. "I wish you the best of luck."

He doesn't like that—my easy dismissal—and all at once the ice melts from his eyes. They're now the searing blue heart of an inferno. The hairs on the back of my neck rise, a primal warning of danger. I muse that it's the same response a deer must have when a wolf is near.

But what he doesn't know is that I'm what he said I'd be.

A queen of the jungle. If he so much as snarls at me, I'm going to take a nice big bite out of his neck.

Something of my inner dialogue must reflect in my face because he tenses, then abruptly relaxes back into his chair. The fire in his eyes fades to a pilot light. I know better than to think he's submitting—more like misdirecting me. He probably uses the technique in business to keep adversaries on their toes while he plans their demise.

"Color me intrigued," he says in a droll tone. "What kind of approach would you take with me?"

I tell him the truth. "I don't know yet. I usually have weeks to consult with new clients and prepare."

"Well, I can tell you right now we won't be needing those last several." He nods toward the frames.

My brows lift. "Are you sure about that?"

He bares his teeth in a facsimile of a smile. "Yes."

I nod, indulging him. "Okay. Have you ever been to any sort of therapy before?"

Instead of answering, he asks, "Can I be frank with you?"

"I'll take that as a 'no.' And by all means, be whatever or whoever you want."

His eyes narrow as he tries to figure out if I'm teasing him. But I have Mona Lisa's perfect poker face.

"I don't want or need to talk about my problems, or my sex life, and I definitely don't need whatever that is."

He points an elegant finger at a certification on the wall. Without looking, I know it's the one that says TANTRIC SEXOLOGY AND BREATHWORK PRACTITIONER. It sits between BOARD CERTIFIED SEXOLOGIST and SOMATIC SEX THERAPIST.

I have the wicked impulse to tell him I'm also certified in erotic massage, intimacy surrogacy, and kink coaching. But he'd probably run, and I don't want him to. I want to give him the same gift he gave me seventeen years ago. If I can.

"What *do* you need, Mr. Hayes?" I ask mildly. "Because from the conversation I had with your sister-in-law this morning, it seems to me you're one misstep from the psych ward or a rehab facility. Given the fact you're here, showered and sober, I think somewhere inside you is a voice crying out for help."

The words are a calculated risk. Or maybe a leap of faith, as alarming as that prospect is.

Full lips compress, then release on a slow exhale. "Fair point."

I hold his gaze. *Hold it... hold...*

Finally, dark lashes flutter as his eyes lower. Relief so sharp it's painful seizes me; I bite the inside of my cheek against a gasp.

There's hope for him, after all.

"I still don't see how this can work," he says.

"It's my job to worry about that."

Momentary surrender forgotten, his eyes meet mine. "I don't think you understand what I'm saying."

The barest edge of helplessness in his voice makes my shoulders relax a fraction even as my heart rate kicks up. I may be a mystery to him—and I'll keep it that way—but he's no longer so much of a mystery to me.

"What I'm hearing is you don't trust me, and that even if you did, you'd still find it difficult to share your private thoughts and feelings. As much as you may want change, you think we're wasting our time."

He nods slowly. "Exactly."

"Out of curiosity, have you ever trusted someone enough to show them the deepest, darkest parts of yourself?"

Another predatory flash in his eyes. He wants to lie. I see the moment he decides not to—there's an infinitesimal release of tension in his jaw and a sardonic twitch of his lips. Another surrender. Smaller but no less important than the first.

"Can't say I have."

His accent is suddenly thick, his voice close to a growl. My long-sleeved blouse conceals another bloom of goose bumps. I've hit a fault line, though I'm not sure which one. *Childhood trauma? Early relationships? Or his marriage?*

I nod, refocusing. "It's perfectly natural to have defenses against vulnerability. I'm not asking you to trust me off the bat. Give me three weeks. If you still think this is a waste of time, we'll go our separate ways."

His fingers clench on his thighs. He forcibly stretches and relaxes them. "Fine."

I retrieve my pad and pen, then jot down an address. "I'd like you to meet me here tonight at nine."

"Tonight?" he asks sharply.

I look up through my lashes. "Yes. Do you have plans?"

His jaw clenches. "No."

"Great." I tear off the paper and extend it.

He grabs it and reads the address. "What is this place?"

I smile fully for the first time, knowing it will unsettle him. It does; he shifts in his chair.

"A rage room." I stand, signaling the end of our session. "Don't be late."

CHAPTER 3

KIERAN

"**Y**our brother and his wife are here."

Looking away from the white caps on the Pacific, I nod at my head of security, Sven. He touches his ear and speaks to one of his men.

"He'll receive them on the back patio. Is the chef still here? Okay, ask him to put something together. Light fare." He pauses. "No alcohol."

I don't dispute the order. Sadly, the person who knows me best is a man whose company I pay for. Sven is a special case, though, and worth every cent. He's been with me for years, has seen me at my lowest and highest—both figuratively and literally—and we share a bond deeper than most conventional friendships. Life-and-death situations will do that for you.

Resigning myself to the coming inquisition, I walk away from the cliff, past the glittering pool, and up a set of steps to

32

the covered deck that spans the back of the house. Sven follows, ever my shadow.

I drop onto a padded chaise, cross my ankles, and fold my hands over my stomach. Said stomach is gurgling, still recovering from the obscene amount of booze I've poured into it over the last week. My liver's protests, at least, are silent.

My head feels like wet cotton sits between my ears, my typically whirring thoughts subdued. I have no idea if it's the hangover catching up to me or the oddness of this morning. The office. The woman.

It's been a long time since I was so unnerved by another person. Or felt as challenged. I can't shake the suspicion that everything she said and did was carefully orchestrated, from the too-small chair I sat in to her every movement and word.

Who the fuck is she?

And why does she seem familiar?

The latter question I can thankfully answer—my hungover brain was clearly hallucinating. There's no way I could have met and subsequently forgotten that woman. Not when she dug under my skin in seconds and made my fucking bones vibrate.

Alistair walks outside first, followed by his wife of five years, Gail. While the effusive chatterbox is perfect for my brother and I generally like her, I also find her utterly exhausting. They settle close together on the outdoor couch opposite my chaise, looking like the cover photo of a magazine profiling lives of the rich and beautiful.

Gail smiles and waves at Sven; Alistair gives him a brief nod before shifting blue eyes a shade lighter than mine to me.

"Well?" he barks, ever the battering ram. "How'd it go?"

I ignore him and narrow my focus on Gail. Her smile wavers and her eyes don't quite meet mine. Anxiety rolls off her in waves. *Killer instinct,* my brother calls it. My innate ability to hone in on a person's mental state has served me well in life. It's second nature now, so fine-tuned that meeting someone I can't read is highly unusual.

It's been a highly unusual day.

"How do you know Dr. Stirling?" I ask Gail.

A personal favor is the only conclusion that makes sense for why I was seen on such short notice on a Saturday. While I couldn't sense much of anything beneath Stirling's Fort Knox exterior, instinct tells me she doesn't give a rat's hairy ass about my money, celebrity, or even the fact I'm, as she expressed, "one misstep from the psych ward or a rehab facility."

Moreover, according to the preliminary profile my private investigator scrounged up this morning, most of her clients are rich and famous. He's the one who likened her to the Wizard of Oz. As much as it irritates me, having met her, I see merit in the comparison.

Pink infuses Gail's cheeks. She glances at Alastair and laughs nervously. Realizing my error, I swear silently; it didn't occur to me until this moment that she might be one of Stirling's clients.

You're slipping, Kier.

I'm scrambling for a way to pull my foot out of my mouth when Gail says in a too-high voice, "Funny story, actually. We were roommates in college. Until this morning, I hadn't spoken to her in years."

As I absorb this unexpected information, Gail turns to Alistair with a contrite expression. His brows rise, curious rather than suspicious, and he reaches for her hand. I look away.

"Sorry for not mentioning it, honey," she murmurs. "I didn't intend for it to be a secret."

Even with my gaze on a potted plant, I feel her furtive glance at me. She *did* intend for it to be a secret. From me, at least. Curious. More importantly, *why*?

Before Alistair can reassure her—he can do that shit out of my sight—I ask her, "Undergrad at UCLA?"

Gail has a communications degree, but to my knowledge, she didn't do any post-graduate work.

She nods. "I was a junior when I moved into the apartment. Talia was already living there. I think she was a year or two ahead of me? I can't honestly remember." She giggles breathlessly. "College years, you know?"

Frowning, I compare that to the bullet points from my PI. Gail and Stirling—I can't think of her as *Talia*—are the same age, thirty-one. Her PhD would have taken five or six years, which means she graduated anywhere from two to four years ago. But it doesn't add up. The woman I met today was far too confident and successful for what should be a relatively new career. Which either means she graduated high school years early or accelerated her degrees. Or she didn't complete her degree and is a fraud.

I make a mental note to text my PI to go ahead and compile a more extensive dossier. With dates and receipts.

When I surface from my thoughts, I find Alistair staring at me over the rim of a glass of iced tea while Gail munches on a small plate of grapes and berries. I look at the nearby table on which trays of food and pitchers of water and tea sit —none of which I noticed being delivered.

Another slip.

Rubbing the throbbing spot on my forehead, I brace myself. Alistair has been surprisingly patient, but the look in his eyes tells me his patience is dangling by a thread.

"How was it?" he asks, more demand than question this time.

I lower my hand back to my stomach and shrug. "Fine."

Just because he's genuinely concerned about me doesn't mean I won't make him sweat. He's my brother, after all.

"Just fine?" he grumbles, glancing at Gail. She blinks wide eyes at me. Interestingly, her color is still high.

"I have another session with her tonight."

Alistair's confusion is as telling as Gail's suddenly blank expression. My brother glances at her. "Is that normal? To see a therapist on a Saturday night?"

She hurries to swallow the food in her mouth. "I don't know," she says, but it comes out like a question.

This time, Alistair's stare on his wife is laser focused. "Gail?" he asks in a voice I know means business. It's made grown men's balls shrink across many a conference table.

She cracks instantly. "I'm sorry. I had the idea of calling her and it snowballed from there. Maybe I didn't really think it through." She glances wildly between us. "It's just... Talia has always been an unconventional woman. Brilliant to the point it's kind of scary. I saw an article last week about her and I thought... I don't know, that Kieran might benefit from someone like her. An out-of-the-box thinker."

Alistair glances at me in bafflement. I shrug back at him. Gail's distress isn't comfortable to witness, strumming the brittle strings of my protective instincts, but I want to hear where she's going with this. Obviously, she knows about those disturbing certifications on Dr. Stirling's wall and just as obviously, she withheld that information from my brother. His reaction would have been far more inflammatory than mine. I have no doubt he would have quashed the idea outright.

Oddly, it makes me respect my sister-in-law more.

"Honey, what are you not saying?" Alistair's effort to sound gentle misses the mark, probably due to the thunderous scowl on his face.

Gail glances at me. The panic in her eyes is too much for me to take. I clear my throat, bringing my brother's attention to me. "I think she's dancing around the fact that Dr. Stirling is best known as a celebrity sex therapist."

Alistair laughs, but when neither Gail nor I join him, the

sound abruptly stops. He turns horrified eyes on his wife. "You sent him to a sex worker?"

Gail gasps. "Of course not! Sex *therapist*."

"What's the difference?" he cries. "She asks about your feelings while she tickles your pickle?"

There's a slight scuff of a shoe behind me, between five and seven feet away. Intentional. I'm sure Sven's face is impassive, but inside he's having a good laugh at my expense and wanted me to know it. *Arse.*

While Gail explains to my idiot brother the difference between sex work and sex therapy—while thankfully stressing the fact Stirling is also a regular psychologist—I rub at my forehead again. If I'm going out tonight, I'm need to catch a few hours of sleep beforehand.

Facing Stirling with weakened faculties is not an option.

"...dominatrix on the weekends."

Catching the tail end of Gail's whispered words, my head whips up so fast a muscle twinges in my neck.

"*What?*"

They stare at me. Gail flushes again, this time bright red from jaw to temples. My brother looks constipated. There's another scuff behind me, a little louder. Sven's version of dying of laughter.

Dropping my feet to the ground on either side of the chaise, I lean forward. "Repeat that."

Alistair squares his shoulders. Color creeps up his neck. "Gail was merely telling me that Talia paid for college by working as a—" He swipes a hand over his face, a wheeze escaping as his fingers pass his mouth. "Fucking hell, this is too much."

"Dominatrix and kink educator," finishes Gail, refusing to meet my stare.

There's a suspicious gasping sound behind me. I throw a glare over my shoulder at Sven, whose eyes are dancing so hard they're sweating.

Alistair murmurs, "She's not going to, ehm, whip him or anything, right?"

"Don't be an ass," Gail hisses back.

I cradle my pounding head in my hands and groan. "What has my life come to?"

THE QUESTION still floats in my mind eight hours and a restless nap later as I slip into the back seat of my BMW and Sven settles behind the wheel. He refuses to let me sit in the passenger seat; I gave up arguing with him about it years ago.

He starts the car and circles the drive, heading toward the gate at the bottom where he pauses to push a button on the visor. As the massive wooden slab slowly moves aside, his eyes meet mine in the rearview.

"You sure about this?"

At least he's not laughing anymore. He has his game face on—or game *voice* since his face never changes.

While he didn't attempt to talk me out of this arguably insane venture, I can tell he's not happy. He doesn't like taking me to some random address in the Valley despite the fact the other two members of his team left ahead of us to scope it out. I also doubt my relaying what Stirling said at the end of our session—that we'd have the place to ourselves—gave him any comfort.

It didn't give me much comfort, either.

"Just drive before I lose my nerve," I tell him.

He drives.

About ten minutes in, he gets a call from one of his men, Gabe. I listen to the report: the location is a small, nondescript warehouse, just as the satellite image search indicated. There's approval in Gabe's voice as he tells Sven the building is highly secure, with an abundance of external video surveillance and high boundary walls topped by barbed wire. The entrance and three emergency exits—both sides and rear of the building—have keypad security and more cameras.

I tune the rest out. I appreciate Sven's vigilance, as always, but if I delve too deeply into what he and the other two do for me on a daily basis, I run the risk of a swift slide into paranoia.

Been there, done that.

Instead, I think about how public record listed the address we're driving to as owned by Shadow Healing Arts LLC. A rather ominous business name, but a fitting one based off my first impression of the woman who owns it. And, you know, the fact she dominates men sexually.

No fucking wonder she raised my hackles.

I close my eyes and try to think calming thoughts, but instead, I see Stirling's smile at the end of our session. It came out of nowhere, like a summer downpour after a morning of blue skies in Galway. Shocking, impossible to evade, and as irritating as it was captivating.

Her teeth weren't entirely straight, the most notable imperfection a left eyetooth that sat slightly forward, overlapping the tooth beside it a bit. I have no idea why the detail bothers me to the extent I'm thinking about it hours later. Maybe because the rest of her was so objectively flawless.

While not my type in the least, I can still admit Stirling's a stunning woman. Tall and willowy in stature, but with a fluidity of movement that speaks to physical strength. Natural breasts, average in size from what I could glean with a quick glance. Rose-colored lips, the bottom plump, the top bowed. Eyes caught in the rare space between brown and yellow, their shade all the more impactful for the dark lashes and brows framing them.

I agree with my brother's knee-jerk assessment after he insisted Gail show him Stirling's photo—that her looks are reminiscent of a young Brooke Shields. But while Shields's beauty is warm, inviting even, Stirling's is somehow off-putting. Like a modernist painting that captures your attention but leaves you with a vaguely unsettled feeling.

My lack of physical response to the woman doubtlessly puts me in the minority of men—or women for that matter

—who find themselves in her path. Even Alistair and Gail looked a bit dazed after staring too long at her photograph.

Despite my verbal agreement to give her three weeks, I haven't decided one way or another whether I'll continue her so-called therapy after tonight. Not because I think she's bad at her job. I'm sure she helps all sorts. Disturbing extracurriculars and certifications aside, I can even acknowledge an intellectual curiosity about her methods. It isn't often I see that razor-sharp awareness in someone's eyes outside Lumitech's labs. Like knows like—just as I do, she sees the world as a puzzle to solve. Or perhaps a foe to conquer.

The simple truth is I don't believe what's wrong with me can be fixed. If it weren't for Alistair and my purely scientific curiosity, I wouldn't be entertaining this madness at all.

"We're here," says Sven, jolting me from my thoughts.

He drives through an open chain-link gate and parks beside a black Lexus. The gate rattles as it slides closed behind us, obeying a remote in the hand of the woman standing near an open door.

Her dark hair is still pulled back, though she's changed into athletic leggings, a fitted long-sleeved shirt, and trainers. Shadows make her cheekbones stark and eyes dark. Light from the building behind her defines her statuesque form, paying special homage to the tuck of her waist, the flare of her hips, and long, shapely legs.

Even the stalwart Sven stares a few seconds too long before turning off the car and exiting—and he bats for the other team. As for me, I'm gratified to realize I might as well be looking at Mrs. Murphy, the elderly lady who lived in the flat above ours growing up and who used to ring us for sugar without pants on.

As I get out of the car and walk toward Stirling, however, I have a disturbing thought.

I wouldn't terribly mind seeing that crooked eyetooth again.

CHAPTER 4

TALIA

Kieran walks toward me across the shadowed cement, every inch a wolf on the prowl. Long, loose limbs in the same sweatpants from this morning. A hooded sweatshirt encasing his torso. Broken-in sneakers. Squared shoulders with no hint of tension. His walk tells me he knows his own body and the impact of the space he takes up, but that he isn't cocky about it. His grace suggests a history with martial arts but also vividly reminds me of watching a younger, skinnier man float backward over cobblestones.

A man shadows him, the same one I glimpsed in the hallway outside my office this morning. Mid to late forties. Blond buzzcut. A few inches shorter than Kieran but substantially more muscled. His expression is watchful as he scans our surroundings. There's a notable bulge at his hip under a light jacket.

I'm confident this is Sven Akerman, the man who called me two hours ago to introduce himself as Kieran's chief personal protection officer and let me know his men would arrive ahead of time to "sweep and secure" the location. They were polite and professional, identifying themselves immediately at the gate. They, too, were armed.

I address Sven first. "Dylan and Gabe are currently inside and should be done momentarily. I've given them remote access to the outdoor security cameras. The interior feeds are automatically purged every night to protect my clientele."

His roaming gaze pauses on me. "Thank you for accommodating us, Doctor." His voice is a deep, distinctive gravel; I recognize it from our call. "We'll keep out of the way."

He looks at Kieran, who extrapolates meaning from a subtle shift in the man's expression.

"Thank you, Sven," he murmurs.

Sven nods, turning his back to us. Despite his bulk, it suddenly feels like he's merely another shadow in the night— albeit a lethal one.

While I'm used to clients having security personnel, these men are on a different level. Clearly ex-military, highly trained and hyper focused on Kieran's safety. All of which leads me to deduce being the CEO of Lumitech isn't only about innovation and board meetings.

Putting my curiosity aside, I focus on the here and now. "Follow me, Mr. Hayes."

As I walk into the building, his footsteps follow me down the central hallway lined by false walls. Industrial-sized can lights on the distant, unfinished ceiling provide ample light to the partitioned rooms on either side of us, each denoted by a brightly painted door.

Dylan and Gabe emerge from the last room on the left. The former gives us a nod and slips past us toward the entrance. The latter pauses to say, "All clear," to Kieran before giving me a parting smile. "Thanks, Doc."

When I hear the front door close, my curiosity becomes too much. I slow and turn to face Kieran. He stops and regards me impassively, but there's a knowing glint in his eyes.

"Are you in danger?" I ask.

"You tell me," he drawls.

When I merely stare at him, he releases a small sigh. "Not right now, no." He pauses, his voice lowering. "I trust those men with my life, and so should you."

I consider this and finally nod, knowing better than to ask for details. Like whether there have been threats or attempts on his life. We're not there yet—might never be—so for now I file the information away.

Down the hallway, I stop at the third door on the right. Kieran stops behind me, close enough that I feel the heat of his body. I glance over my shoulder and crane my neck, waiting for him to notice the invasion of my personal space. His eyes widen slightly, like he's surprised by how close we are. He doesn't apologize, but he does take a smooth step backward so he's no longer looming over me.

Blue eyes dance over my features before veering over my

head. "Interesting place you've got here." His bland tone doesn't fully disguise his skepticism.

I smile slightly. "It gets better."

I open the door and step inside, waiting for him to follow before closing it. The long room boasts a single large table, the surface cluttered with a disjointed mix of items: old televisions, computer monitors, glassware, lamps, cheap pottery, empty wine bottles, and more. Past the table is an empty space with a giant X spray-painted on the floor. Unlike the other three walls, which are plywood and plaster, the wall behind the X is thick cement.

Kieran looks around, a faint line between his brows as if he's just now realized what he signed up for. As he surveys the rack of protective gear beside us, his shoulders lift a fraction. When he sees the hanging hammers and bats, they lift even more.

His cues of increasing discomfort—as minor as they are—are normal for those who have extreme, repressed emotions. An invitation to unchain the beast that lives within each of us is an inherently scary prospect. When it's not a little frightening? *That's* a cause for concern.

"Never been to a rage room, I'm guessing?" I ask as I pull a jumpsuit off a hook and hand it to him. XL because the man is a literal giant.

"No," he grunts.

He stares at the coarse fabric in his hands long enough that I wonder if he's going to bail. Then he blinks and turns away to pull off his sweatshirt, tossing it to the floor beneath the bats. Hesitance leaks from every jerky movement of his limbs as he steps into the jumpsuit and zips it up.

I make a split-second decision and grab one for myself, pulling it on swiftly over my clothes. Another break from habit; I usually let my clients have the space to themselves, observing via CCTV from my onsite office. I don't dwell on it—every client is different. And this one might be the most *different* I've ever had.

I swipe a pair of protective glasses and gloves, and he does the same.

"What are the rules?" he asks, voice as tense as his shoulders.

Striding to the table, I grab a wine bottle and hurl it hard at the cement wall. It shatters on impact, raining glass over the X.

I smile back at him. "Who said anything about rules?"

AN HOUR LATER, I hand Kieran one of the water bottles I retrieved from the fridge in my office. He accepts it with a mumbled, "Thanks," and drains it in a series of convulsive swallows.

A bead of sweat drips from his hairline to his jaw. His skin is flushed. The top half of the jumpsuit hangs loose around his waist, exposing a damp black T-shirt that clings to his chest and stomach. After an initial, purely selfish perusal of his muscled arms, I make it a point to ignore them. Especially the veins in his forearms and the freckles strewn across them like grains of sand.

"Your sweat smells like alcohol," I say after taking a sip of water.

A smirk tilts his lips. "I'd be surprised if it didn't."

I take another sip. "How do you feel?"

He studies the mess we made. The painted X is barely visible beneath the destruction. Behind us, the table is empty.

A delayed chill skates down my spine as I reflect on Kieran's rage. Mostly silent. Deceptively mild. Like an earthquake deep in the ocean that isn't felt until its result—a tsunami—hits land.

I broke the wine bottle, a lamp, and a porcelain bowl.

He obliterated everything else.

"Tired," he answers. There's a long pause. "I still don't want to talk about my problems."

"I don't recall asking about them."

He huffs, eyes alighting briefly on my face. "Do you want me to say I feel better? I don't. But I'll probably sleep tonight, so that's a positive."

I nod. "Fair enough. What do you normally do on a Saturday night?"

There's a minuscule pause. "Drink and fuck."

My stomach flutters, but my voice stays calm. "And what's a normal Sunday like for you?"

A line appears between his brows. "Why?"

"Just answer the question, Mr. Hayes."

Amusement flares in his eyes. "For Christ's sake, call me Kieran."

I take an aggressive step toward him. He stills, eyes hardening, fingers clenching on the water bottle and making the plastic crackle. I stare up at him, showing him the predator inside me and how utterly unimpressed she is.

"I'll call you by your first name when you stop being a brat, *Mr. Hayes.*"

His eyes widen, then narrow, glittering. But the worst of his rage is already spent, the beast inside him too tired to do more than snarl. Which doesn't mean the aftermath isn't still a viable threat. He's going to crash hard. Since I set the process in motion, it's my responsibility to try to defuse it before he leaves. If I can't... well, he has three babysitters. Hopefully they can contain him tomorrow.

When his lips twitch, I breathe a mental sigh. He maintains the stony expression for another moment, then gives in and laughs. A real laugh, warm and deep. I ignore the pleasant vibrations of it in my chest.

He finally calms. Someone new looks out of his eyes. Or perhaps someone old—a memory of a different, more lighthearted man. An echo of a boy I didn't really know but whose irreverent optimism probably saved my life.

And I wonder if he can be resurrected.

"You sounded just like my mam."

"I like her already."

He laughs again, but it lacks the previous warmth. "Do

you call all your clients brats when they don't dance to your tune?"

I shrug. "If the shoe fits."

All traces of humor vanish from his face, replaced by unnerving focus. My heart thuds a warning that my mind translates and my instincts confirm. I suddenly know where this conversation is headed and have a good idea who's to blame.

He shifts half a foot closer. If I were anyone else, I might take a step back. But I'm not, so I only tilt my head more to maintain eye contact.

"The shoe does *not* fit," he murmurs. "But out of curiosity, how do you require brats to address you in return?"

I was right.

Dammit, Gail.

I'm not ashamed of my past work as a dominatrix—especially since it helped pay for my degrees—but it's also not something I advertise, especially to male clients. It creates... problems.

"I assure you there will be no scenario in our work together for which you'll need to call me anything but Dr. Stirling."

He growls, "Good to find we're on the same page."

Subduing the urge to roll my eyes, I redirect. "Now that that's settled, I have some homework for you."

His brows lift. "Is that so?"

I cock my head. "Unless you're no longer willing and would prefer to end things now."

The spark in his eyes tells me I've pissed him off again, but the heat fades after a moment.

"What's the homework, Dr. Stirling?"

I don't miss the slight emphasis on my name. Nor am I able to completely ignore a burst of dangerous curiosity. An image flashes in my mind—alarming, provocative—and I pick it up and throw it much as I did the wine bottle. Thankfully, it, too, smashes on impact.

"No drinking. Monday morning, you'll go back to work. Keep your workdays under ten hours. Exercise in the mornings. Eat three healthy meals. Go to sleep early. Be at my office at seven p.m. on Wednesday."

He bares his teeth. "Oh? Is that all?"

I lift a hand. "Before you throw another tantrum, consider something for me. Would you be this offended if a man of my qualifications gave you the same instructions?"

His chest rises, then falls as he slowly exhales. Chagrin darkens the skin of his neck. "Probably not, no."

I smile. "Kudos for self-awareness. You have my number. Feel free to call me if you need to. Otherwise, I'll see you Wednesday. Any questions?"

He sighs. "No."

"Then we'll call it a night."

I step outside the room and wait for him to join me. He emerges a minute later sans jumpsuit, his sweatshirt back on. The hood is up, dark hair fanning his cheeks. My heart snaps against my ribs; I stare a beat too long.

"What?" he asks, eyes wary.

I think fast. "Just deciding whether or not to tell you I'm proud of the work you did tonight."

He smirks. "Better not. Might go to my head."

My lips press against a smile. We don't speak as I walk him out. He doesn't say goodbye, just slips into the back seat of his car after Sven opens the door for him. The man gives me a long look, then a nod that probably means something I'm too rattled to decipher. Dylan and Gabe hop into an identical BMW and I open the gate for their caravan.

Once they're gone, the gate closed again, I lock up the warehouse and retreat to my car. I don't start it, knowing I can't drive until I allow myself to feel the effects of the last hour. To purge the emotional transference from watching Kieran destroy property with the same ruthless savagery he might have displayed against a hated enemy on a long-ago battlefield.

Fine tremors take ahold of my muscles. Energy with no outlet zings beneath my skin while delayed fear softens the edges of my vision. Inhaling slowly through my nose, I count to four, then release the breath from my mouth. I do it several times until intellect overcomes the primal response.

I'm not afraid of Kieran Hayes. I'm afraid *for* him—and, if I'm honest, for myself.

I've traveled many dark, twisted roads with my clients over the years. Some would say it's my specialty. I'm an excavator of hidden realms, a hunter of the psyche's most warped, stubborn treasures. But I've never felt so out of my depth. Never struggled so hard to remain safely outside the vortex of their pain.

And it's only the first day.

Closing my eyes, I relive the peak of his rage. The repeated swing of a bat against a computer monitor on the floor. Muscles straining, lungs heaving like bellows. Blow after blow. A mindless machine. Then like a switch was flipped or a plug pulled, he stopped. The head of the bat clanked on the floor, the grip loose in his fingers. For thirty seconds, he stared at what he'd done.

Then he looked at me, and what I saw in his eyes... He might as well have been on his knees, begging me to save him. For those brief moments, he was unveiled. Raw and helpless and so exquisitely broken. Our prior roles fundamentally reversed.

"Fuck," I whisper, thudding my forehead repeatedly against the steering wheel. The physical jolts are jarring rather than painful. As intended, they drag me from the rabbit hole of my thoughts.

Straightening, I start the car.

TALIA

A thirty-minute drive later, I punch in a code beside a black door in an alley off Wilshire in Beverly Hills. The pad turns green and I walk inside. Another hallway stretches before me, this one with soft, recessed lights and plush carpet. Abstract black-and-white photos hang in huge frames in the white spaces between four doors. A final door stands opposite me, padded in black leather. Muted thumps of music come from the attached club.

A door on my right opens and a man pokes his head out, a guarded expression melting to surprise and happiness when he sees me. Emerging fully, he closes the distance between us.

Tall and slender and almost inhumanly gorgeous, his white-blond hair is short on the sides and long on top, flopping artfully over his brow. The smile on his face soothes the burn beneath my skin—just like I knew it would.

"I could hardly believe it when I recognized your code. Welcome back."

I want to smile but make myself frown instead. "You cut your beautiful hair."

It used to be long, almost to his waist. When we were involved, one of my favorite things to do was brush and braid the silky strands. The new style makes him look his age—thirty-three. It also makes him look less like an angel who accidentally fell from heaven and more like one who dove intentionally. I'm not sure I like it.

His grin grows. "Two years since you've stepped foot in Crossroads and that's the first thing you say to me?"

"I've missed you, Nate," I murmur.

His smile turns impish. "If that's the case, I'm due for a break and my office door locks."

More tension drains from me as I laugh. "I'll take a hug."

Obeying, he pulls me into his deceptively strong arms. I inhale his familiar, citrusy scent and the last tendrils of my tension fade away.

He palms the back of my head beneath my bun, skilled fingers pressing lightly on pressure points. "Never thought I'd see the day when you came to me for comfort."

My lips curve. "Don't be silly. You've always brought me comfort."

His chuckle vibrates beneath my ear. "Oh, I know. I just wanted to hear you say it."

"Cheeky," I admonish lightly, then lift my head to see his face. "How have you been, lovely one?"

The pet name slips out. His eyes darken, gaze latching briefly on my mouth. I shake my head chidingly; he smiles slowly, unrepentant.

"I've been good, Mistress," he whispers.

A frisson of awareness tingles through my center, accompanied by a slideshow of memory of how good Nate is. Ending things between us had been hard for both of us, but we knew it was time. As much as we cared for each other, we couldn't give the other what we really needed long-term.

"Still unattached?" I ask against my better judgment.

His gaze flickers. "Somewhat."

I step back immediately. "Nathan," I snap, using his full name because it annoys him. "Tell me you didn't disrespect someone by touching me."

He shakes his head, eyes wide. "I didn't. That's not what I meant." He blows out a heavy breath, then laughs a little as he studies me. "God, I forgot the impact of that voice. I'm not committed to anyone at the moment, promise."

"What did you mean, then?"

He flushes and looks down. "It's new. Nothing official. And they share, anyway."

He looks at me and I'm once again surprised by the directness of his stare. I'm even more surprised by his next words.

"I recognize the look in your eyes, Talia. You know I can give you what you need."

Though his presumption is startling, it's the use of my first name that makes my brows shoot up. "You've changed."

He nods, still intriguingly defiant. "Some shit went down not long after we parted ways. Personal stuff. My sister was in trouble." At my expression of concern, he shakes his head. "She's fine now. Better than fine. But that's when I started growing a backbone."

I reach out and grab his hand. "You've always had a backbone."

"Thank you. But I needed to find one the world could see, so I started working on it. You heard about me taking over daily operations for Dominic?"

I smile warmly. "Yes, Charlie told me. Congratulations." My smile falters. "I'm sorry I didn't reach out."

He smiles faintly, squeezing my fingers. "It's okay. I understand why you didn't. Anyway, Dominic and Charlie taught me a lot." His smile turns wry. "Including how not to freak out over using a Domme's first name."

I smile at the thought of the owners of Crossroads, Dominic Cross and Charlie Rhodes—the latter my mentor during my college years—teaching Nate how to boss people around.

"How's the transition been?"

"A few ruffled feathers initially but nothing extreme. The hardest part has been stepping back as a patron of the club. My position makes submissive behavior confusing for the staff, even if I'm not on the clock."

"I'm sure."

We turn as the door to the club opens. Music fills the hallway—a dark and erotic tempo that thrums in my bones

—before the door shuts again. A woman in a latex catsuit glances at our joined hands and smiles.

"Break time," she chirps to Nate.

He glances at his watch before nodding. "Thanks, Ginny. See you back in fifteen."

She waves and disappears through an adjacent doorway.

"Charlie's gone for the weekend," Nate says, his tone carefully neutral. "If that's who you came to see."

"I came for you, silly."

I say it without thinking, only realizing what I've done when Nate steps closer. He tugs my hand up, splaying my fingers on his chest. I stare at my hand in bemusement; two years ago, he hadn't possessed the confidence to touch me like this.

I drove here expecting to have a drink, to get out of my head, and unwind a bit. And yes, I was hoping to see Nate, whose presence has always centered me. What I didn't expect was for him to be single, exhibit a new, intoxicating blend of behaviors, and to flat-out proposition me.

My fingers curl a little, my nails depressing his shirt and the skin beneath. His breath catches. Need and determination war in his expression.

"You haven't given me a hard no yet, so I'll try again. Please come to my office and let me serve you. For old times' sake."

The awareness that fluttered earlier returns in a bright, heated flash, soothing all the pieces of me that have been fraying since yesterday. Since Kieran Hayes walked into my office with his predator's grace and broken soul. The thought of him—errant, unwanted—makes my arousal skyrocket, mocking me with blatant proof of how attractive I find my new client. How attractive I've *always* found him.

"Whoever you're thinking about," Nate says urgently, "use me instead. Please. I want you so much my legs are about to give out."

I suck in a breath as a knot inside me unwinds, bringing calm and clarity. Right now, in this moment, I can either spiral out about something I have no control over—my body's response to Kieran—or I can accept the gift being offered. And the wonderful man offering it.

"We can't have the boss collapsing in a hallway, can we?"

Relief and triumph shine in his eyes before his gaze drops. He steps back and bows his head, clasping his hands over his groin. Anticipation makes him tremble, makes his breath come fast. The throb between my legs intensifies at the sight.

"Don't be modest, lovely one."

His hands fall to his sides, revealing how excited he is at the prospect of my care. Closing the distance between us, I palm the evidence. He jerks, breath hissing through his teeth. I feel a swell of power mingled with a familiar gravity. One of the hidden treasures I've discovered in this life: even in dominance, there is surrender. As surely as Nate will surrender to my whims, I'll surrender to his.

Leaning forward, I place a gentle kiss on his smooth, warm cheek. Then I squeeze him as I murmur in his ear,

"Here are the rules: we're not fucking tonight, but I'll let you make me come. If it's good, I'll return the favor with my hand. If you exceed my expectations, I *might* put my mouth on you. Do you remember what my mouth can do?"

He makes a strangled noise. "Yes, Mistress, I remember."

I smile. "Then I expect you'll work hard for your reward."

IN NATE'S LOCKED OFFICE, I find succor and respite. He earns my mouth—I never had any doubts—and I give him aftercare in the form of cuddling on the oversized couch. His head rests in my lap as I scrape my fingernails lightly across his scalp.

Peaceful and replete, he gazes up at me. "Do you want to talk about it?"

I smile softly. "Thank you, but no."

Unoffended, he closes his eyes. "Well, if you ever need to *not talk* about it again, my door is always open."

I laugh and draw the pad of my thumb over his brow. He sighs and mumbles, "We still haven't replaced you, you know."

"I know. Charlie calls once a month solely to order me to come back."

He smirks. "Of course she does. You're the best kink educator in the city. A fucking legend." His lashes part, eyes finding mine. "One hour twice a month on Saturdays. Or a seminar every six weeks. Think of it as paid community service."

I roll my eyes. "You're under standing orders from Charlie, aren't you?"

He grins. "Yep. If I see you, I'm required to bring it up." His smile fades, eyes turning serious. "Do you still feel the way you did when you stepped back? From the club and me?"

"Yes to both questions," I say gently, then narrow my eyes. "Tell me Charlie hasn't implied that you're in any way responsible for my leaving."

He shakes his head quickly. "She hasn't."

"Good."

My reasons for giving up my role as an educator at the club were simple—I was stretched too thin, exhausted all the time, and wanted to focus on my career as a therapist. That I ended up stepping back from the lifestyle at the same time wasn't premeditated; it just happened that way.

"So you haven't...?" He trails off, his cheeks reddening.

I lean forward to drop a kiss on his forehead. "No, lovely. You're my last sub. I can't see that changing."

I'd hoped the words would be comforting, but sadness clouds his face. "I'm sorry," he whispers. "Even with all the work I've done, I'll never be able to top you. I just... can't."

My heart squeezes. "I never wanted you to change, Nate. I'm sorry if I ever made you feel that way."

He reaches up and captures my hand. "You didn't. I

guess I'm feeling nostalgic." His eyes twinkle. "No one edges me like you do."

I laugh, but it fades quickly.

"Besides," he adds more softly, "we both know it was mutual. I needed more, too."

Around the same time I started realizing being strictly a Domme wasn't fulfilling me anymore, Nate was coming to terms with his desire for polyamory. He wants to be shared and to share. I want monogamy and sex that allows me to explore both dominance and submission.

"We were almost perfect, weren't we?" he muses, melancholy tainting the words.

I palm his face. "You deserve more than *almost*. Never forget that."

His lips curve. "Yes, Mistress."

A strident knock on the door makes us jump.

"Nate?" calls a male voice. "We have a situation in playroom seven. Non-emergency, but I need some help."

Nate launches to his feet and tugs on his pants. "Coming!"

I pull my shirt on over my bra, then throw my hair into a quick ponytail. When Nate glances at me for permission to open the door, I nod.

The man on the other side is vaguely familiar. He smirks at the sight of Nate—mussed hair, barefoot, and bare-chested, with visible bite marks peeking out of his waistband—then his eyes flicker to me and widen. He blanches, head lowering.

"Professor," he says in an awed voice. "I'm sorry for the interruption."

I wince at the nickname I tried and failed to quell. "It's fine. We're done."

Nate murmurs, "Told you you're famous."

Shaking my head, I settle back on the couch to put on my socks and shoes. I listen as the man relays that a scene went off the rails. A sub is crying hysterically. Her Dom is distraught but not violent. He can't calm her down but also won't let anyone else try.

Nate scrambles to pull on his shirt. "Jesus, Lionel, you said it wasn't an emergency!"

"She's not hurt—"

"Not physically," I mutter at the same time Nate scoffs.

"—but the curtains are open and a crowd has gathered."

"Where the fuck is Adam?" Nate demands.

"Middle of a scene. Playroom four, I think."

Nate curses as he struggles with a shoe. "What about Irene?"

Lionel is finally grasping the seriousness of the situation. "I don't know," he says in a wavering voice. "I came on an hour ago and haven't seen her."

"Why hasn't another Dom gone into the room and asserted control?" I ask, frowning. "The doors don't lock."

Lionel won't meet my eye. "A few have tried, Mistress, but the door is blocked from the inside. Should I—should I get security?"

"You're only now considering that?" yells Nate.

I sigh and stand up.

"Nathan, take a breath and put on your shoe."

He freezes, then nods and does as I say.

I turn my attention to Lionel. "What's the sub's name?"

"M-Mandy, Mistress."

"Both of you, follow me."

THERE ARE consequences for stepping into our former selves. No matter how hard we try, our present-day feet can never perfectly align with the imprints we once made in the world. The result is dissonance. A jarring feedback loop between who we once were and who we've become.

When I finally get home at 1:00 a.m., I'm wrecked. I stumble through my dark house, shedding clothes as I make my way to my bedroom. I manage a brief detour to the bathroom before falling face first onto my bed and curling into the fetal position.

My consequence, my pain, is eerily close to what I felt when I was young—an innate sense of not belonging— which in my case formed a core belief that I'd never belong anywhere.

Finding my place didn't happen overnight. It took years. Like Lewis Caroll's Alice, I had to experiment until I found the correct door for me. Ironically, it took walking through the *wrong* door at UCLA when I was twenty. What I thought was an evening seminar on cognitive neuroscience was in fact an introduction to BDSM. By the time I realized my error, it was too late. I was frozen in my seat and riveted by the lecturer, a professional dominatrix named Charlie Rhodes whose magnetism enthralled me.

Charlie told me later I stuck out like a sore thumb that night. Not because I looked radically uncomfortable—though I was—but because I absorbed her every word like I was starving and had finally found a feast. She spoke about sexual dominance and submission. Safety, consent, communication, power, and pleasure. She had what I wanted: confidence, innate sensuality, and deep understanding of human connection and the intersection between the mind and body.

That was my true beginning; the following nine years, my history.

Donning the mantel of the Professor tonight was like walking into my childhood home and finding that even though all the furniture was the same, I was looking at it from an impossible angle. Although I played the necessary role—asserting control over the Dom in the playroom, soothing the sub and counseling her when she calmed down —I felt upside down in a right side up world.

I don't fit at Crossroads anymore, in the first place I felt like I belonged, and it fucking hurts.

But something else hurts more. A truth that sneaks up in the darkness and silence between my muffled sobs and falls over me like a weighted blanket when my tears at last ebb. A twisted treasure unearthed in my very own psyche by tonight's dissonance. Reflective and inescapable, it glows across all the footsteps of my past.

There's a reason why the men I've always been drawn to look like Nate. Tall and slender and faintly untouchable. Because they resemble the first male who quickened my sexuality.

Eighteen-year-old Kieran Hayes.

All these years, I've been trying to make a memory kneel.

At least I finally understand the underlying reason I pulled away from Nate, from Crossroads. Because after so long searching, some part of me must have accepted I'd never find what I was looking for.

He isn't real.

My heart has been hunting a ghost.

CHAPTER 6

KIERAN

Despite my best attempts over the last four days to talk myself out of this appointment, at 6:59 p.m. on Wednesday, I knock on Dr. Stirling's office door. When there's no answer, Sven and I exchange a glance. Her car is in the parking lot. She even reminded me via an impersonal text service of the date and time.

Like I could have forgotten.

I'm about to knock again when the door opens. Slightly mollified that she didn't summon me from inside again like I'm mutt begging for scraps, I open my mouth to make a sarcastic remark.

But no words come out.

"Mr. Hayes," she says, nodding. "Hello, Sven."

"Doctor," he rumbles.

Honeyed eyes return to me. She's so tall in her sky-high

heels, we're almost at eye level. A dark brow cocks. "Are you feeling all right?"

I clear my throat. I *never* clear my throat unless I have a fucking cold.

"Fine," I bite out.

Her eyes narrow at my tone, but she steps aside slightly and waves me in. I force my suddenly leaden feet to move past her. For exactly two seconds, I feel the heat of her body all the way through my suit. Her perfume coils around me, the fragrance notes like dancing snakes born to hypnotize men. The scent clings to me as I cross the office. I want to shower immediately.

My blood boiling, I unbutton my jacket and drop into the too-small chair. I think I might hate her. Especially when the soft *snick* of the door closing makes my cock stir. Fucking idiot body part doesn't know any better. Not when Stirling looks like every horny teenager's illicit wet dream about a naughty schoolteacher.

The top half of her shiny dark hair is clipped back, the lower half falling in long waves that form parenthesis around her breasts. Completing the honeytrap is a pseudo-conservative white blouse—silky and thin enough to hint at lace beneath—a skintight black skirt that skims the top of her calves, and heels so tall they could double as spears. Oh, and red lipstick. Because everything else wasn't obvious enough.

The worst of it is she pulls it off. *Some-fucking-how* none of it looks contrived. Even though I damned well know everything this woman wields—her mind, her words, her body, her clothes—is a weapon.

"Is something wrong?" she asks, floating to her chair like a dancer, then sinking onto it like it's a throne.

"No."

Her blood-red lips don't move. Her face is a static painting. Only her eyes are alive, studying me like I'm an equation she already knows the answer to. A queer feeling takes hold of me—that odd wave of familiarity I felt the first time I saw her. I must have met someone with eyes the same color before, but I have no idea when or where.

"How was returning to work?" she asks.

"Fine."

It's been better than fine. Returning was surprisingly easy thanks to Alistair's efforts the last month. As far as anyone at Lumitech knows, I stepped away to work on an ultra-private project at home. I'm not even mad I'll need to pull something out of my ass to support the lie. It doesn't matter whether or not I bring forward something actionable. My project leaders know full well that half my ideas are science fiction, anyway, either wildly impractical or downright implausible. They're used to my eccentricities.

For the last three days, I've felt stirrings of the same excitement I had in the early years. A sense of possibility and purpose. Even the never-ending project meetings that had become painfully monotonous felt less so.

"Close your eyes, Mr. Hayes."

I glare at her. "Why?"

She tilts her head. Her hair swings forward, hugging the curve of one full breast. Lamplight makes her skin unnaturally luminous. Polished alabaster.

I need to get laid. That's obviously the reason my eyes keep straying. I can't be attracted to her. I like women who are soft, warm, and compliant. Who have nothing to hide—unlike the woman across from me, who more and more reminds me of a Japanese puzzle box. With spikes that take blood at every wrong move.

"Because I asked you to," she answers.

"You didn't *ask*." I sound deranged. Mean and angry. I feel a pinch of shame.

"Correct," she says. "Do you know why?"

Blowing out a breath, I swipe a hand down my face. I knew this was a mistake. "I bet you're gonna fucking tell me, huh?"

"Because when I ask you a question, you rarely answer. When I give you an order, it irritates you, which at least leads to an honest response. Now close your fucking eyes."

Startled, I laugh. Her lips curve.

"Jesus. *Fine*."

I close my eyes.

"I want you to think about the last time you were happy. Don't focus on details like where you were, who you were with... that's background noise. I want you to isolate the *feeling* of happiness. Let me know when you have."

My first thought is of my wife, but I shut it down before I even picture her face. My mind goes blank.

"This is impossible," I mutter.

"Did you have a pet as a child?"

I immediately envision the ugliest dog in the world. A small, geriatric mutt with the foulest breath who followed me home from the river one day and inserted himself into our family. But he loved me first and most, rarely straying from my side.

"Aye. Dilly." A genuine smile spreads on my face. I fucking loved that dog.

"Good. Hold onto that feeling as you take an internal step back from it. Think of it as a ball of light that you can walk around and observe. Now take one more step back until you can feel *where* that happiness is. Where it lives in your body. Once you find it, tell me."

It's surprisingly easy to follow her instructions.

"My shoulders," I say softly. "The front side of them. And, ehm, the bottom of my chest around my ribs."

I feel like an absolute fool, but she says, "Good," with a warmth in her voice I haven't heard before. "Take a deep breath and open your eyes."

I open my eyes to her smile and that annoyingly charming eyetooth.

"Now," she says lightly, "how was returning to work?"

My lips tug into a begrudging smile. "You win, Doc."

Once I start talking, it's like a dam breaks. More and more pours out, and at some point I forget that she's... *her*. I talk to her like I would a colleague, outlining a few of the more exciting ventures in the works. Advancements and new applications for current technologies, all the expected impacts on the market over the next few years.

Stirling listens with her whole body. Legs crossed, she leans forward with an elbow on a knee and her chin on a fist. Her eyes stay pinned to mine, slightly widened. She looks like I'm giving her proof that fairies are real. It's a heady feeling and likely to blame for what comes out of my mouth next.

I tell her what I've been personally working on for the last five years with a specialized team of ethicists, neuroscientists, nanotechnologists, and biomedical and robotics engineers. Information so privileged even Alistair doesn't know all the details. Beyond the initial press release years ago—that I'd argued vehemently against—we've kept the project behind literal vault doors.

"Neural nanorobotics," she echoes in an awed tone. "I vaguely remember there being a media splash years ago when Lumitech announced funding research on it, but I haven't seen anything since."

"That's intentional."

After the first round of death threats, I'd put my foot down with the board. Given that some of the threats weren't specific to me but rather promises to bomb our headquarters, I hadn't needed to push too hard.

She frowns. "There were protests for a while, right?"

I nod. "People hear 'artificially intelligent robots' and 'brain,' and assume nefarious intent. Then fear-mongers spread more misinformation that, unfortunately, is far more palatable to the masses than scientific research."

"I can't remember if you released the intended application. Is there one?"

I smile wryly. "We're not developing mind-control, that's for sure. Our goal is nanorobots that repair damaged neurons and remove amyloid plaques associated with Alzheimer's disease."

Stirling blinks and sits back, a softness in her expression that makes my skin itch and my fingers twitch. My tongue swells with another detail—how close we are to a working prototype. But I've already said too much.

"That's amazing," she says. "I'm assuming you haven't publicized your ongoing research because of competition?"

"We have no competitors," I tell her with a small smile. It's not arrogance—it's fact. No one has the team I do. Other companies are working on similar technologies, but they're light years behind us. "It's for security reasons."

She nods. "What you've told me won't leave this room."

"I'm not worried about that." Oddly, it's true.

"Then what *are* you worried about?"

My mind ices over, the spreading numbness a welcome buffer between me and this new, mystifying urge to confide in her. I shouldn't have told her about the project to begin with.

There is no project. Not anymore.

Not since a phone call in the middle of the night accomplished what two assassination attempts hadn't.

"Did something change five weeks ago?"

I loathe how easily she can read me—a feat even those closest to me have never managed.

Sharing time is over.

"I've been working my ass off since I was eighteen. I was bound to crash eventually." I shrug. "I'm feeling back to normal now."

Her eyes sharpen. *Lion eyes.* The second my mind makes the connection, something in me relaxes. There's now a valid explanation for that niggling familiarity I feel around her. Dilly was the single canine exception to my lifelong love of big cats. When I was little, my parents used to have to drag me away from the lion enclosure at the Dublin Zoo.

"So that's what over a month of daily drinking and isolation were? A vacation?"

"Apparently so."

Stirling stares at me for another beat. "I think we should stop here for today."

Music to my ears.

Standing smoothly, I button my jacket. She rises as well, gliding past me to the door. My eyes have a mind of their own, skating over the dark mass of her hair, lingering on the curve of her ass, trailing down her legs. Her bare calves are works of art.

"Mr. Hayes."

Shit.

Stirling stands at the door, hand on the knob, her expression reproachful. For a shocking second, I wonder what she looks like when she comes.

I'm so rattled by the thought, I snap, "You're not my type, but I'm not dead. Out of curiosity, what did you hope to accomplish by wearing that getup? Did you think I'd fall to my knees and ask to be spanked?"

Shock blankets her expression, swiftly encompassed by anger. Shame floods me like toxic waste. *Why the fuck did I say that?* She's really done nothing except try to help me.

"Stirling, I—"

"No," she snaps.

She crosses to me and gets right in my face, so tall I barely have to dip my head to maintain eye contact. And I do—I deserve whatever she's about to unleash.

"Listen very carefully because I'm not going to repeat myself. That's the last time you'll reference my past, which you know less than nothing about. Moreover, our sessions are outside my normal working hours—which, as I mentioned to Gail, are booked solid for the next two months. If I'd had time to change between my last appointment of the day and this one, believe me, I would have."

My voice bypasses my brain entirely, emerging hoarse. "You wore that for another client?"

Her eyes flare. She takes an abrupt step back, then swivels and opens the door. Not looking at me, she says in a frosty tone, "Good night, Mr. Hayes. If you'd like to book another session, you have my phone number."

I clear my throat and walk past her into the hallway. The door doesn't slam, but the sound is jarringly final. I acted like a fool, and I don't blame her for putting me in my place.

Sven's gaze shifts from the door to me, then flickers down before snapping back to my face. His brows lift.

"Don't say a fucking word," I growl.

He grunts—the equivalent of a gleeful howl.

I stalk past him toward the exit, refusing to acknowledge or adjust my rock-hard cock.

CHAPTER 7

TALIA

"This is... a complicated situation."

I groan in the direction of my phone, currently on speaker on my bathroom counter, while I apply mascara. "Come on, Leo. You can do better than that."

Dr. Leo Chastain, Mia's husband, is a colleague and a friend, but right now he's my therapist. I even sent him five dollars before calling to seal the deal. Not that I doubted he'd agree to counsel me on demand—he owes me.

Once upon a time, Mia was his client. I was the colleague he turned to when the shattering of his ethics nearly broke him. Because of me—and my brilliant insights, thank you very much—he eventually forgave himself and pulled his head out of his ass before Mia disappeared from his life.

"Do you have feelings for him?" he asks finally.

I almost stab myself in the eye with the mascara wand.

Reinserting the applicator, I screw the top closed and throw it into the open drawer. "This isn't a you-and-Mia repeat. Not even close."

"I'm still asking."

I sigh. "Like I already told you, at fourteen I had a fantasy-based obsession with a memory of him. From my first sexual experience onward, I gravitated toward the physical archetype of him as an eighteen-year-old."

"You're pissed about that."

My mirror agrees with him. "Not as angry as I was when I realized it, but yeah."

"Why? Are you still attracted to eighteen-year-olds?"

I roll my eyes. "You know what I mean."

"I think I do. You're insulted that you made decisions subconsciously steered by childhood experience. Because you think you're smarter than the rest of us and should've been exempted from ordinary psychosocial development."

I growl, and the jerk laughs.

"What's past the anger, Talia?"

Grabbing my phone, I carry it across my bedroom to the closet. As I step into heels, I tell Leo, "Sadness."

"Why does this new information about yourself make you sad?"

"Because it's tainting beautiful memories. Time I've spent with incredible men. And I guess it makes me worry I wasn't totally authentic with them."

"That's bullshit," he says crisply. "Just because a formative experience led you to be attracted to a certain body type doesn't mean you treated any of your partners like stand-ins for someone else. Unless you're saying you were actively replacing them during intimacy with fantasies of Kieran?"

I grimace. "God, no."

"I didn't think so. Also, you dodged my question. Do you or do you not have feelings for your client?"

"Absolutely not. He's volatile, emotionally stunted, thinks therapy is a waste of time, and *chauvinist* might as well be stamped on his forehead. Every conversation we have leaves me with a headache and second thoughts about my career choice."

He whistles softly. "In that case, do you foresee your past experience or current personal opinion of him preventing you from being an objective, effective therapist?"

"Maybe the first one," I admit.

He hums thoughtfully. "You're attached to the idea of saving him, which makes sense given the experience in Ireland and your preoccupation with equal reciprocity."

"Dang, don't pull punches on my account."

The problem with receiving therapy from someone who's known you a long time is... they've known you a long time. Leo is well aware of my family history. After years of my mother and sister *taking* and me *giving,* I finally set boundaries. I have reduced contact with my mom but haven't spoken to my sister in almost two years. I don't speak with my father often, but at least it's for the simple reason we don't have anything to talk about.

I can hear his smile as he adds, "All I'm saying is you

don't owe him, Talia. Nothing beyond your skills as a psychologist. As much as the line sometimes blurs, it's not our job to save anyone. We simply do our best to light the way for them to save themselves."

I deflate with a sigh. "You're right."

"Of course I am. I'm smarter than you."

I laugh. "You're such an ass."

Leo chuckles. "You mean I'm the older, wiser brother you always wanted."

"Yeah, that too. Thanks. Say hi to the family for me."

"Will do. One final question."

"Yeah?"

"You're sure he doesn't recognize you?"

"Absolutely sure."

"Hmm. I find that hard to believe."

I smile. "Trust me, I look drastically different than I did at fourteen. I'll show you a picture sometime. It's been seventeen years, Leo. Not only that, it was dusk, raining, and he'd just smoked a joint. I'm confident what was a memorable meeting to me was something quickly forgotten for him, a random American girl he found in a graveyard and walked back to her hotel."

There's a pregnant pause, and I know I'm not going to like what he says next.

"And how does *that* make you feel?"

I was right—I don't like it at all.

My phone buzzes with a text, and I read it with no small

measure of relief. I quickly turn off the speaker and bring the phone to my ear.

"Sorry. My date is here. I've gotta run."

"Uh-huh."

My laugh is a tad shrill as I grab my purse and leave the bedroom. "I'm not lying. He's taking me to the Philharmonic. Ask Mia. She was the one who set us up. He's the principal of her school."

He groans. "Oh, no. Tell me she didn't."

I jerk to a stop in the foyer, eyeballing my front door. "What?" I whisper-hiss. "Leonardo Chastain, tell me right now if I need to get out of this."

Leo coughs. "No, no, Alan is great. You'll have a splendid time."

"*Splendid?*" I screech through my teeth.

My doorbell rings.

Leo's laughter ends abruptly as he hangs up.

CHAPTER 8

KIERAN

I can't believe my eyes. Or my ears. Or anything really about what's happening as Dr. Stirling settles gracefully in the seat directly in front of mine at the LA Phil. The man with her looks like white toast with strawberry jam smeared on his cheeks. It takes him three tries to hold down the retractable seat long enough to actually plant his ass on it.

My brother bumps my shoulder. "Isn't that—"

"Shut up," I hiss at the same time Gail whacks his arm from the other side.

Toasty is sweating and babbling about the architect of the concert hall while Stirling smiles at him. She needs to stop smiling or he's going to have a coronary. I actually feel a bit bad for the guy.

"That's fascinating, Alan," she says warmly.

Jesus. Is there a more tedious name than Alan?

Toasty grins like she offered him a blow job. His gaze flickers down to her breasts and he gets even redder. The skin around Stirling's eyes tightens. I bite the inside of my cheek to keep in a cackle.

"Do you know her?" whispers the woman next to me. I think her name is Claudia. Maybe Flavia. She's a petite, pretty blond. Exactly my type.

I lean over so I can keep my voice low, regretting the move when I get a nose-full of flowery perfume. "No, but she looks familiar. Is she an actress or something? Should we ask for an autograph?"

Claudia-Flavia giggles. "No. She's some celebrity sex therapist. Buzzfeed did an article about her and it kinda blew up."

"Sex therapy, huh?" I grin, and she blushes like I knew she would.

I'm relieved when the musicians file across the stage and take their seats, then the first chair violinist. As the orchestra begins warming up, I close my eyes to listen. A prickling sensation overtakes me at the familiar, harmonious chaos. My eyes stay closed as the conductor's entrance garners more applause.

Alistair whispers to me, "You okay?"

I nod, murmuring back, "Just miss her."

"Same."

Our mother loved classical music with a passion. Baroque, Renaissance, Opera, it didn't matter and changed by the day. She played it so much—all the damn time, really

—that Alistair and I hated it as teens. Little shits that we were, we'd crank heavy metal in our room to drown out the record player that sat outside the kitchen.

Now the music is a barbed comfort. For five years, we've come here every month to feel close to her. Even though most days she doesn't remember her love of music. Or even her love of us.

Shubert's Symphony No. 6 in C major unfolds, carrying me back to a rainy afternoon in our flat. Mam in the kitchen, the smell of a roast floating out. Dad dozing on the couch with a book open on his chest. Alistair and I running around attempting to murder each other as silently as possible.

The music swells and ebbs around the memory. I float on the surface of it, out of place and time.

A kick to my shin jerks me from my stupor. My eyes fly open to find everyone standing and applauding. I join them quickly and put my hands together. The vestiges of dreaminess cling to me as my gaze drifts to the back of Stirling's head. A wisp of hair curls against her bare neck, the rest drawn up in a loose bun. I have the sudden, ridiculous urge to rip out the clip and watch her hair spill like a waterfall.

The applause tapers off, voices rising and bodies shuffling toward the lobby for intermission. Stirling's date—I've already forgotten his name—says something about using the restroom. When Stirling nods, he just stands there like an ape.

She finally says, "I'll stay here, thanks," and he beats a retreat. She sighs and sits back down.

Alistair and Gail have also disappeared. Clavia presses close to me, her fake breasts against my arm. "Do you want to grab a quick drink, Kieran?" she asks, her voice unpleasantly loud.

Out of the corner of my eye, I see Stirling's spine stiffen to a plank.

"Go on ahead," I tell her, pulling out my phone. "I have to answer a few emails."

"On a Saturday night?" she whines.

I grin. "No rest for the wicked."

Wrongly interpreting the words as foreshadowing, Clavia blushes and titters, then finally leaves. I sit down and scoot to the edge of the seat, leaning forward until I'm close enough to Stirling to count the individual hairs in that little wisp and the tiny gold links in her necklace.

"Psst."

Her head falls forward a moment—in resignation, most like—before she straightens and turns around. "Hello, Mr. Hayes."

Goddamn.

Surprise punches me, like my brain deleted how beautiful she is so it could appreciate her again for the first time. Or maybe it's the fact my wall of defensive denial crumbled at the end of our session Wednesday.

As aggravating as it is to admit, I'm attracted to her. Very, very attracted.

Bronze eye shadow makes her eyes look like pools of gold, and the subtle, rosy tint on her lips somehow packs a bigger punch than red lipstick. A few loose tendrils of hair frame her face. The snug, long-sleeved green dress doesn't show nearly as much skin as I imagined from Toasty's drooling; on the other hand, I can't blame the man. This woman would make a burlap sack sexy. At the base of her throat sits a tiny gold pendant of a bird, vibrating above a fluttering pulse.

I clear my throat. "I was a jackass on Wednesday. I'm sorry."

The coolness in her eyes shifts to wariness. "Is that so?"

I nod gravely. "I meant to call you today to apologize, but between all the healthy meals and exercise, I didn't get a chance."

I'm rewarded with the barest of close-lipped smiles. I scoot even closer, almost falling off my seat. The need to see her eyetooth is fierce.

"So—"

Stirling's gaze snaps to my right, and she smiles broadly. *For someone else.* "Gail!"

My sister-in-law shoves past Alistair and commandeers his seat, chattering a mile a minute to a grinning Stirling. I push backward until my spine hits the chair and glance at my brother, who stares at the women like he's never seen female friends reunite before.

Flowery perfume and a whiff of Chardonnay invade my nose as Clavia returns. She asks me a question that I have to ask her to repeat, and I immediately forget the exchange after. It's almost a relief when Toasty finally returns from the bathroom—probably after nervous shits—and Gail and Stirling wrap up their conversation.

Intermission ends and the orchestra begins Beethoven's Symphony No. 7. Even though it's one of Mam's favorites, I struggle to immerse myself in the music. Stirling's fault. I'm distracted by her neck, obsessively imagining what my hand would look like wrapped around the smooth, pale column.

When the final applause of the night tapers off, I tap Gail's shoulder. "Take Flavia home, will you?"

She blinks, wide-eyed. "Um, sure. Okay."

An annoyed voice chirps, "It's Claudia."

Alistair and I share a wince before I turn around. "Sorry, pet. It's been a long week. I'll reach out another time."

Unable to help myself, I glance one last time at Stirling, blinking when I see she and Toasty are already gone. I scan the aisle but don't see her. My bones start to burn with urgency—our conversation wasn't finished.

Claudia makes an insulted noise as I brush past her, hurrying down the row and throwing out "sorry" left and right as I jostle people. I'm usually more cognizant of my size, but I need *out*. The human flow thickens at the back of the hall, and I have to resist the urge to shove through.

When I make it into the lobby, Sven and Dylan appear to either side of me. Gabe is likely on his way to fetch the car. A few people call my name as I cross to the exit doors. I ignore them, not slowing, and push outside.

I spot her standing alone at the curb. My legs eat the distance in seconds.

"Stirling."

She spins on a heel, surprise flashing in her eyes before they flicker around me. Her throat moves as she swallows. "You shouldn't be seen with me."

My brows shoot up. "Who fuckin' says?"

She rolls her eyes, the gesture so at odds with her usual poise I have to bite my lip to stop a grin.

"Where's Toasty?" I ask.

She frowns. "Toasty?"

The grin sneaks free. "The white bread you're with."

Her head bows, and I think she mutters, "For fuck's sake," before sighing. "Mr. Hayes—"

"You should call me Kieran or Kier in public if you're worried about people thinking you're my therapist. Though I guarantee that's not what they're wondering seeing us together."

Her eyes widen a bit and veer to Sven. I have no idea what she sees on his face, but to my everlasting shock, a stain of peachy-pink spreads across her cheekbones. The sight is astounding. Revelatory. I'm a worthless sinner witnessing a miracle.

Like a fool, I say, "You're blushing," and it sounds like I've told her she's spontaneously grown a third arm.

She takes an abrupt step backward. "Enjoy the rest of your evening, Mr.—"

"Kieran."

She scowls. "—Hayes."

A car pulls up to the curb behind her. I see Toasty sweating in the driver's seat. Stirling sees him, too.

"Go easy on him, Doc. He looks breakable."

As the words come out, I grimace. *Idiot.* I could slap myself. But as I open my mouth to apologize, she shocks the hell out me by laughing. It sounds like fucking bells.

Eyes sparkling, she shrugs. "Win some, lose some."

My burst of laughter is loud and startles us both. Stirling stares at me, lips parted, then seems to remember where she is and who's waiting for her.

She starts to turn, then glances back. "Wednesday at seven?"

My nod is swift. "Sounds good."

She clears her throat. "Okay. See you then."

"Kieran," I whisper.

She shakes her head, too amused to be irritated, and walks toward the car. I tuck my hands in my pockets and watch the sway of her hips. Because I've clearly lost all sense.

Behind me, Sven rumbles, "Open her door."

I jerk into motion, overtaking Stirling before she reaches the car. As I pull open the passenger door, my hand falls to her lower back in a move so natural I don't realize I've touched her until she jerks forward. My fingers tingle; I curl them against my palm.

"Thank you," she says in a stilted voice, slipping into the seat.

Once she's settled, I lean down to make eye contact with Toasty. "Gentlemen open doors for ladies."

He pales.

"Drive safe, yeah?"

He nods, throat convulsing.

"Enough, Kieran," murmurs Stirling.

My gaze snaps to hers, my giant grin triggering another roll of her eyes. I relinquish my hold on the door and she pulls it closed. They drive away.

I'm giving Sven a raise.

CHAPTER 9

TALIA

Kieran slouches on the sofa in my office, making it appear child-sized. His arms are spread over the back, long legs splayed. The suit jacket and tie he came in wearing hang on a hook by the door. A white button-down is open at the collar and rolled up his forearms. He finally had his hair trimmed, and he shaved this morning.

He looks content, powerful, and smug.

"Does this mean you've forgiven me for last week?" he asks with an endearingly crooked grin.

His entire demeanor is different today, but the most drastic change is in his eyes. Vivid and lively, they virtually glow. From a professional standpoint, his attitude is a massive step in the right direction. No one wants a client who resents every session. But I'm also not naive enough to think my prowess as a therapist is the cause.

I shouldn't have engaged with him Saturday night. Used

his first name. Let his charm get under my skin. I gave him an inch and now he's taking a mile—or thinks he is.

"The seating arrangement today had nothing to do with you, Mr. Hayes."

His smile widens at my formality and the reminder that he's not my only client. "You had time to change."

I rearranged my damn schedule to make the time. No more skirts—no skirts ever again with this man. I'm wearing wide-leg trousers and flats. Full coverage blouse. Black, black, all black. My hair is in a severe bun, my lips bare except for Chapstick.

"You're in a good mood today," I remark with a smile—a slight one, my lips staying sealed. I haven't missed his fixation with my teeth.

He shrugs. "I guess I am."

"Still exercising daily?"

He nods. "Judo and laps in the pool every morning. My sensei sends his thanks, by the way. He loves kicking my ass almost as much as he loves ringing my doorbell at four a.m. Crazy fucker."

"I'm glad to hear it. And how's work?"

"Back to the grind, as they say." His tone is light, but his eyes flicker away from me. A second later, he crosses his legs at the ankle.

Fault line.

There are two roads ahead of me, both with risks. I can lean into the work angle, try to find out what set him off in our last session. What happened five weeks ago. Or I can aim somewhere else. If I dig from a different angle, I might reach treasure faster.

Decision made, I internally brace for conflict. "And how was the rest of your date Saturday night?"

His eyes snap to me, sparkling and dark. The moment he touched my back rises between us: his breath catching, my graceless escape. To keep from reacting—or God forbid, blushing—I think about Alan's fumbling, failed attempt to kiss me at my front door.

"Whatever do you mean, Doc?"

Here we go.

"Did you take her home?"

He disguises a flash of surprise with laughter. "Are we really going there?"

I nod serenely. "We are."

He sobers, sitting up and crossing his arms. *Direct hit.* Conscious or not, he senses what's coming. I wait for him to either attack or attempt to redirect. But he doesn't do either.

"No," he says shortly. "Gail and Alistair drove her home."

"What was her name?"

"Fla—no, Claudia." He winces. "In my defense, it was a last-minute blind date."

"Are blind dates typical for you?"

His eyes narrow. "Are they typical for you? Because we both know Toasty was one."

"We're not talking about me."

His teeth grind, the movement of muscle along his jaw

pronounced. I almost wish he'd kept the beard. Part of me wishes, too, that his guard were still up. That I couldn't read him as easily as I now can.

"I wouldn't say they're typical, no."

"How do you normally find dates?"

"An app," he says through his teeth. "You know, Tinder for billionaires."

I tilt my head. "Can you tell me about your dating habits the last few years? How many dates per week?"

"Two or three," he says flatly. "Sometimes more, sometimes less."

"In that time, have you ever dated the same woman longer than a week?"

Blue flames spark and begin to burn. "Several. In fact, there are three women I've been seeing for over a year."

"But you're not seeing them exclusively. Are they aware you're dating other women in addition to them?"

The flames erupt. "They know the score, all right? We're adults."

I take a breath, then throw an axe right at his fault line. "Did you struggle with monogamy during your marriage?"

His eyes freeze over and he goes preternaturally still. "No. And that's all I'm going to say. We're not talking about Liz."

My heart throbs at the pain he's trying so hard to hide. I don't have to pretend sympathy; it seeps from my pores.

"Kieran," I say gently.

Ice cracks, a tiny silver of flame burning through. "What?" he asks roughly.

"I'm not going to counsel you about opening yourself back up to a meaningful relationship." *Yet,* I add privately. "Your grief journey is your own. What I'm concerned about is the fact you might be using casual sex to avoid the journey altogether."

"Who says it's casual? Maybe I have no interest in a conventional romantic partnership. I'm sure you can relate."

I ignore the jab. "Okay, then have you seen any of your regular partners in the last six weeks?"

I already know the answer; I can recognize a man in dire need of sexual release. And not the type that comes from his own hand.

"What does that have to do with anything?" he grinds out.

I sit back and cross my legs. "Were you attracted to Claudia?"

"Sure was. She's a fine thing."

"Then why didn't you take her home?"

He leans forward, eyes like chips of ice. "You want to know, Stirling? You sure?"

"If I wasn't sure, I wouldn't ask."

The words come out confident despite a sudden sensation that I've lost traction and am sliding right into the open mouth of a wolf.

Blue flames obliterate ice. "Because for some insane reason, I couldn't stop thinking about your neck and what it would feel like to squeeze it while I fucked your throat."

The air vacates my lungs in a whoosh. Heat burns my

centerline in a searing wave. It takes everything I have—absolutely everything—not to physically jerk in place.

"You're blushing again."

"I'm not dead."

I throw his words back at him without thinking. As soon as they release, I freeze in consternation. I've lost control of the dynamic and myself. It's never happened before in this office. In any private space. With any man in my adult life.

Kieran's smile is slight and satisfied as he slouches back again, arms extended, knees falling open in an arrogant extension. The amount of willpower I exert to keep from glancing down his body is tremendous.

"You're aroused, Stirling. I can see the wild pulse in your neck." His rough, lyrical voice makes another pulse—the one between my thighs—pound harder.

I force a nonchalant shrug. "I could just as easily be repulsed. You were looking for a reaction, Mr. Hayes, and you got it. Congratulations."

"Oh, it's Mr. Hayes again, is it?"

I suck in a breath and release it slowly. "Yes. While what you said was highly inappropriate, I'm glad you shared."

His teeth scrape across his lower lip. "I can't wait to hear why."

"Two reasons. One, you lashed out defensively because the topic was making you uncomfortable, which tells me it's an important one to revisit."

"Cute. Reason two?"

"The fact you've fantasized about me sexually is troubling. If we can't resolve it, I'll have to refer you to another therapist. I have someone in mind who I think would be a good fit."

Sorry in advance, Leo.

"No."

I blink. "No?"

"I'm not seeing another therapist. It's you or no one."

Worry unfolds under my breastbone. "It would be a mistake to end therapy."

His gaze meanders leisurely down my body before he scoffs. "Come on, Doc. I guarantee I'm not the first to think about you. Besides, we both know I don't actually want you. I prefer bedmates about a foot shorter and without claws."

"Enjoy your stay, Birdie. And maybe lay off the whiskey until your claws grow in."

The memory punches me and I flinch—a reflex I can't control or mask. My only choice is to ignore it right along with Kieran's suddenly acute focus.

I yank the shreds of my control to me.

"That's a worthwhile observation." My voice is too weak; clearing my throat lightly, I continue, "Given the nature of your fantasy—that of you exerting power over me—I'm willing to consider it was a subconscious defense against the threat I pose."

A muscle in his jaw jumps. More control flows sweetly into my hands. I don't bother waiting for him to reply.

"I've clearly touched some core wounds, and your emotional defenses identified me as an enemy. Combined with your recent stretch of celibacy and hetero-normative traits..." I shrug. "Makes sense."

Kieran shakes his head slowly; eventually, his lips twitch. "You're a trip."

"Does that mean you agree?" I ask levelly.

He stares a few moments, then sighs and scrubs his hands down his face. "Fuck, I don't know. I guess." Head down, he mumbles something under his breath.

"What was that?"

Blue eyes flash up. *Open. Raw. Tortured.*

"I wouldn't blame you if you told me to get out and never come back."

I tilt my head, bemused by the sudden shift. "Why would I do that?"

"Because I..." He can barely get the words out, his head bowing as if under mighty weight. "I told you I thought about forcing myself on you. I'm sorry. God, I'm so sorry."

My heart softens as years of experience in the kink community and as a sex therapist roll through me in a tender wave. He doesn't deserve to feel guilt over a harmless fantasy. Using it as a weapon against me? That was a dick move. But I can't let him beat himself up over the fantasy itself.

Knowing the root of his shame is in the idea of my lack of consent, I ask, "Was I enjoying it?"

His head whips up, eyes wide. "What?"

"In your fantasy, did you see my face?"

Ruddiness stains his cheekbones. Long fingers clench on his knees as his gaze veers to my throat. I'm powerless over a reflexive swallow. He sucks in a breath, blackness spreading through blue as his pupils dilate.

I stiffen against an answering rush of heat and yank the mantel of the Professor around my shoulders. I don't even care if I pay for it later.

"Focus, Mr. Hayes."

He twitches, gaze dropping. "Yeah, Doc. I saw your face."

"Was I giving cues of a struggle?"

His shifts restlessly, a foot coming up to the opposite knee. I keep my gaze firmly on his face.

"No," he finally says.

"Then you weren't forcing me," I tell him. "I'm willing to move past it if you are."

He nods, still not looking at me. "Yeah, good." He blows out a breath. "Can we call it a day?"

"Yes."

He jumps off the couch and is out the door before I can muster the energy to stand.

CHAPTER 10

TALIA

When I was thirteen, the monster inside me woke up. By the time I turned fourteen, she was constantly with me, flexing and scratching. The pressure was tangible, so agonizing, I'd curl into a ball on my bed for hours and shake with the effort of containing it.

In the months prior to our trip to Ireland, I was so exhausted from my nonstop efforts to manage the monster that my grades started slipping. My teachers grew worried. The school counselor talked to me, but I couldn't tell her what I was feeling. I'd never been taught how.

Conversely, my parents failed to hide their relief when I brought home my first C. They'd always said they were proud of my academic achievements—especially when it came up around other adults—but I knew they weren't. Not really. Even if I didn't have the words to communicate my own feelings, I'd spent my life observing them and others. Always slightly apart from my peers, my family. Looking in from the outside.

My parents loved me, but it was an obligatory kind of love. I made them nervous. A little scared. I was the changeling who'd dropped into their home and upset their perfectly predictable lives. I was too much effort, too different. And when they thought I didn't notice, they looked at me like the problems in their marriage were my fault.

If only she'd been a normal child.

When we returned home from Ireland, I grew even more depressed. I barely left my bed, preferring to sleep and float in daydreams of the boy I'd met in a graveyard. The first person I'd ever opened up to, who'd seen the real me and shown no fear or revulsion. When I thought about him, my monster was quiet.

My fantasies grew to epic proportions, each more grandiose than the last. My favorite was the one where his father was an Interpol agent with a computer program that could find anyone, anywhere. Kieran hacked the computer and tracked me down by cross-referencing passports with reservations at the hotel in Galway. He showed up outside my house in the middle of the night and tossed pebbles at my window. Our reunion was always the hardest part for me to envision as I had no life experience to draw from. There was some sort of embrace. A confession from him that he couldn't stop thinking about me, either. It ended with a hazy epilogue of us running away together.

Then, about two months after our trip, my father moved out. Watching from the living room window as he packed boxes into a rented trunk while my mother drank wine in the backyard and Olivia hid in her room, I realized that fantasies were pointless.

No one was coming to free me, save me, or love me. I had to do it myself.

That was my awakening. The moment I stopped fighting the monster and her baby claws popped through my skin. It hurt like a muscle stretching—there was pleasure in the pain. Power I'd never felt before.

I was done kneeling to the world.

THE SESSION with Kieran stays with me like a mosquito bite, driving me half-mad over the next two days. I scratch at every word spoken. Struggle with the unprofessional urge to call him and make sure he's okay.

I try and fail not to hijack his fantasy as my own. In a weak moment, I kneel naked in the shower and close my eyes to a vision of him doing exactly what he said. I imagine what he'd feel like. Sound like. I squeeze my own throat as I stroke myself to an explosive orgasm, then collapse in gasping, tearful shame.

I almost call Leo a dozen times. What stops me is the fear of the questions he'll ask. The fear I'll lie to him because I'm not ready to face the truth. My monster—tamed for years—is restless. Pacing. Her claws tickle the underside of my skin, an imminent threat.

I don't sleep well Wednesday or Thursday, my dreams filled with vague catastrophes I don't remember when I wake. My only relief comes at work. In my office, I'm not Talia, a woman still worried I'm not enough, that I'm failing. That I still haven't found where I fit in the world. I'm Dr. Stirling: therapist, life coach, wizard. I'm compassionate and honest. My best self. I cradle my clients in my palms and stroke their tattered feathers. I feed them, soothe them, and help them learn to fly again.

The strain of balancing the schism within me catches up Friday evening. I'm so drained when I get home that I skip my normal after-work ritual of a shower and ten minutes of meditation.

Without bothering to change clothes, I make myself popcorn and grab a beer from the fridge, then slump onto my living room couch. Pulling a blanket around my shoulders, I close my eyes, telling myself I'll open them in a minute. Eat a little. Watch a show.

In a minute...

The incessant vibration of my phone wakes me hours later. The room is dark, my popcorn cold, the beer warm.

"Okay, okay," I mumble groggily, digging into the couch cushions where the device slipped. I manage to extract it. Squinting against the brightness of the screen, I see the time first—a quarter till midnight—and then the name of the caller.

Sven Akerman.

My stomach nosedives and I swipe to answer. "Hello?"

"Sorry to call so late, Doctor." He sounds the same as always. Gravel in the desert. There's a fair amount of background noise wherever he is: feminine squeals, male laughter, and... was that a splash?

I'm now fully awake. The urge to ask if Kieran's okay is pressing, but I force myself into therapist mode. "What can I do for you, Sven?"

He hesitates, then sighs. "I couldn't reach Alistair and frankly, I'm at the end of my rope. I'd take a bullet for Kier, but right now I want to strangle him. I need help."

In the background, there's another loud splash, followed by laughter.

"Where is he?"

"Home. With fifteen guests." The slight emphasis on the last word tells me these people aren't friends so much as co-signers on Kieran's bad ideas.

I hang onto professionalism with both hands. "I'm Kieran's therapist, not his babysitter. What are you asking me to do?"

"Nothing, Doctor." His voice is too dry. "Just thought you should know he started drinking Wednesday when he got home from the appointment and hasn't stopped since."

My heart skips.

"Give me the address. I'm on my way."

SOMETIME IN THE last four years, Kieran moved to Malibu. His home is a sprawling, single-story retreat on a bluff overlooking a private beach. Alan could probably tell me who the architect is. All I know is it's lovely, quintessentially modern but still inviting, the grounds overflowing with palm trees and greenery.

When I pull up to the closed gate, I put my car in park and grab my phone to text Sven. I'm about to press Send on the message when there's a knock on my window.

"Shit!"

Palm to my chest, I roll down the window.

"Thanks for coming," Sven rumbles.

"Thanks for the heart attack."

His lips twitch before he walks a few steps and punches a code into a keypad. The gate starts to slide open, and he returns to my window. "Everyone is gone, as per your request."

It was closer to an ultimatum. "Where is he now?"

"In the pool last I saw. Gabe's keeping an eye on him."

"How drunk is he?"

Sven shrugs one massive shoulder. "He's Irish."

I choke on inane laughter. "Was that a joke?"

"Nope." One of his eyelids flutters, and I'm almost positive it's a wink.

"And his mental state? Angry, happy, sad?"

"Irish," he says blandly.

He turns and walks ahead of me down the driveway. Torn between the urge to laugh and scream through my teeth, I put the car in gear and follow. I pull around the loop and park adjacent to a four-car garage, then join Sven at the front door. He opens it for me and stands aside.

Nerves tickle in my stomach. I'm on *his* turf now. My composure is a toddler's paper mache project—sloppy patchwork over a balloon of anxiety.

Desperate for more time to pull myself together, I ask, "When do you guys sleep?"

"When we're tired."

"Do you live here?"

He nods. "Guesthouse. Are you done stalling, Doctor? Because we're not getting any younger."

The drawled admonishment startles a laugh out of me. "I guess I am. Thanks for the pep talk."

"Anytime. Walk straight through—can't miss the pool. I'm going to turn on the boundary security system now. It's motion activated, so shoot me a text when you're ready to leave or you'll wake up the West Coast."

"Great," I mutter, stepping into the house.

The door closes behind me. I drop my keys and phone onto the entryway table, then take in the expansive floor plan. The open kitchen, living, and dining area are done in soothing, cool-toned neutrals. A wood-beamed ceiling soars overhead, and airy hallways branch to either side of the great room. Opposite me is a series of dramatic, floor-to-ceiling glass panels, the middle a sliding door. I'm sure the view is spectacular during daylight; right now, all I can see is a shadowy outdoor entertainment area backlit by a blue glow from a pool beyond.

The air reeks of alcohol, food, and weed. Off to my right is a chef's kitchen, the enormous island cluttered with dozens of bottles and cans, half-full glasses, and takeout containers. The rest of the space—a central, U-shaped collection of long couches and an enormous dining table to the left—are likewise trashed.

I step around a bikini top and sopping wet swim trunks. Skirting the couches, I approach the sliding panel. It's open a crack. I listen but don't hear any splashing.

Breathe. Hold. Exhale.

This isn't the first house call I've been on for a client. It's rare, but it happens. The process of healing isn't gentle. There are always ups and downs, sometimes even U-turns and backflips. But in every way that counts, I know this is different. I'm not objective. I feel responsible. Guilty. Because this is *him*.

My soft-soled flats are silent as I slip outside and cross the deck, then walk down a set of steps to the pool. Cold, damp air sneaks under my blazer and makes my skin pebble.

A quick scan of the empty turquoise pool leads my gaze to the attached jacuzzi and the man sitting in it. His arms are spread over the cement behind him, his face shadowed. I can sense rather than see the force of his stare.

Pulling air into my tight lungs, I walk toward him. My heart drums in my ears, my breaths shallow and too fast. The closer I get, the less I know what to say. Not helping is the visual overload of him half-naked and wet, steam rising around him. He's all muscle but not bulky, every inch of him beneath and above the clear water lean and defined.

A bead of red flares at his mouth. Smoke trails from his nostrils, curling upward and dispersing, and a breeze brings me a distinctive, pungent aroma wrapped in chlorine and brine from the Pacific.

I halt a few feet from the jacuzzi. Kieran pulls the joint from his mouth and taps ash onto cement behind him.

"If you call me Mr. Hayes, I'll throw you in the pool." His flinty expression and the flat, uncompromising tone tell me he's not joking.

A few seconds pass before I find my voice.

"Noted."

A tingle of awareness along my right side snaps my gaze toward a dark figure as it rises from a deck chair. I startle and for the second time tonight, my heart almost explodes.

"Jesus Christ," I snap. "Make some noise, Gabe."

Kieran chuckles softly.

"Sorry," Gabe says, his dimpled smile belying the words. He glances at the jacuzzi. "Be nice, boss."

Kieran grunts. Gabe gives me a parting nod and strides past me, disappearing up the stairs toward the house. I fantasize about following.

A heavy sigh brings my attention back to Kieran's hooded eyes. "Either get in the jacuzzi or sit down. You're putting a crick in my neck."

I'm not sure which of us is more surprised when I toe off

my shoes and roll my four-hundred-dollar trousers over my knees. I sit on the smooth lip of the jacuzzi—a safe distance from him—and drop my legs into the water. My eyes flutter shut on a sigh of somatic pleasure.

"Imagine what it feels like when more than your feet are in it," he says dryly.

For a moment, I picture it. A different me in a different life, one wherein I wouldn't hesitate to strip down and join this man in the water. In this alternate reality, I'd be softer, sweeter, my mind smooth curves instead of sharp angles. I'd ease his pain with my body. Quite possibly with my heart.

"Why'd you come, Stirling?"

Clearing my throat, I open my eyes. He takes another long drag of the joint, inspects it briefly, then flicks the nub at the row of deck chairs.

"Sven asked me to."

He shakes his head. "He didn't. He knows I'd fire him."

"Would you?" I ask curiously.

He looks away. "Nah, but still."

I stare at his profile. His furrowed brow. "I came because he told me this started after our session Wednesday." I pause. "I wish you'd called me."

He snorts. "I bet you do."

"Kieran." The use of his name—or more likely the note of pleading in my voice—turns his head. "Just tell me."

"Tell you what?" His lips barely move.

Why your eyes are so angry and sad.

"The truth."

His head falls back, eyes sightless on the night sky. "It's the damnedest thing," he says, so softly I'm not sure he actually intends for me to hear. "I want to say, 'I'll tell you if you get in the water.' Why? Why is it whenever I see you, I feel instantly defensive? Like we're about to do battle and I need to attack first."

I don't speak. We both know why. Because this *is* battle. A war for his life and future.

His head rolls toward me. "I know you want to help me. I just don't think you can."

His words, his eyes, his tone—all empty, vacant—shatter my patchwork persona. For the first time in I don't know how long, I'm just me. Just Talia. And he's the boy who saved me in a rainy graveyard.

And goddammit, I'm going to save him back.

CHAPTER 11

TALIA

As I take off my blazer and toss it onto a deck chair, Kieran's jaw goes slack. He chokes when I step out of the water to unbutton my slacks.

"Stirling—"

"Turn, please."

Water splashes as he pivots. I strip off my pants and chuck them. Still semi-decent in a thong, bra, and a black silk tank top—all of which are about to be ruined—I slip into the water. Heat cocoons me with prickling pleasure, the contrast of cold air on my face and shoulders near-euphoric. I settle against the smooth seat, tugging my floating tank down and tucking it between my legs.

"You can turn around."

Kieran's wide eyes—no longer empty, thank God—take me in. He laughs roughly. "I can't believe you did that."

I shrug. "Compromise rarely kills. Now you have to hold up your end of the bargain."

His smile fades but doesn't entirely vanish. "Can we renegotiate? Maybe if you take the top off."

"Kieran," I chide.

He swipes hands over his face and through his hair, then gives his cheeks a few light slaps. At my questioning look, he says, "Trying to sober up enough to remember why I can't touch the pretty lady."

"Cute," I mimic him.

Another short laugh, then a grunt as he hauls himself out of the water and drops onto the tiled border. Steam spills off his flushed skin. Water sluices along cuts of muscle in his arms, chest, stomach...

"Like what you see?"

I swallow and drag my gaze to his boyishly crooked grin. He's so beautiful it hurts, a tightness in my chest and a sharp ache between my legs. My inner conflict must be on my face because his grin disappears. Predatory intensity replaces it. His muscles quiver like he's a second from launching at me.

"Just say the word," he murmurs.

A modicum of reason returns.

My complicated response to him notwithstanding, he's my *client*. He's high and drunk—even if he does have a Herculean constitution—and teetering on a cliff of emotional and professional disaster. He also uses sex as a weapon to avoid real intimacy.

He doesn't want *me*.

Maybe in another life... but not in this one.

"No, Kieran. For many reasons, not the least of which being I'm your therapist."

The intensity melts away. He watches me another moment, then shrugs in indifference. "Worth a shot."

I release a slow breath, my heart convulsing as it accepts its newest bruise. "Why don't you come back in the water? You're shivering."

He slips in without protest, dunking and surfacing before slouching against the opposite wall, head canted against the edge. I don't push him, instead staring into the darkness beyond the bluff, visualizing the waves whose muted roar rides the breeze.

"I should have been there."

My mind kicks into focus. I remember what I asked him for—the truth. "When?"

His eyes are closed, voice thready. "In the car that day. Liz didn't want to go to the store. She felt nauseous from the pregnancy and was craving peanut butter. It was a Saturday, but I'd stayed up all night working. She hated it—the fact I couldn't switch off my brain on command, just go to the office then come home like a normal husband. Anyway, I blew her off when she asked me to go, told her to order a delivery."

His throat bobs, brow furrowing slightly. "I think she wanted to spend some time together, you know? Maybe get breakfast or something. She was never good at asking for what she wanted. I had to guess a lot. I think... sometimes I think she was afraid of me. Not physically. Just, dunno, emotionally maybe."

"Why do you say that?"

He shrugs. "We didn't date long before we married, and I worked all the time after. Could be she was starting to figure out she'd made a mistake. I'm a bit of a moody bastard, if you hadn't noticed. A hothead."

"Moody—maybe. But you're not a hothead. That would imply you're easily swayed to violence."

He lifts his head and offers a humorless smirk. "Pretty sure you saw what I'm capable of in that warehouse."

I hold his stare, letting him see how serious I am. "There's a definitive line between passion and uncontrolled rage. Intensity and cruelty."

"I've been cruel to you, haven't I?"

It's obvious he wants to direct the conversation away from his wife, and I let him. While I'm glad he shared what he did, he's not in the right headspace to delve deeper.

Neither am I.

"No, Kieran. You've been an asshole a few times, sure, but it's nothing I haven't seen before and nothing I can't handle. I was poking emotional sore spots—you were protecting your secrets."

A bit of lightness returns to his face. "Like a child who doesn't want to give up the dirty blankie for a wash."

I smile. "You said it, not me."

His answering chuckle fades quickly. "You're letting me off too easy. Men shouldn't speak to women like—"

"Your inner misogynist is showing," I interject. "You're hung up on the fact I'm the so-called weaker, fairer sex. But I'm not. I'm your equal, and some part of you knows it because when you're not being a brat, you treat me like one."

He makes a pained face. "Bloody hell."

"Am I wrong?"

"I'm starting to think you rarely are," he mutters, then huffs a laugh. "My mam would've loved you."

My focus narrows at the past tense—she's still alive as far as I know—but I file it and ask, "Why's that?"

Humor creases the corners of his eyes, but their depths hold a sudden edge that puts me on alert. "She was a straight-talker, like you. Never held back an opinion. Always made sure my dad knew when he displeased her." His voice lowers to a throaty purr. "Can't lie, I'm starting to see the appeal of displeasing a woman. One in particular."

I'm defenseless. Summarily defeated. All I can do is lower my head as my body revolts: tingling, tight nipples, throbbing clit, and a mental slideshow of a hundred different ways I could prove to him that displeasing me is mutually beneficial.

"You all right?" There's enough heat in his voice to turn up the temperature of the ocean. "Let me know if I can help."

"Stop talking," I snap.

His dark chuckle only makes matters worse.

I finally resort to thinking about Alan—who hasn't stopped calling me despite my clear communication that we aren't happening—and the unsolicited dick pic he sent me this morning. On my to-do list for the weekend is a phone call to Mia, as I'm pretty sure he sent the photo from his office at the middle school.

The mental image of Alan's underwhelming, half-erect penis does the trick, instantly shutting down my libido. After a few deep breaths, I glare at a smug Kieran.

"Would you like to explore why you're so comfortable loading innuendo into a conversation about your parents?"

His laugh is immediate, loud, and long. While his delight is intoxicating, I keep a straight face. *Thanks, Alan.*

Kieran sobers with effort, wiping tears from his lashes. "I'm sorry," he says, trying not to laugh again. "God, I can't seem to help myself around you. Getting a rise out of you is too satisfying."

"Let me know when you're done."

"Yep. Right. Carry on with the interrogation."

I swallow an exasperated sigh. "How did your father typically respond when your mother confronted him?"

A grin flashes. "He'd sputter until she laughed him from the room. My dad's more the traditional sort. Stereotypical gender roles and all that. Not to say he was bad to our mam. He thought she hung the moon, just..." He trails off.

"Sometimes he treated her like she was breakable instead of powerful enough to control tides?"

Surprise flickers over his features. "Nail on the head. But

I don't want you to get the wrong idea. They had a happy marriage. Loved each other madly. I know I'm lucky."

I press a mental bookmark to the fact that despite his clear admiration and love for his mother, he's habitually chosen partners who emulate a different type of woman.

"I need to apologize," I tell him softly. "I shouldn't have called you a misogynist. I know you don't hate women, Kieran."

I half-expect him to make a joke, but he doesn't. "I appreciate that, but I don't blame you for saying it. I still feel bad about the unhinged shit I've said to you." He grimaces. "That I keep saying to you."

Before I can think better of it, I tell him, "Think about what happens when two alphas of the same species meet."

His eyes narrow, glinting with the type of intelligence that intoxicants can mellow but never truly dent. "Competition. Are you're implying we're in a war for resources and breedable females, Stirling?"

"Hypothetically speaking, yes. Me being a woman is merely information you've exploited in an attempt to assert dominance over me. We're animals, Kieran. And we're alphas."

He stares me a beat, then shifts in his seat and looks away. "Jesus. How do you do that?"

"Do what?"

His eyes pin me, almost accusing. "See me so clearly?"

A crack appears in the wall around my heart; I patch it, then pick my next words carefully. "Ever since I can remember, I've been fascinated with people. What makes them tick. It started with my family and expanded from there. Growing up, I heard 'stop staring, Talia' multiple times a day." I shrug. "You could say I turned my voyeuristic tendencies into a career. I understand people instinctively. I see their layers, fault lines, and strengths. All the hidden treasures of the psyche. My first impressions are rarely wrong."

He stares at me. "Huh."

"What?" I ask tentatively.

"Just... all of that. *Talia.*"

My heart rattles. "Dr. Stirling."

"Stirling," he says unsmiling. "And your first impression of me?"

Fierce and fractured. A footstep from the void. A puzzle of constantly moving pieces, each of them breathtaking beyond words.

Aloud, I say weakly, "A man who needed my help." He grunts. This time, I look away first. "I have one more question if you're willing."

"One more," he agrees.

"Is your mom okay?"

"Knew you'd catch that," he murmurs, then sighs. "She has Alzheimer's."

My lungs compress. *Of course.* That's why he's devoted himself to finding a cure. "Diagnosed five years ago?" I ask, remembering when he told me he started working on neural nanorobotics.

"Thereabouts, yes. Rapid onset and progression. I'll give

you one final truth for free: she loved classical music. That's why my brother and I attend the Phil once a month."

I say the only thing I can.

"I'm sorry, Kieran."

Eyes shuttering, he stands up and sweeps his hair back. "I'm dehydrated, hungry, and too fucking sober." He glances at me. "You should get out, too. You're all red. I'll get towels."

Moving to the elevated boundary between the jacuzzi and the pool, he leaps onto it in a feat of agility that looks supernatural, then dives into the cold water. I push myself to the edge and watch his powerful body glide toward the shallow end. He surfaces near the distant steps and extends to his full height, then throws a smile over his shoulder at me.

Time stops.

I still blink. Still breathe. But the fabric of history pauses to absorb the sight of him into my immutable memory. That crooked grin the magazines never see. The body of a living god glowing blue under the pool lights. All the wild, haphazard beauty of him—inside and outside—stuns me so deeply I start to shake.

"Do it!" he calls. "That's the price. Swim to me and I'll get you a towel."

This is a bad idea.

The thought floats away, chasing my inhibitions off the nearby bluff. My tank top seals to my chest and stomach as I lift from the water. Even wet, it barely skims my hips. I don't look at Kieran as I hoist myself onto the ledge. When I find my balance and stand, I finally glance his way—and immediately regret it.

In the next seconds, I feel every place his eyes touch: my ankles, calves, knees, thighs. They pause on the front panel of my thong, then flicker over my chest and arms before starting back down.

"I don't know where to look," he says cheerily. "It's like a candy shop."

My heart pounds at its cage. I can't help a quick glance at his groin, visible above the water. His swim trunks are plastered to the answer of whether or not he's proportional everywhere. His cock is hard, long, and thick, bound by wet fabric to his thigh.

My mouth waters and I almost lose my balance on the ledge.

He's horny. It's a reflex. I could be anyone.

None of the thoughts help because even though I could be any woman, he's not any man. Not to me.

"Get out of the pool," I say shrilly, not caring that the demand reveals I don't trust myself. Him. Either of us.

"Not a chance. We're at war, remember?"

"From the look of your swim trunks, I'd say I'm the one with all the weapons at the moment."

It's a futile counterattack—he grins and shrugs. "Can't blame the poor fella. He hasn't gotten the memo that you'd bite him instead of kiss him."

I laugh; God help me, I laugh. Then I dive from the ledge into the water and swim toward a disaster in the making. The cold registers but in a distant way, barely cooling the heat inside me. At least I have the sense to angle away from him, surfacing on the opposite side of the shallows. Staying submerged from the neck down, I yank out my wet bun and studiously avoid looking at the man standing less than six feet away.

"I win," I say with forced levity. "Where's my towel?"

There's a beat of silence, then he says mutedly, "You're lucky I've spent the last two days drinking and barely sleeping."

"Because you wouldn't have opened up to me otherwise?" The second the words are out, I realize I've walked into a trap. My eyes screw shut as I wait for his jaws to close, for my defenses to take another blow.

But there's only silence.

I open my eyes. He's staring blankly toward the jacuzzi. Muscles locked. Jaw tense. Brow furrowed. A burst of worry has me straightening and moving toward him.

"Kieran?" My teeth chatter over his name. "Are you okay?"

He startles. "Yeah, sorry. I'll be back."

He hauls ass out of the pool and up the steps, taking them two at a time, then disappears into the house without a backward glance.

I wait. And wait some more.

The cold sinks through my skin and penetrates my bones. With it comes the bitter realization that I may have really fucked up. Destroyed all the progress we've made.

I shouldn't have jumped in the pool.

Anxiety propels me toward the steps with a plan to make a run for the jacuzzi. I'll warm up for a minute, then grab my clothes and flee for my car. I'll call Leo tomorrow and he'll help me find a way to fix this.

I'm halfway out of the water when a man—not tall or graceful enough—leaves the house and heads down the steps, something voluminous and pale in his arms. I sag onto the first step as he approaches.

"Hi, Sven."

My voice is raw with disappointment and resignation, but I can't bring myself to care.

"Doctor," he rumbles.

Eyes averted, he stops a few feet away and holds open a luxurious towel robe. I walk up the steps and slip my arms inside the sleeves, turning to wrap it around myself. A small, pitiful sound leaves me. The robe is out-of-the-dryer hot and feels so incredible my eyes fill with tears.

"Thank you," I croak. "What time is it?"

"Close to two."

No wonder a hot robe is making me cry. I haven't had a good night's sleep in days, and all I had for dinner was a packet of almonds on the drive over here. Add to that mix my actions and defeats tonight, I feel like I could sob for an hour and sleep for the next ten.

"Kier wanted me to tell you he didn't forget you. He was running the dryer." Sven makes a noise in his throat that could be laughter or annoyance. "He's in the shower now."

I barely hear him. "I'll get my clothes. Can you show me where I can change, then let me out of the gate?"

"I'll grab your things. Go up to the house and get warm. Then we can talk about how you're in no shape to drive."

He walks toward the jacuzzi.

No fight left in me, I do as he says.

CHAPTER 12

KIERAN

Hot shower spray beats on my back, more punishing than pleasurable—same as the grip I've got on my cock. My forehead thuds against the tile wall, water misting from my mouth as I gasp and tug in quick, graceless jerks. Against the darkness of my eyelids, I see her on her knees, soft golden eyes looking up at me with surrender. Messy hair and flushed cheeks. That fucking mouth swallowing me down. My balls tighten and I chase my release, then groan in misery as it dances away.

"Talia," I whisper.

The fantasy shifts. She crawls up my body wearing a wet black tank top and a tiny thong. Unsmiling. Her hair in that goddamn bun. I can't move—don't want to—as she settles with her knees on either side of my head and pulls the scrap of black away from her pussy.

"Eat me out, Kieran," she demands before smothering my face with heaven.

I detonate with a hoarse shout, my hand cramping, ropes of cum hitting the glass, my legs, a bottle of shampoo. My knees almost go out and I lurch sideways, my shoulder smacking into marble. The pain makes me laugh, a crazed sound that echoes in the bathroom.

There's a stitch in my side that makes every breath hurt. *Everything* fucking hurts, all the time. I've grown so used to pain and guilt, I can't handle that I've started feeling something different. Something like dawn after four years of twilight.

Because of her.

Leaving her shivering in the pool was the hardest thing I've done in ages. I don't even care anymore whether she needs to tie me up or smack me around to get off. I'd tie *myself* up if it meant any part of me could be inside her. I'd punch myself in the fucking face.

I want her to destroy me.

I think it might be my only road to salvation.

BY THE TIME I get myself dry and into some sleep pants, I feel relatively sane again. The itch under my skin is gone. I may even be able to sleep tonight.

Then I open my bedroom door.

"Motherfucker!" I holler at Sven. "You tryin' to put me

in a wooden box? What're you doing lurking outside my door?"

He sighs. "I was about to knock, jackass. I came to let you know I set up Dr. Stirling in the second guest room. She's in the kitchen now."

My face goes numb. "What? She's still here? I thought she left."

He glowers at me. "Whispering now isn't going to erase the squealing you did two seconds ago."

I laugh in spite of myself. "Fuck you."

He rolls his eyes. "She can't drive home, Kier. When I brought her the towel, she could barely keep her eyes open."

"Okay," I say, even though none of this is remotely okay. *She's still in my house.* "Why is she in the kitchen?"

"For one of the smartest people on the planet, you sure can be an idiot. She needed food, so I told her to have at whatever she could find."

He's right; I'm a jackass.

"All right. Thank you. I've got it from here."

He squints at me.

"I'll behave myself, okay?"

He grunts. "Gabe's on duty if you need him."

I nod. He gives me another withering look, then finally ambles away. I listen for the sound of the front door closing and three beeps as he sets the main house alarm. Then I walk silently down the hallway, pausing at the corner so I can spy on Stirling without her seeing me.

Sitting on a couch with a plate in her lap, she nibbles

half-heartedly on a peanut butter and jelly sandwich. She looks tired and adorable and *real*. Her face is clean of makeup. Her hair is a disaster: wet and frizzy and piled atop of her head in a listing knot.

I'm so charmed by her hair it takes me too long to realize what she's wearing. Then I almost rub my eyes because I can't believe it. Sven must have raided my closet while I was in the shower, the wacko, because she's got on one of my old Stanford pullovers and a pair of my sweatpants.

I've never seen a woman look good in my clothes. *Ever.* They've always been too big. It's weird when your girlfriend looks like a child wearing her daddy's T-shirt. Stirling, however, looks perfect. Exactly like a woman in her man's clothes should.

She'd probably call me sexist if she knew I thought that, but it's not a gender prejudice thing. It's biological instinct, one a thousand times more intense than I've ever felt. Quite simply, I want to mark her, mate her, and breed her.

I rub my chest, wincing at the sting of heartburn, and step into her line of sight. Her eyes lift from the sandwich, widening a little. Her lids are puffy. *Was she crying?*

The sting in my chest intensifies. "Ehm, hi." Internally, I cringe. "Sorry I didn't come back to the pool. I—"

"Sven told me," she says with a small smile that doesn't reach her eyes. "It's okay. Thank you for the heated robe."

"You're welcome. I'm just gonna..." I point toward the kitchen.

"It's your house." She looks ten types of uncomfortable. "This is really..."

"Weird?"

Her eyes sparkle for a second. "Yeah. Pretty weird. I can finish my sandwich in the room." She makes to stand.

"No, stay," I say quickly. "I'm going to grab a snack and crash."

She slumps. "Thanks. I'm sorry about this. I don't know why Sven wouldn't let me order an Uber. Or why I listened." The last bit is mumbled.

I'm not sure why she listened to him, either, but the longer I look at her, the more grateful I am for Sven's persuasive powers.

"No apologies necessary," I say casually. "He's got oversized protective urges to go with his oversized biceps. Best to just go with it. Avoid his temper tantrums."

I'm lying through my teeth. Sven's protective urges have never extended to any of the women in my orbit. Stirling has no idea how rare it is for him to even speak with anyone besides me, Gabe, or Dylan. If I didn't know my head of security is gay, I might wonder if he has a thing for her.

Jerking into motion, I cross to the kitchen, ignoring the unholy mess. Tomorrow is soon enough to feel embarrassed on behalf of my entire genetic line. The fridge is stocked with prepackaged meals from my chef, though most of the food sits untouched because I've been drunk or high for the last two days.

I grab the first thing I see—yogurt, unfortunately—and

snag a spoon from the drawer. Knowing I should leave her be and retreat to my room, I still round the couch and sit a few feet away from her. Moth to flame, tides to moon.

I'm so fucked.

"Yogurt?" she asks skeptically.

"Too tired to make anything."

I peel the seal off the cup and lick it clean—slowly, because I can't fucking help myself. Out of the corner of my eye, I watch her try her best not to stare at my moving tongue. She finally resorts to pretending something interests her across the room, but her pink cheeks betray her. My blood surges south, only without the needy edge of before. Fucking strange, but all I really want to do at the moment is tuck her under blankets and kiss her forehead.

Frowning, I toss the circle of foil on the coffee table and start shoveling yogurt in my mouth.

She scoots to the edge of the couch. "I'm going to—"

I swallow fast. "Did you graduate high school early or do accelerated degrees?"

She stills. "Graduated early."

I think of the email from my PI that for some unknown reason I haven't opened. "What were you, sixteen?"

"Yes."

She sounds hoarse; I glance at her, bemused by the wariness in her eyes. I belatedly realize why it's there—she still thinks we're in a normal therapist-patient relationship where she stays untouchable while I spill my guts.

It makes me smile.

"When'd you get into the kink stuff?"

"Kieran..."

I focus on eating to keep from laughing at the whining pitch of my name. When I finish the yogurt, I drop it on the table, then lean back and tuck my arms behind my head. She tries not to look at my bare chest. Oh, she tries. *Adorable.*

"Humor me, Stirling. You won't be able to sleep right now, anyway."

She frowns. "Why not?"

I nod to her half-eaten sandwich. "If you sleep now, you'll have shit dreams. Give it thirty minutes."

She sighs, then slides her plate onto the table beside my yogurt cup. I close my eyes and wait, feeling almost... content.

"I was twenty," she finally says. "I accidentally walked into a seminar on BDSM."

My eyes fly open. "Accidentally?"

Her lips twist into a half-smile. "I thought it was a lecture on cognitive neuroscience."

"Of course you did." I chuckle, imagining a wide-eyed, twenty-year-old Stirling. Super nerdy. Maybe a little awkward.

"It was a shock," she says dryly.

"I bet. So, what? You heard about tying people up and got a tingle?"

She glares at me, which only makes me smile wider.

"I'm messing with you. I know I've given you shit about

it, but I'm not totally ignorant. Even been to that club down on Wilshire a few times."

"Crossroads?" she asks in a strangled voice.

I nod, eyeing her. Then it clicks. "You worked there?"

"Yes, as an educator. Until two years ago." She finally sits back but looks unbelievably tense.

"Relax. I probably won't remember any of this tomorrow, anyway."

I'm lying. She knows it. To my surprise, however, she blows out a breath and melts into the cushions, crossing her arms over her chest. It hits me that she's probably naked under my clothes since she wore her underwear in the jacuzzi. *Jesus Christ.*

I lower my arms and shift to face her, hiking a knee up to create some breathing room in the crotch of my pants. Given the topic, I have a feeling I'll need it.

"Paint me a picture—you went to the seminar and decided you wanted to be a dominatrix?"

"Ha. No. But I did trade contact information with the woman who spoke, Charlie Rhodes. She became my mentor a few months later."

"Took you that long to get the nerve to call, huh?"

She huffs a little laugh. "Sure did. Anyway, she took me under her wing. She had a space where she saw her clients, and I ended up working there with her while I got my PhD. Then she and Dominic Cross opened Crossroads."

"Yeah, I know Dom. I've met Charlie a few times, too."

Her eyes widen. "*What?*"

Damn, I love surprising her. I might be slightly obsessed with seeing that look on her face. "Dom's a friend of a friend. He's actually who connected me with Sven after—" My teeth click as I snap them shut.

I thank my lucky stars that Stirling's so tired she doesn't notice my almost-slip. She frowns thoughtfully, her eyes soft and unfocused.

"That makes a lot of sense, actually, given Dom's military background and Sven's, uh, extreme competency."

I smirk. "I'm gonna tell him you said that. And then I'm going to get him a keychain that says 'Extremely Competent Bodyguard.' He'll treasure it always."

"Very funny."

I grin. "Thanks. I thought so."

She shakes her head at my childishness, then looks me in the eye. "I never saw you there. At Crossroads."

I can't read her tone. If I didn't know better, I'd say it was disappointed. "It was only a few times right after they opened. I didn't participate in any of the... festivities."

She smiles.

Eyetooth.

"Do I sense an undercurrent of squeamishness, Mr. Hayes?"

I chuckle. "I won't yuck your yum, but I haven't been back since I saw a naked woman tied to a cross and whipped while fifty people watched. Granted, I did enjoy watching her come repeatedly afterward."

A haughty brow cocks. "Is this more of that 'women should be treated like porcelain' mentality?"

"Maybe. Or maybe I was born vanilla." I pretend to have just remembered something. "I *did* take a class at Crossroads back in the day. An intro to rope bondage. Some crazy Dubliner taught it."

She sputters. "Liam Roark?"

"Sounds familiar, yeah. He said I was a natural."

She looks dubious, but there's real curiosity in her eyes when she asks, "Have you ever used what you learned?"

"Nah. Choking is about as freaky as I get."

She fights a laugh. "Choking isn't vanilla."

"You would know, wouldn't you?"

She rolls her eyes. God, I love it when she does that.

"I bet I could still find my way around some knots. Liam was a good teacher. Almost too charming, though. I was half in love with him by the end of it and I'm straight as an arrow."

Her tinkling laugh is so pretty it makes my chest squeeze.

"That's Liam for sure. A lot of hearts broke when he moved back to Dublin a couple years ago."

"Yours?"

"Definitely not."

I fake affront. "It's the Irish accent, isn't it? Total turn-off."

"Shut up."

She can tell me to shut up all day if she keeps smiling. "What then? Blue eyes don't do it for you, either?"

She groans. "Stop. Liam and I were friendly, but we were both dominants. I didn't have a submissive bone in my body back then."

She gasps a tiny bit, then flushes. Not in embarrassment, though—more like horror.

Buzzing fills my ears. "Back then?" I repeat.

My brain stumbles as it struggles to process what she's revealed. *Back then* she didn't have a submissive bone in her body, which means now...

I can almost feel the *snick* as a section of her puzzle box unlocks.

I've tortured myself wondering how I could be so attracted to her if we're as sexually compatible as opposing magnets. The argument she's fond of—that it's my subconsciousness defending itself by objectifying her—is a load of horseshit. She doesn't know how hard I've fought it. How many fruitless hours I've spent trying to convince myself she isn't my type, that I feel nothing when I look at her, that it's merely her mind that intrigues me.

Fact is, three weeks ago she lit the book of *my type* on fire and started writing a new one. Now every damn page is her. I can't even look at other women because I'm obsessed with the one in front of me.

She's not immune to me. I've seen glimpses of interest from her over the last weeks. Sparks that have drifted past her ironclad control. The blushes. That wild pulse. But I've been mostly resigned to the fact she likes the look of my face and body, maybe entertains fantasies of dominating me.

Tonight threw me for a loop because her mask came off, and what I saw beneath it contradicted what I thought I knew. In the jacuzzi, I saw a woman afire with simple, uncomplicated lust. And when she saw me in the pool, she looked like she could already feel me inside her.

Maybe this thing between us is twisted. Scratch that—I know it is. She's my therapist and I'm a fucking mess. But it doesn't change the fact our bodies are screaming to thrust and sweat and fuck. And it doesn't change the fact I lied to her on Wednesday about my fantasy. Yes, I've thought about her sucking me off. I'm human. But when I pictured—*picture*—my hand on her throat, we're face to face. Belly to belly. Chest to chest.

Equals.

"Can you forget I said that?" Her voice is weak as a kitten's, her eyes panicked.

I clench the back of my neck, feeling like I'm a shaken bottle whose top is about to pop off.

"We have to stop talking about this," she rambles. "I'm sorry. This whole conversation is inappropriate. I don't want to give you the wrong idea."

Too late, Stirling. Far, far too late.

"Tell me what you mean." My voice snaps with command, but unlike every person who's heard this tone from me, she doesn't back down. Her spine straightens instead, fire kindling in her eyes.

Something inside me bends. Breaks. Before she can shut

me down completely, I whisper, "Put me out of my misery, Talia."

She blinks rapidly. I must imagine it when her eyes look glassy for a second.

After a hard swallow, she says, "I haven't been a paid dominatrix for four years. Two years ago, I stopped working as a kink educator and took a break from the lifestyle to... figure things out." She picks up her plate and stands. "That's all I'm going to say. Good night, Kieran."

I watch her walk away. Her head held high. Elegant and magnetic despite her exhaustion, despite the sagging chaos of her hair and my too-big clothes.

Slowly, I become aware of my harsh breathing and tense body. I relax in increments—legs, stomach, shoulders, neck. Finally, hands and feet.

Then I close my eyes and smile.

TALIA

Mia stares at me, eyes showing white, the end-piece of a croissant stalled halfway to her mouth. Leo, conversely, sips his coffee sedately, pale blue eyes thoughtful.

I just told them what happened last night and how it led to the drastically out-of-character behavior of me ringing their doorbell on a Saturday morning wearing my client's sweatshirt over wrinkled slacks. From their reactions at the door, I look exactly how I feel. Like I got four hours of shitty sleep and am in the midst of an epic personal crisis sans underwear.

"My bad," Leo says finally. "When we talked last, I should have warned you to never, ever get in a jacuzzi with a client. Or hot springs. Basically, water is a bad idea."

I make a face at the reminder of their first, disastrous sexual encounter. Mia sputters and chucks her croissant, which smacks him in the chest. He grabs it and shoves it in his mouth, then gives his wife a look that pinks her cheeks.

"Guys," I whine.

Mia winces. "Sorry. Pregnancy hormones are out of control."

I push my fingers into my hair, then give up when they hit knots after a few inches. "Don't apologize. I'm the one who barged in here. I'm sorry—I should have called. I wasn't thinking straight."

"We're glad you're here," she protests.

"Your timing, though..." Leo grumbles.

Mia punches his arm. "Talia, we love you so much we made you the godmother of our unborn son. You're family, and you're always welcome here. Selfishly, I'm thrilled you've come to us. I was starting to worry about you."

I frown. "You were? Why?"

She shrugs, glancing at Leo. Apparently, they have telepathy because he says, "She's referring to the fact that we have similar temperaments. We don't open up easily and usually only share our problems in the rare instance a situation spirals out of our control. Basically, she thinks you're a control freak like me and that it's kept you from being happy."

I don't know whether to laugh or scowl. "Seriously?" I ask Mia.

She nods. "I've never seen you like this."

"A hot mess?"

She smiles slightly. "Some chaos every once in a while is

good for the soul. It shakes things up. I think you should fire your client and date him."

My insides twist. Groaning, I palm my cheeks. The skin is too hot. *Fuck*, I'm blushing.

She continues, "It's painfully romantic. I'm going to daydream all day about when he realizes you're the girl from the graveyard." She sighs dreamily. "Kismet."

While I didn't share Kieran's name or the reason he's seeing me, I did recap the overlap in our histories for her.

My gaze swings to Leo. He blinks back at me, expression bland. "She's been reading a lot of romance novels."

Mia tears off another piece of her croissant, mumbling, "He's right, but whatever. Still romantic."

Leo sets down his coffee. "Do you want my advice as your friend or as your colleague?"

"Colleague."

"Either fire him or restore the working relationship."

"I can't fire him."

Leo nods. "Thought so. Then let me remind you that you've made a career out of unorthodox therapy methods. Your client wants something from you. Why don't you use that as currency to get what you want—namely, his investment in the process?"

Mia shifts in her seat. "Whoa. As hypocritical as this sounds, that seems risky. Professionally speaking."

I glance at her, a smile tugging my mouth. "I don't think he's suggesting I use sex."

"I'm not," Leo confirms with a wry glance at his wife. "Head out of the gutter, Amelia."

She flushes and laughs. "Never mind, then. Continue."

"That's not to say this isn't without risk," he tells me. "The tightrope you'd be walking is a narrow one. You'll have to be vigilant. The closer you get to him—the more you give him—the greater the intimacy will feel. You might lose perspective."

"And your heart," chirps Mia.

Leo asks gravely, "Can you handle that?"

Can I handle that?

I spend the next four days asking myself the question and don't come up with a definitive answer. Not that having an answer would change the path in front of me.

Whether or not I can handle the aftermath of emotional intimacy with Kieran, I'm going to attempt it. The potential payoff is worth the risk. And I'm not without support. At Leo's insistence, we now have a standing phone appointment Thursday mornings. He's my safety net, bound by a promise to tell me if he thinks I've lost balance on the tightrope.

Wednesday evening, I wait for Kieran outside my office door. I know he's coming because since Saturday, Sven has taken it upon himself to send me daily updates. The texts are unsolicited and I don't respond to them, but I don't tell him to stop sending them, either. It's because of them I know

Kieran trashed all the booze and drugs in his house when he woke up on Saturday. He spent the weekend cleaning, napping, and eating. He returned to work on Monday.

The back door opens. My pulse jumps as Kieran strides inside, his presence instantly sucking the oxygen from my lungs. He left his suit jacket and tie in the car this time. His hair looks like he's been running his hands through it all day, but he seems well rested and sober.

Pacific blue eyes find mine, a touch wary. *Good.*

"Mr. Hayes," I greet him dryly.

His lips twitch. "Dr. Stirling."

I look past him. "We're going to be in a different room tonight, Sven. Do you want to check it out first?"

He nods. "Thanks."

I lead him to the door opposite my usual office. As I unlock it with a six-digit code on the mounted keypad, I almost smile at the sudden focus from the men behind me.

"The door will lock behind us," I tell Sven. "Did you see the code?"

He nods again. I hold the door open just enough for him to enter. It takes him approximately five seconds before he returns.

"All clear," he says in a too-dry tone, then stations himself against a wall and stares pointedly at a painting mounted opposite him.

"After you, Mr. Hayes."

With visible hesitance—and a parting glare at Sven—

Kieran walks into the room. I follow, letting the door close and auto-lock behind us.

Kieran wanders around the space, dimly lit and scented heavily with aromatherapy. He finally turns to me. "I don't know what I was expecting, but this isn't it."

"Don't lie," I chide. "You were expecting a BDSM dungeon."

He throws me a crooked grin. "Maybe. Why the fancy lock?"

I nod toward the room's other door, also locked but with a standard deadbolt. "Files." I pause. "Also, this used to be a dungeon."

He laughs a bit uncertainly because it's not clear whether I'm teasing. I am, but I like that he can't tell.

"Don't tell me we're doing yoga. My sensei wiped the floor with me this morning and my muscles are pulverized."

"No yoga." I grab a few round pillows from a cubby and place them opposite each other on the central area rug. "But no chairs, either. Or shoes."

His brow cocks. "I'd rather do yoga than guided meditation, Stirling." He points at a massage table, currently folded up against a wall. "*That*, I would volunteer for."

"No meditation, either. And no massage." I lower onto one of the pillows, crossing my legs in front of me, then pat the other pillow. "Come on, don't tell me you can't sit criss-cross apple-sauce."

He toes off his shiny Italian shoes. "Can't promise my feet don't stink."

I smile. "That's why I pumped the air full of oils."

He comes to the floor easily, as flexible as I knew he'd be from observing the way he moves. I purposefully put the pillows close together, so I'm prepared for the moment our knees touch. It still makes my breath catch.

Kieran stills, looking a question at me—*Are you going to move back, or am I?*

I don't answer him. Nor do I move.

"Comfortable?" I ask.

"I am if you are."

"I am, thank you."

I'm actually the opposite of comfortable being this close to him. Close enough to smell his faded cologne and the clean musk beneath. Close enough that his broad shoulders take up most of my line of sight. And close enough that the heat of his body seeps through his slacks and my leggings into me.

But I'm committed.

His eyes narrow. "What are we doing?"

"This is our talking circle."

"Our what now?"

"Think of it as a space where we come to resolve conflicts, make compromises, or simply share unfiltered thoughts. Today, we're going to use it to broker a deal."

"A deal," he repeats, clearly mystified.

I nod. "Will you hear me out?"

His shadowed gaze scans my face. "Yes."

I take a deep breath, then leap into the unknown.

"As you know, our professional relationship took an unexpected turn Friday night."

He stiffens and opens his mouth, but I lift a hand.

"You said you'd hear me out."

Lips compressing, he nods.

"There are many people who'd say my behavior was grossly unprofessional. I shouldn't have gone in the jacuzzi, shared details of my private life, or stayed the night in your guest room. I'll admit, initially, I shared that mindset. But I've since given it a lot of thought and come to the conclusion that our experience was in line with my general methodology. Maybe it's not something I've done before, but it nevertheless built trust. You shared more with me Friday night than you have before. Do you agree?"

"Don't suppose you'll accept the excuse I was high?"

I crack a smile. "No, Kieran."

His jaw clenches as I say his name. "Then yes. I agree."

"I think I made a mistake in how I've approached our time together. As I mentioned at our first meeting, I normally have weeks to prepare for new clients. Maybe if we'd done the usual interviews, we could have avoided this. Maybe not—it doesn't matter. What matters is I've realized you're a lot more likely to share with me if you see me as a friend rather than an adversary."

"A friend?" he scoffs. "You can't be that blind. How many more times do I have to get a hard-on looking at you for you to admit I want you? Under me, above me, sideways, upside-down... Doesn't matter."

My face flames. So does my body. I don't bother hiding my reaction; instead, I meet his challenging gaze head-on.

"I'm not blind. I understand you think you want to have sex with me."

"I *think*? There's no thought involved." He leans back on his hands. "Look down and you'll have the proof. It's not fuckin' pleasant, I'll tell you that much. I'd turn it off if I could."

By force of will, I don't look at his lap. "I don't want you to be uncomfortable," I say softly. "The opposite, really. If you agree to my proposal, I think it will help."

"Not likely—unless it involves you sitting on my face."

The erotic visual makes my core clench hard; it also annoys me. "Enough, Kieran."

"It'll never be enough, Stirling." He glances between my crossed legs. "Are you throbbing for me?"

"Goddammit! Stop!"

My yell surprises me more than him. While I struggle with dismay, he struggles not to laugh.

"Do you know why I'm so good at chess?"

I clench my hands together to prevent them from reaching up and pulling my hair out. "What does chess have to do with anything?"

"I'm good at chess—brilliant, really—because I can see the future. The variables, the probabilities. The more I know about who I'm playing, the easier it is for me to win."

"What are you getting at?"

"I know what your proposal is. You want to have more

exchanges like we had on Friday. I tell you something, you shrink my brain, and then you reward me with details about your life because you've figured out I want to know everything about you."

Son of a bitch...

He sits up, shifting forward until our knees bump again. "You know what the flaw in your plan is? You think the more I know about you, the less I'll want to fuck you." He chuckles, low and menacing. "I guarantee that won't be the case."

My stomach sinks, taking my pride with it. He outmaneuvered me before I even managed to set pieces on the board. As my illusions of control crash and burn around me, all I can think is how foolish I was to imagine I could win a battle of wits with a king.

With no other options, I pull off my masks and lay down my weapons. My resigned sigh makes his focus narrow.

"You're right, Kieran. I do think that because I'm not the woman you've built a fantasy world around. That woman is your idea of me. The sex therapist, the former Domme, the first woman since your mother to call you on your shit... whatever is causing this infatuation, it isn't *me*."

His eyes glitter. "Agree to disagree."

I wave the words away. "Fine. My proposal stands. You give me the truth—unfiltered and honest—and commit to exploring the underlying causes of your binge-drinking and drug use. If you do that, I'll give you a truth in return."

"What if I want something other than a truth from you?"

I shake my head. "We're not negotiating. You can ask me one question, and I'll answer honestly." I pause, then add, "Unless I deem it inappropriate."

I don't trust the look on his face. Confident. Borderline ruthless. He's ignoring my white flag and readying a final volley.

"There's always negotiation in business deals, Stirling. Always."

He leans forward another inch, bringing us eye-to-eye. Too close. Our mouths are only a few inches apart. I can feel his breath. See the individual bristles on his jaw. His eyes are midnight seas reflecting the flickering lights of the fake candles on a shelf behind me.

"I'll give you this week's truth, and you'll come with me to a benefit for Alzheimer's on Friday night."

My eyes widen. "Absolutely not."

"Even if I tell you why I lost my shit two months ago? Full disclosure. The whole, ugly truth."

I open my mouth. Then close it.

Kieran smiles, slow and victorious, and whispers, "Checkmate."

CHAPTER 14

TALIA

Friday evening, I approach the sleek black limo parked outside my house. Sven walks beside me, Gabe a few steps ahead. Kieran is waiting in the car with Dylan. Not that I expected or wanted him to appear at my door like a suitor, but I now know why he's tucked behind bullet-resistant glass.

I know why he has full-time security and lives behind perimeter alarms. Why, with the exception of the LA Phil and the occasional charity event, it's rare for him to be seen outside Lumitech's highly secure headquarters. I know the reason for Sven's hyper-vigilance. Why he, Gabe, and Dylan carry guns and wear Kevlar vests under their lightweight jackets.

Since Lumitech announced their intent to research neural nanorobotics five years ago, Kieran has received countless death threats. Multiples per day, every day. The company's security division handles them, tracking down sources when they can and passing their findings to the LAPD. It's a never-ending game of whack-a-mole with minimal results.

At the initial, shocking windfall of threats, Kieran struggled with paranoia, fearing for his and Liz's safety. He updated their home security system and had wanted to hire a driver for her. She refused, stating she'd grown up in the public eye and already lived with restricted freedoms. Eventually, she cooled his worry, half-convincing him that the threats weren't serious, simply a price for him being an industry leader. He let it go after she promised to carry mace and agreed that if a serious concern arose, she'd accept increased protection.

Then she died, suddenly and shockingly, while driving his car to the grocery store.

He didn't say it aloud, but I could see it in his eyes—he doesn't think her death was random violence. He also believes it's his fault for not insisting on an armed driver.

At the urging of his father and brother, shortly after Liz's death, Kieran hired a close protection officer to accompany him everywhere outside his house. Good thing, too, because not six months later, there was a very real attempt on his life that put Sven in the hospital with a stab wound. A year and a half ago, Sven took a bullet to the shoulder when someone shot at Kieran as he stepped out of the elevator in Lumitech's parking garage.

Both would-be assassins were apprehended and are currently in prison. Open and shut cases. But despite confessions stating they were working alone and hated Kieran's guts for wanting to tamper with human brains, something didn't sit right with Sven. The men's stories were too similar. Too scripted. They fit the profile of muscle for hire, both of them with long criminal histories. It was a stretch to believe either of them even knew what neural nanorobotics was. Still, without proof or leads connecting them, there was nothing to do but move on.

Gabe and Dylan were hired, and the team moved into Kieran's guest house to provide round-the-clock security.

Life went on. Kieran kept working toward his dream of curing his mother's Alzheimer's. All was quiet until two and a half months ago, when he received a call in the middle of the night from an unknown number. Disguised by distortion, a voice told him that this was his final warning. If he continued working on neural nanorobotics, others would pay the price for his hubris. The caller hung up, and a text followed with an attached image: Alistair and Gail out to dinner, both of them oblivious to the photographer.

The police were called, a detective assigned. But since the threat was made from a burner phone, it was untraceable. The detective dismissed a possible connection between Liz's death, the assassination attempts, and the phone call. Without outright saying it, he told Kieran he was overreacting. Sven dragged him out of the precinct before he did something to get himself thrown in jail.

The following morning, he hired a high-profile private investigation firm. They accepted the case immediately and promised results, but it was too little too late. Kieran couldn't sleep, was suffering renewed bouts of paranoia, and could barely function at work.

Already dangling at the end of his rope, he fell into the self-destructive spiral that landed him in my office.

I pause on the sidewalk and ask Sven, "Do Alistair and Gail have a security team?"

His lack of surprise tells me Kieran shared what we discussed on Wednesday. "Not twenty-four seven like Kier, but yes. They have top-of-the-line home security with remote monitoring and armed escorts for social engagements—though they've limited those since the call."

I nod distractedly, thinking of Gail and how much all this must be affecting her. Does she live in fear? Maybe I should recommend a therapist if she doesn't have one already.

"Do you have concerns for your safety tonight?" asks Sven.

I meet his eyes, dark and steady. "No," I answer. It feels honest but also not quite the truth. I'm more rattled than anything else. The last two nights, I checked every window and door in my house twice to make sure they were locked before bed.

"Dr. Stirling?" Gabe questions. "Your chariot awaits." He stands at the open back door of the limo with his usual dimpled grin. I'm sure it's meant to be reassuring, but it only reminds me that he's trained to put himself between Kieran and bullets.

"Thank you," I murmur, lifting the hem of my dress and maneuvering onto the leather seat.

The door closes and the interior lights dim. I can barely look at Kieran; he's a black hole in a tux, alluring and lethal, sucking out my sanity. My pulse flutters alarmingly fast, my body struggling to remember this isn't a date.

This is war.

"Nice to see you again, Doctor," says Dylan, seated opposite us behind the front partition.

I seize the distraction. "Likewise. I'm assuming Sven or Gabe know how to drive this thing?"

White teeth flash in his darkly handsome face. "Gabe took a course not long ago. I guess we'll find out if he learned anything."

"Ringing endorsement."

Dylan chuckles.

The limo pulls sedately away from the curb. I buckle my seat belt, then take my phone out of my clutch to make sure it's on silent before tucking it back inside. When I realize I'm fidgeting, I stop and sit still. So still I can hear my heartbeat pounding in my ears.

"No hello for me?" purrs the man beside me.

I make myself look at him—a wolf in the guise of an elegant man.

"Hello, Kieran."

His gaze flickers down my body. "You look exquisite, Talia."

Even though I agreed to him using my first name

tonight—neither of us wants to explain why he calls me Stirling—I still physically react to the shock of it. Or maybe it's the honesty in his voice. Either way, my body temperature rises.

"Thank you." I sound like I'm chewing glass.

He grins. So smug in his victory. I look away, staring at the passing scenery outside. Still, as uncomfortable as I am, I can't regret agreeing to this. From the moment I conceded defeat on Wednesday, he was extremely candid. Despite the heavy topic, the more we talked, the more relaxed he became. By the end of the session—which went almost two hours— he was lying on his back with the pillow under his head. Therapeutic catharsis at its best.

I have a much clearer picture now of what he's been dealing with for the last five years and how it all came to a head. While I'm glad about that, it also revealed an unforeseen obstacle. One no amount of therapy can circumvent.

As long as the threat to his life and loved ones exists, he'll be caught between the drive to continue his research and a very real fear of the consequences. To deal with the constant guilt and helplessness playing tug-of-war inside him, he seeks escape through substance abuse and meaningless physical pleasure.

I knew I had my work cut out for me, but... *damn.* My only hope at this point is that the private investigation firm figures out whoever made that horrifying phone call and whether they're connected to the assassination attempts.

"You seem tense tonight," Kieran remarks. "I'm off

alcohol at the moment, but there's champagne in the bar. Can I offer you a glass?"

"No, thank you. I won't be drinking tonight."

"Do you ever?"

Kieran's expression reminds me of the first time he walked into my office. Distant. A little haughty. Now I know it means he doesn't want to show me what he's feeling.

"Yes, I drink occasionally."

"But never to excess," he surmises.

More of my already fragile nerves snap. I return my gaze to the window. "Not since a few unfortunate evenings in college, no."

His sigh is so heavy I feel it against my bare shoulder. "Can you at least try to enjoy yourself tonight? Melt the outer layers of that ice-queen mask you've got on? It's for a good cause."

I welcome a surge of annoyance. "If you wanted a yes-girl to giggle and hang on your arm, you should have used Tinder for billionaires."

Dylan coughs over the word, "Burn."

"Really, man?" Kieran huffs, then mutters, "Impossible to find good help these days."

Dylan chortles.

"Go ahead, laugh it up."

"Oh, I will," replies Dylan smoothly.

They continue lobbing insults until both are laughing. I listen with half an ear, my mind on the unique relationship between Kieran and his security team. Their camaraderie is more like that of friends or brothers than boss and employees.

I remember Gabe's easy smile and the comment at the jacuzzi: *"Be nice, boss."* How Dylan—who I've interacted with least and thus far has seemed even more stoic than Sven—laughed at Kieran's expense. And I remember Sven saying, *"I'd take a bullet for Kier,"* so casually, like it was a foregone conclusion. And I suppose it was. He's already done it once.

They would die for Kieran, and not out of obligation because he pays their salaries. At least not wholly. They love him. Protect him like they would a brother-in-arms.

As the reality of that sinks in, I finally come to terms with what I've avoided accepting for two days. Someone has tried to kill Kieran. *Twice.* The last time, if Sven hadn't jumped in front of him at the perfect moment and taken the bullet meant for his heart, he'd be dead.

Dead.

"Hey. Look at me."

Kieran's concerned voice startles me. I turn to find him halfway across the seat, one hand hovering in the space between us like he was about to touch me.

Shit. I must have really checked out.

"Sorry," I say weakly.

He scans my face, his hand falling to his knee where it clenches into a fist. "This is one of the reasons I didn't want to tell you. I don't want you to be afraid for your safety when you're with me."

I'm not afraid for me.

I'm afraid for *him*.

Swallowing back the truth, I frown. "There's more than one reason?"

"There you are," he murmurs, then smiles. "The other reason is it means I've lost at least eighty percent of my mystique. I'm no longer a charismatic, handsome stranger with secrets."

My laugh is involuntary. "Wow."

He sits back with a self-satisfied smile, looking like a contented—and very dangerous—predator. His gaze flickers between my eyes and my mouth. No, not my mouth. My teeth.

I suddenly can't take it anymore.

"What is your obsession with my teeth about? It's weird, and that's coming from a kink expert."

Dylan has a coughing fit. Kieran ignores it.

"Not your teeth," he answers readily. "Just the crooked eyetooth. It's so fucking charming I can't stand it."

My face warms. "Again—wow."

He laughs. "Not that I'm complaining, but why no braces when you were young? I feel like parents these days slap those things on kids whether they need them or not. It's like a rite of passage."

"I had them," I admit. "Retainers, too. My wisdom teeth didn't come in until my mid-twenties. The dentist thought I had enough room. He was wrong." I run my tongue over my eyetooth. "It's never bothered me enough to get it fixed.

Until recently, that is. Thanks to you, I have a complex in the making."

Kieran doesn't laugh. "Please don't ever straighten that tooth."

My mind blanks at his fervent tone. Warmth, dense and soft, floats through my chest.

Dylan clears his throat as the limo rolls to a stop behind two others outside the Beverly Wilshire. Ahead of us, couples in evening wear stream inside over an iconic red runner, though thankfully, the paparazzi presence is minimal.

"Dr. Stirling," Dylan says, his game face firmly on. "If you'll scoot back a little, I'll exit now."

I unbuckle my seat belt, then gather my hem and shift a few careful inches toward Kieran. Dylan pauses, half bent over as he approaches my door, and I realize he doesn't have nearly enough space to get by.

"I don't bite unless asked," whispers Kieran.

Gritting my teeth against the reaction in my traitorous body, I shift back again. But this time my gown's slippery material works against me and I slide right into Kieran's chest. Large hands clamp on my waist. He makes a soft, guttural sound that vibrates between my legs. My breath stalls as sensation overloads me—his hard thigh against my ass, the strength and promise in his hands, the furnace-like heat he gives off. Even the brush of his jacket against my bare skin feels erotic.

Dylan bolts from the limo. The door closes.

"No touching," I force out.

But I can't move, and he doesn't release my waist or even snark about the fact I touched him first. He looms behind me, huge and dark and virile. His fingers twitch, digging into the soft bodice of my gown as he tugs me harder against his thigh. I suck in a harsh breath that wants to release as a moan.

The limo rolls forward slowly.

"Talia," he whispers, hot breath on the back of my neck. "Tell me you feel this."

"I can't." The voice that comes out of me is tortured, clogged with desire.

"Why?" he lashes back. "I'll get another fucking therapist. Just say the word."

"That won't change anything."

His frustration comes out in a growl. "Are you seeing someone? Is that it?"

I grasp the excuse with both hands. "Yes."

His hands drop immediately. I scramble across the seat, almost hugging the door as we pull to a stop at the red carpet. My thighs are slick, my breaths fast and shallow.

"At least tell me it's not Toasty."

It takes me a second to place the ridiculous nickname. "No. Not Alan."

The limo stops. The back door opens. Dylan offers me his hand, and I lunge for it like I would a lifeline.

Chapter 15

Kieran

She lied about seeing someone. I know that now. If I'd been thinking straight, I wouldn't have even asked. My gut tells me Stirling is a loyal woman; if she'd met someone in the last two weeks and was invested in a new relationship, she never would have come to my house last Friday. She certainly wouldn't have stripped to a thong and joined me in the jacuzzi, no matter how dedicated she is to my therapy. And she wouldn't keep looking at me with such desperate, conflicted need in those golden-brown eyes.

On the other hand, I'm a grown man. I was raised to respect a woman's words and boundaries, and Stirling has been clear—*repeatedly*—that she doesn't want to explore what's happening between us. Even if her body is screaming the opposite—that she wants me as much as I want her.

I'm still mulling the mess of it all an hour later. Seated next to my brother at a table near the stage, I sip a glass of sparkling water and watch Stirling. She stands fifteen feet away with Gail in a pocket of empty space. My sister-in-law chatters nonstop, oblivious to the undercurrent from nearby tables. The side glances and outright stares—curious, covetous, and in a fair number of cases, scandalized. All directed at the woman who shines brighter in her silky black gown and tiny bird pendant than those wearing sequins and dripping diamonds.

If I didn't know Stirling, I'd think she was relaxed and comfortable. Enjoying herself, even.

She's not.

Beneath her beautiful mask of congeniality is a snarling animal pacing in its cage. She's highly aware of the stares, the whispers that accompanied our entrance and continue to follow her like a mist. She hates the attention.

Right now, she probably hates me. But I'm not her enemy. Half the reason I blackmailed her into coming tonight was to wrap her in the legitimacy of my name. Okay, maybe not *half* the reason. But a solid fifteen percent.

She'll hate me for sure if she realizes I'm trying to protect her. But for all her understanding of the human psyche, she's never been run through the toxic grinder of trash media. She may not even know that her cover of anonymity—which cracked with that first article—was officially blown three days ago.

Someone from her old life sold her out for a quick buck. Her career as a dominatrix is now circulating, including an anonymous interview that doesn't skimp on details. And the details are... inflammatory.

As far as I know, Stirling hasn't felt the repercussions yet. But it's only a matter of time. As gifted a therapist as she is, her famous clients will be second-guessing their association with her. Their publicists and managers will be demanding they cut ties.

I have someone tracking down the anonymous asshole's identity. While it would feel lovely to break his face with my fist, I'm mature enough to know there are less violent and more efficient ways to make him regret being born.

"I'm curious—" starts Alistair.

"No, you're not," I snap.

He grins behind his cocktail glass. "Sure am. Never seen you this rabid over a woman." His smile vanishes. Clearing his throat, he looks away guiltily.

My stomach clenches. I feel sick, his guilt a splash in the sudden ocean of mine.

Because he's right.

I loved Liz deeply. From the moment I met her, I knew she was going to be my wife. She was soft and gentle and kind. An antidote to my rough edges; clear skies to my storm. Her death and that of our unborn child destroyed me. I'd never felt that kind of pain. Some days, on anniversaries or when I see something that reminds me of her, I still can't believe I survived her loss.

But maybe that in itself is a kind of explanation for this fixation I have with Stirling. Like an earthquake that exposes a hidden cave system, perhaps grief opened parts of me that weren't visible before. Brought oxygen and life to the darkest recesses of my spirit. I'm too feral now for anyone gentle. Too sharp for anyone soft.

Whatever the reason, Alistair's right. I've never felt need like this. Obsession. A primal directive to take and claim a woman. Not subdue her—never subdue. More like unfold. I want to unwrap her and lick her secrets. I want her to trust me and need me and challenge me.

I want more than her body.

I want her fucking soul.

THE NIGHT WEARS ON. There's a dinner I don't taste because I'm too focused on watching Stirling eat. A performance by a Broadway star I don't hear because Stirling accidentally touches my hand reaching for a glass of water and afterward, I can't stop thinking about her fingers, long and delicate, and how they'd feel wrapped around my cock.

"Stop staring," she hisses.

"I can't." I sound so annoyed by the fact, she gives me a startled look. I almost grab her by the chin and kiss her. She flushes and turns her attention to the stage.

The auction begins. An incredible amount of money is raised, a good portion of it via paddles from our table.

In addition to my brother and me, three of Lumitech's executive officers are present with their partners. Oliver,

Danielle, and Henry have been with us since Lumitech's infancy. They've met our parents. I've been to their homes. Attended birthday parties and weddings. They grieved with me when Liz died, have supported me through professional highs and lows, and kept the company running with Alistair when I was drinking myself to oblivion.

They're so loyal that none of them have blinked an eye tonight at the permanent frown on my face or my inability to hold a conversation for longer than ten seconds.

I would give them raises, but they don't need more money. Plus, I froze executive salaries six years ago in order to push funds into our workforce wage packages. Maybe I'll send them fruit baskets.

After the auction, there's a lull for dessert and coffee. When Talia and Gail disappear to the bathroom, I finally tune into the discussion at the table.

"...putting everything he has into it," Henry says, throwing a loaded glance my way.

I frown at Alistair. "Who and what?"

"Lyle Porter at SubFusion," he says in a low voice. "Rumor is he's personally sunk eight figures into their nanorobotics project. Same objective we have." He winces. "Sorry, *had*."

Schooling my expression, I shrug. "Good luck to him. Knowing Lyle, though, he might as well have lit the money on fire. He has a third of his father's braincells and probably doesn't know the difference between a biologist and a botanist."

Across the table, Oliver has a coughing fit and his wife, Jenny—drunk as she always is at these events—pats half-heartedly at his back. He waves her off and gulps down the rest of his wine.

"You're really not bothered, Kier?" asks Henry.

My smile is forced. "Nope."

It does bother me. Not because I begrudge another company going after the same objective as us. Competition equals faster innovation in our field, after all. I simply don't like Lyle, who took over SubFusion when his father retired four years ago. In our limited interactions, he's come off as the type to smile at your face and talk smack behind your back. He's also a shit boss according to the numerous SubFusion ex-employees Lumitech has absorbed over the years.

If I'm brutally honest with myself, though, I'm mostly jealous Lyle has the freedom to fund and research whatever he wants because his company isn't a global heavyweight like Lumitech. He flies under the radar in a way I can't, which means he probably sleeps like a baby because no one is threatening to kill him or his family members. Lucky fuck.

The lights dim for another performance. Talia returns to the table, distracting me with nothing more than her nearness. After the applause dies down, the head of the organization gives a speech. At the end, she thanks their primary donor. Lumitech, of course. Alistair goes onstage to accept the plaque that will hang next to the ones from previous years in our corporate lobby.

Then he gives a short talk about our mother. Even

prepared for it, I'm still sucker punched as he tells two hundred people about the woman who birthed us. How she defied her parents' expectations of joining the family alterations business and went to university for her teaching credential. How she loved dancing, classical music, dark beers, and teaching little hellions to read.

Alistair's voice cracks. His words blend together as I remember the same crack in my father's voice from our phone call a few days ago. The anguish he couldn't hide as he told me that for the first time since her diagnosis, Mam hadn't recognized him during their morning visit.

Fingers clamp on my hand, which lies fisted on my thigh. My gaze snaps to Stirling. Her eyes are warm pools of bronze, her expression soft but fierce as she pries my fingers apart, threads hers between them, and holds tight.

The itch under my skin fades. My next breath unravels the tightness in my chest. I don't let go of her hand until it's time to leave.

We say our goodbyes to the table, and Sven escorts us to the waiting limo. We don't speak as we buckle in. Dylan gives me a questioning look that I return with a glare. Minutes pass. Wrapped in shadows and the background hum of the road, the silence simmers.

I want to thank her for what she did but don't know how. Not without making her uncomfortable, possibly defensive. She broke her own rule and touched me tonight. And we both know she didn't do it as my therapist.

Too soon, we enter her neighborhood. Suddenly

desperate to hear her voice, I ask her if she's seen the new article. I immediately want to kick myself, but she merely nods and sighs.

"A friend sent it to me."

I want to tell her I'm working on a retraction but know she won't appreciate my meddling. I also don't want her to feel like she owes me anything.

I clear my throat, feeling awkward as fuck. "Is there anything—that is, are you all right?"

Smooth, Kier.

She studies me, eyes gleaming, passing streetlights flickering across the side of her face. "That's kind of you to ask, but I'm fine. In fact, I'm kind of glad it happened."

The limo stops outside her house. Dylan launches off his seat and shoves me aside to exit through my door. I don't think his elbow to my gut is accidental, the force of it knocking the air from me in an undignified grunt.

"Sorry," he lies, then slams the door.

I cough. "Fucker."

"Are you all right?" asks Stirling, her lips fighting a smile.

"I will be when I fire him."

She laughs softly. "Sure you will."

I grin at her like an idiot until she blinks and picks up her little purse. My heart leaps as she reaches for the door handle.

"I'm sorry I made you come tonight."

She hesitates, then shifts to face me. "I'm not. You were right. It's a worthy cause."

"Thank you, by the way, for the donation check you snuck off to write."

Her eyes flare as she realizes how closely I watched her tonight—every damn second except when she was in the bathroom. I would have watched her there, too, if I could have.

Her expression smooths. "Is there anything else, Kieran, or can I go?"

The wry tone makes me want to grin again, but I bite it back. "Yeah, one more thing. You said you were glad about the article. Why?"

I'm breaking the rules. She doesn't owe me a truth. But she gives it to me anyway.

"It made me realize how important that part of my life was. If I hadn't walked that path, I wouldn't be where I am today. I'm not ashamed of my history with the kink community. I'm proud of it. The fact it's triggering so many people only highlights the ignorance and shame around the topic."

She trails off, eyes flickering like she's surprised she said so much. "Anyway, you could say I've been reevaluating my career goals over the last few days." Her lips twist. "I found myself with some unexpected free time when two clients fired me."

I wince. "I'm sorry."

She shrugs. "Like I said, I'm okay with it."

"You think everything happens for a reason?"

Her eyes find mine and a zing of awareness flashes down

my spine. I never want to stop looking at her. For her to stop looking at me.

"Not exactly. But I do think challenges break off pieces of us we don't need anymore. If we want to, we can use those pieces to lay the groundwork for a new path forward."

I have a feeling she intends the words to apply to me more than her, but I can't think past how they relate to her life. When I put two and two together, my stomach bottoms out.

"You're going back to it?" I ask hoarsely. "The lifestyle?"

She hesitates. "Not as a Domme, no."

My relief is embarrassingly obvious, but the potency of the emotion leaves no room for self-consciousness. "Teaching, then?"

After another pause, she nods. "Part-time. But who knows, maybe it will expand from there. My inbox has been equal parts hate mail and invitations for speaking engagements. There are even two offers for book deals."

My mouth dries up, my relief flattened between awe and anxiety. It doesn't surprise me that others can recognize what a brilliant light she is. She's a comet whose fiery tail shines on me now, but eventually, she'll fade from my sky and illuminate others'.

I don't have her, but I feel like I'm losing her.

"Well, I'm not firing you," I say gruffly.

She smiles. "Thanks. See you Wednesday?"

I nod, and she exits the limo with smooth grace. Sven appears and escorts her to her front door. Even though I know he'll wait until he hears a lock turn, I twitch as I wonder if she has an alarm system. If she has the means to defend herself if someone breaks in.

I torture myself with fears until Sven joins me in the back, occupying Stirling's seat. Then I torture myself wondering if he can feel the fading heat of her body.

"You've gotta figure this out," he says as the limo pulls away from the one place I want to be.

My teeth clench. "I offered to find another therapist. She said no."

He hands me his phone. I stare at the screen, not understanding what I'm reading at first. When it registers, my fingers spasm.

CROSSROADS IS PROUD TO WELCOME BACK

DR. TALIA STIRLING
AKA THE PROFESSOR

SATURDAYS 6PM - 8PM

REGISTER <u>HERE</u>

Once I've read it a hundred times and cycled through the same number of emotions, I toss Sven the phone. Crossing my arms over my chest, I slouch in my seat and glare out the window.

A solid minute later, he drawls, "How's the pouting going?"

Fucker always makes me smile when I don't want to. Shaking my head, I ask, "Why even show me that?"

"You giving up?"

"Giving up on what?" I'm angry again. "Maybe Stirling's right. Maybe this... thing I feel doesn't have anything to do with her as a person. Maybe it's some weird side effect of the therapy or the illicitness of it—of her. I don't even know her. Not really."

"But you want to."

"You're fired."

"Thank God. I can finally take that vacation to Maui."

Now I'm laughing. When it tapers off, I clear my throat. "Did you...?"

"Take an Uber to her house during the benefit in order to break in and assess her security?"

I nod, ignoring a pinch of guilt.

"Sure did. She has a standard alarm system. It's functional. I confirmed with her that she sets it every night and suggested she set it during the day as well. All doors, windows, and crawl spaces are secure."

I breathe a sigh of relief. "Thanks."

He's quiet for a while, then says, "You match."

I scowl at him. "What?"

Shrugging his gargantuan shoulders, he gives me a look I've never seen on his face. Close to sympathy. Then he blows my mind with the most emotional speech he's ever made.

"You and Stirling—you fit. Anyone with eyes can see it, hear it when you talk to each other. Maybe this shit has always been easy for you in the past, but you're not an easy man anymore, Kier—if you ever really were. And if Stirling were easy, she wouldn't be your match."

My throat feels funny. "You've gone soft, big man."

He glowers. "I know it's not an ideal situation, her being your therapist. Maybe if she were horrible at it, but she's not. You're at least twenty percent more tolerable since you started unloading your demons in her office."

"Thanks," I grouse.

"All I'm saying is I don't think you should give up. Use that high IQ you supposedly have. Solve the equation or whatever." He makes a disgusted sound. "The first event is next week. I'm done talking."

I look away. Stare at nothing. Think about everything.

Finally, I say, "Set it up."

Sven doesn't reply; he doesn't need to. This was his hare-brained idea, and I'll be sure to remind him when it blows up in my face.

Guess I'm going back to Crossroads.

CHAPTER 16

TALIA

On Wednesday, Kieran meets me at the warehouse. I take him to a different room, one aligned with creation rather than destruction.

"You have some options," I tell him as he surveys the worktables. "You can make a mosaic, sand and prep furniture for repainting, or carve a piece of wood. If none of those appeal to you, I can teach you the basics of crochet or we can move to a room with canvases and paint."

He gives me a disbelieving look. "I'm not an artist."

"It's about the process, not the end result. No one expects you to have a showing at LACMA next month." I pause. "I think you should try carving something."

"Why?"

"Just trust me."

His gaze narrows. I hold eye contact, projecting calm

when inside I'm a whirlwind. Finally, he nods. "Okay. As long as you do it with me."

"Deal."

We settle side by side on stools at the woodcarving station. After I go through the basics—what tools to use, how to carve with the grain, and different types of cuts—I give him a laminated sheet with easy instructions to make basic shapes out of a two-inch block.

"What are you going to make?" he asks, twirling a V-shaped chisel in his fingers.

I grab a block for myself. "No idea."

He smirks. "Let me guess, the wood will speak to you and tell you what shape it wants to take?"

"Definitely not. I'm horrible at carving, actually." I lift my hand to show him the small scar at the base of my palm. "Case in point."

Before I can read his intent, warm fingers encircle my wrist and draw my hand toward his face. Heat radiates up my arm, sparkling energy that swirls to my nipples and chokes my airway. My mind blanks.

"I know," he murmurs, eyes on the scar that hovers dangerously close to his mouth. "I'm breaking rules."

His thumb drags over the scar, making me shiver. Blue eyes flash to mine, roaming my face and neck with intense focus. Then he drops my hand and picks up his chisel again.

"I know what I'm going to make."

"Good," I say weakly, grabbing my own tool.

He goes to work, each movement methodical and confident—too confident for someone unfamiliar with the tools.

"You've done this before," I guess.

He smiles slightly. "Not since I was little. I went through hobbies as fast as I outgrew my clothes. There was a whittling phase, a spear-fishing phase, an astronomy phase. You name it, I probably tried it when I was a kid. There was even a snake phase, though that was shut down fast. Eventually, I started tinkering with all the electronics in the house. Mam threw a fit, so Dad started bringing home broken ones for me to fix. Toasters and coffee makers, mostly." He chuckles. "When I found he was charging people for my services, I made him give me a cut."

I smile at this insight into his relationship with his father. "I love that. Are you two close now?"

"Yes."

The crisp reply tells me it's a sore point at the moment, likely due to his mother's illness. I don't press him. Although the topic is integral to his therapy, I'm tackling a different one tonight.

Chipping aimlessly at my block, I surreptitiously watch him process the emotional discomfort. Eventually, his shoulders relax and the tightness around his mouth disappears.

Then I begin.

"What do you see your life looking like five years from now?"

His focus doesn't leave the block, but his eyes crinkle. "Really?"

"Humor me."

He hums, chewing on his lip a moment, then frowns. "I honestly have no idea."

There's vulnerability in the answer—he didn't like admitting that—so I gentle my voice. "Has envisioning the future been easy for you in the past?"

He nods shortly. "I've always had a pretty clear idea of what I wanted in life. Not the specifics, necessarily, but the end goals. The specifics came when I started making five- and ten-year plans in my teens. Kept using them for the bulk of my twenties."

"Did you always achieve your goals?"

His carving pauses, then resumes. "Professionally, yes. And for a while, personally, too."

I give his answer a moment to breathe, for the acknowledgment of his grief to be felt.

"Would it be correct to say you value strategy over spontaneity?"

He smirks. "I'm an engineer and a scientist, Stirling."

"I'll take that as a yes." Changing tracks to a seemingly random tangent, I ask, "Do you have a history of alcoholism or drug addiction in your family?"

A smile curves over his face. "Because I'm Irish, I must be an alcoholic?"

"Come on," I admonish.

His teasing eyes briefly meet mine. "The answer is no. But I did have a friend in college who was a recovering addict.

Even went to some meetings with him. I know the warning signs."

"Is your binge-drinking and drug use a strategy rather than unplanned impulse, then? Do you consider it normal?"

"What's normal about my situation?" He scoffs, then sighs. "Yes, I'm aware I've overdone it a bit lately. But there are a few distinct differences between me and an addict."

Something an addict would say, is my first thought. But I've learned that generalizations are dangerous where this man is concerned. And my instincts have been off before.

"And those differences are?"

He sits back and inspects his carving, which looks more or less like a lumpy blob with a smaller blob attached to one side. Exchanging tools, he begins shaving off long, thin curls from the bigger section.

"One, it doesn't make me feel better or help me forget. Two, I don't crave it when I stop or obsess over when I can have the next drink. Three, I don't experience a marked change in thinking. Four, I don't make excuses for it or manipulate, deceive, or blame others."

I study his profile, fascinated by his answer.

"You've clearly given it some thought."

He smiles slightly. "Scientist."

"Then why do it?"

He shrugs. "Boredom tops the list. In case you missed it, I basically live in a cage. A nice one, but one that's grown substantially smaller in the last few months. And sure, sometimes booze and a blunt can *blunt* the emotional edges." He smirks at his play on words.

"By emotional edges, you're referring to feelings of stress, grief, or profound powerlessness?"

"Tomato, tomahto," he mutters, then glances at me from beneath his lashes. "Yes, Stirling."

"Does casual sex achieve the same result for you? Relieve those feelings?"

"No," he says, then hesitates. A moment later, his expression twists with irritation. "Shit. I hate it when you do that."

I give up the thin pretense of carving, setting down my tools and swiveling to face him. "Can you admit that maybe you've fallen into the habit of using sex like you use drugs and alcohol? Perhaps even as your primary tool to escape boredom or overwhelm?"

His lips thin, but he doesn't say anything.

"How long has it been this way?" I ask softly.

Brows drawn together, he mumbles, "Really gonna make me say it, are you?"

"Yes."

He sighs. "Since Liz died."

The treasure of his growing self-awareness floats into my hands. I'm so proud of him. Whether he realizes it or not, the work we're doing is giving him back some of the power and control he's lost.

The next part, I know, won't be as easy.

"Have you attempted intimacy with a woman since the threatening phone call?"

His fingers clench on the carving. "Besides you?"

"Kieran."

He flicks an irritated look at me. "What are you getting at?"

"That like drugs and alcohol, casual sex isn't a healthy long-term coping mechanism. Some part of you recognizes this, otherwise you'd still be using it. I'd like to understand your reasons for cutting yourself off from a new relationship."

"Who says there's a reason?"

"Your personality says there's a reason." I tick off on my fingers. "Scientist. Engineer. Strategist. Planner. Methodical to a fault—"

"Fuck, I get it."

"Well?"

The chisel slips, carving off more than he intended. His jaw clenches. "Pass," he growls.

"This isn't a trivia show."

Another switch of tools, this time to a finer-tipped chisel. He resumes working, but there's a calculating tilt to his head.

"I'll answer if you answer a question first."

My back straightens. "Okay."

"Are you really seeing someone?"

My stomach flips. "No," I admit. "I'm sorry I lied to you about that. It was the wrong way to set a boundary."

He nods to himself, expression neutral. I stay tense in expectation of a follow-up question, but he surprises me.

"It wouldn't be fair to ask a woman to deal with the restrictions in my life right now."

I pause a beat, weighing the words. By this point, I know him well enough to decipher when he's holding back. He's not lying, exactly, but he's also not being honest.

"Can you dig deeper? What's the emotion behind that?"

His eyelashes flicker. "Fear."

"Of what?"

"Death, obviously. I'd prefer that no one else dies at the hands of a deranged stalker."

"More, Kieran. This is an established pattern that spans four years. Your fear is valid, but there's another component to it."

"Maybe I haven't met a woman I'd like to chat with after fucking," he grinds out.

"More."

Air hisses through clenched teeth. Stormy eyes find mine. "I'm not the same man who married Liz. I don't feel capable of it."

"Capable of what?"

He throws his tool to the table, swiveling to face me. "You win, Stirling. Here's the truth. It's not that I haven't tried dating anyone. It's that when I have, I lost interest within days. I don't know how to be normal anymore. I'm too angry, too... jagged. I'm so different, if Liz were still alive, I don't even know if she'd have me. And worse, so much fucking worse, I don't know if I'd want *her*."

Anguish screams in his eyes, his face. I want to touch him

so badly. Push my fingers into the tense muscles of his shoulders and neck. Brush the hair back from his face and tell him, *It's okay, you're okay, you'll be okay.* A fine tremor moves down my spine, my fingers curling together in my lap as I resist the impulse.

"That's grief," I murmur. "The inescapable tragedy of time passing and carrying us away from the people we've lost. It doesn't diminish the love. We can only accept that our hearts have different shapes now. You're as capable of love as you were then. And just as deserving."

Holding eye contact has never been harder. Even though he's the one who exposed a core vulnerability, I feel flayed open by his steady gaze. I'm terrified he can sense that my words are more than helpful rhetoric. That I meant them not as his therapist, but as a woman in awe of him.

The tightrope slips under my feet.

Kieran's rapt expression softens. With a small shake of his head, he turns back to the worktable and picks up his tool. I let him work in silence for a few minutes, both to let the heaviness pass and to give myself time to remember what the hell I'm doing.

Once I feel solid again, I clear my throat.

"Ding, ding, round two," he murmurs, lips twitching.

My sigh is half relief, half laughter. "Okay, let's circle back to coping mechanisms. Do you have any hobbies outside of work? Judo doesn't count."

He frowns, glancing at me. "Why not?"

I arch a brow. "You tell me."

He sighs. "Because it's a strategy I employ for health and longevity and not strictly for enjoyment."

I grin. "Exactly."

He glances at my eyetooth; I close my mouth. Smiling to himself, he returns to his carving. Though the blob is more refined now, with striations and a tapered side opposite the narrow protrusion, I still can't figure out what it is.

"Hate to disappoint you, Stirling, but I do have hobbies. I swim. Cook. Read. Those are for pleasure."

"That's good," I say encouragingly. "How else do you manage stress?"

"I get the sense you'd love it if I said meditation or Tai Chi."

I laugh. "Yeah, that'd be great. But self-care doesn't have to be active. Bubble baths and massages work, too."

He throws me a wicked smile. "Know any masseuses? I'm very picky these days. Has to be a woman with lion eyes, one crooked tooth, and a personality like a minefield."

I suck in a startled breath. My balance, so recently recovered, suffers a fatal blow.

Kieran watches me for a long moment, his smile slowly fading as his gaze caresses my hot cheeks. Then he nods to himself and returns to his project.

I spend the next few minutes trying to crawl my way back to control, but it's no use. My thoughts are clogged, my senses in charge. I'm hyperaware of every breath he takes, every movement of his hands. The way he bounces his knee when he's planning his next approach to the carving. How he stills with focus before each careful shave of wood.

Conceding that we've accomplished all we can today, at least from a talk therapy standpoint, I slip off my stool and wander to the mosaic table. I could—and probably should—step outside while he finishes, but I can't. My base self is still in control, compelling me to stay close to him. Share space with him as long as I can.

I can already hear Leo's response when I call tomorrow. *"Recenter and reassess."*

Desperate for equilibrium, I select a handful of small, irregularly shaped tiles and begin fitting them together like puzzle pieces. The similarity to my mental landscape doesn't escape me, nor does the fact that my efforts in both dimensions are futile. Mosaics aren't puzzles. Their components don't often connect, and even if they do, seamlessness isn't the goal. The point is to organize their chaos to create something new.

I wish organizing my thoughts were as easy as shifting tiles, but too many of my thoughts have impossible shapes. Still, I keep trying. Somewhere inside the chaos is reason. I only have to find it.

A dim tile shot through with orange veins reminds me of how his dress shirt looked as we sat knee-to-knee last week, fake candle flames flickering.

"How many more times do I have to get a hard-on

looking at you for you to admit I want you? Under me, above me, sideways, upside-down..."

More memories come forward. All the overtures, subtle and not, he's offered with increasing urgency since the night at the Philharmonic. The undeniable chemistry we have. How his touch lights me up with an intensity I've never felt before. How fascinating he is to me—not as a client, but as a man.

Part of me wants to stay with these thoughts, rub their edges and soak in the twinkling light they reflect. Lose myself in fantasy the same way I did when I was young. God knows I have—most nights, in fact, alone in bed with my vibrator.

But at the end of the day, I haven't slipped that far. I'm not fourteen anymore. I don't believe in fantasies. So even though it hurts to put them aside, I make myself recenter and reassess.

I go back further, to our session a few days before the Phil. Kieran started off combative, but something unlocked and he shared candidly about his work for most of the hour. It was the first time he opened up to me. Then just as abruptly, he shut down. The trigger was asking him what had happened five weeks prior—the threatening phone call.

Following the trigger, I find its two-pronged origin: the death of his wife and his mother's diagnosis. The losses of the two women he's loved most in his lifetime.

In my mind, Leo says, *"There it is. You're back on solid ground."*

What Kieran's feeling for me is transference. He's unconsciously projecting the powerful emotions he has for his late wife and mother onto me. After four years without experiencing emotional intimacy with a woman, it makes perfect sense for him to confuse our professional relationship with a personal one. My personality and looks, so different from his wife's, were unintended catalysts.

I shift a few more tiles around on the table, wishing—as I do every time I go through this exercise, which at this point is almost daily—that the conclusion brought me relief.

It never does.

"WHAT ARE you thinking so hard about over here?" asks Kieran from behind me.

I turn quickly on my stool. "Just playing with tiles. Are you finished?"

He nods and holds out his hand. "Here. It's for you."

When I see what lies nestled in his palm, a wave of cold cascades down my body. The world tilts. My vision momentarily dims. There's no tightrope at all anymore—only a free fall.

He made a hummingbird.

Memory tiles slip and slide from the past into the present, destroying the work I just completed. They clatter together in happy chaos—the same that permeated a long-ago conversation on a rainy night in Galway.

"You look like a wet hummingbird."

"Someday the world will kneel to you."

"I was wrong. You're not a bird, after all."

"You're a lioness."

"Birdie. Your name is Birdie."

"Go on, take it." Kieran nods to my neck. "I figured you liked them since I've never seen you without that necklace."

"It's beautiful. Thank you. But I can't accept it." The words are the right ones, but I sound all wrong. Flustered. Upset.

His gaze sharpens. "It's a bird. You like birds. Accept the gift."

I don't like birds, actually. At least not any more or less than other animals. If I were strapped to a table and tortured, I'd still be hard-pressed to explain why I've been wearing a necklace with a hummingbird pendant for the last ten years and have only taken it off to clean it.

Is it because of him? No doubt. But it's just as much true that it's not about him at all. It's about me. My metamorphosis. My growth. My pain and the claws I grew to protect myself from more.

It makes no sense.

It means everything to me.

Swallowing the absurd urge to laugh until I cry, I reach out. My fingertips graze his palm as they close around the small figurine. The wood is warm from his hands, the shape a little lumpy and rough.

It's perfect.

"Thank you." I make myself set it down on the work-table, then stand. "And thank you for your candor tonight. I feel really good about where we are with your therapy. How are you feeling?"

My voice still isn't quite right, but there's nothing to be done about it. I'm in free fall. I need him to be gone before I hit the surface.

Kieran's gives me another thoughtful look—the one I'm beginning to fear more than any other. To my relief, he finally answers, "I feel good, too."

I force a smile. "Great. I'll walk you out."

CHAPTER 17

TALIA

Saturday evening, I smooth my hands down the front of my blouse, checking that it's tucked seamlessly into my pencil skirt, then resume pacing the same five feet of carpet before the desk in Charlie's office at Crossroads. I'm anxious about tonight, but at least I'm not spiraling anymore. I'm focused. Ready.

I owe my sanity to Leo, who reminded me Thursday morning of the Stop Sign Method. I've spent the bulk of the last three days practicing the simple but effective exercise. When thoughts of Kieran intruded, I visualized a stop sign. The first day was the hardest, the red octagon virtually living in my head. By this morning, though, I felt back in control.

"Nervous?"

Charlie's dark eyes track me from the red velvet couch where she sits nibbling on strawberries, looking like

Aphrodite in a white dress, her dark hair loose around her tanned shoulders.

"A little," I admit.

"Why are you wound so tight? You've done this a hundred times."

I glance at her. "Not helping."

Her smile is vulpine. "If you wanted your ego or clit stroked, you should have gone to Nate's office."

I grimace. "Really not helping."

"Talia." She waits until I stop and look at her. "When was the last time you were properly fucked?"

I sigh. "It's been a while."

Longer than a while, actually, but if I tell her how long it's really been, she'll lose her mind. As it is, I already know she's going to lecture me.

She doesn't disappoint.

"For God's sake, let me find you a Dom. One who's known you a long time and will be sensitive to your needs." She pauses. "Speaking of, Adam asked about you after your visit a few weeks ago. He's always had a thing for you, even before you started leaking Switch vibes and ran away from us like your ass was on fire."

For a few seconds, I think about it. The night of the playroom fiasco, Adam appeared as I talked the distraught Dom into unblocking the door. He took control of the man so I could attend to the sobbing woman. When all was resolved, he invited me to get a drink at the bar and catch up. I was momentarily tempted—I'd always liked him—but a warning look from Nate made me reevaluate. It was then I realized that despite the mantle of the Professor on my shoulders, Adam wasn't looking at me like I was a Domme but a potential submissive. The change was weirdly off-putting. Like being a predator for years and suddenly waking up in the body of a rabbit.

"Besides," Charlie continues, "I've seen him fuck. It's glorious. He'll fix you right up."

He won't, though. As talented as Adam is—I've seen him fuck, too—he won't fix anything. He's not who I want, and no substitute will do. Until Kieran and I go our separate ways, I'm resigned to self-pleasure only. I have to believe that someday I'll meet someone who makes me feel as wild and alive as he does. The alternative is too depressing to consider.

"Thanks for the offer," I tell Charlie, "but no."

She sniffs. "Your pussy's loss."

There's a knock on the door. I hurry to open it and find Nate on the other side. He looks me over and smiles, big and genuine, and relief loosens the tension in my shoulders. I was worried he'd want a repeat of the last time I was here, but all I see in his eyes is uncomplicated affection and the comfort of our shared history.

I hope it means he's found what he's looking for.

"You look hot as fuck, Talia."

I grin. "Thanks. So do you."

Charlie grumbles, "Sometimes I really miss the old Nathan."

"No, you don't," he says lightly, then offers us his arms. "Come, ladies. The Epicenter of Sin awaits."

THE EPICENTER, a recessed, circular stage where live scenes take place at midnight, dominates the back third of the club. Right now, it's occupied by me and a slim podium. My rapt audience stands three-deep behind the waist-high railings above me, their faces shadowed due to the spotlight over my head and the club's dimmed background lighting.

My nerves faded within the first few minutes, overtaken by my passion for the topic. Before I know it, I'm wrapping up the lecture, an updated version of one I gave years ago about the intersectionality of psychology, gender, and kink. While the crowd has been responsive, laughing or murmuring at appropriate moments, I'm still shocked by the thunderous applause when I finish.

A grinning Nate descends into the pit and hands me a water bottle, then lifts my free hand into the air.

"The Professor, everyone! Let's hear how glad you are to have her back!"

His voice is amplified by the small microphone on my blouse. I turn it off, glaring at him as the audience roars anew. He laughs and tugs me into his arms for a hug. More whistles pierce the air.

At my ear, he says, "Ignore that. You're amazing. You were always impressive, Talia, but that was next level."

My ire melts, and I kiss his cheek. "Thank you, lovely."

We break apart as Dominic Cross walks down the steps, his powerful aura dampening the crowd's cries. Dark eyes crinkled with warmth, he offers me his hand. I shake it, surprised by a sudden surge of emotion. Stern, protective, and honest, Dominic is as much responsible for who I am today as Charlie is. I've always thought of him as a giant, grumpy big brother and his wife, London, a quirky big sister.

"Good to see you, Talia," he says, his handsome face open in a rare smile. "That was exceptional."

"You, too, and thank you. I'm so flattered you came."

"London and I wouldn't have missed it for the world." He glances up at where she must be, but all the faces blend together outside the spotlight. "She'll hunt you down after, I'm sure. Are you ready for the Q&A?"

I nod, aware of the simmering excitement from the crowd. "It's always been my favorite part, actually."

"Mine, too." He looks at Nate, and my heart warms at the respect in his eyes. "You good?"

Nate nods serenely and pulls a microphone from his pocket, switching it on.

"Testing, testing, motherfuckers."

His voice bounces around the club. Laughter sounds. Even Dominic chuckles before he climbs the stairs and disappears into the shadows. After confirming that my mic is back on, Nate follows him.

For the next forty-five minutes, Nate moves through the audience. There are questions that fill the air with more laughter, others that demand silence and a careful response. Most aren't even questions about kink. A woman asks what to do if she and her partner have different love languages, and a man asks for advice because his husband is resistant to couples counseling. Some voices are nervous or desperate. Others witty or dry. All are honest and vulnerable, and together they abolish the last of my doubts about coming back.

My conviction grows that this is what I'm meant to be doing. Small groups, large scale, it doesn't really matter. There's nothing that feels as profound and meaningful to me as a community coming together. Learning about themselves and each other.

Eventually, Nate announces that the next question will be the last.

There's a moment of silence, then:

"How would you counsel someone who's falling for their therapist?"

As the deep, musical voice fills the club, the blood drains from my head. I reach for the nearby podium, my fingernails digging into the wood so hard it splinters. A sliver pierces the skin beneath my thumbnail—a lightning strike to my senses that focuses me and clears the ringing from my ears.

In the absence of shock, rage floods every inch of my body and mind. *This can't be happening. He can't be here.*

It's too much.

"We're ending here today," I say tightly. "Thank you, everyone."

I rip off my microphone and stalk up the stairs into the crowd. The look on my face works better than a flamethrower, clearing an immediate path from the Epicenter to my target: a tall man wearing fake glasses and a baseball hat.

Ignoring Nate's shocked face and Sven's grimace, I grab Kieran's arm.

"Come on, Clark Kent," I snarl, then drag him across the club through the archway leading to the playrooms.

TALIA

"**W**hat are you doing here?"

Kieran's gaze moves away from a row of dildos displayed in a plexiglass drawer. I brought him to the least extreme of the play-rooms, but it's still Crossroads. The space radiates eroticism from every inch. If I'd been thinking straight, I would have taken him to one of the offices.

His eyebrows lift. "Is the silent treatment over, then?"

My teeth clench. I'm too spun up to even attempt under-standing why I'm so angry. All I know is that I feel like every-thing's falling apart.

Like *I'm* falling apart.

When I can unhinge my jaw, I spit out, "It took me a minute to remember how to speak without screaming."

His lips thin, eyes sparkling.

"If you laugh right now, I swear to God I'll lose my mind. And take off those stupid glasses."

I regret the demand when the undiluted force of his blue eyes hits me. "Better?"

"No," I snap. "Now answer my question. Why are you here? More specifically, what did you hope to accomplish by inserting yourself into my private life and derailing the entire evening for me?"

He winces. "Ouch."

My anger softens the tiniest bit. "Dammit, Kieran. Why?"

He walks to the wide, padded bench in the middle of the room and sits. From his grave expression, he's finally realized how close I am to strangling him.

"Remember what I said about why I haven't dated anyone?"

My heart skips a beat. "Yes, of course."

"I wasn't being totally honest. I *did* feel that way. Until very recently. Now I can't stop thinking about you. I want to know you. I want you in my bed and my life. It's as simple—and complicated—as that. I've decided I don't care that you're my therapist. In fact, you're fired."

My breath catches. "Don't."

A spark of amusement lifts the corner of his mouth. "You can't tell me what to do anymore."

"Like I ever could," I growl.

He fights a wider smile. "Let me amend my statement.

There's one scenario in which you can order me around to your heart's content."

Panic sparkles over my skin. "We've made so much progress the last few weeks. Wednesday night was huge. Didn't you feel it? We really got somewhere."

"I did. You're a great therapist, no question. I just don't want you to be mine."

"Please reconsider," I say, not caring that I sound desperate. "I can still help you."

The vestiges of humor vanish from his voice. "If you want to help me, Talia, tell me why you're fighting this so hard. I already know you're attracted to me. Fireworks don't hold a candle to what happens when we touch." Darkness passes through his eyes. "Is it the security issues? My restrictive lifestyle? I know it's a lot. I'm selfish for asking you to accept—"

"That doesn't have anything to do with it!" I explode.

He leans forward, expression taut. "What's the problem, then? I'm smart, fit, and relatively charming. I don't have any STDs or illegitimate children. I'm a good cook. I do my own laundry. My bank account balance has an obscene number of zeros. Most importantly, I want to eat you out until you pass out and then go back for seconds." He pauses, head tilting. "You're blushing. You like the idea, don't you? My face between those beautiful thighs?"

"I'm *frustrated*," I hiss.

"You're aroused."

"You're delusional!"

His voice lowers to a growl. "I'm perfectly sane, and you know it."

I hit the red zone of emotional overload. My eyes start to sting. Horrified, I spin away before the first tear falls and swipe angrily at my face.

"Talia," he whispers. "I know you feel something for me."

Forgetting my tears, I whip around. "It's in your head!"

He stands and swallows the distance between us in three strides. I suck in a breath as his fingers curl around my throat, tilting my face to his. My knees weaken; I lock them but can't prevent a full-body shudder. His palm is hot and dry, the press of his fingers excruciatingly gentle. My heart pounds in my ears, my neck. Between my legs.

"This is in my head?" he whispers, his mouth dipping toward mine but stopping a hairsbreadth away. "Your pupils just blew. I can feel your racing pulse. Try another lie, or admit you want me and I'll kiss you."

More tears leak from my eyes—of resignation, this time—as I stare up at the man who's consumed me in one way or another since I was fourteen.

I've been such a fool. I really thought I could be his thera-pist. I thought if I could teach him to bend, I'd be able to prevent him from breaking. I could save him. Repay him.

I was so wrong.

He's the resilient one. The king who bows to no one. And I'm the one breaking against the walls of my own mind.

My fall was always a foregone conclusion, the tightrope

an illusion. Deep down I'm still the girl in that graveyard, overweight and acne-prone with braces and bad hair. And he's still the beautiful boy who took my secrets and gave me the courage to grow claws.

Now those claws flex, ripping through scar tissue to the girl beneath. Freeing her to experience her first and favorite fantasy coming true. Awe spreads through me, honeyed and hot. And it suddenly doesn't matter that his feelings for me are transference.

My feelings aren't.

I'm done fighting them.

Pushing forward against his hand, I fit my mouth to his. For a moment, I hear rain. Feel it. Then there's only the soft, hot texture of his lips against mine, and his gasp of surprise or maybe relief. He was right—fireworks don't hold a candle to what happens when we touch. This is the birth of a universe.

I lick his perfect lower lip. His groan is gasoline on the inferno inside me, and my restraint snaps. I yank his hand from my throat and surge against him, grabbing fistfuls of his hair for leverage as I devour his mouth. He tastes like every sin I've ever craved. Better than even my wildest fantasy. He kisses me back like he feels the same but keeps his hands on my waist. They tremble and flex like he's holding back. And he is. For me.

I press harder against him, angling one leg between his and twisting against his erection. He grunts. Trembles harder. His fingers dig into my waist. But he still lets me lead. Somehow, he knows what I need.

When a new need arises, I push him backward until his legs hit the bench. Then I gently tug his hair until he sits. The seal of our mouths breaks. I gaze down at him, my hands framing his face. Swollen lips, flushed cheeks, his hair sticking up, he looks at me like I'm his salvation.

He doesn't know he's always been mine.

"Take off your pants," I tell him.

His eyebrow cocks. "Say please."

I kiss him again, quick and hard, because I can't resist. "If you do, I promise it will be worth it."

His pupils dilate even more. "Close enough."

As he takes care of his jeans, I take care of privacy, flipping the switch by the door to turn on the red Occupied light. The curtain is already drawn, the lights dimmed. Part of me wants to turn them to full brightness. So I can see more. *Everything.* But shadows are more apt. This is the void of space, after all, and we're a silent explosion.

When I turn back to Kieran, I almost trip at the sight that awaits me. As it is, I blink a few times in sheer disbelief and wonder.

"I love that look on your face," he murmurs, "but I won't lie, it feels a bit awkward sitting here with my dick in my hand."

Laughter burbles out of me. His answering chuckle ends in a groan when I hike my skirt over my knees, push his legs apart, and drop to the plush rug between them. Dragging my nails up his thighs, I close my eyes to memorize the heat of his skin, the tickle of sparse hair. A slow inhale traps his scent in my lungs.

His breaths grow harsh. "Wait. Let me—"

"Shut up, Kieran. I already know what you want. This is what *I* want."

I gather spit in my mouth, then lick my palms, one after the other. He watches me do it, lips slightly parted, eyes glittering and dark.

I'm suddenly, acutely happy he's the first man I've gone to my knees for. The secret is a treasure, pulsing and joyful. He doesn't know how important this is, how vulnerable I'm making myself. What it means.

But I do, and that's enough.

"Equals don't kneel."
"I think they do. But only to each other."

I take his cock in my slick hands, sliding them down until they meet his body. He's thick, the skin flushed dark with blood, so hard and needy. A vein throbs against my fingers. Pre-cum leaks from the tip. He's so close already and I love that it's because of me. Leaning forward, I pump my hands as I swirl my tongue over the broad, flared head. The silky texture makes me moan. The flavor of his want makes my pussy ache and drip.

He chokes. "Jesus fucking—"

I take him in my mouth.

"—Christ!"

I find a rhythm with my mouth and hands, relishing his needy grunts and the small, greedy thrusts of his hips. When I pay special attention to the vein on the underside of his shaft, he hisses and loses a bit more control. His fingertips graze my jaw, nose, cheekbones, throat. Like I'm priceless art. Delicate and easily shattered.

Silly man, I'm a lion.

Hollowing my cheeks, I take him into my throat and swallow once, twice. His fingers spasm against my head. With an agonized shout of my name, he comes apart. His pleasure heats my throat and fills me with vibrating, liquid power.

I uncurl my fingers slowly, then lick him root to tip, all the way around, until he topples backward onto the bench with an arm over his face. He's shaking, his chest heaving.

"I can't fucking see—holy—what on earth—"

Moving to my feet, I round the bench and brush a lock of hair from his forehead. The urge to cry reappears, almost undoing me, but I smother it. *Just a few more seconds.*

His arm slips over his head and he looks up at me, eyes unguarded and tender, full of everything I wish so badly were true. The connection is painful, so I focus instead on locking in every detail I can. I trail my thumbs over his eyebrows, down the peak of his nose, across the faint freckles on his cheekbones.

I don't feel the tear until it falls.

Kieran's eyes widen. "Talia—"

"No," I whisper.

Bending, I kiss his forehead. *Goodbye.* Then I take a long step back from the table and smooth down my skirt.

"Go home, Kieran. Please consider reaching out to a new therapist. I personally recommend Dr. Leo Chastain."

At the forced detachment in my voice, devastation flashes across his face. It hurts me, too. Like a fucking stake to the chest. But I don't have the luxury of living in fantasies anymore. And that's what this is—or was.

Kieran sits up slowly, gripping the edges of the bench until his knuckles turn white. Even certain he won't, I shift back another step in case he tries to reach for me. His head bows, his arms flexing.

"Why do I feel like you just saved my life and then broke my heart?"

My entire self, soul to cells, fractures. Numbness spreads through me—endorphins after pain.

"Look up transference."

His eyes shutter, face hardening to granite. With a curt nod, he hops off the bench and pulls his pants on.

"I'm sorry."

The words slip from my lips and tremble in the air. All I can give him. I fracture deeper. Harder. Helpless to do anything but watch as he grabs his hat and glasses off the floor and walks past me.

Pausing at the door, he says softly, "That's the shittiest part of it. I know you're sorry. Cowards always are."

My monster wails and screams, fighting me tooth and

nail. But she, too, is a creature of fantasy. She won't rule me ever again.

"Goodbye, Stirling."

I flinch at the name.

Then he's gone.

NATE FINDS me a few minutes later. I haven't moved. It isn't until he gathers me in his arms and starts whispering words of comfort that I realize I'm crying.

"I knelt."

It takes me four tries to get the words out. They slice off more pieces of me as they go. Soon enough, there'll be nothing left.

The hand stroking my back stills. He knows exactly what that means. "Then he's an idiot," he says finally.

My short laugh rattles with tears. "Not him—me."

He leans back, showing me wide eyes. "Not possible. Why would you say that?"

"I pushed him away. I thought I was saving him..." I shake my head. "I don't know anymore. It hurts."

His expression softens. "You weren't trying to save him. You tried to save yourself."

A fresh wave of tears rises. "That, too."

He smiles sadly and strokes my cheek. "Go easy on yourself. You might be an expert on the heart, but you've never been in love before. Welcome to the jungle, Talia."

CHAPTER 19

KIERAN

"You're very calm, Kier. It's weirding me out."

I look up, meeting Sven's eyes in the rearview before he refocuses on the road.

"Should I be raving?"

"Guess not." He clears his throat. "Do you, uh, need me to listen or whatever?"

A smile cracks my frozen face. "Fuck off."

His shoulders drop with relief. "Home, then?"

"No." I brush imaginary lint off my jeans. "Stirling's."

Sven brakes too hard approaching a stop sign. "What? I thought—when you came out, it seemed like…"

I chuckle. "Take a breath, buddy."

He swerves to a stop outside a dark storefront on Wilshire and twists in the seat. "What the fuck happened?"

"What happened is she thinks it's transference." My voice

is eerily calm and sounds a bit freaky. "Remember me ranting to you boys about it last weekend?"

Sven grunts.

I shrug. "She doesn't know I've already disproved the hypothesis."

He drags a hand over his buzzed head. "Are you sure about this?"

I'm not. There's a knock-down, drag-out fight going on inside me, my conviction clashing with doubts. But I hold tight to what she couldn't hide from me tonight. Her passion. Her tears. The pain in her eyes before she shut down.

The fact she knelt for me.

She *knelt.*

Tonight is just one more battle, but I'm going to win the war. And when I do, when she surrenders to this, I'll give her the crown. Everything I have. Everything I am.

I'll lay it all at her feet.

"I'm sure."

"Your funeral," mumbles Sven as he puts the car in gear.

I spend the drive planning out exactly what I'm going to say and exactly what I'm going to do to her first—bury my face between her thighs until she comes. Twice.

By the time we reach her house, I'm so hard it's painful. Not helping are the near-constant flashbacks of Talia on her knees, swallowing my cock and cum like they were candy. I've had some great blow jobs in my life, but every single one of them faded into obscurity the second she put her mouth and hands on me.

Because Sven is a sneaky bastard, he drives past her house to the next side street and parks. We have a line of sight to her house, but she won't see us when she turns onto the street. He keeps his thoughts to himself as we wait, probably because he knows that when I set my mind to something, nothing short of a missile will stop me.

Twenty minutes pass, then thirty. Around the forty-minute mark, I almost change my mind as doubt creeps back in. I start thinking about that blond who hugged her after the lecture. Who she smiled at and whose cheek she kissed to the delight of the crowd. There was a physical familiarity between them that told me they were lovers at some point. I'd wager money on him being her last submissive.

"Why are you muttering about blond men? What did we ever do to you?"

I look up at the rearview, taking in Sven's bored expression and dark, knowing eyes.

I'm spared an embarrassing answer when headlights flash across the tree we're parked behind. Unlike the last dozen times, the car doesn't drive past. I recognize her Lexus as it slows and pulls into her driveway. The garage door rises. She parks inside.

"Sven," I say tightly.

"What?"

"If the blond is with her, you have my permission to tackle me and get me back in the car by any means necessary."

He cusses. Colorfully.

The garage door rolls downward. The second the sliver of light disappears, I'm out of the car and jogging down the sidewalk.

A door slams behind me. "Goddammit, Kier!"

"Stay back," I throw over my shoulder. I cut across her front yard, take the steps to the porch in a leap, and pound my fist on her bright red door.

From the shadows of the driveway behind me, Sven grumbles, "She's gonna call the cops."

"No, she won't."

The side of my hand is starting to hurt, but I don't let up until the door swings open on Talia. Dark hair spills riotously over her shoulders, freed from its high ponytail. Her feet are bare, her skirt wrinkled. And her silky white blouse is untucked on one side, the bottom two buttons undone.

Everything I planned to say to her flies out my ears.

Her eyes widen. "Kieran? What—"

"Are you alone?"

"Yes, why—"

"We have unfinished business."

She rocks back half a step. The movement brings her face beneath the soft glow of a ceiling light, and the jealousy searing my veins extinguishes instantly. Her eyes are puffy, her face flushed. She doesn't look unkempt because she fucked someone else; she was getting ready to crawl into bed because she's been *crying* since I left her.

"What—"

"Let me in."

My voice isn't gentle. Nothing about this moment is gentle. I want to destroy the world—destroy myself—for making her cry. And I want to fuck her so hard she cries again.

Her delicate nostrils flare, eyes spitting fire. "If you interrupt me one more time, I'm going to break your nose."

Elation lights up my body. I can't help the grin that spreads over my face. I probably look deranged, but I'm past sanity and firmly in the realm of *Fuck It All* at the moment.

"I'll take it. Anything you dish out." I soften my voice as much as possible. "Just let me come inside. Your house. You. One night. That's all I'm asking for, mo ghrá."

Her eyelashes flicker at the endearment. I wonder if she knows what it means, then decide I don't care. Nor do I care whether she seriously thinks I'll be satisfied with one night. Let her believe the lie.

This is war.

I take a step forward, the toes of my shoes smacking against the metal sill of the door. Two feet away, she stands her ground like the queen she is. But her chest moves faster. Against the silk of her blouse, her nipples are hard points begging for my attention.

"Kieran."

My name is a whisper cracking with the same desperation that shines from her eyes. Desperation for me to stay, to leave, to give her what she needs and deny her. All of it.

"One night, Talia."

Emotions fly across her face like swift moving storms. Longing. Guilt. Pain. Desire. She's still fully clothed, but she's never been this naked. Never shown me this much.

I told myself a lot of things on the way over here—that I'd give it my best shot and let her decide, that I wouldn't force it even if her words and eyes didn't match. But that was before, and this is now. I understand her inner conflict, the pressure and weight of feeling like you always have to maintain control. The fear of what might happen if you lose it.

This isn't the Talia who told me to take off my pants and deep throated me like she was born to do it. *This* Talia needs me to help her let go.

I've never been more qualified for anything.

One more step brings me across the threshold and chest to chest with her. My fingers dive beneath her hair, curling unerringly around the back of her slender neck. I force her head up and she gasps, arching for me, her breasts soft and warm against my chest. I know she feels my cock; she squirms against it. She's panting, neck flushing, eyes dark and glassy with arousal. All strung out with need for me. *Beautiful*.

I lean forward just enough to whisper in her ear, "I'm going to fuck you raw. Your pussy, your ass—they're mine. You're going to let me do whatever I want to you, and you're going to fucking love it."

She whimpers.

"You're going to close the door now and set the alarm. Then you're going to take me to your bed. Okay?"

"Okay," she whispers.

My eyes close in relief. "That's a good girl."

I uncurl my fingers and step to the side. She slips past me to close and lock the door, then taps the console mounted beside it. A light flips from green to red. She looks at me, eyes dark and huge, and a hard swallow convulses her throat. My cock twitches in memory.

Energy coils in my muscles, runs like electricity in my veins. "Your bed," I remind her.

Her breath hitches. She nods, the movement jerky, then guides me across a living room, through a shadowed kitchen, and down a hallway. The closer we come to her bedroom, the more she relaxes. She's accepting the inevitability of this. Softening in anticipation.

I'm having the opposite reaction, my tension mounting further every second. It's all I can do not to throw her on the runner beneath our feet and claim her like a beast.

"Is your cunt wet, Talia?"

Her quick glance over her shoulder makes my balls tighten. There's no conflict anymore. Only hunger as acute as mine.

"You know it is," she whispers.

We cross into her bedroom. I'm only dimly aware of a lovely, airy space. Plants, dimmed lights, soothing colors. All I really see is the king-sized bed. When we reach it, I turn her around roughly and finally, *finally*, unleash myself.

Delicate buttons tear from their threads as I pull the halves of her blouse apart. Her heaving breasts sit in pale lace.

I yank the cups down and fill my hands, my thumbs teasing firm, rosy nipples.

"Perfect," I whisper, bending to circle a pert bud with my tongue. The sound she makes is exquisite, between a sigh and a groan.

As I knead, tongue, and bite one breast, then the other, her pussy gets the message I'm sending. Her hips push frantically against me. *Soon, love. Soon.* I reach around her back and undo the clasp of her bra, then pull it off and toss it. My shirt comes off with a swift yank and then my hands are on her again, stroking up her belly, over her breasts. Her nipples are darker after my ministrations. I pinch them.

She gasps my name and I crush my mouth to hers, tasting the last syllable. This time, I control the kiss. I take everything I want with one hand anchored in her hair and the other on her jaw to hold it open. Breathing becomes a secondary need to exploring the origin of so much of my obsession. Her voice. Her sharp tongue. That goddamn tooth—when I trace its contours, I groan like a man on the verge of collapse. My cock throbs, ready to blow just from kissing her.

Backing off a bit, I nip at her swollen lips, then kiss along her jaw to her neck. She smells so fucking good. Feels perfect against me, her height and curves custom-made to complement my frame. My hands roam her torso, memorizing the silk of her skin and the bow of her spine. I find the zipper at the back of her skirt and pull it down. With a tug, the fabric clears her hips and pools around her feet. I palm her ass, spreading her cheeks. My fingers find the string of her thong and follow it to her center.

Petal-soft, swollen, and so fucking wet.

"You're dripping, sweetheart."

She nods against my shoulder. "Please, Kieran."

Her soft, beseeching voice wrecks me. Lifting her by the waist, I throw her onto the bed. She lands on her back, hair a dark pool around her shoulders. Her lips are parted, eyes hot with surprise and lust.

"Never been tossed before, have you?"

The shake of her head fills me with savage satisfaction. Her hands come to her breasts, kneading and tweaking her nipples. I grunt at the visceral impact. For one second, two, I stare at the vision laid out before me. My jaw clenches. My hand finds my cock, squeezing it through denim in hopes of relieving some pressure. It doesn't help.

"Spread your legs."

She does so instantly, without shame. Rooted in her feminine power and sexuality. I'm humbled by it. And more turned on than I've been in my entire life.

I pop the button on my jeans and toe off my shoes and socks. "Touch that pretty pussy for me."

One hand dips between her legs, pulling aside her thong, while the other trails across her chest and belly. Staring into my eyes, she strokes herself with drugging confidence, her hips swiveling, making little noises that urge more pre-cum from my cock.

She has no idea how possessive she looks right now. Her

eyes tell me she owns me. That I own her. But it's all right—the rest of her will figure it out eventually.

"Fuck," I hiss, pulling down the zipper on my jeans. "I was going to eat you out, but I've changed my mind. I have to be inside you right fucking now. You have the most perfect pink pussy I've ever seen. Is it for me, Talia? Does it belong to me tonight?"

She nods eagerly. "Yes."

"Show me what's mine."

She gets rid of her lacy thong. Her knees lift and drop open again, even wider than before. She trails a hand down her stomach, making a V of her fingers to spread her glistening folds. Her middle finger dips inside her body. Her back arches off the bed.

I can't fucking breathe. "After I make you come all over my cock, I'm filling your ass," I warn.

She moans. "Please."

My jeans and briefs hit the floor. Higher brain function turns off. I crawl atop her, throwing her hand out of the way. I don't even have to line myself up—it's like my body knows hers already. Her hips lift, legs framing my thighs. White lights sparkle across my vision as my cock finds the source of her heat. I might be having a stroke. I don't care.

One vicious thrust brings me all the way in.

"Oh God," she cries, her face contorting and eyes closing.

She's tighter than her fists, her throat. Hot as molten metal, as familiar and miraculous as rain on my upturned face.

"Look at me," I snarl.

My brave girl does as I ask, opening her eyes. Everything she can't say and won't admit swims inside them. I'm utterly lost.

Drawing back, I push inside her again. Hard. Again. *Harder.* I find her mouth with mine and spear it with my tongue as I fuck her mercilessly. She's still too tight, struggling to adjust to my size despite how wet she is. I'm probably hurting her, but I'm too far gone to care. So is she.

"Yes, God, yes," she sobs. "Harder."

Her nails dig into my back, my ass. I come down to my forearms, giving her my weight and the grind of my pelvis against her clit. Sweat drips from my forehead to her face, running into a line of fresh tears. *My tears.* I lick them off her cheek as she coils tighter and tighter, her moans almost continuous.

Half a dozen more thrusts and she incinerates with a choked scream. Her body convulses beneath me, pussy clamping down so hard I see white again. Warmth gushes around my cock.

Willpower holds back my own release as I ride out her orgasm, never letting up. The moment she goes supine, I pull out and throw her onto her stomach. I smack her ass so hard the pale skin instantly blooms red, then drag her to her knees and shove two fingers into her still-fluttering pussy. She whimpers, writhing against my hand as I fuck her hard and fast with it.

I'm a madman. She's a succubus. Heaven can't compare to this and if this is Hell, I'm never leaving.

My thumb gathers her cream and lifts to massage her asshole. Her pussy spasms, soaking my fingers anew.

"Such a good girl," I whisper. "You want it so bad, don't you?"

I increase the pressure and she whimpers, rocking back harder. My thumb slips inside. Our synchronized moans sound like a goddamn harmony.

"Lube?" I rasp.

She looks at me over her shoulder, dark hair curtaining half of her face. "I don't want it. Spit on me."

I almost come right then. It's a miracle, in fact.

Grabbing her hips, I lube her with my tongue and spit. Her groans are so guttural they vibrate against my jaw.

I retreat to push a finger into her and pump it leisurely. As soon as she adjusts, I add another. Then a third. I spit twice more to keep her nice and wet. Her head tosses back and forth against the mattress, her cries verging toward sobs again.

"With me, Talia?"

"Do it already," she snaps.

My laugh is villainous. I bend forward and clamp my teeth on the muscle between her neck and shoulder. She yelps and thrusts harder against my fingers.

"Please," she whispers. "Please fuck my ass, Kieran."

I lick the inflamed skin. "That's my girl."

I dip my cock back into her pussy, not staying long

enough to distract myself, then fit myself against her asshole. I forget how to breathe as I start gently pushing. She's wet and prepped but still shakes beneath me, muscles tensing and releasing. A thought surfaces, one that seems impossible but rings as undeniable.

She's never done this before.

It's domination, plain and simple, and she's giving this first to me. The realization brings a wave of possessive tenderness, softening my urgency just enough for me to force out the words, "Relax and bear down a little, mo ghrá."

She takes a shuddering breath, then another slower, deeper one. She softens. Opens. Taking the gift of what's already mine, I sink into her a few inches. She can't help but stiffen at the intrusion; her breathing speeds up.

Stilling, I stroke and massage her back and hips. "You feel so perfect. So tight and warm. I'm so fucking pleased. Thank you. Thank you, sweetheart."

The final threshold of her resistance falls. The choking grip on my shaft loosens a fraction. I bottom out inside her with a growl. Her answering moan is music to my ears and snaps my control.

I begin fucking her in earnest, hard and steady. Her moans get louder, her pussy drenching my balls. When she begins rocking with me, I see stars. Familiar pressure builds inside me, only it's more intense than I've ever experienced.

This orgasm might kill me, but I'm at peace with it.

"Work your clit for me," I grind out.

Her hand dives beneath her, the other clenched on the

bedding. She strokes herself with two fingers, fast and sure, gasping and keening. Her nails graze my balls on every thrust, spiking the pressure in them to catastrophic levels. My thrusts start to lose rhythm. I'm seconds away.

Miraculously, so is she.

"Oh, fuuuuck," she cries through a sob.

She screams my name, jerking and contracting around me. It's too much; too intense. Lightning streaks through my limbs, coalescing and detonating in a flash that swallows my sight.

I roar my gratitude to God and the Devil both as I fill her with cum.

CHAPTER 20

TALIA

I wake to sunlight on my face and a languor in my body so pervasive it's a challenge to open my eyes.

Then recall hits.

I jerk upright, blinking fast as I take in the empty room, my empty bed. The air hums with stillness, the type of quiet I'm most accustomed to. I'm alone.

A weight descends on my chest, compressing my lungs. I don't know why I'm surprised. Disappointed. No—*devastated*. He offered me one night, and that's what he gave me. Not once did we speak of anything past the present. He didn't ask me to date him again, didn't try to convince me his feelings weren't transference.

Maybe he realized they were, and last night was about the challenge. Dominating the dominatrix. Proving to himself and me how much I wanted him. How much I'd be willing to submit.

Does he know I gave him parts of myself I've never given anyone? I think he does.

Still, I'll never regret it. Not the discomfort in my body right now, not my tears or my begging last night. He deserved it all. He proved himself worthy with the care he took. The tenderness he showed. Real or not, last night he acted like he was mine. Last night, my oldest dream came true.

Pulling my comforter to me, I curl into it and close my stinging eyes. Memories flood me, sensation following each winding path. A shower. His hands washing me, tender and thorough, then the ease with which he lifted me against the tiled wall. His laughter when I couldn't hide my shock.

"You may be built like a goddess, but lucky for you, I'm built to worship one."

Water misting between our mouths, our chests and stomachs flush. His eyes pinning me as surely as his cock and his hand on my throat. No words, just the silent language of our bodies. My orgasm, sudden and explosive. Then my knees against the tile, his cum painting my neck and chest. He hadn't asked for it—I hadn't given him a choice.

We slept for a while after. It was still dark when I woke up to his tongue on my clit and his fingers massaging my G-spot. He edged me until I was sweating and cursing him, then brought me to the deepest, most shattering orgasm of my life.

I didn't mean to fall asleep again, but when he tucked me against the warm, hard planes of his body and stroked my hair, my mind slipped away.

It's no surprise I don't remember him leaving. The grogginess in my head and the stupor in my body signal I was probably catatonic. I wish I'd woken, though. Even if I have no idea what I might have said or done. Asked him to stay? Begged him for another night? I wouldn't have.

But at least I could have said goodbye.

My phone buzzes once from the nightstand on the opposite side of the bed. I glance at it, momentarily indifferent, before my heart leaps to my throat. I scramble across the sheets and pluck it from its cord.

Sven Akerman.

My exhale is a pained wheeze as I swipe to read the message.

> We're on a plane to Galway. Back in two weeks. He'll fire me if he finds out I told you, but I like you better than him. Take care of yourself, Dr. Stirling.

Swallowing a geyser of misery, I blink fast to keep tears at bay.

I guess I have my answer.

THE SUMMER of the trip to Galway, after we came home and my dad moved out, I put aside impossible fantasies and grew claws.

That's how I like to remember it, anyway.

Not even Leo knows the full truth of the following two years. The closest I've ever come to telling someone who wasn't a professional was after I met Charlie. After I discovered that fantasies themselves weren't the problem—that as long as there were boundaries around them, I could stay safe.

The first months of Charlie's mentorship were glorious. I was on Cloud 9, in love with exploring kink both physically and psychologically. I lost my virginity in exactly the way I wanted: to a gentle, beautiful man who obeyed my every command.

As my education and experience expanded, Charlie often shared that she'd never met a more natural dominant or a woman so free of shame.

I never corrected her, never told her there's more than one type of shame.

The night I came close to telling her the truth, she'd invited me to join her in a session with one of her long-time clients. I'd never met him before and she didn't give me any prep. A part of me will never forgive her for that, though I understand why she made the choice.

I knew by this point that serious pain wasn't something I enjoyed providing, but it was part of the job. Even though I didn't enjoy full-strength whipping, caning, or more extreme forms of bondage, I found immense satisfaction in mastering the skills. Even more in providing a safe space for those brave enough to explore desires that society deemed perverse.

The client that night, however, was a true masochist. His desire for sexual gratification was inexorably linked to his desire for pain. Halfway through the session—already a challenging one for me—Charlie unrolled a velvet pencil case. Instead of pencils, though, the thin slots were filled with plastic-encased scalpels.

The man started sobbing at the sight of them—sobbing in *relief*.

I froze in abject horror.

"So you do have a limit."

Charlie's voice was unexpectedly gentle, the most sympathetic I'd ever heard it. She whispered something to the man, who nodded, and then she guided me from the room. Once outside, I started shaking so hard my teeth chattered. She brought me to a couch and held me in her arms until finally, minutes later, I started to sob.

I could have told her. She would have understood.

But I didn't.

WHEN I TURNED off my fantasies at fourteen, I turned off my ability to hope. To dream. In some ways, it benefited me. I was able to let go of the need for acceptance from my family. I put my focus back into my education and excelled in my final two years of high school. I stopped caring that I had no friends, stopped seeking validation from anyone but myself.

My claws grew long and strong, but they had no outlet.

Their first victim was me.

College offer letters started flowing in during my senior

year, and I felt nothing. I was merely going through the motions. Ticking off boxes on a sterile list of what I thought I should be doing. Even when I received an offer and substantial scholarship to UCLA, and my mother hugged me, I felt nothing.

While my future prospects grew bright, my inner world grew dark. I rarely saw my father, but when I did, there was invariably a phone call to my mother later in the week demanding she put me in therapy. She always refused.

"You're overreacting as usual, Patrick. She's exactly the same as she's always been."

I wasn't.

Without fantasies, without dreams, without friends or real family, I was completely alone with my monster. As she grew, so did the pressure under my skin.

My mother was an esthetician at a spa in Beverly Hills, but she also went on house calls. Sometimes, if she didn't have appointments outside the spa that day, she left her travel bag at home. A bag that included tools for the popular service of derma-planning.

Scalpels.

No one ever saw outward evidence of my inner torment. I was intentional about where I cut and used butterfly sutures to minimize scarring. My mother was disorganized to a fault and never noticed when a scalpel disappeared.

I was lucky. So very lucky. Before my addiction could progress from a weekly ritual to a daily compulsion, my father finally won the argument. The summer before I started at UCLA, I found myself in a therapist's office.

That therapist not only saved my life but changed the course of it, finishing the job an Irish boy inadvertently started. She gave me a new outlet. A focus that became my life's vocation.

At twenty-two, I used my savings from working with Charlie for plastic surgery to remove the scars. It was a relatively easy process, the scars themselves minimal due to my obsessive diligence. But even though my inner thighs are smooth now, there's no surgery invasive enough to erase the marks my claws made as they matured.

If I hadn't fought so hard to control my monster, would she have cut me so deeply? Would she be cutting me even now, slicing over and over again into my heart?

I don't blame her. What wild animal doesn't crave freedom? It's not her fault she lashes out. I was the one who put her in a cage. Who took away the only thing that mattered to her.

Now, curled on my bed, my body empty and aching, I wonder what would happen if I freed her. If I finally let her have what she's fought so hard for all these years.

Dreams.

CHAPTER 21

KIERAN

An hour into the flight, Sven drops a thick folder in my lap. "Here's the light reading you requested. I'm going in back to get some sleep. Don't wake me up unless this tube is going down." He pauses. "Actually, don't bother."

"Thanks." I tap a finger on the folder before placing it on the table in front of my seat. "And you're welcome."

He scowls. "For what? Making me sit in a car until four a.m., then informing me with psychotic cheerfulness that we're getting on a plane in two hours?"

I smother a smile. "Not that." I nod my head back and to the left, where Dylan currently sits reading a novel. His eyes are focused on the book, headphones covering his ears.

Sven's glare intensifies to nuclear levels even as his bristled cheeks darken. "I have no idea what you're talking about."

226

I chuckle. "By the way, our usual suite at the hotel was unavailable. You two will be sharing a room. I can't remember if I requested two beds or not. Guess we'll find out."

His face is starting to resemble a beet. "Since when do you book flights and hotels yourself? You have an assistant for that shit."

"I was going to call Doug, but I thought I'd let him sleep. Since I'm such a great boss."

"Yeah, you're a fucking peach." His voice lowers to a tense whisper. "Is this payback for butting in with Stirling?"

My brows rise. "Of course not. I'm grateful for that. So grateful, in fact, I'm thinking you'll be the best man in our wedding. And before you start worrying about anyone's job, I've known about you two for months and have zero problems with it. You've done an admirable job of being discreet."

Sven stares at me for a pregnant moment. "Sometimes I forget what a scary sonofabitch you are. Not even Gabe suspects."

I grin and tap my temple. "Genius, remember?"

He makes a sound of disgust. "Only if genius somehow rhymes with meddlesome little shit. I'm going to sleep. Enjoy violating Stirling's privacy."

He stalks toward the bedroom at the back of the plane. Dylan doesn't look up as he passes, but his fingers tighten around his book.

Poor, lovesick fools.

All three of us.

An attendant slips down the aisle toward me. "Would you like more coffee, Mr. Hayes?"

What I'd like is to take a nap and wake up with Talia sitting on my face, but in the interim... "Please. Thank you, Samantha."

Once she's gone, I turn my attention to the folder. On our drive home this morning, I woke up Dylan to tell him to pack a bag for Ireland and to print out the attached files of a certain email. Inside the folder is everything my PI has dug up on Talia, the last update having arrived yesterday. From the thickness of it, he went the extra mile. Given what I'm paying his team every month, I expected nothing less.

I should be taking this time to review the latest report on their investigation into the phone call. Sven's been trying to talk to me about it for days. But I keep blowing him off. I'm too distracted. Something else dominates my thoughts—*someone* else.

Setting down my coffee, I pull the folder onto my lap and open it. The first page is a list of the contents.

"Jesus," I whisper.

School transcripts from elementary school onward. Articles in local newspapers and online in which her name has appeared, the oldest more than fifteen years ago and the newest from yesterday. Employment records. Credit history. Properties purchased and sold. Copies of expired and current drivers' licenses, ID cards, and passports. He even included the abstract for her PhD dissertation.

With a guilty grimace, I close the folder. Sven's right—

this is a major violation of her privacy. A thousand times worse than having him break into her house to assess her security. I should destroy it as soon as humanly possible. It's the right thing to do. What a good man would do.

Only apparently I'm not a good man, because a minute later I'm reading a series of remarks from early teachers suggesting her parents have her intelligence levels assessed. Her first IQ test was at seven. Another at thirteen. The last at sixteen.

When I see the numbers, when I realize what they mean, my cock stiffens. No fucking wonder I was obsessed with her brain first. Her sharp eyes and sharper tongue.

She's smarter than me.

So fucking hot.

I'm grinning as I browse deeper into the file, eventually stopping on an article about her graduating high school at sixteen and being accepted into UCLA. There's a grainy, black-and-white photo of her in the top corner. My smile slowly fades as I stare at a young Talia. With the exception of her coloring, she looks shockingly different—her eyebrows thicker, her face rounder. She's barely smiling, but I see a hint of braces.

Déjà vu prickles over my skin, the same familiarity I felt when I met her. Only this feeling is a hundred times more potent.

I *know* this girl.

Which makes absolutely no sense.

I flip through pages without really knowing what I'm

looking for, only that I have to find it. My search becomes chaotic—papers hit the floor as I throw entire sections to the side. A cluster slips off the table to the aisle. The sheets scatter, a few sailing across the floor under another seat. Glimpsing color and the curve of a pale face on one of them, I launch out of my chair and land hard on my knees.

"You all right, man?"

Ignoring Dylan, I grab for the pages, ripping through them until I find it: a color copy of her first passport, issued when she was fourteen.

And my heart

fucking

stops.

Somewhere past the boundary of my dying brain, I hear voices.

"I just got to sleep, Dylan."

"I'm sorry, but you're the only one who can handle this type of shit."

"What type of—*Christ.*" Footsteps pound toward me, and Sven's hand clamps on my shoulder. "Kier? What happened?"

I whisper hoarsely, "I've died of shock."

Then I start to laugh.

I laugh and laugh until tears stream from my eyes, while Sven and Dylan gape at me like I'm a lunatic.

But if I'm a lunatic, then so is she.

My match—my queen.

Birdie.

I REMEMBER THE DAY WELL. It was a Saturday. Early evening. Mam told me to go for a walk and stay gone for an hour. When I'd grinned and asked if she wanted me to act surprised when I came back and found a party, she smacked me upside the head.

I was leaving for Oxford on Monday. Alistair had helped me pack over the last few days, bitching the whole time that I should have enrolled at Galway University with him. It was a great school, but I'd been set on for Oxford for years.

Before I left the flat, I knocked on my brother's door. He was on the phone with his on-again, off-again girlfriend; I could hear her belligerent yelling from six feet away. I pantomimed a walk and smoking a joint, but he winced and shook his head.

I shrugged and went on my way, extra-glad I was entering university unattached. Girls were great fun for a night or two, but any longer and they became a distraction. With the five-year plan I had, I couldn't afford distractions.

The rain outside was more mist than downpour, perfect for a stroll. Content to wander, I didn't have a destination in mind until I came around a corner and saw the graveyard.

It'd been a while since I'd visited Gran, and it seemed fitting to say goodbye before I left for England—and smoke a joint on her behalf.

THE GIRL LOOKED like a wet bird curled up in front of Gran's headstone. A *hummingbird*, I decided, because even though she was sitting, she was in perpetual motion. Twitching feet. Jerking shoulders. Repeated swipes of pale hands across her face, smearing wet bangs.

She was making noises like sobs only angrier, and she was mumbling to herself about someone named Olivia. American accent, if my ears weren't misleading me.

Was she drunk? Crying? Or lost?

I scared the shit out of her when I asked. She jumped up, then almost toppled right over. Drunk, then. Or maybe all three: crying, lost, and drunk. A winning combination. As I contemplated whether or not I was annoyed by this unexpected diversion, the girl stood there, staring at me like I was someone famous. She was cute in a crazy way, with frizzy hair, big eyes, and red cheeks.

Then she giggled out of the blue—a husky sound that made me up her age by a few years—and slapped a hand over her mouth. The abrupt motion almost took her to the ground. It was hard not to laugh, but I managed it.

Resigned to helping her, I killed my joint and tossed it to the ground. The little bird chirped that I shouldn't litter.

"You shouldn't be hammered and wandering around a graveyard at dusk, Birdie, but here we are."

Her eyes got even bigger at my nickname for her. She wobbled sideways, toward the row of headstones.

"My name isn't Birdie," she slurred angrily.

"It is now." I grimaced as she swayed again. It would be a

real shame if she fell and cracked her head open on Gran's final resting place. "You'd better sit back down before you fall, *Birdie*."

Like her bones turned to liquid, she melted downward and slumped back against the headstone. Despite the dreamy drunkenness of her expression, to me she still seemed angry. Sad and angry.

I'd always been good at reading people.

Sighing, I trudged along the row of graves. I'd give her a while to sober up, then get her back to the parents who'd pissed her off.

Plopping down next to her, I misjudged my trajectory and ended up closer than intended. My shoulder bumped against hers. I thought about moving but decided against it. Her arm was soft and warm, Gran's headstone rough and hard, the ground cool and wet. I wasn't a danger to her—and she was clearly harmless.

She was staring at me again. Smirking, I let her. I didn't think there was anything special about my face, but I'd figured out a few years ago that girls liked it. Plus, this girl was American; they went crazy for an accent.

I waited to see if she'd be brave enough to talk to me.

"Do you have another joint?" she asked in a weird, forced voice.

Oh, she was brave. Possibly stupid, too. I decided against lecturing her about asking strangers for drugs.

Smothering another laugh, I looked at her. "Not a chance, Birdie."

She gazed into my eyes, swaying toward me like I was gravity. A vibrating, drunk, sodden bird who didn't know where the ground was.

Cute. And sad.

"How old are you?" she slurred. At least her voice was normal-sounding this time.

"Eighteen."

I could tell she wanted me to ask how old she was—probably so she could lie. I didn't ask. It didn't really matter. Even if I wasn't leaving town in two days, she was far too young. An innocent kid. From the way she kept looking at me, all bashful and awed, I doubted she'd ever kissed a boy.

Daylight was fading fast, making it hard for me to see the color of her eyes. Light brown, I thought. They were pretty. Her mouth was nice, too. I had a feeling she'd be a stunner one day.

Her shoulders slumping even more, she dropped her gaze. Loneliness radiated from her like a perfume. She stared at the ground like she wanted to sink through it and have a chat with my gran.

It made my heart hurt.

I coughed a little to get her attention. "What brings a wee bird out of her nest to fly among the dead this fine evening?"

"Vacation."

Obvious, Birdie.

"Let me guess where the bird flew from." I squinted at her, pretending to decipher something from her clothes, then guessed California. It was the first place that popped into my head, probably because it featured heavily on my five-year plan.

She made a face that told me I was right, and I grinned. But instead of my smile coaxing one out of her—as I'd hoped it would—she wilted even more. Suddenly, I had to know. I had to understand why this little bird was drunk, sad, angry, and alone in a graveyard.

The fact she'd chosen Gran's grave out of hundreds suddenly struck me as portentous. Like maybe there was a reason she was here, that I was here, that we'd met each other. I'd never been religious or superstitious, but goose bumps rose on my arms.

"Go on then, tell me," I said.

She frowned at me. "Tell you what?"

"Why your eyes are so angry and sad."

And she did.

By the end, I knew one thing for sure: this little bird was going to be more than okay. She was going to make the world kneel.

Just like I would.

I was an hour late to my own party, though my parents forgave me when I explained what happened. Only I couldn't explain it—not really—because what happened was far more than helping a lost girl find her hotel.

I'd been given a gift. Maybe from Gran, as fucking wild as the notion was. The gift was witnessing the beginning of an evolution. The makings of a force to be reckoned with.

As I drifted to sleep that night, my last thought was tinged with regret.

I should have let her tell me her name.

"No way." Dylan leans back, gaping. "That's crazy. Are you sure it's her?"

"As sure as the heart attack I had when I saw that passport photo."

I take a sip of the fresh coffee Samantha brought out after I stopped raving and waving a piece of paper around. The woman looked half a breath from a panic attack, and my reassuring smile only made her blanch. I make a mental note to up her tip.

Sven's dark eyes probe mine. "It was seventeen—almost eighteen years ago."

"It's her."

The hummingbird necklace. The way she freaked out when I gave her the carving. And her eyes... it was dusk to dark when we met all those years ago. I never got a good look at their color. But the shape of them. The *fire* in them.

Talia Stirling is Birdie.

I know it to my very bones.

I turn my gaze to the clouds outside, my head a mess of jumbled thoughts. I remember a lot about that night, but I wish I could remember every single detail. Every word she spoke. Every response I gave. But Sven's right. It was almost two decades ago.

My life changed dramatically right after. In the following months, the memory of the young, drunk girl in a graveyard was painted over by new experiences and challenges. As the years passed, I only recall actively thinking about her one other time.

It was after Alistair and I moved to Los Angeles. We'd been grocery shopping, aimlessly wandering aisles and missing our mam's cooking. I'd seen a girl in a baggy sweatshirt. Dark hair and bangs. And for a second—the briefest blink—I'd thought it was her. My graveyard girl all grown up. I'd almost followed her. Then Alistair asked if we could afford steaks, I lost sight of her, and life went on.

"All this time, she knew it was me," I muse aloud. "That's why she saw me hours after Gail called her."

Sven makes a skeptical noise. "Your face was on the cover of Forbes last year, Kier. It's not like she didn't know who you were. Not saying you weren't memorable at eighteen, but that's... She was drunk and very young."

"She was still Talia," I murmur, my mind half in the conversation and half in a rainy graveyard. "She had an IQ of 150. She memorized my face—I told her my name. God, it seems so obvious now. I can't believe I didn't recognize her."

Dylan clears his throat. "Don't beat yourself up, man. She looks completely different."

Sven adds, "If she does know you've met before, there's a reason she never said anything."

Because she wanted to help me.

I think back to that first session. Those long moments when we stared at each other. Had she been waiting to see if I'd recognize her? Had she been relieved? Disappointed? It's impossible to say. She was a beautiful statue back then. An unsolvable equation.

More memories of the graveyard float to the surface of my mind. Greedy for them, I grab one. Then another.

And suddenly there's a flood.

"My parents look at me like I was switched at birth. I don't fit into their pretty, perfect aesthetic. I don't care about anything they care about, and they don't care about me. Sometimes I hate them, but most of the time, I just want to be who they want me to be. But I can't. I've tried."

"I don't fit anywhere. I'm always on the outside looking in. I don't have anyone to talk to. Sometimes it feels like I'm watching a movie of everyone else's lives. I'm separate. Formless. With no life of my own."

"I feel this pressure inside me. Like there's a monster trying to get out. Sometimes it hurts so much I can't breathe."

"No one talks to me at school except my teachers. Not even the nerds will let me sit with them at lunch. I'm a

freak to them. It's not like I can help the way my brain works! It's not my fault I remember whatever I read, that I understand stuff."

"I wish I were normal. I just want to belong, to feel like I'm a part of the world. But I'm scared I never will."

My heart feels like fire in my chest as the last levels of her puzzle box unlock, the construct unfolding like a lotus flower in my mind. As I knew they would be, her depths are beautiful beyond words.

"I see you," I whisper. "And you do belong, Birdie. You belong with me."

CHAPTER 22

TALIA

Tucked in our usual corner at Rhubarb, I sip black tea while Mia nibbles distractedly on avocado toast, her gaze glued to her phone as she reads the article that came out in the *LA Times* this morning.

"Holy shit," she says for the fifth time. Unlike the previous instances, however, this time she expounds on it. "I'm at the part where you drop the statistics about how many people have either tried or fantasized about BDSM or admit to having kinks. This is wild. It's the norm not the exception. Everyone needs to know this."

"That's the idea," I say wryly.

When the journalist, Alicia Reynolds, first emailed me last week, I almost trashed the message. But that was *before*. Before Crossroads and Kieran and Sven's text.

I called her early Monday morning. She came to my office that afternoon and grilled me for close to three hours. The result is an article entitled, *Meet Dr. Talia Stirling, L.A.'s Most Controversial Therapist.*

"I like this journalist," Mia murmurs. "She did right by you."

I murmur agreement, keeping to myself that Alicia did right by herself and her community, too. I hadn't recognized her name, and it took about twenty minutes into the interview for me to realize why she seemed familiar—because when I'd seen her at Crossroads over the years, she was generally blindfolded and wearing a lot less clothing.

I didn't say anything when I recognized her and outside silently acknowledging the moment with a nod, neither did she. Based on the first few questions she asked, I had no doubts she'd be able to remain professional. In fact, she was brutal. Her very first question was, *"Have you ever had sex with a therapy client?"*

Thanks to Kieran firing me Saturday night, I didn't have to lie.

Mia finishes reading and her sparkling eyes meet mine. "I'm so proud of you, Talia."

I make a face. "Ew."

Her smile widens. "Get used to it, woman, because this is only the beginning. I can feel it. What are the latest book offers up to?"

My face warms. "A lot."

She rubs her hands together. "Wait until this hits national publications. Hello, bidding wars."

I shift in my chair. "Can we talk about something else?"

She laughs knowingly. "Sure. Have you reached out to you-know-who?"

I wince, realizing I set myself up. Shaking my head, I look into my tea so I don't have to see her sympathetic expression.

After waking up on Sunday and losing my mind, I wound up calling her instead of Leo. In the moment, I'd needed a female friend far more than a therapist. She showed up at my house an hour later and stayed all day.

She knows everything, down to the fact I let Kieran dominate me and enjoyed—no, *loved* every second of it. And every day since, she's been bugging me to contact him. For closure, for clarification, or for—as she optimistically believes—confirmation that Saturday night meant as much to him as it did to me. That his trip to Ireland wasn't him trying to get as far away from me as fast as he could.

Every day, I've woken up a little less opposed to the idea. A little less scared.

But I'm not brave enough yet.

"I have no idea what I'd say," I say with a sigh. "'Are you over me now that you had me?' Or there's always, 'Statistically speaking, your desire for me is likely a projection of complex, unresolved feelings for your dead wife, but I'm down to have my heart smashed, so let's go.'"

Her brows lift. "Maybe start with, 'Hi, how are you?'"

A smile tugs my lips. "What a novel idea."

She grins. "I thought so."

A figure moves into my periphery, approaching my side of the table. Mia glances at them first. From the shift in her expression, I know it's not our server. Bracing myself, I turn my head.

A man smiles down at me. Generically handsome, blond, around Kieran's age. It takes a second to place his face: Oliver McCann, one of Lumitech's executives. He and his wife were seated across from us at the Alzheimer's benefit. I didn't speak to him outside of introductions and goodbyes, though I remember his wife drank too much.

"Hi, Talia. I don't know if you remember—"

"Oliver," I say with manufactured politeness. "Nice to see you again."

His smile becomes more confident. A touch smug. I almost tell him not to take it personally—I didn't remember him because he made an impression. I just have a photographic memory.

"Great to see you, too. I thought I'd pop over and say hello. See how you've been."

My gaze narrows; I'm officially annoyed. "I'm fine, thank you. How's Jenny?"

Instead of the mention of his wife turning off the gleam in his eye, it only grows. "Great. How's Kieran?"

Caught off guard, I ask, "How should I know?" Then I wish I could retract the words as interest flares in his eyes.

"Oh? Sorry for assuming." His chuckle is insincere, as is the abashed expression that follows. "I was confused because I thought Kieran was in the Maldives with his girlfriend, but then I saw you and thought maybe you two had stayed local." He grins. "Does this mean you're single?"

I glance at Mia, who looks incensed. Before she can say what's on her mind, I tell Oliver, "No. I'd like to get back to breakfast now."

He blinks in that baffled way some men do when a woman is too direct. "Oh, sure. Sorry to interrupt. Take care."

With a final, lingering glance, he retreats around the wall of greenery behind me.

"What the fuck," hisses Mia. "What a sleaze ball. You know he was lying about Kieran, right?"

"Yes."

And I do. Not only would Sven not lie to me about where they were going, Kieran wouldn't have had sex with me and taken someone else on vacation the next morning.

Taking another sip of tea, I frown.

"What's the conclusion, Doctor?"

Shaking off an unsettled feeling, I answer, "Oliver feels like he's in competition with Kieran. They've had conflicts over women in the past. He was fishing to see if I'd be open to sleeping with him, probably because he thought it would annoy Kieran."

"Have I told you how much I love your brain?"

I smirk. "Yes."

She glances in the direction Oliver went, her mouth twisting. "I'm glad you handed him his ass. Idiot actually thought you'd jump to offer him yours."

I shudder. "That would never happen."

Her grin is wicked. "You know what will happen?"

Catching sight of our server turning the corner behind her, I shake my head quickly. She, of course, pays me no mind.

"More mind-blowing anal sex with a hot Irishman, that's what! Do you think he'll let you peg him? Ugh. So hot. I've definitely thought about fingering Leo. Should I ask him? If he says yes, can you give me pointers on finding the prostate?"

I drop my forehead into my palm.

"Can I get you ladies anything else?" asks our server, his voice cracking and his face bright red.

Mia erupts in giggles as I swiftly pull out my wallet.

"Just the check."

WHEN I PULL into my driveway, the first thing I see is the last thing I expect: Gabe standing on my front porch. He gives me a wave. I pull into the garage, then quickly grab my purse and meet him in the driveway.

"Hey, Doc," he says with an easy smile. "Bet you're wondering what I'm doing here."

Despite his smile, my heart pounds a mile a minute. "Is everything okay?"

Is Kieran *okay?*

"Everything's fine. Do you mind if we step into the garage?"

My senses prickle. "Why?" I ask sharply.

Gabe takes an immediate, large step backward. "Sorry, Dr. Stirling," he says, voice soft and careful. "It's a habit in my line of work to avoid high exposure areas. We can stay here if you're more comfortable."

I take a slow breath and force myself to relax. "No, I'm sorry. I'm not afraid of you, Gabe. I've just had a weird morning."

"Totally understandable, and it was smart of you to ask. I'll get to the point—Sven said he tried to text you this morning but none of his messages went through. Consider me your wellness check."

I relax a little more. "I was at the warehouse for a while. My office there has horrible cell service."

Gabe nods and pulls out his phone. "If you're willing, I'd like to give him a quick call now so he can speak with you."

I glance around the yard, the street. A car drives by slowly; the driver glances at us. The hair on the back of my neck lifts.

"Jesus, now I'm paranoid. Come inside."

Gabe winces. "Sorry."

"Stop apologizing for doing your job," I say as I lead the way. Once the garage door is down, I let us into the house and punch the code to change the alarm from Away settings to Home.

"Glad to see you're serious about security," he says cheerfully as he follows me into the kitchen.

I can't help but laugh. "Sven's fault. You want some water?"

He shakes his head, already dialing. "Thanks, I'm good."

I watch his face, seeing the moment the line connects. He listens for a few seconds, then says, "Yeah, hold on," and hands me the phone.

My heart skips a beat as I lift it to my ear. *What if...*

"Hello?" My voice is breathless.

"Dr. Stirling, thanks for humoring me," rumbles Sven.

I swallow a pulse of disappointment. "Call me Talia, Sven. I'm not your boss's doctor anymore. What's going on?"

"Just a minor security concern that was brought to my attention this morning."

My heart, barely recovered, starts thumping again. "What does that mean? What kind of concern?"

There's a long pause, like he's weighing his words. "Since we left town, the same security company that monitors Alistair and Gail's home has been monitoring yours."

"*What*? Did you just say my house is being monitored without my knowing or approval?"

Out of the corner of my eye, I catch Gabe's wince. Sven's sigh filters through the phone.

"I would have told you, but I think you can guess why I didn't. That being said, I agreed with him that it was a good idea."

I rub the bridge of my nose, feeling conflicted. On the one hand, I'm angry at Kieran's autocratic presumption. Another, more primal part of me is delighted because it means he's thinking about me. That I'm important enough to protect.

"Okay," I finally say, "let's put a pin in that issue. What's the security concern?"

"The two-man team assigned to you made note of a car driving by repeatedly over the last three days. The plates and registration are dead ends. There were several times the car slowed or stopped on your street right outside your house. Single male driver. Caucasian. Dark hair. They got some photos but so far facial recognition isn't pinging."

Disquiet ripples through me. My armpits prickle. I'm suddenly very glad Gabe is standing five feet away with a gun under his jacket.

"I, uh, wasn't expecting that."

"I know." The phone buzzes in my hand. "Will you take a look at the photo I just sent and tell me if you recognize him?"

I pull up the text and zoom in on the photo, studying the man. He's wearing a baseball hat and sunglasses and looks like anyone. Generic. A shiver rolls down my arms.

"No, I don't. Sorry."

He sighs. "It's all right. Worth a shot."

"You think it has something to do with..." I can't say his name, but thankfully, Sven doesn't make me.

"It's doubtful. There were some pictures of the two of you from the benefit, but they were scrubbed before circulation. And I'm very careful when I drive. No one followed us to your house Saturday."

I flush at the reminder that Sven was here that night, probably just out of sight from the porch. If he was close enough, he could have heard everything Kieran said to me before I closed the door. The prospect doesn't embarrass me, exactly, but it does make me wonder how many times he's heard Kieran say similar things to other women. Which in turn pisses me off.

I curl the hand not holding the phone, digging my nails into my palm to refocus. "You think someone might be stalking me?"

"It's possible. You're quite the hot topic at the moment and not everyone is a fan."

That's putting it lightly. The article that came out this morning was my first in-depth interview, but there's been a snowball effect since my former client decided to 'out' me a week ago. From online forums to clickbait articles, my name is popping up a dozen times a day. I've become an unwilling figurehead for incendiary debates on morality, ethics, and sexuality.

I've lost three more clients, two of them women who've been with me for years. Those hurt a lot worse than the previous losses. The consequences have spilled over the boundary of my career, too. After a disastrous incident at my neighborhood market on Tuesday involving a woman and a Bible, I've started grocery delivery.

Breakfast with Mia this morning was the first time I've been anywhere but my home or offices this week. In weaker moments, I've considered options ranging from cutting and dyeing my hair to closing my practice, selling my properties, and leaving the country. Even the consistent, supportive phone calls I'm getting—both from my network at Crossroads and professional colleagues—haven't dented my underlying anxiousness.

I'm losing control of the life I built for myself over the last decade. No matter how many times I tell myself I'm okay with it, I'm not.

I'm really, really not.

Sven interrupts my dark thoughts. "Are you still doing the event at Crossroads tonight? If you are, I'd like you to let Gabe escort you there and home."

There's a *snap* in my head.

"No."

"Talia, listen—"

"You listen to *me*, Sven. I understand you're caught between a rock and Kieran's cement head, but you aren't responsible for my safety. Thank you for the heads-up about the car, but I want the watchdogs at my house gone. I'll find my own security company. As for Crossroads, there's probably nowhere on earth I'm safer at the moment. Now put your boss on the phone because I have some words for him."

There's a weighted pause. "I wish I could, but I can't."

"Why not?"

"He's indisposed."

My anger fizzles as I realize where he must be—with his mom.

"Fine," I grumble.

"I'd be happy to pass along a message, though," he says in the ultra-dry tone that signals his amusement.

"Please do. Tell him if he thinks I'm flattered by his high-handedness, he's lost his damn mind. And if he has something to say to me, he can put on his big-boy pants and call me himself."

"You got it." His voice is warm with approval. "One last thing. Just a suggestion, because I would personally hate for something to happen to you. Stay at a friend's place for a few nights, okay? Until you can get your own people hired and monitoring."

I sigh. "Yeah, all right. Here's Gabe."

I hand over the phone.

CHAPTER 23

TALIA

Just after midnight, I punch in a code next to a black door with gold stenciling reading *Private*. This hallway at Crossroads is uncarpeted and utilitarian, its only features the door before me and a rolling metal one for deliveries, currently closed and dead-bolted.

The low, sensual beat of the club's music snuffs out as I let myself inside and close the door. Under the soft glow of a security light mounted over my head, I follow London's instructions, securing the locks and setting the alarm system. Then I head up a narrow flight of stairs, flipping a wall switch at the top to bring on recessed lights in the living area.

I'm relieved to see the one-bedroom loft hasn't changed much in the years since I've been in it. It looks like a cross between an expensive hotel and a residential brothel, the latter owed to the wall with a gleaming St. Andrews Cross and an impressive display of whips, ropes, and floggers. In reality, the loft is something in between, primarily a safe haven where close friends of Dominic and London can retreat, relax, and play.

I drop my purse and small overnight bag on the couch and head for the kitchen, finding the cabinet with glasses. Behind a stack of cloth napkins in a different cabinet, I find the bottle Dominic told me would be there: his favorite brand of very expensive, eighteen-year-old Scotch.

"Thank you, Dominic," I whisper as I pour a few fingers into the bottom of my glass.

Retreating to the sofa, I sit listlessly next to my purse. A few swallows later, I finally begin to relax.

Tonight's lecture was fantastic, the crowd even more responsive than last week's. But it took serious mental effort to shut away the memory of my conversation with Sven. The man in the car outside my house. The possibility that someone who wishes me harm knows where I live.

My head falls back to the cushion. I close my eyes. Silence buzzes in my ears, a sensation I normally love but right now feels oppressive.

Or maybe... maybe I've never loved being alone. Maybe it's a lie I told myself so many times it became true. A defense against feeling like I'd never have a place in the world.

Stop. Not tonight.

Giving myself a shake, I sit up and finish the Scotch in two long swallows. I'll take a shower. Get some sleep. Things will be different in the morning—or maybe my perspective will be different. Either way, nothing good will come from me dwelling on all the shit I can't change.

Recenter. Reassess.

I push to my feet and grab my bags, then take them into the bedroom and toss them onto the bed. Halfway to the bathroom, I hear the distinctive *bzz, bzz* of my phone ringing. Figuring it's Nate or Charlie checking to see if I made it into the loft okay, I fish the device from my purse.

Kieran Hayes.

My heart throws itself against my ribs, flooding me with adrenaline.

"Shit, shit, shit."

I sit on the bed, then jump back up. Walk a few paces. Sit again. My finger hovers over the screen.

"He's a man. Just a man."

But my subconscious knows he's not *just* anything, and I'm freaking the fuck out.

The phone stops buzzing. My head hangs. I'm relieved. I'm bereft.

It starts buzzing again.

This time I don't let myself think. "Hello?"

"Hi, Talia."

It's a good thing I'm sitting down because my legs turn floaty.

"Kieran," I manage.

"How was your speaking engagement?"

I can hear the smile in his voice. He sounds relaxed. Perfectly calm—the opposite of me. The contrast sharpens my voice. "Fine, thank you."

He hums, and I feel the sound between my legs. "Is this a good time?"

"A good time for what? Your apology for hiring security for me without telling me?"

He chuckles. There's a rustling sound on his side. Sheets, I realize. Glancing at the nightstand clock, I do a quick calculation: it's early morning in Ireland. He's in bed.

Fire races under my skin at the thought.

"I'm not sorry," he murmurs. "I only wish I were there so I could see to your safety myself."

My lungs freeze. "What does that mean?"

Another humored exhale. "It means whatever you want it to mean." He pauses. "Did you miss me this week? Think about me?"

Yes. Constantly.

"Is there a point to this phone call? I was about to go to sleep."

"Now there's a lovely thought. Yes, there's a point—I wanted to hear your voice. Give me five minutes. How are you? Tell me about your week."

"I'm..."

I rub my forehead, wishing I hadn't indulged in that drink. Those two little words—*tell me*—are a seventeen-year-old trigger only he can push. My tongue loosens.

"I'm struggling. I lost three more clients and was accosted in the grocery store by a woman who said I was the Devil's whore. Apparently, she found her husband looking at photos of me online. There's... uh, more have surfaced. Some old promotional shots Charlie and I did for Crossroad's opening."

"I've seen them." He pauses, voice lowering. "You look stunning. Like a goddess of vengeance with that whip in your hand."

Golden warmth slips through me, melting my thoughts. His voice is better than whiskey, a rough burn on my senses.

Into my stunned silence, he asks, "Do you want me to get them taken down? I have people for that."

I make a sluggish connection. "You got that article pulled, didn't you? The one from my former client?"

"Would you be angry if I said yes?"

I sigh. "No."

"Then yes, though it took longer than I hoped. Viral media is like a fast-spreading rot. Hard to contain. They're still working—"

"It's okay," I interject. "Really. I appreciate the effort, but I'm sure your tech wizards have more important things to do. There's no point, anyway, not after the feature in the *Times* this morning."

"Another thoughtful sound. "Just finished reading it before I called. It was great, Talia. You should feel proud."

"Thank you," I whisper.

"Do you miss it?" His voice has a new edge. "Dominating men?"

A fantasy flashes, technicolor in my mind. His muscles straining against rope. I shift on the bed to relieve the ache between my legs, but it doesn't help.

"Sometimes." My voice scrapes; I clear my throat. "Not the work side of it. I enjoyed fulfilling the needs of my clients, but it wasn't personal."

"You mention that in the article," he muses. "I think you blew a lot of minds when you said you've never engaged sexually with a client. That kink isn't even strictly about sex."

"Did I blow *your* mind?" I ask recklessly.

His swiftly drawn breath makes goose bumps waterfall down my body.

"You did. You do. All day, every day."

There are five long, tense seconds of silence wherein all we do is breathe. He recovers first.

"What do you miss about it?"

Another mental flash of him hits. This time he's bound and blindfolded on his knees, his face upturned to me in perfect trust.

"The connection," I say hoarsely. "Knowing my partner feels safe and trusts that I'll take care of them physically and emotionally."

His soft groan cuts off sharply, like he tried to stop it from emerging but couldn't. I bite the inside of my cheek, my pulse pounding hard and low.

"The blond with the microphone. He was your sub, wasn't he?"

I blink at the abrupt transition. "Nate, yes. We ended things two years ago."

"For good? When was the last time?"

There's something raw in his voice, but I'm too muddled to analyze it beyond how it makes me feel: like if I touched myself right now, I'd explode.

"I saw him last month. After our session at the rage room."

He laughs, the sound strangled. Pained.

I can't handle it.

"I went to him because I wanted you. It was the last time."

The following silence is so thick I can hear the blood rushing in my ears. Then he asks with soft wonder, "You wanted me then?"

I've always wanted you.

"Yes. From the first time I saw you."

In a graveyard in the rain.

Relief thickens his slow exhale, then fervent words fill my ears, my body, my soul.

"I didn't want to leave your bed on Sunday, much less the country, but you needed time and space. If I hadn't gone, I wouldn't have been able to stay away from you. It's not transference, Talia. I promise you. It's your eyes, your voice. Your beautiful fucking brain. The fact you can read me like a book when no one—*no one*—has ever been able to. When we met, I was slipping away. I mean that literally. I was losing time, losing myself. You were the fire that melded the pieces of me back together. It wasn't the therapy—it was *you*."

I can't breathe, much less speak.

"You asked me in our first session if I'd ever trusted someone enough to show them the deepest, darkest parts of myself. I said no, and at the time it was the truth. But it's not true anymore. Do you understand? I trust *you*. I see *you*. I..." He sucks in air. "I want to tell you why I came to Ireland. The real reason."

My head spins. "Your mom—"

"Isn't herself anymore," he says with finality. "She doesn't know me. She's safe, as content as the finest care can make her, but she isn't why I came. My lab is here."

I blink in confusion. "Lumitech has a headquarters in Ireland?"

"No. This is privately funded. So completely off the books not even the custodians in the building know what's under their feet. When I got that call and the photo of Alistair and Gail, I thought it meant they knew about the lab in Limerick. The *real* lab."

I gasp. "The project here is a diversion."

"So fucking smart," he whispers.

"Kieran!"

He chuckles. "Yes. Lumitech's project has been officially shelved for three months, but it's never been more than a think tank. My people are here—the brightest minds in the world. They don't even need me. They never have. I come every six weeks or so under the pretense of visiting family, but I spend most of my time underground with them."

I thread this information with what he's told me before and muse, "You never stopped working on it because they never stopped."

"Correct. I've spent the last three months agonizing over whether to shut everything down. To give up. I was close—so close—to pulling the plug. Then I was watching you sleep Sunday morning, and I realized I couldn't ask you to be brave if I wasn't willing to take risks myself. So I did it."

My ears ring. "Did what?"

"Gave the green light. Preclinical testing begins in five weeks. We've done it. Too late for my mam, but not too late for others. For everyone."

"Holy shit," I whisper, my eyes stinging. "Kieran, I'm so happy for you."

"Thank you, mo ghrá."

I try to repeat the word but mangle it. He chuckles.

"What does that mean?" I demand.

"You didn't look it up?"

"It sounds like gibberish. Tell me how to spell it and I will."

His laughter grows. "Not a chance. But it's two words, not one."

"Not helpful," I grumble.

"Don't worry. I'll tell you someday."

I huff. "I'll call Gail and have her ask Alistair."

"No, you won't. You love the frustration. Prolonging the

tension. Don't you, mo ghrá? Didn't you love how I made you writhe for an hour before I let you come on my tongue?"

My breath stutters out of me. "Kieran," I whisper.

"Yes, sweetheart?"

"Next time..."

"Mmm, yes?"

"I'm in charge."

I hang up on his guttural curse.

CHAPTER 24

KIERAN

Stretching out my legs, I cross my ankles and let my head fall back against rough stone. Sven and Dylan are out of sight but nearby. They've been on high alert since I told them I gave the go-ahead for preclinical testing. If it were up to them, I'd never breathe fresh air again for my own safety.

"Hey, Gran. It's been a while."

Wind whistles through the bare branches of a nearby tree, each gust heavy with impending rain. I run my palm over the cold grass beside me where Talia once sat, sad and angry and vibrating like a hummingbird.

"Thank you for bringing her here that night. Don't know how you did it, but I'm grateful." I sigh heavily. "I'm scared, Gran. Not of her—she's the only thing that makes sense right now—but of something happening to her, to

Alistair and Gail or others because of me. Because I can't let go of the project, of the possibility of saving…" I trail off, my eyes screwing closed.

I can't save my mother.

It's too late.

But my heart doesn't understand the timing.

Leaves crunch under footsteps nearby. I open my eyes expecting Sven, but instead, it's my father. He was always the biggest man in any room, but these days, he's a tree permanently reshaped by storm, craggy-faced and whittled down.

"Thought I'd find you here."

He waves a hand at me and I scoot over so he can sit. For a few minutes, we merely exist side by side, together but alone with our thoughts.

Then he stirs and says, "Your gran was a magical woman, but I don't think even she's capable of dispensing advice from beyond the grave."

"I didn't want to bother you."

He scoffs. "What bothers me is that you think I'd be bothered. Now tell me about the woman."

My head swivels. "What?"

"You dinna think I'd be able to tell my son was in love? Go on, then. Tell me about her so I can tell Sorcha in the morning. Since you won't do it yourself."

I grimace. "I know you think Alistair and I should visit more, but she doesn't know who we are. You saw yesterday— I only agitate her."

"Because she can sense you're upset."

"She doesn't know me!" I explode. Sucking in a breath, I rub my face roughly. "Sorry. *Fuck.*"

"Kier." His voice is as heavy and full as the clouds overhead. "I shouldn't have said that. Forgive me. I didn't... I didn't always understand your pain. I was selfish, hanging onto the fact she still knew who I was. I thought... I had hope."

Lifting my knees, I hook my arms over them and bow my head. "I tried to fix her. I tried so fucking hard, and I did what I set out to do. But I wasn't fast enough."

He stills, and guilt is a thousand spikes piercing my heart.

"You're ready for the next phase?"

I nod despondently. "Preclinical testing, yes. If all goes well, we could be starting clinical testing and trials within a few years."

"But she can't be in them," he guesses.

"No," I whisper. "Her disease has already progressed too far."

"Kier. *Son.* Look at me."

I lift my head slowly. His blue eyes are bright with the grief he can't hide, but he's smiling. He grabs my face in big, warm hands and pulls my forehead to his.

"You did it, kid. You did it."

My eyes burn. "But at what cost? We've lost Mam. Liz. Some fucker tried to kill me twice and threatened Alistair and Gail. And God help me, if something happens to Talia, I'm afraid of what I'd do. Who I'd become."

He draws back enough to show me a raised gray eyebrow. "Talia, eh?"

I smirk tiredly. "Yeah."

"Tell me about her."

"She came out of nowhere." *Twice.* "Long legs and lion eyes. She's a psychologist. Her IQ is higher than mine. I'm a goner."

He chuckles. "She doesn't let you get away with shit, does she?"

My smile widens. "Nope."

He sobers. "And she isn't a checkmark on a five-year plan?"

I flinch. "Jesus, Dad."

He cups the back of my neck, squeezing gently. "I'm too old for tact. I know you loved Liz. She was a sweet girl. But Sorcha always thought you needed someone as hardheaded as you and twice as clever. As you know, she was rarely wrong."

Grief punches me; tears blur my sight. "I'm sorry I wasn't fast enough to save her."

His stern mouth pinches, his jaw working to hold back a tide of tears. "I know," he says gruffly. "But do you remember what she said that day? After she was diagnosed and you flew over here full of fire to tell her you were gonna find the cure?"

I remember, but I can't fucking speak or I'm going to scream.

"She told you all she wanted was for you to be happy. That's all either of us has ever wanted. Not a cure, not cars or houses or trips to fuckin' Tahiti. So for the first time in your life, stop trying so goddamn hard. You deserve to live, Kier. Let it go. Just let it go. You've got nothing left to prove."

The words shatter me, which shatters him. We sob and cling to each other's faces like drunks. We don't notice the rain falling in thick, freezing sheets, or the wind that screams through headstones—only the space between us where a life of love is ending and another finally begins.

THE SECOND THE plane reaches cruising altitude, Sven marches up the aisle to loom over me.

"Are you ready to talk?"

I crack an eye open. "Bully."

Dylan snorts somewhere behind us.

"Avoidance isn't going to make this go away," Sven snaps, lowering into the seat facing mine.

I sigh and sit up straighter. "No, you're right."

I've been putting off this conversation for nearly two weeks, purposely staying focused on the lab, my parents, and —for the last five days—exchanging texts with Talia. I've kept them completely innocent, mainly to fuck with her head. But the payoff is she's been opening up to me. Giving me access to her day-to-day life. I know about the publishing house she's in talks with and the fact her client list has shrunk to the point she's reduced her hours to three days a week. I know her hopes, her worries, her fears. Her *guts*. And every day, she grows more beautiful to me.

Now that we're headed home two days earlier than planned, all I want to think about is surprising her. Kissing her. Holding her. Shoving my nose in her hair and breathing her in.

Never letting her go.

"There's good news and bad news. Which do you want first?"

With effort, I set aside thoughts of Talia. "Doesn't matter."

"The threats being sent to Lumitech have dropped off over the last month."

"Starting with good news, then?"

He grunts. "Gabe also confirmed that Talia had video surveillance installed at her home and hired a security company. Same one that did the work at the warehouse; solid reputation. Patrols pass the house every three hours."

"Yeah, she mentioned that a few days ago."

Sven's mouth curves the tiniest bit.

I roll my eyes. "Moving on."

"Tom has a list of suspects he wants you to look at. Do you recognize any of these men?"

He hands me his phone. I scroll down the series of photographs, then shake my head. "No. Wait—" I scroll back up and show Sven the photo that gave me pause. "Doesn't this guy work at Lumitech?"

He nods. "He's in IT. Jared Green. Fits the profile of someone who'd have access to your private number and the skills to make the call. He also called out sick the day after."

I study the man's face. "I'm not seeing it. What's his backstory?"

"Divorced single father working full-time and going to law school at night. He's under watch but at the bottom of the list. There are some serious contenders there, though. Moralist radicals with national followings, fringe religious purists."

I hand him the phone. "Have we switched to bad news, then?"

"Good, bad, whatever. I only said that to get you talking."

I smirk. "Bastard."

"You must be rubbing off on me," he quips. "There's something else, too. Tom found a link between the two hit men."

Every muscle in my body tenses. "What? Or who?"

"It's a money trail. The families of both men have been making cash deposits every month. Same amounts each time. Not enough to raise suspicions, but the totals are adding up to a substantial payout."

"Hush money." I pinch the bridge of my nose, waiting for relief that doesn't come. "We need more than that. We need to know who's paying them."

"The grandmother and sister are being tailed to see if we can catch the next handoff."

"Good."

Sven rubs his jaw, eyes avoiding mine.

I sigh. "Spit it out."

"I was asked to run another group of suspects by you."

"Who?"

"Executive leadership at Lumitech across all departments."

I blink, then laugh shortly. "Not this again."

His expression hardens. "Tom wouldn't be worth his price if he didn't consider every angle. And before you ask, no, I didn't bring it up. Whether you want to face it or not, the list of people who have your private number isn't long. The list of who has access to your daily movements is even shorter. And then there's the list of who has the money and connections to hire hit men."

I frown out the window, tension riding my body as I think about the scars Sven carries because of me. A jagged line on his side. A starburst on his shoulder. Neither wound stopped him from disarming and cuffing the attackers or snapping at me to stop trying to help him and "Fucking call nine-one-one, Kier!"

The crack of a gunshot in my memory still wakes me up sometimes. The horror of Sven's body jolting against mine. The way time vacillated between hyper-speed and slow motion.

We weren't supposed to be leaving the office for another hour that day, but my last meeting had been canceled. I shouldn't have even been in the parking garage. He normally pulled the car around to a secure exit at the back of our building, but I'd gone with him because I was an impatient ass and hadn't wanted to wait.

Faces cycle through my mind, a carousel of people I've trusted for a decade. Who know my cell number, who knew my meeting was cancelled. The same people who knew where Liz and I lived and that I went running every morning, which was when the guy came at us with the knife.

Sven's right. He's always been right. That the person behind everything is a stranger simply isn't logical.

What's my continued denial worth? Is it worth Sven's life? Dylan's or Gabe's or mine? My brother's?

Is it worth Talia's?

I pull a breath into my tight lungs and turn back to Sven. "Tell Tom to focus on Lumitech. And hire more people. As many as necessary for twenty-four seven security on Alistair, Gail, and Talia. I don't care if they don't like it."

He stares at me, his surprise contained to a slight squint. "Done. I want two more on your personal detail as well."

I nod, having expected the request. All the money and power in the world can't keep word of the impending testing phases under wraps forever. For better or worse, the target on my head is about to get bigger.

Moreover, Sven knows my stint as a hermit is finished. I have a company to run. A disease to cure with a technology that will forever alter landscape of modern medicine. And I have a woman to love.

I don't want fear to control me anymore, but thanks to

Talia's work in my head, I'm aware of my limitations like never before.

I need help.

I'm finally ready to ask for it.

Grabbing my phone, I pull up the browser and type in: *Dr. Leo Chastain, Los Angeles.*

CHAPTER 25

TALIA

Istare across my kitchen table at the two women who rang my doorbell five minutes ago. They're twenty-five years apart but look like sisters thanks to spray tans, the same hair stylist, and cosmetic surgery.

Six minutes ago, I was running on my treadmill and trying not to overthink the fact I haven't heard from Kieran since yesterday afternoon. Now I'm trying to figure out how to kick my mother and sister out without sounding like a complete bitch. I'm not sure I can manage it. The gray roots in my mom's artificially blond hair and my sister's chipped nails suggest they've run out of money. Again.

I tune back into the one-sided conversation as my mom says, "It's a shame, what they're saying. We just want you to know you have family support."

She's trying to sound genuine, but she keeps glancing at

my sweat-drenched sports bra and leggings. Her lips purse in distaste every time, like she thinks I leave the house like this.

It's my own fault I'm in this mess. I haven't gotten into the habit of checking the app on my phone when the doorbell rings. If I'd looked first and seen them, I could have ignored the summons and kept running—the only activity that's doing anything for my stress.

Instead, I'd bolted for the door thinking maybe, illogically, that it was Kieran, only to be slapped into another dimension. One in which I hadn't set an explicit boundary with these women; namely, *I'm not giving you any more money, so don't call me, talk to me, or show up unannounced at my fucking house.*

I should have closed the door in their faces.

I'm not exactly sure why I didn't.

"I appreciate that, but I'm doing fine. I have an incredible support network." One that doesn't include them and never will.

My mom smiles. "That's great, Talia. We're so relieved to hear you're landing on your feet. Did I read somewhere that you're writing a book?"

It's her smile that does it—specifically the fact it doesn't reach her eyes. At least Olivia isn't bothering to hide the fact she was dragged here. She's said less than a sentence and keeps looking around my house like she's assessing its market value.

"Why are you really here, Mom?"

She turns red. Olivia's head whips toward us, her eyes

narrowing with interest. The dynamic is as old as we are. She's always loved conflict, instigating and escalating it whenever possible. Especially when it promises a divide between our parents and me and keeps her in the position as the favored daughter.

A memory surfaces of our trip to Ireland, one of the first and the absolute last time we traveled as a family. The night I met Kieran, when I returned to our hotel room, Olivia was already there, sobbing about how I'd stolen shots from someone at a bar and then disappeared.

What she doesn't understand—can't seem to wrap her head around—is that I'm not her victim anymore, and I haven't been for a long time.

"See?" chirps Olivia as she palms our mom's shoulder. "I told you not to get your hopes up. She hasn't changed. She only cares about herself. Zero appreciation for how hard you worked to give her what she needed to succeed. She owes you everything, but she wouldn't help us if we were begging on the streets."

I count to ten in my head, then stand up. "We're done here. I'll walk you out."

My mom sniffs and clutches her purse to her chest as she stands. Her eyes are red and wet as they meet mine, but I'm immune to her manipulation. My armor is impenetrable these days, reinforced with bricks of the countless times I needed a hug, a kind word, a soothing touch, and none arrived. Her emotional displays—or lack thereof—no longer dictate my self-worth.

Most days, I have compassion for her. Her own mother was a highly critical perfectionist, her father remote and cold. She can't love me because she was never taught how. Olivia is easier for her to show up for because they're cut from the same cloth. I'm too... me. And I'm all out of fucks to give.

They follow me to the foyer, Olivia whispering furiously the whole way. I don't bother listening.

I open the door but block the exit, staring at my sister until she scowls at me. "When I said no contact, I meant it. Don't show up here again." I shift my gaze to my mother. "If you want to talk to me, call next time."

"She's going to lose her house," snaps Olivia, getting in my face. "She was afraid to tell you because you're such a judgmental bitch. You think you're better than us? What a joke. I always knew there was something wrong with you, and now the whole world does. The high and mighty child prodigy grew up to be a glorified prostitute!"

"Get out," I whisper, "before I say something I'll regret."

My spine tingles just as Olivia's gaze snaps up and over my shoulder. Her eyes widen.

A deep, lilting voice says, "I don't have Talia's qualms, so fuck off right now or I'll call a judge and have you both thrown in jail for harassment and trespassing."

Kieran's fingers curl around my shoulder and squeeze gently. Half of me wants to turn and cling to him. The other half of me wants to elbow him in the stomach and run. All of me is mortified. I stay stock-still, afraid if I see his face I'll do something insane like start crying.

My mom, pale-faced, gapes at Kieran like he's a god appearing in the flesh. "That's... you're..." She smacks Olivia's arm. "Isn't he—"

"Kieran Hayes, oh my gosh!" Olivia's laugh is forced. "How embarrassing that you heard our little sisterly squabble. You have a brother, don't you, Kieran? Can I call you Kieran? You know how it is—"

"No, you can't call me Kieran," he says flatly. "And no, I don't know *how it is* because I'd never speak to my brother that way."

Olivia turns white as a sheet.

Kieran steps into the house, his front pressing flush to my back. With a tug on my shoulder, he maneuvers me sideways until the doorway is clear. His other arm wraps around my waist, bare forearm against my bare stomach. Calm and comfort shower me like cleansing rain. My muscles automatically relax.

He feels so *right*.

"Are you... together?" asks my mother in an awed voice.

Kieran says, "Yes, we are," as I answer, "None of your business."

He chuckles and presses a kiss to my head.

Olivia stammers, "Let's—let's start over. We clearly got off on the wrong foot." She extends a hand, her eyes pinned on Kieran, her smile saccharine. "I'm Olivia Stirling, Talia's big sister."

"No, thanks," says Kieran mildly. "Anyone who speaks to Talia like that is no one I want to know. Now do I need to repeat myself, or should I have my security escort you to the nearest police station?"

I shiver at the very real threat in his voice. Olivia is too numbed by Xanax and her own self-importance to hear it, but my mom does—or she sees Sven and Dylan standing at the base of the porch, watching us with sharp eyes. She grabs my sister's arm and pulls her out the door. Kieran kicks it closed behind them, then turns me around and wraps me in his arms.

He nuzzles his nose into the sweaty hair over my ear. "Mmm, you smell good."

"You're full of shit."

He licks the shell of my ear and I shudder, my senses coming alive and flooding with him.

"You taste good, too, even if I'd rather be the cause of your sweat."

Ignoring the sudden hammer of need between my legs, I lean back to see his face. His eyes are soft—the vivid blue of a clear, deep sea. I want to kiss the curl of his lips so badly my mouth burns. I can't believe he's here. That he's looking at me like this. That *he* wants *me*.

"You're home early." I'm breathless, my voice choked by emotion I'm no longer capable of masking.

He nods, his gaze caressing my features with such focus I feel peeled open. He's hard against my stomach, but his hands are unmoving on my spine.

"Are you done fighting, Talia? Are you ready for me?"

I suck in a breath. "I... I want to be."

His mouth twitches. "I can work with that. Do you want to talk about what just happened now or later?"

"How about never?"

"Later, then."

His lips graze my forehead, then dip to my neck. He takes another deep inhale. I'm too turned on to care that I haven't showered today, that I'm not wearing deodorant. He sucks me in like he can't get enough, his cock twitching against my stomach.

"I need to fuck you, mo ghrá. So, so badly. Do you want me back inside your perfect little pussy?"

I suck in a breath, my body temperature skyrocketing. He chuckles darkly and licks a line up my neck. My knees weaken.

"You like my filthy mouth, don't you?" His voice lowers even more, rumbling through me. "It's you—you did this. You make me an animal. If you told me you wanted to shower right now, I'd say it's not fucking happening. I want you sweaty and dirty. Sloppy. *Soaking*. Wild."

An unhinged moan leaves my mouth. He jerks me against him, a hand diving beneath the waistband at the back of my leggings, fingers seeking until they find my center. One long finger sinks inside me, then two. I'm on my tiptoes, helpless to do anything but cling to his shoulders as he rocks me on his hand.

Lips against my temple, he murmurs, "All this cream for me, sweetheart?"

I gasp. "Yes."

"Only for me?" he growls, almost lifting me from the floor.

"Yes!"

"I know you said you'd be in charge, but I—" His breath shudders out of him, and I register the tremble in his frame. How hard he's trying to control himself.

You make me an animal.

I turn my head, taking his mouth. Soft to soft. Heat to heat. I bite his lower lip, then lick it. "I'm an animal, too. Let's see who's more vicious."

The sound he makes raises the hairs on the back of my neck and makes me pulse around his fingers. He lifts me from the floor, one arm around my waist, his hand still anchored in my pussy. I spend the walk to my bedroom painting his taut throat with my lips and tongue. When I bite down on muscle, he gasps. Then we're falling onto my bed.

He withdraws his fingers and drags my sports bra over my head. It catches on my hair tie, pulling it and several strands of hair out. At my wince, his eyes flash to mine.

"Shit. Sor—"

"Shut up." I grab his face and guide it to my chest. He devours my breasts with hands, lips, tongue, and teeth. Throwing my head back, I writhe against him, the base of his hard cock gliding against my clit. Another minute of this and I'll come.

"Good boy," I purr.

Kieran freezes. A smile spreads on my face as his head lifts from my chest, blue eyes an inferno.

"I'm not sure I like that."

I bat my eyelashes. "Oh, you like it. Because you want to please me. Don't you?"

His forehead drops to mine, a groan in his throat as he thrusts against me. "Honestly, it makes me want to spank the shit out of you."

I grab his ass, then smack one cheek. *Hard.*

"Jesus fuck," he hisses.

I laugh as he yanks my arms over my head, pinning my wrists in one hand. Wrapping my legs around his waist, I undulate against him. He pivots his hips away, not giving me friction. I snarl up at him.

He laughs even as black swallows more blue in his eyes. Staring down at me, he drags his free hand down my torso. His gaze falls, narrowing on the sweep of his thumb against my waistband.

"Are you on birth control?" he asks abruptly.

I bite my lip. "You want to fill my cunt with cum, Kieran?"

His eyes flare in surprised lust. My smile is knowing.

"Oh, did you think that word was only for you? *Cunt*," I draw out, my tongue snapping the T. "It's mine. Just like your cock, your hands, and your mouth. I want them. Now."

He mutters something I can't understand—more Irish— then rears back and slaps my pussy. I yelp at the sting in my clit, then groan at the flood of heat. It's punishment but feels like a reward.

"Vanilla, my ass," I mutter.

He smirks and rocks against me, giving me the lightest tease of friction. Torturing us both.

"More." I gasp.

"Answer the question and I'll give you what you want."

"Fuck. Fine. Yes, I'm on birth control."

His jaw clenches, his thumb resuming a teasing path across my abdomen. "Another question." His eyes meet mine. "This one is for Dr. Stirling."

He says my name with such heat my pussy clamps down on nothing. "What?" I ask breathlessly.

"Tell me why, for the first time in my life, the thought of wearing a condom is abhorrent."

The words, coupled with the look in his eyes, make the breath stall in my lungs and pours molten lava into my core. *Holy shit.* I open my mouth, but my voice is nowhere to be found.

Kieran leans down and licks the corner of my lips, then peppers kisses over my cheek and jaw. He whispers, "What's it called, Dr. Stirling? I'm sure there's a name for it. When everything in me wants to fill you with cum, over and over?"

"Breeding kink," I answer breathlessly.

"Huh. Sounds about right."

He gives me a deep, drugging kiss, then draws back. I try to follow him, but his hold on my wrists keeps me in place. He plays with my nipples, tugging them until I'm panting and twitching. I'm seconds from begging.

"Does that scare you? That I feel that way?"

"Of course not," I manage. "It's perfectly normal."

"Hmm." His hips settle against mine. I groan in relief at the pressure. "And what if I told you I wish you weren't on birth control? Does *that* scare you?"

My mind stalls out even as my body reacts. Goose bumps ripple across my chest. My nipples tighten painfully. And my hips circle and lift for him.

I'm terrified—and beyond aroused.

Kieran stays still, his eyes holding mine. I'm more naked than I've ever been beneath his steady stare.

"Yes," I finally say. "And... no."

His shoulders relax a fraction.

Overwhelmed, I snap, "Are we done talking yet?"

He grins and releases my wrists. Climbing off the bed, he pulls off his T-shirt and unbuttons his jeans. *Finally.* I kick my shoes off and yank my leggings down. They get caught on my feet and I almost scream in frustration. He laughs and pulls them off with one hand, flinging them down. Another few seconds and he's naked, the afternoon sunlight kissing every hard slab of muscle. Mussed hair, wild blue eyes. The most perfect cock I've ever seen.

He wraps one hand around himself, stroking from base to tip. The sight distracts me and I almost miss the shift in his expression. When I catch it, I gasp and scramble up—not fast enough. He flattens me to the bed, sweeping my legs up until my knees press to my shoulders and pin my arms.

The thick, blunt head of his cock presses right where I need it. I jerk my hips up, chasing penetration, but he stays out of reach.

"Uh-uh, mo ghrá. I won. I'm in charge."

"You're going to pay for this," I growl into his grinning face.

"I look forward to it," he murmurs. "For now, though, you're going to shut your beautiful mouth and take my cock like a good girl."

He fills me slowly, a devilish smirk on his lips, his eyes absorbing each minute shift in my expression. By the time our hips are flush, I'm shaking and panting. He groans, eyes closing briefly.

"It's like coming home," he whispers, then his mouth seizes mine as he slowly withdraws and pushes back in at the same, excruciating pace.

I buck against him. "I thought you wanted to fuck me like an animal," I mumble into his mouth.

His lips curve against mine as he withdraws and fills me again, each inch taking a thousand years.

I whimper. "You're killing me."

Now he's almost laughing. "*'Desire to us/ Was like a double death,/ Swift dying/ Of our mingled breath.'*"

"Langston Hughes? Really?" I cry.

He does laugh, then, but stops when I shove my knees into his chest, freeing my arms, then grip his face in my hands. "Fill me with your cum and push it back inside me when it leaks out."

Every muscle in his body tightens, predatory light sparking in his eyes. A shiver rolls down my spine—pricking elation, anticipation sweetened by a sprinkle of fear. With a guttural growl, he breaks, driving into me fast and hard. My eyes roll back in my head.

"Like this, Talia?"

My answer is a desperate moan. I've never been so full, so consumed that I can't feel where I end and he begins.

"You take me so perfectly, sweetheart. Grip me so tight. God, do you hear that? How wet you are for me? This cunt was made for me—you know that, don't you? That you're meant to be fucked by me and only me?"

Lost in the sensual assault of his body and words, I barely notice my wrists being pinned over my head again or his other seizing the back of my neck. His thumb hooks into my mouth, pressing my jaw open for his tongue to invade. My tender nipples drag against his chest with every thrust, his pelvis slamming into my clit over and over again. Daunting sensation builds, a sparkling, spiraling torrent.

"Yes, yes," I moan. "Right there. Don't stop."

He doesn't, even when I almost bite off his tongue as I come, screaming and shaking beneath him. As the last contractions fade, he makes a small, rough noise. His hips lose their steady rhythm.

I lick into his mouth, nip at his lips. "Give me every drop. Don't close your eyes. Let me see you fall apart."

His features sharpen, eyes blazing. "Tá mé i ngrá leat, Talia," he whispers.

I don't know what it means, but I feel it like a shot of heat to my chest. He drives into me one more time, his cock unyielding steel. When I feel the first heady pulse of him inside me, a second climax hits me like a freak lightning strike.

"God, oh God," I sob, bucking against him.

His arms scoop beneath me, clutching me tight as we ride out our twinned pleasure. I gasp for air against the slick heat of his neck, his equally harsh breaths in my ear. Our hearts pound at the barriers of flesh and bone separating them.

"If that's death," he says thickly, "I'll die every day for you."

I stroke his sweat-damp hair, his shoulders and waist, the still-twitching muscles along his spine. "Kieran," I whisper, my voice cracking with everything I can't say or don't have words for. My fears. My dreams.

All of them... *him.*

He presses soft kisses to my eyelids, my cheeks, and finally my mouth before he looks into my eyes. And as though he heard every word my soul wrapped around his name, he says, "I know. It feels like too much and never enough, doesn't it?"

I swallow hard and nod.

He smiles a little and drags his nose along mine. "I think it's supposed to."

Before I can process that, he pulls out of me and shifts down, spreading my legs open. "So pretty and swollen from me, more red than pink." He strokes me gently, gaze avid as he parts my folds. I gasp and shiver.

"Squeeze for me, sweetheart."

I do. He groans, two fingers catching his cum as it drips out. I know what's next—I want it more than anything—but nothing can prepare me for the soft, reverent look on his face as he pushes his fingers carefully inside me. Like his cum belongs there. Like he does. Like he's the only man who ever has and ever will.

His dark head lowers. He presses a kiss to my tender clit. Then he looks up with a crooked grin. "I'll wash your hair if you wash mine."

I want to cry, but I smile instead.

"Deal."

CHAPTER 26

TALIA

"Are you hungry?" calls Kieran.

Squeezing moisture from my hair with a towel, I walk into the bedroom to see him lounging against my headboard with his phone. His hair is wet, too, a messy halo around his face. Jeans and no shirt, bare feet crossed at the ankles.

I almost pinch myself.

"Sure." I pause. "Do Sven and Dylan want to come in the house? We should feed them, too. Right?"

Kieran doesn't look up. "Gabe relieved them a bit ago so they could go home. We came straight from the airport."

My lungs squeeze. *He came straight to me.*

"Oh, okay. So should I invite Gabe inside?"

He finally looks up, revealing a hint of wariness around his eyes. I toss the towel into a nearby hamper and perch on the edge of the bed.

"What is it?" I ask.

He clears his throat, then laughs a little. "Don't know if I'll ever get used to that." I frown, and he clarifies, "How you can see what's going on in my head."

"I can't, though," I say mutedly.

His eyes soften even as his expression grows grave. He tosses his phone to the sheets and pats the bed next to him. Despite a small trill of alarm in my body, I crawl to him and settle against his side. His arm hooks snugly around my waist. My leg falls naturally between his, my head coming to rest on his chest.

A sigh of contentment escapes me.

"Feel that?" he murmurs. "How we fit?"

"Yes." My fingers trail across his clavicle; he catches them and holds my hand over his heart.

When he doesn't immediately speak, I glance up to see his shuttered expression. Stiffening, I say, "You're making me nervous."

"Not my intent." He kisses my forehead. "Just organizing my thoughts. And trying not to think about taking off your clothes again."

"Do I need to sit up?"

"I dare you to try."

I hold back a smile. "*Kieran.*"

Darkness shifts in his eyes. "That's the voice, isn't it? The one that makes men beg?"

Denying the impulse to ask if it makes him want to beg, I ask instead, "Is that what's bothering you?"

"No," he says.

I close my eyes in relief, then open them when he releases my hand to cup my face. His thumb skates across my cheekbone.

"I called that therapist. The man you recommended."

I blink in surprise, then grin. "Dr. Chastain?"

He nods. "The very one. I must have said something alarming because our first appointment is tomorrow morning at nine. He's coming to the house."

Thank you, Leo.

"That's amazing."

He smirks. "Turns out I'm not as hardheaded as my former therapist thinks I am."

I open my mouth, then close it, suddenly uncertain of the new dynamic between us.

"Be you, Talia. That's all I want."

A knot inside me relaxes. "What changed your mind?"

He gives me a little squeeze of approval. "I had five weeks of therapy with a brain dentist. She chipped away until all my nerves were exposed, then blew on them."

I make a face. "What a horrible visual."

He smiles slightly, then his gaze clouds and drifts to our entwined legs. "I guess it took a while to settle—all the shit we talked about. My issues. How I cope. How I... avoid. My dad really drove the point home yesterday when he told me I should stop trying so goddamn hard, that I've got nothing left to prove."

He sighs. "Fact is, I've gone most of my life with a giant

chip on my shoulder. This feeling that I needed to be the best. The smartest. Change my family's circumstances in the most pronounced way possible. Force the world to know my name. Every step I've taken since I was fourteen has been calculated to move me toward my goals. My dad was right—I wasn't living. I set aside what was important to focus on what I could accomplish."

"What you've accomplished *is* important, Kieran."

"I know," he admits, then frowns. "In theory, I know that. But I don't feel it. Maybe that will change with successful testing, but all I can focus on is that it's too late to save the person the treatment was meant for. Her disease is too advanced."

My heart thuds in sympathetic pain. "I'm so sorry."

He blinks fast, then clears his throat. "Now that it's happening—now that I've reached this impossible benchmark—I'm realizing how many years I've wasted ignoring the giant hole inside me. A hole that's suddenly filling up. Overflowing. And I've never been more scared in my life."

My pulse accelerates. Even as my brain tries to find ways to make what he said *not* about me, my heart knows—hopes, wants—otherwise.

"What are you most afraid of?" I ask softly.

His eyes close. "Right now? Telling you the truth of how paranoid I am, what I've done because of it. I'm afraid of smothering you, poisoning you with my fears. I'm afraid you'll end up hating me for it. But I don't know if I can stop myself. Even if it means losing you."

When I sit up, he doesn't try to stop me. His dark lashes lift, eyes reflecting the same emotions that thickened his confession. Fear. Anxiety. Raw, desperate desire. I grab his hand, threading our fingers and squeezing. The urge to tell him there's nothing he could say that would make me walk away from him pounds at my teeth. I swallow it down, scrambling for a logical response instead of an emotional one.

"Thank you for being honest with me. I do need to know what you mean by 'what I've done,' though."

He inhales slowly. "The night of the benefit, I had Sven break into your house to assess your security. You already know about the company I hired to watch your house—I didn't fire them like you told me to. I've also hired personal protection for you. Sven is briefing them right now. There's more, too. What I haven't done yet but want to."

My mind and heart racing a mile a minute, I ask weakly, "What do you want to do?"

"I want to convince you to move in with me. Close your practice. Relinquish your freedom. Stay in my line of sight at all times. I can't stop the fear. Can't help it. I'd chain you to me if I could, Talia. And yes, I fucking mean that."

My breaths rasp in the sudden quiet. It takes a solid thirty seconds for me to sort through why those ideas are bad. Finally, I'm able to divorce myself from the thrill of his possessiveness.

"I guess it's a good thing you have therapy tomorrow."

He blinks, brows lifting. "That's it?"

I hesitate, then nod. "Since Sven told me about that car,

the man watching me, I've felt vulnerable in a way I never have before. Even though there haven't been any more sightings of him, I still feel the weight of it. I can't imagine how much worse it's been for you, what you've dealt with for years—the threats, Liz's murder, the attempts on your life, the phone call... If it eases your mind to have a security team follow me, I'm okay with it." I pause. "You'll tell Dr. Chastain all this, right?"

"Yes," he says without hesitation.

I swallow past my dry throat, nodding. "Good."

He stares at me for several moments. "I shouldn't be surprised, but here I am, my mind once again blown."

I laugh, a soundless burst of air. "You're surprised I'm not freaking out? Oh, believe me, I am."

Just not for the reason you think.

His gaze sharpens. Pierces. He sees too much. Hears what I can't say. Heat rolls through me. Unable to hold his gaze, I look down.

The next seconds are a blur as he pins me to the mattress. His forearms caging my head, he kicks my legs apart and settles his weight. His eyes hold mine from inches away.

"Don't hide from me ever again, mo ghrá," he whispers. "Tell me."

I gasp for air. For words. Courage.

"Please."

His voice cracks—I crack with it.

"I'm freaked out because I'm *not* freaked out!" My voice is too loud, fraught with agitation. "The idea of giving up everything for you—my whole life—doesn't seem nearly as insane as it should. What if you change your mind, Kieran? What if you wake up one day and realize I'm not as fascinating as you think I am, or you really do prefer petite blondes? I've already given you more than I've given anyone!"

"I know," he whispers, gaze tender as it roams my flushed cheeks, my tearing eyes.

"That's just it—you don't know. I'm a *Domme,* goddammit. Do you have any idea what it means that I went to my knees for you? That I let you fuck my ass? That you're pinning me like this and I haven't scratched your eyes out? I have one submissive bone in my body. One! Out of two hundred and six!"

He bites his lower lip so hard it turns white.

I sag back to the bed, the fight draining out of me. "You're laughing. Unbelievable. I hate you right now."

A crooked grin spreads on his face. "No, you don't. What we feel for each other is the furthest from hate you can get."

I freeze. He chuckles and kisses my nose, then rolls away and climbs off the bed. His hand extends toward me. My brain still half-melted by his pronouncement, I scoot toward him and let him draw me to my feet. A finger under my chin lifts my face for his kiss—soft, almost chaste, a tingling exchange of heat and breath.

"You're perfect," he whispers. "Every molecule. All two hundred and six bones. You are and will always be a miracle to me."

He strokes my cheek before taking a deliberate step back.

When I register the intent in his eyes, goose bumps explode across my skin. My fingers clench. My heart stampedes.

I gasp his name.

"I'm yours, Talia. All of me."

With smooth grace, he lowers to his knees before me and bows his head.

I wrench open Talia's front door and glare at Gabe. As much as I like the guy, right now I want to choke the life out of him.

"You have the worst fucking timing."

He grimaces. "Sorry, boss. Sven insisted."

Seconds—fucking *seconds* after my knees hit the carpet, my phone started blaring with the distinctive alarm only a code from my security team can trigger.

"This had better be good."

Talia steps up beside me. My arm curves around her waist, drawing her close. Her hand settles on my lower back. For a second, her nails press into my skin.

"Give him a break," she murmurs. Her touch is grounding, but it's the low command in her voice that makes my anger bleed away—and my cock swell.

She thinks that tone doesn't affect me; I can't wait to

show her how wrong she is. The first few times I heard it, it made my bones vibrate with annoyance because it rattled the paradigm of who I knew myself to be. Now it makes me vibrate in a different way. With desperation and lust. I want to be back on my knees. I want to worship at her feet.

I may never be able to be her 'good boy,' but I'll be everything else—her pet, her slut, her fucking slave. Anything and everything she wants.

Her nails dig into my back again, making me jolt. I realize I'm breathing hard and sporting a massive tent in my jeans.

Gabe looks positively giddy. I'm never going to hear the end of this.

"Everything okay?" asks Talia in a normal tone. And thank fuck for that because if I ever hear her talk to another man with *that* voice again I'm going to—

"Relax," she whispers.

I take a breath, hold it, and release it slowly.

Gabe shifts on his feet, looking between us like he isn't sure who he works for anymore. It almost makes me smile.

"What is it?" I ask.

He focuses on me. "Sven and Dylan are wrapping up the onboarding of the new, uh, team members... " His gaze flickers to Talia.

"It's all right," I interrupt. "I told her."

He smiles. "That makes things easier." He looks at Talia. "Two of them will be assigned to you, so it would be ideal if you could meet them today or tomorrow."

"I want three watching her, Gabe."

He has the sense to put away his dimples before he meets my stare. "There will be. I'm taking point." He pauses a beat. "If you're okay with that."

Am I? Do I want this twenty-something, muscled, dimpled kid shadowing Talia day and night? Going with her to all the places I can't? Errands and her office and fucking Crossroads every Saturday?

Talia leans close, her mouth grazing my ear. "It's Gabe," she whispers, so softly it's barely more than a breath.

A fraction of my sanity returns. She's right—this is *Gabe*. He was Sven's star pupil at the training academy I poached him from. He's close to his black belt in Judo, juggles knives for fun, and can incapacitate a man in four seconds. Most importantly, he doesn't look at Talia like he's attracted to her. If anything, he gives off little brother vibes. He's also a thousand times more preferable than three total strangers.

Feeling me relax, Talia kisses my neck and drops down from her tiptoes.

I meet Gabe's calm gaze. "Thank you for taking point on her protection."

He nods soberly. "Absolutely. I'm sure the new guys are good, but the three of us thought you'd appreciate the shift of personnel."

"Now that that's settled," Talia says lightly. "Give me five and I'll be ready to come with you."

I catch her hand as she turns to leave. "Pack a bag?"

She smiles, showing me that perfect eyetooth. "Okay. For the night or the weekend?"

For the rest of forever.

"Weekend," I manage to say.

She nods and glides away. When she turns a corner, I drag my gaze back to Gabe.

"I'm probably never going to forgive you for interrupting what was about to happen."

He blows out a breath, coasting a hand over his hair. "Frankly, Kier, I don't blame you."

"No one comes in the house tonight." I pause. "Audio off, too."

His lips twitch. "You got it. I'll brief the new kids."

As NIGHTFALL PUSHES a sunset of fiery orange and magenta into the Pacific, I step onto the back deck and approach Talia.

"Everyone's gone."

She looks over her shoulder with a wry smile. "They're never really gone, though, are they?"

She tips her head to the right. Following her gaze, I squint into the shadows past the deck and see two shadowed figures walking down the property line.

I grimace, my gut sinking. "Once we're inside and the alarm is on, they won't come in unless there's an emergency. But, ehm, you should know there's video and audio surveillance in the house. Not the bathrooms, obviously, and

I've already turned it off in my bedroom. I'm sorry. I know it's a lot."

My skin prickles with apprehension, dark thoughts intruding. *What if she changes her mind? Decides it's too much?*

Talia closes the distance between us with purposeful steps. She flattens herself to my chest, her arms snaking around my middle and tightening. Gratitude and relief almost take me to my knees. I palm her head, sinking my fingers into her soft, unbound hair. *God, she feels perfect.*

"It's okay," she says. "You're worth it. Your safety means as much to me as mine does to you."

The sunset shifts from the sky to my chest, filling me with streaks of flame. My mouth opens, the words I want to tell her rising fast. *I know who you are, Birdie. I've spent my life waiting for you. I love you. You belong with me.*

Something holds me back. Fear, maybe. Or I'm just a manipulative asshole who wants her to be the one to confess. To abolish the last barrier between us.

I clear my throat. "Care for a swim?"

She laughs and draws back. "I'm not into exhibitionism."

I smirk. "I can turn off the lights in the jacuzzi."

"Can you plug their ears, too? Because if you haven't noticed, I'm loud." Her head cocks. "So are you, actually."

I'm suddenly grateful for the deepening shadows and the fact my back is to the lights from the house, because I'm blushing like a virgin boy. She still sees it—or senses it. Her grin is wicked and causes a chain reaction in my body.

"It's your fault," I mutter, my hands roaming down her back to her ass. I pull her against me, thrusting lazily into her stomach. "Did you get enough to eat?"

"Mmhm." Her breath skates over my neck, my ear. "It was nice of your chef to come feed everyone tonight. How do you feel about the new guys Sven hired?"

"They seem competent. You ready to talk about what happened when I showed up today?"

She stiffens slightly. When she tries to draw away, I hold her tighter. "Kieran," she huffs in annoyance. "I don't want to talk about my family."

I already know far more than she thinks—more of what she said that night in the graveyard has come back to me. Almost like my psyche preserved the details knowing I'd want the memories back someday. I remember why she was there in the first place. Her abusive older sister, Olivia.

"How much money have they guilted you into giving them over the years?" I murmur.

She stiffens more, fingers clenching on my back. Finally, she relaxes with a sigh. "A lot." She shakes her head shortly, frustration and stubborn sadness in each twist of her neck. "I told my mom the house was too big for her. That property taxes would keep going up. She didn't listen. She asked for help with the down payment. It was stupid of me to say yes. I'm sure Olivia was in her ear, too, angling for a cut like she always does. Who knows if all the money even went to the down payment."

"It wasn't stupid, Talia, just human. Your sister is a bitch, by the way. She probably needs therapy."

She laughs shortly. "That she does."

I stroke her back. Hold her tighter so she knows how grateful I am for her honesty. "What about your father? Do you talk to him?"

"Not really," she says mutedly. "He's actually not a bad person. We're just very different. When I had some issues as a teen, he got me into therapy, but when I turned eighteen and visitation and child support weren't mandatory anymore, we drifted apart. He was remarried by then. I usually hear from him around the holidays and my birthday."

I want to know what issues she had as a teenager but refrain from asking. She'll tell me eventually, and I'm playing the longest game—the one that lasts a lifetime.

Almost as an afterthought, she adds, "I wouldn't be surprised if I don't hear from my dad again, though."

I frown. "Why?"

"He's become very religious over the years." She clears her throat but doesn't say more. She doesn't need to.

It breaks my heart, thinking of the young girl I met who felt so alone in her own family—and the woman in my arms who, despite the intelligence of a rocket scientist, hasn't managed to completely give up hope that someday they'll accept her.

"They don't deserve you," I tell her, my voice gruff with the effort of holding back more.

She drags her forehead over my chest, then looks up. For a second, I think she's going to tell me—what, I'm not exactly sure. But something big. Then she swallows, her gaze dropping to my mouth. My cock jumps. A Pavlovian response to seeing her throat move that I doubt I'll ever be cured of.

"Anything else you want to know?" she asks wryly.

"Yes. Every-damn-thing about you."

Her nails drag down my spine, eyes a beautiful prism of vulnerability and darkness. "Are you sure about that?"

It's the *voice*.

I clear my suddenly parched throat. "Yes."

Her pupils expand. "Okay. Let's go inside and talk."

"Talk?" I bark.

An eyebrow arches. "You've never been topped before, have you?"

I shake my head.

"Then yes, Kieran, we're going to talk first," she says in that damn voice that makes my brain short-circuit. "I'm going to ask you some questions, and you're going to give me honest answers."

I take a short breath. My heart races and *Jesus Christ* my palms are damp.

"I trust you to—"

She presses fingers to my mouth. "This is nonnegotiable. I need to know your limits—what you're open to exploring and what you don't want." Her lips curve. "Speaking as someone who was recently dominated for the first time, there could also be some mental challenges I want to prepare you for."

"Did you have them?" I ask, afraid of the answer but needing it, too.

Her voice softens. "Yes, but you kept me present and above all, you made me feel safe and cared for. I don't regret a single second of anything we've done." She hesitates, lashes shadowing her eyes. "I need you to know I don't expect this from you. I don't want you to do this because you feel like you have to."

"I know, mo ghrá," I murmur, "but have you forgotten what happened earlier today?"

A flush rises from her neck to her cheeks. "I haven't," she whispers, "but it does feel like I might have dreamed it."

"Not a dream. I want this—you. All of you. And I..." My throat closes.

Her fingers stroke my jaw, sending pulses of warmth into my chest. "You what?"

"I want to let go," I say, my voice rough with emotion. "For you. For me, too. If that makes sense."

Her eyes glisten. "Yes, it does."

I blow out a breath, relaxing a little. "Let's talk, then. You're the boss." I wince. "Actually, what, uh... what am I supposed to call you?"

A beautiful smile blooms on her face right before she presses her lips to mine. "Just Talia," she whispers into our kiss. "Your Talia."

TALIA

My hands tremble as I cap the tube of red lipstick and set it on the counter. I adjust the clip holding the top half of my hair back, then pull the remainder over my shoulders until the strands frame my breasts. There's nothing else to do but leave the guest bathroom and walk down the hallway to Kieran's bedroom.

Gripping the counter, I stare into the reflection of my wide eyes. "Remember who you are. You've been called Mistress, Goddess, Master, and Queen. You are a Domme. He's given consent. He trusts you to care for him. He's yours to tease and command. Yours to use. Yours to please."

Natural Dominant or not, Kieran *wants* me to take control. He made it abundantly clear this morning and again this evening, and there's an inescapable logic to it I can't ignore. Finally and fully cognizant of the mental load he's been carrying for years, he craves freedom from that crushing pressure. And while as a doctor I'm aware this isn't a lasting solution for him, as a Dominant I know I can give him temporary relief.

"You will give him what he needs," I finish in a whisper.

Slowly, the panicked beat of my heart calms. My breaths grow fuller, my shoulders straighter. Then I think about our conversation an hour ago and my pulse ramps up again. Not with anxiety, though. With excitement. Anticipation.

This time, when I draw the mantel of the Professor fully over my shoulders and let it sink into my psyche, I do it without hesitation. There will be no consequences, no dissonance. This isn't a sacrifice but a homecoming. After nearly two decades of waiting, I am exactly myself with exactly the right man.

With a final, deep breath, I leave the guest room. Except for the measured *click* from my heels, the house is quiet as I walk down the airy hallway toward the distant end. Time is fluid, stretching and constricting. I'm walking forever; I'm turning the doorknob and opening the door to his bedroom.

A small sigh escapes me as I take in the spacious, tranquil sanctum where Kieran rests his head at night. Thick, dark curtains are drawn over the floor-to-ceiling windows to my right. Candles flicker on surfaces throughout: a table before a cozy seating area, nightstands, a floating shelf over a dark fireplace. The dancing lights play across wood floors and creamy area rugs, across pale gray walls interspersed with framed artwork and a massive bed stripped of everything but the fitted sheet.

Across him.

He's exactly where I told him to be, sitting on his heels on the floor at the foot of the bed. Freshly showered. Naked. His head bowed, eyes closed.

A king on his knees.

For me.

"Beautiful, Kieran. Thank you."

I watch as he processes my arrival, my voice. His chest begins to rise and fall at a faster pace. A tremble moves through his frame. As I walk toward him, my gaze roams his shoulders, his arms, the hands that hang loosely at his sides. I'm looking for signs of tension, but there are none. He's relaxed everywhere except one place—his cock is hard against his thigh, flushed with blood. Pre-cum glistens on the tip and on his skin where it dripped.

Elation soars in my veins.

"Have you touched yourself?"

"No, Talia."

Dear God, his voice. Smooth whiskey. Lilting, soft music. Reverent. Almost euphoric. I've heard the tone before, many times, but it's never affected me this way. Because it's him.

"Do you remember the rules?"

He nods.

I move even closer, the tips of my stilettos a few inches from his knees. "Repeat them."

His throat moves in a heavy swallow. "You give, I receive. I'm not to speak unless spoken to. No touching you unless invited. No coming without permission. If you ask me for my color, Green is continue, Yellow is slow down. Red is my safe word and means stop."

"Very good," I purr.

He shudders, a noisy breath escaping his mouth. I reach forward, stroking a hand over his soft, damp hair, fingering the strands and tugging them lightly. He grunts, his hips shifting forward, his cock twitching.

My other hand joins the first. I grab fistfuls of his hair and jerk his head up. His eyelashes flutter, staying closed with effort.

"You have permission to open your eyes."

He blinks, blue eyes focusing, features sharpening as he takes me in. His mouth opens, then closes, his lips thinning as he struggles against the impulse to speak. Dilated pupils tell me the challenge of obedience is only heightening his arousal. The pulse in his throat is a living creature seeking escape.

"Are you pleased?" I ask, scraping my fingernails over his scalp.

"Yes," he whispers hoarsely.

I'm wearing the exact outfit that elicited such a strong reaction from him weeks ago: black pencil skirt, white blouse buttoned to my neck, my tallest heels. My lips are red as blood.

"Before you left my office that day, I put you in your place. It aroused you, didn't it?"

"Yes."

"Mmm. Did you jack off when you got home, Kieran?"

He makes a small, rough noise. "Yes."

"Tell me what you were thinking about while you stroked yourself."

The muscles of his arms bunch, then relax. "I thought about bending you over that too-small chair you made me sit in. Pulling up that fucking skirt and shoving inside you. Wrapping my hand around your throat. Making you come no matter how badly you tried not to."

Arousal slicks my thighs at the visual. My hand falls to his neck. It's too wide for me to grip completely, but I apply pressure with my palm and a teasing threat with my nails.

"Do you know what I was thinking about that night? When I rubbed my clit until I came?"

He groans softly, eyes closing. "Tell me." My hand tightens on his throat. "Please."

"Since you asked nicely." I lean forward, my hair brushing over his shoulder and chest. Angling my mouth to his ear, I whisper, "I thought about bending *you* over. I thought about fucking *you*. And tonight, I'm going to do just that."

He jerks. I glance down at his lap and snap, "Don't come."

He sucks in a breath and releases it slowly. One by one, his muscles relax. I lick his earlobe. Squeeze his neck one more time, then release it.

"Good, Kieran. Very good. Before I fuck you, I'll give you something you want. When I step away, get up and lay on your back on the bed. Clasp your hands above your head."

Denying myself the pleasure of watching him move at my command, I walk to the door to retrieve the black case I gave him earlier. Behind me, I hear the friction of skin on soft sheets. It makes me smile as I unzip the case and retrieve what I need, but I wipe my expression as I turn and approach the bed.

I set the rope, lube, and silicone toy on the mattress beside him, then let my eyes roam over every beautiful inch displayed before me. His jutting cock. Heaving chest. Heels that dig into the mattress, thick thigh muscles clenching. Fingers that curl and relax over his head. Tight jaw. Dark, glittering eyes—almost angry as they flicker between me and the items. The dildo and lube are by far the hardest for him to accept.

My control shivers as the one submissive bone inside me —so newly awakened—balks at the notion of asking such a powerful man to submit. I want to tell him about the toy, that it's made specifically for male anatomy, the best product money can buy, and is perfect for beginners. That it will blow his mind.

But I don't. Instead, I take a deep breath. My headspace calms. Recenters. *You are in control. Reestablish trust. Bring him back to you.*

"Color?"

His jaw works for a few seconds. "Green."

"Hmm. Let's try that again." Pulling my skirt over my

knees, I climb onto the bed. Once I'm within reach, I grab his cock and squeeze. He jackknifes, gasping out my name.

"Tell me again what color you are, Kieran."

"Green! So fucking green."

I release him and shimmy my skirt over my waist. He groans when he sees my bare pussy. My touch, and now the sight of his ultimate reward, land him back in the present. He licks his lips, causing an answering pulse inside me.

"Eyes on my face."

He obeys. I tuck two fingers in my mouth and suck, then swirl my tongue around them. He pants, hands clenching but not moving. Lowering my fingers between my legs, I find my swollen clit, gasping a little at the electric contact. His eyes stay on my face—burning with desire, all resistance wiped away.

I tuck my fingers back into my mouth, tasting myself. As expected, the tease is too much for him. Animalistic need alights in his eyes. His arms start to lift, abs clenching as he begins to sit. I slap his stomach hard, then grab his balls. He grunts, freezing, eyes wide on my face. Dropping my middle finger to the skin behind his sack, I apply pressure.

He makes a soft sound of protest. "Fingernail," he rasps out.

"Excuse me?" I squeeze harder, push a little deeper. His chin lifts, eyes rolling up as the sting of pain blends with pleasure.

Air gusts from his lungs. "I take it back," he gasps out.

"Color?"

"Green."

"Good," I croon, releasing his balls. Grabbing the spool of rope, I crawl up his body. "I'm going to bind your arms now. If you touch me without permission or speak out of turn again, I'll wrap your cock, too."

He makes a choked noise, his eyes squeezing closed.

"Do you understand?"

"Yes."

The rope is bamboo, silky and soft but with reliable hold. Perfect for low-risk sensual play. I take my time wrapping his wrists and forearms, bending lower than necessary so my hair and breasts graze his face. Besides flaring nostrils and twitching lips, he stays perfectly still.

"I'm so proud of you," I say as I sit back on my heels. "You look so beautiful with my knots on you."

I unbutton my blouse, exposing my braless breasts, then lean forward again with my hands braced to either side of his head. Arching downward, I drag a peaked nipple across his lips. His brow furrows in agony.

"Suck," I demand. "No biting."

Wet heat surrounds my nipple. He sucks hard, his tongue swirling. A delicious current forms between my breast and pussy. I give it a few seconds, then offer him the other nipple.

"Again."

He complies eagerly—so eagerly that my head falls forward and the ache between my legs grows distracting.

"Stop."

He releases me. "Thank you," he whispers.

"You're welcome." Smiling, I trail a fingernail down his forehead, follow the proud peak of his nose, the indent beneath, and finally press against his full lower lip. "Are you ready for your first reward?"

His eyes drift over my flushed face. "God, yes."

I tap his lip and warn, "If you come, I'll punish you."

I don't give him a chance to reply, swinging my leg across him so I'm on my knees above his face. "Make it good, Kieran," I say as I lower myself to his mouth.

With a greedy moan, he devours my offering. Within seconds, I'm rocking against him, soaking his chin and whimpering as his tongue alternates between fucking me and lashing my clit. When he finds a rhythm that makes my legs shake, he doesn't deviate from it. Not until I have to grab the headboard so I don't fall over, not until I buck and cry out as searing waves of pleasure liquify my limbs. He flattens his tongue against my clit as I ride the orgasm to its trembling end.

As hard as it is, I drag myself off him, sinking onto my heels next to his shoulder. His eyes follow me, roaming my exposed breasts, my glistening pussy beneath the skirt bunched around my waist.

"Are you pleased, Talia?"

I consider punishment, then decide to give him a pass—I feel too good at the moment. "Yes. Are you?"

He licks his wet lips. "Very."

Our gazes connect and hold. I can't help the smile that

curves over my face. His eyes crinkle, a precursor to the main event: crooked grin.

I love you.

I swallow the words with effort. His eyes soften like he heard them anyway, and our smiles slowly fade. I breathe through the unfamiliar sensation in my chest, the deep burn of an intimacy I've never felt before when dominating someone.

"Mo ghrá," he whispers.

Snapping out of it, I twist his nipple. He grimaces, then laughs shortly.

"Sorry, sorry."

I soothe the reddened skin with my fingertip, then trail my hands down his ridged stomach to his pelvis. Keeping my eyes on his face, I give his pubic hair a tug—he winces—then wrap my fingers around him. He shudders in relief. I stroke him up and down, my grip loose. When my thumb grazes sensitive nerves, his hips come off the bed.

"You've been very patient," I murmur. "Was it hard not to come with my delicious cunt on your face?"

He swells even more in my hand, a vein throbbing against my palm. Tortured eyes meet mine. "You have no idea."

I squeeze him once, then back off the bed and stand. He groans in protest, the sound cutting off abruptly as I step out of my shoes and shuck off my clothes.

"Open your legs for me. Wider. One knee up, heel on the bed. Yes, like that."

When I pick up the toy and lube, his brows draw

together again. Another struggle commences. His breathing becomes choppy, anxiety tightening the skin around his eyes. I crawl to him, settling between his legs and stroking his warm, tense thighs.

Then I lean up and grab his jaw. "Look at me, Kieran."

Once I have his gaze, I hold it mercilessly, letting him see and feel my control. My calm. My desire that equals his. My absolute certainty that he will enjoy what I'm about to do to him.

His agitation fades. Arousal surges. Desperation peaks.

He's ready.

"Do you trust me?"

His eyes bore into mine. "With my heart and life."

My mouth falls open; I take a steadying breath so my voice doesn't waver. "Thank you. I promise I won't abuse that trust."

Resuming my position between his legs, I uncap the small bottle of lube and pour a generous pool into my hand, then draw the front half of the dildo across my palm until it's completely coated. With a push of my thumb, it begins to vibrate. I lower it to his cock, running it along the underside of his shaft, then lightly across his balls.

He groans, eyes closing. A stream of Irish words hisses through his teeth. I don't admonish him, too riveted by the involuntary jerks of his hips. When his lower abdomen tenses, I back off until he relaxes again. I repeat the process until he's glistening with sweat, in that lovely space between agony and ecstasy. Only then do I lift his tight, heavy sack and run my thickly lubed fingers down to his asshole.

Triumph fills me as his bent knee instantly widens, his hips lifting to give me more access. I massage the tight ring of muscle with the pads of my fingers, my other hand stroking his shaft, squeezing every time my finger pressure increases. All the while, I watch his face carefully for signs of true discomfort. But his eyes, open now and on my face, reflect only trust. Commitment. Adoration and desperation.

His surrender is the most beautiful gift I've ever received.

"Say the magic word," I whisper.

He licks his lips. "Please, my love."

A tornado of heat overtakes my lungs, my heart. "Your wish is my command."

I replace my fingers with the toy, pushing vibration first to the space behind his balls, then to his asshole. There's so much lube already there, and he's so willing and ready, that a gentle push sinks the toy inside him up to the flared middle. He cries out in rapture. Tightening my grip on the base, I draw the toy out, then slide it back in, slowly increasing the rhythm.

More Irish fills the air—a raw appeal that ends with, "Talia! *Please.*"

I don't make him wait. Seating the toy inside him so that its vibration is centered on his prostate, I wrap my other hand around his engorged cock.

"I give you permission to come," I say right before

covering him with my mouth. I suck hard and fast, my throat relaxed for his erratic thrusts.

When he stiffens with a strangled shout, I turn off the toy and slip it out, then devote myself to his orgasm. His cock jumps against my tongue, pulsing and throbbing. I drink him down to the very last twitch and finally release him with a kiss.

Kieran's legs sprawl listlessly, his bound forearms tucked against his face, his stomach flexing as he gasps for air. I crawl up the bed and swiftly untie my knots, unwinding the rope and tossing it off the bed. I massage the reddened skin, then stroke his torso and arms with firm pressure until his breathing slows and evens out. His arms eventually relax and fall to his sides. His gaze is unfocused, his expression tellingly blank.

I stretch out beside him, throwing a leg over his hips and tugging him toward me. He rolls, his arms snaking around me, his head tucked against my chest.

It starts slow—a hitch in his breath, a twitch of muscles. I hold him tightly, wrapping as much of myself around him as I can.

"It's okay," I whisper, stroking his hair, his back. "I'm here. You're safe. Thank you for trusting me. I won't leave you, Kieran. You're not alone. I'm here."

I whisper comfort through his first silent sob, his first hot tear, and through the tsunami that follows. I hold him until the storm fades. Until he falls asleep and until he wakes, stretching in my arms. Even then, it's hard for me to let go.

So hard, in fact, that he ends up having to carry me into the bathroom.

Setting me on my feet, he keeps a strong arm around my waist as he turns on the water in the giant soaker tub.

"I'm sorry," I say helplessly, blinking through sudden, tearful exhaustion. "I should be taking care of you right now."

He gazes down at me with a soft smile and peaceful eyes. "You gave me everything I needed and more, mo ghrá. We do this together—we take care of each other. Okay?"

My heartbeat skips. "Okay."

When the water reaches the halfway point, he guides me into the bath and settles behind me. His arms encircle my waist, heavy and stabilizing. My head drops to his shoulder, a sigh leaving me as his lips trail down my neck.

"How do you feel?" I ask at length.

"Amazing. That orgasm suffocated half of my brain cells, though. I'll have to learn to live with only moderate intelligence."

I laugh. "You poor man."

He smiles against my shoulder. "Worth it."

"I'm glad." I rub my foot over his calf. "I've never heard you speak in full-on Irish like that. Are you actually fluent?"

He nods. "There aren't many opportunities to use it anymore, sadly. The language isn't dead, but it's definitely on life support."

"That's tragic. Even if it sounds like gibberish, it's lovely to listen to."

"Tá grá agam duit, Talia."

I shift so I can look at him. "What does that mean?" When he only smiles at me, I scowl. "At least tell me what you said tonight."

His low laugh vibrates my back. "I honestly don't recall. Probably something along the lines of, 'my brain cells are dying and I don't care,' or possibly, 'I've discovered Heaven on Earth is being fucked in the ass by a goddess.'"

I laugh, unreasonably happy even if he's lying. "Did you teach yourself the language?"

He shakes his head. "My gran did—my dad's mother. She lived with us until she passed when I was fourteen. Taught me Gaeilge alongside English. Alistair didn't take to it like I did, and my parents didn't speak it, so it became our special bond." He smiles softly. "She was a strange, wonderful woman. People called her a witch behind her back because she had a habit of prophesying, usually loudly and without invitation. Things like pregnancies, deaths, divorces, and the like. Didn't win her any friends, that's for sure."

I smile. "Was she ever right?"

He grins, but it fades fast. "Pretty often, actually. She even predicted her own death. The day it happened, I was home sick with a fever. She told me what was coming and said she was sorry I'd have to be the one to find her and tell my parents. I didn't believe her, of course, but knew better than to argue when she had that gleam in her eye. She brought me a cup of tea and sang to me until I fell asleep. When I woke up, I found her in her rocker." He clears his throat. "It was a stroke. Took her at exactly two o'clock, just like she said it would."

Goose bumps prickle my skin. "I'm sorry, Kieran. That must have been so hard."

He strokes my jaw. "It's all right, mo ghrá. She was buried not far from our old flat back in Galway. I spent a lot of time at her grave growing up, just talking to her. And I still visit. It's a lovely spot near the sea. Most of the graves are framed with stone and gravel, but she wanted grass to grow above her so we could sit close. Maybe I'll take you there one day."

My vision sparkles. I face forward quickly as adrenaline sends sizzling rivers into my limbs. Memory assaults me—my stumbling journey through the graveyard, all the gravel-boxed graves, then the beckoning patch of soft grass. I don't remember the name on the headstone, just the rise of wings from the sturdy base and a feeling of comfort.

His grandmother's grave.

Belatedly, I mumble, "That would be nice."

He nuzzles his nose into the back of my head. "I think Gran's magic lingers. One time—this was ages ago, right before I left for Oxford—I even found a drunk American girl nearly passed out on her grave. I had the weirdest feeling that Gran brought her there for a reason. We had the most interesting conversation. I've been thinking about it a lot lately."

My muscles spasm, sending water sloshing against the sides of the tub.

He remembers.

"Cold?" he asks, scooping hot water over my chest and arms.

"A little," I say weakly, even though I'm burning from the inside out. "What, uh—what was so interesting about the conversation?"

"Every second of it, but especially something she said when we parted. I'd told her that equals didn't kneel. She said they did, but only to each other." He pauses, voice softening. "I wish I could tell her she was right, but I never saw her again. Wherever she is, I hope she's found what I have. An equal for whom kneeling is the greatest privilege."

CHAPTER 29

TALIA

After an early breakfast Saturday, Gabe drives me home for a few hours so Kieran and Leo can have privacy for their appointment. I intend to spend the time working on the book I've almost convinced myself to write. Instead, I end up staring at the wall opposite my desk, replaying last night over and over in my mind.

I almost told Kieran the truth. Almost. My mouth was open, the words seconds from spilling, when his hand lowered beneath the water to cup me possessively between the legs. The next few hours were a blur of skin and sweat and finally sleep after we blew out all the candles and dragged his comforter and pillows from the closet.

Now that I know he remembers me, I absolutely have to tell him I was the girl he met in the graveyard. God willing, he won't feel betrayed or manipulated.

On our drive back to the coast, I'm still mulling on the best way to broach the subject when Gabe's voice draws me from my thoughts.

"How are you adjusting to everything, Doc?"

I meet his concerned gaze in the rearview. Realizing he's attributing my subdued mood to his presence and that of the two men in the car behind us, I smile in reassurance. "Talia, please. And I'm fine, Gabe. Honestly. Sorry I'm bad company at the moment."

He shakes his head. "Not at all. Never feel obligated to fill the silence with me. Just want you to know I'm here if you have any questions or concerns."

I shift in my seat. "Now that you mention it, I do have one concern—bringing all three of you to Crossroads tonight."

"What are you worried about?"

To my relief, he doesn't sound disapproving, only curious.

"It's not that I don't trust Sven's judgment—Bo and Elian seem great, and I trust you implicitly. But I'm protective of the club and its members. Things can get very vulnerable and emotional in the Q&A. It doesn't feel right to bring in outsiders. No offense."

"None taken."

Encouraged by his response, I add, "I understand your job is my safety, but I really don't think all of you need to be there. Crossroads has excellent security. All members are background checked and membership is reviewed monthly.

There's electronic surveillance, a security team, and thorough door checks. You can't even bring a pencil inside." I grimace. "Plus, I can almost guarantee people will think you guys are undercover cops."

Gabe nods, expression thoughtful as his gaze flickers between me and the road. "Would you be okay with just me? Believe it or not, I'm pretty good at blending in. Bo and Elian can stay with the car."

I chew my lip, caught between relief at the prospect of him staying close and discomfort over what the relief means —that on some level, I'm scared for my safety. Even in Crossroads.

"Yes, I'd be okay with that." I pause. "I'll call the club and let them know."

"Don't worry about that," he says readily. "If I know Sven, he's already ten steps ahead of this conversation. The man plans for variables the rest of us can't even imagine."

I smirk, relaxing in my seat. "Must be why he and Kieran get along so well."

Gabe laughs. "You should see them play chess. It's terrifying."

I join him in laughter, and a few minutes later, we're pulling through the gate and up Kieran's driveway. My heart swells. As soon as the car stops, I grab my purse, eager to see him. Almost giddy.

"Wait a second, Talia."

Gabe's voice is its usual friendly tenor, but his body language has shifted from relaxed to alert. I still, following his gaze toward a white Tesla. It's not Leo's car; he's long gone, anyway.

Gabe types on his phone. A few seconds later, he puts the car in park and turns it off. "Okay, we're good to head inside," he says, but his brow is furrowed slightly as he exits the car and veers around to my side. Bo and Elian park and join us.

"Who's here?" I ask Gabe softly as he leads the way to the front door.

He glances back at me, still frowning. "Oliver McCann, Lumitech's Chief Information Officer." He looks over my shoulder, looping in Bo and Elian. "Sven says the conversation isn't a pleasant one. We'll take Talia straight to Kieran's bedroom."

I barely notice the fact I'm not a part of that decision. My thoughts have snagged on the name and the odd interaction I had with Oliver at Rhubarb last week.

Gabe opens the front door and an angry voice meets our ears mid-tirade.

"—without even speaking to us! Do you have any idea how this will make us look? Like fucking idiots!"

Kieran's answer is low and measured, the tone more icy than I've ever heard it. "Consider it a courtesy I told you at all, Oliver."

I glimpse the men in the living room. Kieran sits on one of the couches, his arms spread and head cocked. His profile shows me an expression to match his voice. Even though

Oliver is standing, almost looming over him, there's no question who's in charge.

Sven stands by the windows. I catch his gaze for an instant before I'm ushered down the hallway to Kieran's bedroom. Bo and Elian take up positions outside the door. Gabe pauses on the threshold.

"You good here?" he asks.

I nod. "Before you go—quick question. Did Kieran tell his executive team he was going to the Maldives instead of Ireland?"

Gabe frowns. "No. They know he goes back to Ireland every couple of months. Why?"

I tell him about seeing Oliver last week and what he said. By the time I'm finished, Gabe's expression is so neutral I know it's forced.

"Why would he say that? Was he trying to see if I'd contradict him? Reveal the real reason Kieran was in Ireland?"

"I don't know, but thank you for telling me. I'll share it with Sven. Fair warning, he might have some follow-up questions."

My heart skips a beat. "Does that mean Oliver's a suspect?"

Gabe steps quickly inside the room and closes the door. "Excluding Alistair, yes—all Lumitech execs are under investigation at this point."

"Makes sense," I muse. "The people closest to Kieran would have the most access to him."

Gabe opens his mouth, hesitates, and finally says, "So far there's no evidence implicating Oliver or anyone else, but we're on high alert."

I think about the overheard conversation. "He told them about the trials."

He nods. "Early this morning."

I chew my lip. "I don't like him—Oliver. He makes my skin crawl."

Gabe gives me a dry smile of agreement. "None of us like him, but Kieran's known him far longer than we have."

I nod distractedly. "For Kieran's sake, I hope it isn't him."

"I agree."

The door opens behind Gabe. My thoughts evaporate as Kieran strides toward me, his troubled expression melting into one of relief. I barely notice Gabe's retreat or the door closing because I'm enveloped in a crushing embrace.

"I missed you," he mumbles against my neck.

My heart expands like a balloon, pushing against the confines of my ribs. "I missed you, too." Leaning back, I frame his face with my hands. "Are you okay?"

Stormy blue eyes roam my face. "I am now."

"How was therapy?"

"Good."

"Do you—"

His lips swallow my words, the kiss swiftly turning ravenous. Hands flow down my back to my ass, kneading me through my jeans. All my thoughts and worries flee.

"Are you sore?" he asks between kisses.

I pull up his shirt, palming his warm skin. "Does it matter to you? Because it doesn't matter to me."

His answer is a groan.

Our clothes hit the floor and we fall onto the bed in a tangle of limbs. Kieran rolls us and rises to his forearms. My legs frame his hips. I arch into him, eager and mindless, before realizing he's stopped moving. Relaxing back to see his face, my breath catches. Sunlight from the windows turns his eyes to blue flame, and he stares down at me like... like...

"Tá mé i ngrá leat," he murmurs. "I'm in love with you. Tá grá agam duit—I love you. Mo ghrá—my love. You're everything to me."

My vision blurs until I blink, forcing tears from the corners of my eyes.

"I love you, too," I whisper.

No words I've spoken in my entire life have been truer, and from the softening of his beautiful lips, he knows it. Eyes holding mine, he slowly fills me. My body—my heart—my every breath becomes entangled with his.

There's no dirty talk. None of our usual teasing or the power struggles we both enjoy. No sounds but our quiet gasps and the slow slide of skin against skin. We don't even kiss. We make love to each other without breaking eye contact once, as close as we can be, our bodies the sand and waves on the beach below—irreversibly mingled, locked together forever by nature's design.

We shatter as one, trembling in the humming silence. As

our heartbeats slow, he kisses me at last and tells me again that he loves me. And I say it back three times. Once for the girl I was. Once for the woman I am. And once for my monster, free now, purring and content because all she wanted was a dream.

And now she has it.

CHAPTER 30

TALIA

We laze in bed for a while, cuddling and trading inconsequential details about ourselves. Favorite places we've visited, bucket-list vacations, favorite foods, books, movies, and music. I consider telling him a dozen times who I am, but I chicken out. The conversation ends when Kieran gives me a mischievous smile and says, "Now that our first date is out of the way..." then promptly buries his face between my legs.

Alistair and Gail come over for lunch. We eat on the patio, chatting and relaxing. I relish observing Kieran and his brother in close proximity. Despite being older, Alistair exudes a more youthful energy, as quick to smile as he is to frown. Kieran is more serious and introspective. Side by side, it's easy to envision how dynamic they are as business partners, and it's no wonder Lumitech rocketed to global renown in less than ten years.

There's a great deal of laughter, too, as the men regale Gail and me with stories of their childhood. Misadventures. First, disastrous efforts at wooing the opposite sex. They talk about their parents and grandmother, too, and though melancholy floats on the breeze, there's humor and love. So much love.

When we say goodbye, Gail gives me a hug and says, "I knew you'd be perfect for him."

To my surprise, Alistair also embraces me. He's shorter than Kieran, stockier, but there's a familiarity when he squeezes the air from my lungs that makes me tear up. He hugs me like I'm already family.

"Thank you, Talia," he says when he releases me, his blue eyes glassy as they stare into mine. "Thank you for bringing him back."

Kieran grins at my obvious discomfort and stage-whispers, "You're welcome."

"You're welcome," I echo with a wince that makes everyone laugh.

Once they're gone, Kieran takes me to the bluff and down steep cement steps to the empty beach. Dylan follows at a distance. We leave our shoes on the sand and walk barefoot along the water, holding hands and dodging fingers of foam as they rush toward us.

When we reach the end of the small cove and turn around, Kieran stops me with a tug on my hand. Cool fingers on my face, eyes serious on mine, he asks, "Any reservations lurking in that beautiful mind? About this? Us?"

His eyes match the sea to my right, bright blue-gray. My favorite color. I hesitate, then shake my head. "No."

He draws me closer, brow furrowing. "But?"

"I don't have reservations," I assure him. "I just have no reference points for this. What I'm feeling. It's overwhelming." With a breath for courage, I unearth one of my dark treasures and offer it to him. "I've never been in love before."

How could I fall in love with someone else when I've always loved you?

He kisses me, slow and soft, lips grazing and sipping. I melt into his chest, no longer feeling the cold breeze. When I'm buzzing and warm, he hugs me close.

"Your heart is my heart, Talia. I'll never break it. I know you're scared—so am I. But I think this kind of love is supposed to be a little frightening."

I look up at him. "What kind of love?"

He strokes my cheek. "Have you ever read Rilke?"

I nod, and he smiles softly.

"My mam was a big fan. One of the last gifts she gave me was a book of his correspondence with a Viennese concert pianist."

"Magda von Hattingberg," I supply.

His smile grows. "Just so. I'm no poet, so I'll give you his words instead. *'To be loved means to be consumed. To love is to give light with inexhaustible oil. To be loved is to pass away, to love is to endure.'* That's the kind of love this is—the kind that reshapes and remakes us. I've never seen anything as clearly as I see you. All your shadows and beautiful light. I'm your humble supplicant, your faithful worshiper, and I will forever kneel to you and only you. Lean in with me, mo ghrá. Together, we won't fall."

I blink fast against tears. "Liar. You *are* a poet."

He chuckles and draws me back into his arms. "Only for you."

My heart starts pounding. *This is it.*

"Kieran, there's something I've been meaning to—"

"Kier!" Dylan's voice floats across the beach. "Phone call from Limerick!"

He releases me with a huff of annoyance. "I'm sorry. It's the lab. Tell me later?"

I nod.

I FIND the book Kieran referenced, *Rilke and Benvenuta: An Intimate Correspondence,* on a shelf in his bedroom and curl up on his bed. I fall asleep; he wakes me up by pulling my shirt over my head. We make love and nap until the sun begins to set, then have dinner courtesy of his chef, a cheery, rail-thin man who grills the most incredible salmon I've ever tasted.

Before long, it's time for me to get ready for my lecture at Crossroads. Kieran lounges in a chair by the fireplace as I apply my makeup and dress, his mood growing progressively darker the closer I get to leaving. He doesn't ask me to stay. A good thing because I'm not confident I'd be able to deny him.

I didn't lie to him—I've never known emotional intensity like this and it's as frightening as it is thrilling. Being close to him is starting to feel as necessary as breathing. Like inhaling him is the first oxygen my heart has ever had and without him, I'll suffocate.

At the front door, he kisses me with a quiet desperation, then hugs me tightly. "I hope the event goes well," he murmurs. "I'll be waiting up. I love you."

I wonder if I'll ever get used to hearing him say those words. Somehow, I doubt it.

I fill my lungs—my very self—with him. "I love you, too. I'll be back soon."

Every step away from him is physically painful. Gabe escorts me to the car and joins me in the back seat. Bo and Elian greet me with nods and smiles, which I return distractedly. As the car pulls down the drive, I look back to see Kieran one more time. He's standing where I left him, arms crossed, expression withdrawn. Sven stands beside him.

A tree obstructs my view of them, and I sigh as I face forward.

AFTER THE Q&A, I ride the wave of energy and mingle with the crowd, but within twenty minutes, my urge to see Kieran overwhelms my ability to stay focused on conversations. I catch Gabe's eye and nod; he nods back and quickly excuses himself from a woman in a mesh top that displays multiple piercings in each nipple. He stays in my periphery as I make my way across the club, saying goodbye to Nate, Charlie, and several others in the process.

We slip into the employee hallway. I retrieve my purse from Charlie's office, then rejoin Gabe and wait for him to finish a text.

When he looks up, I ask, "So? What did Mistress Marian offer you?"

A telling blush stains his cheeks as he shakes his head slowly. "I'd really, really rather not say."

Resisting the urge to smile, I ask lightly, "I take it BDSM isn't for you?"

He shudders. "Affirmative."

I grin. "I'll spread the word that you're off-limits, if you'd like."

"Please. Thank you." The sheer relief in his voice makes me laugh.

I'm still smiling as he opens the back door and cool air flows around us. Gabe steps outside first, his gaze scanning the shadowed employee and VIP parking lot. Headlights flash halfway down the row of cars, and an engine starts.

He makes an irritated noise. "I texted—they should be pulling up by now."

I step from carpet to pavement, from light to darkness. The door swings closed behind me. "Reception is spotty in the hallway. It's okay, though. The air feels nice."

Gabe takes a step forward and freezes. I follow his gaze and see two figures walking into the parking lot from the street. Fifteen feet away and closing fast. They're wearing balaclavas, only their eyes and mouths visible. Each of them holds something dark and long in their right hands.

Guns.

My lungs atrophy; I can't draw a breath.

"Back inside," Gabe snaps. "Now."

I spin, lunging for the keypad. My fingers shake so hard I get the code wrong. Gabe's spine presses to my back.

"Focus, Talia. You can do it."

I punch my code in again and the light turns green. With a sob of relief, I grab the handle. As I pull the steel door open, Gabe grunts and jerks backward, the impact of his body knocking my head against the door and slamming it closed. I'm dragged downward by his weight, barely managing to turn and catch him as he collapses.

A rough voice growls, "You could have hit her, asshole!"

Gabe blinks up at me, expression twisted in pain. "Run."

Spectral cold consumes me. My hand lifts from his chest. In the orange glow of Crossroad's security light, my palm looks black.

I glance up to see Bo and Elian sprinting toward us across the parking lot. Their mouths are open and moving—they're yelling at me, but I can't hear them. My head is a maelstrom of white noise. There are small flashes around them and they dive behind cars. My gaze swings to the right, finding one of the masked men pointing a gun in their direction. As I watch, his head snaps backward, a geyser of dark matter exploding from the back. He drops like a puppet with severed strings.

A powerful force wrenches me away from Gabe and drags me to my feet. My scream is choked off by an arm wrapping around my neck and squeezing. Something hard knocks into my temple. My ears ring. Ten feet away, Bo and Elian skid to a stop.

"Drop them," snarls the man behind me.

Their guns clatter to the asphalt, empty hands lifting.

"Aren't they good listeners?" The voice in my ear drips with venom. "Tell them, Mistress. Tell them how proud you are."

In a flash of sickening comprehension, I know exactly who's holding me. The same man whose article set flames to my career. The same man who was photographed stalking my house. But for the first time, my memory fails me. I can't fucking remember his name.

"Please, don't do this."

The gun knocks against my head hard enough for me to see stars. "Shut your fucking mouth."

He begins shuffling us sideways, away from the door and toward the street. My vision dims as I gasp for air. I can't remember a thing from the self-defense classes I took in college. All I can see is Gabe's unmoving body. All I can think is that he wasn't armed or wearing Kevlar, that he was defenseless because of me. All I can feel is the crushing pressure on my throat and cool metal prodding my cheek.

"Hey, man, why don't you let her go?" asks Bo loudly. "There are cameras all over this place. The club's security will be here any second, and the cops are on their way. Get out of here while you still can."

The man dragging me laughs. He aims his gun at them and fires, the repeated concussion scorching my ears despite the attached silencer. Elian dives out of sight. Bo lunges for his dropped gun, then shouts and falls, clutching his leg.

The pressure on my throat lessens. In a flash, I remember the man's name.

I scream it as loud as I can.

The gun cracks against my temple and darkness swallows me whole.

CHAPTER 31

KIERAN

Sven's footsteps approach me from behind. I don't turn my gaze from the darkness—the infinite black of the night-shrouded Pacific. On the beach below, Talia's and my footsteps have been long washed away.

"Gabe is headed into surgery. Outlook is good."

Somewhere inside me there's a flicker of relief, but everything else is numb and cold. I'm pinned beneath miles of ice.

"Tom's team has wrapped up at Crossroads. He should be here any minute. Security footage is in line with Bo's and Elian's accounts. Talia was moved into an alley without surveillance, but someone's reviewing cameras in the area to see if they can narrow down the car she left in."

"She didn't leave," I rasp.

He takes a step closer. "What?"

I turn on my heel and snarl, "She didn't *leave*, Sven. She was *abducted*."

He nods, dark eyes full of compassion. "You're right, Kier. That's what I meant. But we're going to find her, okay? Talia did us a huge favor yelling the bastard's name. Tom has people tearing apart Bradley Mills's life right now. His physical description also matches the man we saw stalking her house."

A sharp pain zigzags through my chest. Bradley Mills is who did the anonymous interview and outed Talia as a dominatrix. If he did take her—and her kidnapping isn't directly related to me—then it's still my fault. I was the one who shattered *his* anonymity. My lawyers showed up at his home last week to threaten a defamation lawsuit. Apparently, his wife was there. I probably ruined his marriage. Sent him off the edge.

"This isn't your fault," Sven says.

"Appreciate the effort, but any way you slice it, I'm holding the knife."

"What do you need right now?" he asks softly.

A volcano of rage erupts inside me, abolishing the iceberg on my chest. "I need answers!" I roar. "Where was Crossroads's security team? Who the fuck is the dead man? *And where the fuck is Talia?*"

Someone clears their throat behind us. Sven and I swivel to face Tom Bronson, head of Bronson Investigations. Mid-fifties, with short, steel-gray hair and eyes so dark they look black, he resembles a blade—slim, sharp, and lethal. Six more men are inside the house behind him, four of them setting up laptops on my dining table.

Tom nods in greeting. "The abduction took less than a minute. Crossroads's security arrived seven seconds too late, but as they don't carry guns, I'm not convinced they could have prevented our current situation. They also saved your man's life and likely saved your other man's leg."

"And the dead man?" asks Sven.

"Harvey Elrod. Rap sheet a mile long. Cell records have him communicating with a blocked number via text message. He was hired two days ago to abduct Dr. Stirling and deliver her to an address—"

"Address?" I snap, as Sven demands, "You have a location?"

Tom shakes his head. "No. The address was to be conveyed after a successful retrieval. We assume it was given to Mills. Unlike Elrod, he seems to have been smart enough to trade his personal cell for a burner. That's assuming he's not the person who hired Elrod."

His utterly emotionless voice makes me want to tear him apart with my bare hands. Sven's fingers curl around my shoulder and clench.

Tom's eyes narrow on me. "I'm not going to sugarcoat things, Mr. Hayes. At this point, they're in the wind. No data yet on the getaway vehicle. We'll keep digging into Mills —his cell records, emails, movements over the last week. We're also looking at footage from Dr. Stirling's home to possibly match him to a different car. I hate to say it, but right now the best-case scenario—"

My harsh bark of laughter cuts him off. "The best-case

scenario is that this *is* about me and we'll get a blackmail call."

Tom nods.

I drag my fingers through my hair, squeezing until I feel the pain at the roots. The thought of Talia in that man's hands is too much. *My fault. My fault.* Anxiety curls fists around my lungs, cutting off my air. My vision sparkles.

Sven says abruptly, "Talia doesn't like Oliver."

Shock pulls me back from a full-blown panic attack. "What?"

"Gabe told me Oliver cornered her when she was at breakfast with a friend last weekend. Basically propositioned her. He also said something about you being in the Maldives, possibly a sloppy attempt to find out if she knew why you were really in Ireland. Which means he's known or suspected that you don't go just to visit family." He pauses. "Talia also said he makes her skin crawl."

"The fuck?" I whisper.

"This is Oliver McCann we're talking about?" asks Tom.

"Yes," Sven answers, still looking at me. "He's the only one who reacted badly to the news of the trials."

My ears hum as my mind begins to race, burning off the fogginess of panic and dread. I grab Sven by the front of his shirt. "It's him. That motherfucker. Give me my car keys."

"Not happening," he rumbles.

Tom strides into the house, barking orders to his men. "Get me the current location of Oliver McCann. All known numbers, addresses, and vehicles. *Now.*"

There's a flurry of activity around the dining table.

"Kier!" someone shouts.

Alistair jogs toward me, expression distraught. Gail hurries behind him, pale-faced and trailed by Dylan and two other protection officers.

My brother reaches me and grabs my shoulders. "What can I do?"

"Give me your car keys."

Alistair's eyes widen. He glances at Sven. "Did I hear Oliver's name in there?" Sven nods and my brother's gaze snaps back to me. "Oliver?"

"He makes Talia's skin crawl," is all I can think to say. And really, it's the only thing that matters. The only thing that makes sense. Because *she* makes sense.

And I'll go to war on her word alone.

"I understand people instinctively. I see their layers, fault lines, and strengths. All the hidden treasures of the psyche. My first impressions are rarely wrong."

There's a storm gaining force and intent inside me. A dark vortex of screaming winds and freezing clarity. Slowly, so slowly—otherwise I'll lose control—I turn out of Alistair's hold. One step brings me face-to-face with Sven.

"I love you like a brother."

"Don't," he whispers.

"You're fired." I hold out my hand. "Car keys. Now."

He grabs my shoulders much as Alistair did, but his grip

is punishing. "Think for a second, Kier. You don't know where he has her. If you do find them, you have no idea what you're walking into."

From the open sliding door, Tom Bronson says crisply, "We hacked security feeds at McCann's primary residence. Thirty-eight minutes ago, a sedan with unregistered plates arrived through the service gate. Driver has been ID'd as Bradley Mills. A woman was taken from the trunk into the house by Mills and McCann. She was conscious and struggling." He looks at Sven. "Am I calling this in or are we keeping it in-house?"

"Talia is family," he answers. "We're handling this ourselves."

"Amen," murmurs Dylan.

The storm inside me reaches critical levels. Before I can fracture into a million pieces, Sven grabs me by the back of the neck. "I want you wired and in a vest. You do what I say, go where I say, and you don't fucking deviate. Clear?"

Relief threatens to melt my kneecaps. "Yes. Clear."

Tom steps forward. "Please tell me you're not considering taking your Principal into a high risk—"

"I want five of your guys," Sven interrupts him, his voice steel. "And the arsenal I know is in that van outside."

Tom's thin lips curve. "Is there room for one more on the extraction team?"

Sven nods. "Always."

As Tom retreats into the house, Dylan touches my arm. "Come on. I'll get you suited up."

My brother's wavering voice halts me halfway across the deck.

"Kier? Do you have to go?"

I meet his worried gaze and resist the urge to hug him, afraid I'll collapse in his arms. My voice cracks as I say, "I love her. I won't lose her. I can't."

He watches me a long moment, then nods. "Bring her home, then, yeah?"

"Yeah."

My heart whispers the rest: *If she isn't coming home, neither am I.*

CHAPTER 32

TALIA

My head throbs in time with my heartbeat, my jaw aches from the press of a gag, and my left hip radiates sharp pulses of pain—either from falling to asphalt beneath Gabe's weight or slamming against the walls of a car trunk while unconscious.

The physical discomfort is manageable. The oily fear in my mind is harder to control.

I'm not blindfolded. I know who my kidnappers are— Bradley Mills and Oliver McCann. And I know where we are thanks to my unwilling tour of the downstairs of the house, including a hallway with portraits of Oliver and his wife.

They have no intention of keeping me alive.

Bradley and Oliver argue in low tones on the other side of a massive, ostentatious kitchen—all dark wood, granite, high coffered ceilings, and gilded wallpaper. They've been at it off and on since dragging me kicking and screaming to a chair and tying my wrists behind my back.

Keeping my gaze trained on them, I will them to continue arguing. The longer they don't pay attention to me, the closer I get to freeing my hands. The rope is a cheap, hardware-store variety. Horrible for bondage, it produces bulky knots and abrades the skin. The knots themselves are amateur and would normally be a breeze for me, but my hands are shaking.

Oliver's voice lifts, thick with irritation. "For the last time, I didn't know there'd be three of them."

He looks nothing like the man I've met twice before—his face is pasty and sweaty, his eyes bloodshot with abnormally constricted pupils. I don't know what drugs he's taken, but I hope they give him a heart attack.

"Get the fuck over it," he continues. "You survived and you'll get your payday. We both will."

I freeze as Bradley's gaze shifts to me. Staring into his brown eyes, I see nothing of the man who came to me years ago, equally desperate for and ashamed of his desire for a woman to dominate him. I saw him for three months, until the day he showed up with flowers and a declaration of love.

Charlie warned me early on about the risk of clients developing emotional attachments. The newer they were to kink, the more vigilant we needed to be. I was always careful, maintaining emotional distance while committed to the role I played. My aftercare routines rarely included touching, revolving instead around serving them comfort foods and drinks, heated blankets, and the like.

In my seven years as a working dominatrix, Bradley was one of only three to develop feelings for me, and he's the only one who slipped through the cracks. No warning signs, no red flags. He was perfectly polite, respectful, and never breached the boundaries I set.

As irritated with myself as I'd been for missing the cues of his infatuation, I'd let none of my emotion show as I'd gently reiterated that my actions in our sessions and afterward didn't mean I harbored feelings for him. I then referred him to a kink-friendly therapist. He was disappointed and hurt, which was natural, but he'd seemed accepting. We never spoke again, and I never thought of him again until I read the article in which he basically accused me of brainwashing him.

"I want something else, too," he says.

There's no mistaking the innuendo. Rage smothers my guilt, dissolving the fog of fear from my mind. I hold his stare, unblinking.

Fuck you, I tell him silently. *I'm the bigger predator here. Even if you hurt me, I will never submit.*

His gaze drops, then snaps back to me. Fury flushes his cheeks.

"Fine, whatever," Oliver says, mopping his damp forehead with his forearm. "After I get the confirmation I need, she's all yours."

Ice wraps around my spine. I'm glad Bradley's attention is back on Oliver, otherwise he'd see how terrified those words made me. I'm under no illusions I can stop him from hurting me by glaring at him.

My fingers scramble to loosen the last knots.

"Then quit wasting time and make the call," Bradley snarls.

Oliver gets even redder. "You work for me, asshole."

"We both know that's not true."

Oliver's eyes dart to me before he hisses through clenched teeth, "Shut the fuck up."

Doors suddenly unlock and open in my mind, connecting disjointed observations. Their combativeness. Bradley's attitude; Oliver's anxiety and overall lack of composure. The comment about both of them getting their payday.

Someone else is pulling the strings.

My heart dances from side to side, amplifying the pounding in my temples. Lowering my head, I attempt to slow my breathing.

"Okay. Here we go."

I glance up to see Oliver tap the screen of a cell phone. Ringing fills the kitchen. Three trills later, the line connects. Voice distorted by an app, he asks, "Are you prepared to take me seriously now?"

"Yes," answers Kieran. "I'll give you whatever you want if she's released unharmed."

A whimper leaks around my gag.

"Good," says Oliver. "You have one hour to confirm that the lab in Limerick, including all research and prototypes, has been destroyed."

I expect Kieran to say that's impossible—because surely it is—but instead he says, "Done. I want proof Talia's okay. Let me hear her voice."

Oliver nods at Bradley, who pulls the gun from his belt and stalks toward me. His fingers dig cruelly at the corner of my mouth, pulling the gag off my tongue and yanking it down over my chin. He smiles at my wince of pain, his eyes promising more. The muzzle of the gun taps against my temple.

Oliver approaches and angles the phone toward my face.

"Kieran," I croak. "I'm sorry."

"None of that now, mo ghrá," he says, his low, tender tone bringing tears to my eyes. "Are you all right?"

The gun presses harder to my head, squashing a brief impulse to blurt out Oliver's name. My own mortality overwhelms me. Grief suffocates me, clogging my throat with tears.

"This isn't your fault, Kieran. Remember that, please—" Bradley stuffs the gag back in my mouth.

"Talia? Talia!"

I scream around the gag as Oliver walks away. "As you heard, she's fine. Do your part, and she'll stay in one piece. You have sixty minutes. Goodbye, Mr. Hayes."

Kieran yells three words before the line disconnects.

Oliver frowns at the phone, then sighs and swipes a hand over his hair. "I need a fucking drink." He glances at me, a hint of apology in his expression before looking at Bradley. "No permanent damage. We might still need her."

"No interruptions," retorts Bradley.

Oliver's lip curls. "I'll be in my office. Don't do anything stupid like untie her or kill her."

He strides from the room.

Bradley taps the gun against my head. "Just you and me now."

My stomach tumbles, but the sensation is distant—a physical reflex. In this moment, no fear touches me.

Kieran's three words are my shield.

"Hold fast, Birdie."

He knows who I am.

As the revelation settles, so does the conviction that I will do anything—even sell my soul—to get back to him.

Oblivious to the compass of my morality aligning to a new north, Bradley drags the muzzle of the gun down my neck and across my chest. He's breathing hard, his eyes fixed on my breasts as he rubs the metal roughly against them. My nipples firm under the assault.

I ignore the violation, my mind churning through various plans of action. I'm getting the fuck out of here, and if a life is the price, I'll pour Bradley's blood in the Devil's cup myself.

"Do you know how many times I've imagined this?" he whispers.

At his words, the final puzzle pieces align and lock. My plan solidifies.

I work my tongue against wet fabric in my mouth. "I'm sorry," I say, the words garbled.

His crazed eyes find mine. "What's that? You're sorry?" He grins, sharp and humorless. "You think that will save you?"

I shake my head, my eyes conveying regret and helplessness. "I didn't mean to hurt you."

He stares at my mouth, frowning as he tries to decipher the words. *Come on, asshole, you know you want to hear my voice.* After what feels like an eternity, he lays the gun on the counter behind him and yanks out my gag.

Before I can speak, he grabs me by the throat and squeezes hard. With his other hand, he rips my blouse open. His fingers roughly fondle my breasts. I don't have to fake my cry of pain.

"How does it feel knowing you're not in control?" he spits out.

The last knot on my wrists comes undone. I fist the rope to keep it from falling to the floor.

Finally, his grip on my neck loosens a fraction. I suck in air, my heart thundering and my eyes watering. I gasp out, "I'm sorry, Bradley. Truly. I didn't mean to hurt you. How can I make it up to you? I'll do anything."

He sucks in a breath, eyes full of loathing and lust roaming my face and breasts. "Anything, huh? What if I asked you to lick my shoes? To beg me for the privilege?"

Memory supplies context for his words: his primary kink was degradation, both physical and verbal. I'd given him exactly what he wanted, reading and adjusting to his cues over the course of our appointments. He left my care sated and blissful each time—or so I thought.

Guilt descends like a shroud, but it's sliced to pieces almost instantly. This isn't my fault. I treated him like all my clients, with compassion and care. Whatever twisted him into the mentally unstable person he is now, it has nothing to do with me. I'm merely the vehicle for his self-loathing.

"If that's what you want, I'll do it. You're in charge." I look down so he can't see the lie in my eyes as I say, "Can—can I tell you something? A secret?"

I glance up to see surprise swallow his anger. Glazed eyes meet mine as he nods.

Gotcha, you stupid, sick fuck.

"I'm tired of pretending to be someone I'm not," I whisper.

He shifts his weight, scratching a narrow, bristly cheek. "What do you mean?"

"What I did to you—that wasn't the real me. But I was never taught any other way." The meekness in my voice revolts me, but I stay the course. "All I know is what I'm feeling right now, tied up and at your mercy."

He flushes, hands descending to his belt. "I knew it," he says, his voice trembling with excitement. "I knew deep down you were a slut like her. Like all of them."

And there it is.

Bradley didn't need a dominatrix—he needed therapy for his mommy issues.

"You want to suck my dick, don't you?"

I nod, feigning eagerness even as my stomach lurches. Bile shoots up my throat; I swallow frantically.

Bradley fumbles with his pants, ripping down the zipper and exposing himself. Single-minded in his want. Utterly ignorant of the fact I've laid explosives in his fault line and am about to push the proverbial red button.

Before he can get his junk anywhere near my mouth, I ask hopefully, "Maybe... maybe you can sit in the chair and I can kneel between your legs? I've never done that before—been on my knees for someone."

His groan is thick with phlegm. He shuffles forward and grabs one of my breasts, his other hand stroking his erection. "Since I'm a generous man, I'll give you want you want. Get on your knees like the greedy whore you are."

Decades of practice compartmentalizing my emotions allows me to overcome the urge to vomit all over myself. Shifting my grip on the rope, I allow the middle to unwind and slacken between my hands.

"Can I have a little help? My legs feel super weak." I force myself to glance at his groin. "You're really intimidating."

He grins as he reaches for my shoulders. Adrenaline sharpens my vision and crackles through my limbs.

I let him hoist me halfway to standing before bringing my knee up as hard as I can between his legs, thanking God I wore pants tonight and they were too stupid to tie my ankles together. My full strength isn't behind the blow, but it's more than enough. His mouth gapes in a soundless shriek, his knees buckling. I shove him to the side, away from the counter and the gun. He falls onto his arms, keening breathlessly, hands still cupped between his legs.

Knowing I have only seconds to act, I launch onto his back and whip the rope around his neck. Then I throw my body backward, compressing his trachea and esophagus. He bucks beneath me and twists from side to side, but I simply move with him, avoiding swipes of his hands and utilizing my weight to maintain leverage.

When he realizes he can't unseat me, panic sets in. His hands fly to his throat. He scratches at the rope in an attempt to create slack, but nothing short of a bullet to my head is going to loosen my grip. Rough fibers slice my palms, my blood mingling with Gabe's. I feel no pain—nothing at all—the entirety of my being focused on a single, immutable goal.

I will survive. He will not.

Slowly, his flailing lessens. My muscles quiver with exhaustion, but I keep pulling. Sweat blurs my eyes. Or maybe tears. There are sounds—shouts, running footsteps—but they're muted by the static in my head.

Is someone crying?

Bradley jerks again. I pull harder, gritting my teeth against an explosion of pain in my shoulder and back. My vision washes red.

From far away, I hear a familiar voice. But it sounds wrong, not its usual dry gravel but saturated with worry. "He's almost gone, Kier. Get her off before she kills him!"

Bands of warm pressure surround my chest. It feels like a hug. Like a dream too perfect to be real.

"Mo ghrá," whispers a voice against my ear, "you can let go now. You're safe. It's over."

"Kieran?" I ask, but it comes out as a sob. Another follows, and another.

Oh, I'm the one crying.

"I've got you," he says, voice thick with his own tears. "Let go, my love. I won't let you fall."

My fingers spasm and open.

I'm weightless, lifted up and away.

CHAPTER 33
TALIA

The following night, my phone buzzes from the lip of Kieran's bathtub where I've been soaking long enough for my fingers and toes to wrinkle. After wiping my hands quickly on a towel, I grab my device and read the message.

Done with the cops. Home in 5

My fingers tremble as I type:

I can't wait to see you

Kieran doesn't reply. He doesn't have to. Even separated by miles, I can feel his need.

From the moment I opened my eyes to Kieran's face and realized I was safe, I've anticipated this moment. He was

356

supernaturally calm during my visit to a private doctor and throughout the hours-long process of having my injuries photographed and giving my statement to the police. When his lawyer and Alistair arrived at the precinct, and Sven suggested I be taken home to rest, Kieran gave me a gentle hug and a chaste kiss goodbye.

Mia and Leo were waiting for me at Kieran's. There were some tears but no questions, only relief and compassion. Exactly what I needed. After I took the world's longest shower, they fed me and tucked me into bed, then kept watch over me as I slept. When I woke, the sun was setting. I sent them home, already knowing what was coming.

Now it's here.

The eye of Kieran's storm has passed. It rages inside him, desperate for release.

Stepping from the bathtub, I grab a towel and dry off. The magnesium salt bath and anti-inflammatories I took an hour ago have made my soreness almost negligible. I still keep my back to the mirror, avoiding the sight of the bruises blooming on my neck, shoulder, and hip. I don't look at my hands, either, the abrasions on my palms and wrists minor but stark against my pale skin.

Tomorrow, I have my first appointment with a trauma specialist, a colleague I've known since college. Tomorrow, I'll tend to the bloody tracks left in my psyche by the swinging pendulum of emotional extremes. Terror to hope. Despair to fury. Grief to searing relief when I found out Gabe survived. I'll face, too, the proof of my own capacity to take a life. My lack of guilt. The twisting, aching knowledge that a part of me wishes I hadn't been stopped.

Tomorrow, I'll confront it all.

Tonight belongs to animal necessity, to the natural urge to conquer death with life. Kieran needs physical contact to prove I'm safe, and I need to replace the echoes of nonconsensual touch on my body with the hands of the man I love.

But I need something else from him, too. I need help extracting the poisonous seed I swallowed last night—the lies I told to stay alive. And as difficult as this will be for him, patience and gentleness aren't going to cut it for me. If he treats me like I'm delicate, there will be only one result: the rot inside me will spread.

To obliterate the stain inside me, I need his darkest self. The savage wolf.

As I hang my damp towel on a hook by the tub, the air changes around me. Goose bumps lift on my arms. My pulse begins to drum, fast and furious, as need throbs between my thighs.

He's here.

When the bedroom door opens and closes, I walk out of the bathroom.

Kieran jerks to a stop at the sight of me. With the curtains half-drawn against a cloudy afternoon, the bedroom is shadowed, his eyes dark as they scan me from top to bottom. At his sides, fists form. His rapid, harsh breaths—and mine—are the only sound.

"Talia," he croaks, brow furrowing. "I can't—I shouldn't touch you right now."

I barely feel the floor beneath me as I cross to him. My nipples graze his shirt, emitting tiny shockwaves at the contact. He sucks in a breath, tendons standing out in his flexed arms, broad shoulders shaking as he fights impulse.

Lifting my chin, I stare into his eyes and see *everything*. Our past, present, and future. The floating ribbons of our lives that crossed and tangled by chance seventeen years ago before weaving in separate directions across continents and years. Apart. Distinct. Growing and strengthening and maturing. But always linked by the bond that formed at his grandmother's grave. Now we are braided together, sealed with knots so complex and tight nothing in this world can undo them.

My hand finds his and pulls it to my belly. Flattening his palm against my skin, I guide him to my center. His nostrils flare, lips parting as he sinks two fingers inside me. I gasp, clutching his arms as I arch against him.

"I need you, Kieran. Give me your rage and your love."

Our mouths collide in a brutal union of teeth and tongue. I bite his lip so hard I taste blood. He snarls and bites me back. His fingers curl inside me, yanking me forward and back at a punishing pace. The pleasure is so intense I feel it in the roots of my hair.

Before I lose myself completely, I shove him to make space between our bodies, then rip his pants open and push them down his thighs. Grabbing his cock in one hand and his balls in the other, I squeeze. He hisses, snatching my wrists. Pressure and tingling precede my fingers jerking open.

"No fair," I growl.

His dark laughter is silk on my senses and gasoline on my need. I hook a foot around his knee and pull hard to unbalance him, but I might as well be trying to uproot a tree.

I take a step back, pouting but secretly thrilled by his strength. Watching me with hawklike focus and a smirk, he steps out of his shoes and pants. His shirt goes next, giving me delicious confirmation of how powerful he is. How much bigger and stronger.

I need a different weapon.

He purrs, "Should we arm wrestle next?"

I run my hands up my body, squeezing my breasts together. His eyes soften, instincts dulling. He takes a step toward me, bringing himself within reach. I grab his nipples and wrench them hard.

He yelps but instead of jumping back, he sweeps forward and plucks me off my feet, his arms trapping mine to my sides. "Goddammit, Talia." Amusement and pain roughen the words.

Wiggling to free my arms, I wrap them around his neck and lock my ankles at the small of his back. "Right where I want you," I murmur as I rock against him, finding friction against the trail of hair and hard muscle on his abdomen.

Lips trail along my ear, nipping and sucking, as he palms my ass. "I have something better for you," he whispers, lowering me down his body until the thick root of his cock meets my soaked center. "But you have to ask for it. *Nicely*."

Angling my face to his, I clamp my teeth on his lower lip and tug before releasing it to say, "I shouldn't have to ask for what's already mine. Give me my cock right now."

His features tighten, his entire body hard as marble against me.

My gaze holds his. "Now, Kieran."

Control shattering, he strides to the closest wall. We slam against it, his arms protecting me from the impact. With an animalistic snarl, he fists his cock and notches himself against me. I cry out in relief, but when seconds pass and he doesn't fill me, my moan turns to a growl. A protest on my tongue, my eyes flutter open.

The anguish on his face steals the air in my lungs, wiping away my frustration. "What's wrong?"

"I... God, I don't feel in control. I don't want to hurt you. I'd rather die."

A single tear slides down his cheek, and a deep ache unfurls in my chest. Fighting my own tears, I kiss him softly and stroke his jaw, his brow, his cheekbones. "Oh, Kieran, you can't hurt me. You love me too much. So much, in fact, that you're going to let go of that fear. I need you to remind me what I'm not—fragile or weak. Help me remember who I am."

The darkness melts from his eyes. "I know exactly who you are. My perfect match."

The smile in my heart matches the one on my face. "Yes.

Your match. Your equal. May I have my cock now, please? I want to feel your thrusts all the way in my throat."

Lips curving in promise, he lightly flexes his hips. The head of his cock slips inside me. My eyes roll back in my head at the twinned pleasure and torture of it. He licks my throat, then bites my chin.

"Since you asked so nicely..." Strong fingers hook over my shoulders. "Hold tight, mo ghrá. It's going to be a rough ride."

It's not rough.

It's the perfect storm, and it scours me clean.

THERE ARE MORE storms over the days and weeks that follow. Storms no amount of logic, acceptance, or calls with my trauma therapist can circumvent. They're lightning strikes in blue skies. Impossible to predict or to prepare for. One minute I'm fine, the next I'm not.

The first week is the hardest. I wake up multiple times a night covered in sweat, my heart pounding and a scream lodged in my throat. Sometimes I dream of that kitchen and what happened there. But mostly I dream of blood. Gabe's. Mine. Kieran's. Gunshots and cuts that won't stop bleeding.

Awake, I startle at unexpected noises. A car horn. A door closing. A phone ringing. A Tupperware container dropping to the floor. And when Kieran nicks his finger on a knife in the kitchen, the sight of his blood sends me into a panic attack the likes of which I've never experienced.

My intellectual tools are useless. I can't think or meditate myself out of what's happening. I'm a teenager again, a slave to emotional forces I can't control. All I can do is weather them. Accept the slices of my monster's claws inside me and resist the lure to mirror them on my skin.

This time, though, I'm not alone. Kieran is my cornerstone as I process and heal, just as I am his. We are a seesaw in perpetual motion—each of us strong when the other is not. When he struggles, I am calm. And when I struggle, he knows not to press me to talk. Instead, he draws me baths. Reads to me for hours. Walks the beach with me multiple times a day. When I run into the cold water to feel the shock to my system, he follows me, anchoring me in the waves with his arms as much as the love and acceptance in his eyes.

He doesn't ask me about the nightmares, but one afternoon a week and a half after my abduction, I tell him everything. Or almost everything—I don't bring up the words he yelled over the phone. He hasn't brought them up, either, and the longer we don't talk about it, the more convinced I am that I hallucinated them. I recognize, too, that my emotions are still too chaotic to handle the conversation.

But I do tell him why my father put me in therapy when I was young. About my monster and why blood triggers me. Why seeing Gabe's blood, having it on my hands, cast blinding light onto the shadows of my past.

I show him where I used to cut.

There are tears in his eyes as he traces my invisible scars with gentle fingertips, then with soft kisses. With his touch, he smooths the warped edges of my psyche's darkest treasure. With his words, he turns my vulnerability into strength.

"I love the girl who did this, and I love the woman who survived. You are my miracle."

That night, I sleep soundly for the first time. And the next morning, Kieran leads me to the room that doubles as a dojo and home gym. Sven is already inside. He hands me a Judogi in my size and a white belt.

"Want to learn how to beat the shit out of Kieran?" he asks mildly.

I grab the uniform. "Yes, please."

Kieran laughs and kisses my forehead, then points a finger at Sven.

"Teach her to bring me to the floor in under thirty seconds, and I'll buy you an island to retire on."

Sven smiles slowly. "Done."

CHAPTER 34

KIERAN

"Settle down, folks! This is a press conference, not a circus."

The lighthearted reprimand from Sam Caddel, Lumitech's media relations specialist, causes a ripple of laughter through the small amphitheater and has the intended effect of shutting up the sea of reporters. Beyond them, a wall of cameras from local and national news stations record my every blink, breath, and twitch.

Seated onstage with me at a black-draped table are Alistair and our lawyer, Jameson Sloan. Sven watches over us from a shadowed corner of the stage.

Talia wanted to come, but I convinced her not to, not wanting her anywhere near these piranhas. She and Dylan decided to visit Gabe and watch the live feed from his cushy hospital room. By now, I'm positive she's realized exactly why I insisted she stay away.

A circus is less chaotic.

As much as I'd rather gargle gasoline and light a cigarette than sit here and be dissected for soundbites, it's a necessary evil. Lumitech's stock price took a nosedive when news broke of Oliver's arrest. Another shockwave struck the tech industry three days ago when the district attorney announced that Lyle Porter, CEO of SubFusion Systems, had been indicted on a laundry list of charges including corporate espionage, blackmail, kidnapping, attempted murder, and conspiracy to commit murder.

Once Oliver was cuffed to an interrogation table, he sang like a canary—or a lisping frog since most of his front teeth were broken courtesy of my knuckles. Thanks to his blabbering attempts to save his own ass, and the fact he was paranoid enough to record every phone call, in-person meeting, and transfer of money between him and his puppeteer, the man behind my misery was unmasked.

I've never liked Lyle, but the news he was behind everything stunned me as much as the general public. Mainly because while I've always known he was a shithead, it never occurred to me he was fucking crazy. If someone had asked me even a week ago if I considered Lyle smart enough to orchestrate multiple assassination attempts without getting caught, I would have struggled not to laugh. Now laughter is my last impulse when I think of him. I want to break every bone in his body, put him back together, and break him again.

Given that I'm not interested in a pair of handcuffs,

I'm working on coming to terms with Lyle rotting in prison for the rest of his life. And by working, I mean daily phone calls with Dr. Chastain and going toe to toe with Sven on the mat after he and Talia finish their morning training.

I'm sporting a colorful array of bruises under my suit. So is Sven, who's been kind enough to let me work out my fury on him.

The only reason I'm here today is to show the world—and Lumitech's stockholders—that I'm perfectly fine and mentally stable enough sit at the helm of my multibillion-dollar corporation.

Even though I'm not sure I am. Even though I've been lying through my teeth for the last thirty minutes, projecting false confidence while my bones are burning. All I want to do is flip over the table in front of me, destroy every camera in sight, and sprint across the city to assure myself Talia is alive and well.

Today marks the longest stretch of time I've been away from her since I got her back. I'm actually impressed I've made it this long with nothing but a few texts and a thirty-second phone call before I walked onstage. Even though she's safe and in a much better place than she was two weeks ago, my instincts are still screaming.

Dr. Chastain says the flashes of white-hot rage and crippling anxiety I feel when Talia isn't in my line of sight are normal. Apparently, in addition to the trauma of almost losing her and the shock of Oliver's betrayal, I'm contending with the sudden expulsion of four-plus years' worth of stress, grief, and fear.

"We have time for a couple more questions," Sam continues.

A dozen hands shoot up, and Sam points at a man in the second row. He jolts to his feet, shark eyes on my face and smile oozing manufactured warmth. "Cory Jones with Los Angeles Nightly News. Mr. Hayes, Oliver McCann was your CIO for almost ten years. Since his arrest, it's come out that money was his motive for trying to sabotage Lumitech's nanorobotics research."

Alistair jerks forward. "Let's keep the facts straight, shall we?" His expression is mild, but his voice is cutting. "Lyle Porter and Oliver McCann tried to have my brother killed six times—that we know of—in the last four years. His head of security was shot and stabbed. There were three attempted car bombs and a thwarted property invasion. If Kieran didn't employ the best personal protection on the West Coast, he'd be dead."

I shift in my seat, still peeved that Alistair and Sven colluded to keep me in the dark about the additional four attempts on my life. I understand their reasons—namely, my sanity—but I still yelled at them until I was lightheaded when I found out.

Then I gave my brother a hug and Sven, Dylan, and Gabe raises.

"Not only that," Alistair continues without pause, "they abducted his girlfriend for the purpose of blackmail, sending her security team to the hospital in the process. Their accomplice to that crime has confessed he was contracted to kill her and dispose of her body no matter the outcome. So I think the situation is a bit more serious than *sabotage*."

"You're absolutely right," Cory concedes with a tight smile for me. "My apologies."

I want to tell him where he can shove his apologies but instead nod shortly and dip my hand into my pocket. My thumb smooths over the small hummingbird pendant Talia removed from its chain and gave to me before I left this morning.

"Do you have a question, Cory?" asks Sam drolly.

The crowd titters. Cory's neck flushes, his gaze narrowing on me. "Yes. Mr. Hayes, did you know that when Mr. Porter first approached Mr. McCann, Mr. McCann was in severe debt due to a long-term cocaine and gambling addiction and his home was about to go into foreclosure?"

"No, I did not."

Hands and voices fill the air, but Cory shouts, "One more question, Mr. Hayes! Can you explain to us how you never once suspected that Mr. McCann—one of your closest colleagues—was a drug addict who wanted you dead?"

I hold my thumb to the hummingbird as tomblike silence descends on the room. Faces stare at me with varying degrees of anticipation. It's the multibillion-dollar question. How can Lumitech's biggest contractors—including the U.S. government—continue to trust my judgment if I was oblivious to a viper in my own house?

Cory Whoever from Wherever smiles smugly. When I smile back at him, his expression melts into a confused frown. I allow myself a moment to enjoy being underestimated; it hasn't happened in years.

While I may not be in peak form, I'm still almost as smart as the genius I'm in love with.

"First, Cory, I'd like to address your underlying and flattering assumption that in addition to being the head of a Fortune 500 company with close to forty-two thousand employees, I'm also omniscient."

There's a smattering of laughter. Not from poor Cory, though, whose face has drained of color. He opens his mouth, but I don't give him a chance to stick his foot back in it.

"I'm sorry to say that in his daily emails regarding our internal software systems, our bi-monthly meetings, and the occasional charity benefit we attended together, Oliver never mentioned his cocaine habit or the fact Lyle Porter promised him fifteen million dollars to either end my life or blackmail me into destroying groundbreaking research. Thankfully, he proved inept at both tasks."

The mood shifts, faces grimacing in second-hand embarrassment, eyes dropping guiltily. I run my gaze across the crowd, knowing that Sam is taking note of who won't meet my stare. I almost feel bad for Cory, who's probably starting to realize his higher-ups offered him to me for slaughter.

Maybe I'll send him a fruit basket.

"The bottom line," I continue gravelly, "is that no one

really knew Oliver McCann. Not the people who interacted with him far more than I did, including two PAs and a dozen upper management IT staff members. Not even his wife, who he shipped out of town prior to kidnapping my girlfriend and who's been cleared of involvement. And certainly not me, his extremely busy boss." I release a measured sigh. "All of us at Lumitech are shocked and saddened by the revelations of the last week, but there's only one person responsible for Oliver's choices and that's Oliver himself."

I stand, buttoning my jacket, and Alistair and Jameson follow suit.

"To those harboring concerns for Lumitech's future, let me put your worries to rest right now. I'm proud to announce publicly that our neural nanorobotics initiative is entering preclinical testing. I'm confident that a few years from now, we'll be able to say as a global community that there is a safe, effective cure for Alzheimer's disease."

The room instantly erupts.

"That's our cue," murmurs Alistair, throwing me a wink before he leads the way offstage.

THE CAR RIDE home is a blur, every mile shaving another layer off my civilized self. By the time we get home, I'm a beast on a breaking chain. As soon as I enter the house, I strip out of my jacket and tie and stalk onto the back deck.

To my relief, Talia is exactly where her text said she'd be.

Tall and majestic, she stands a safe fifteen feet from the bluff, her gaze trained on the gunmetal-gray Pacific and the rippling curtain of rain obscuring the horizon line. Her arms are crossed loosely at her waist over a sweater, her wild dark hair whipping around her torso.

Urgency beats in my blood, but I make myself walk slowly down the steps, savoring the singular gravity her soul exerts on mine. Each step toward her feels like moving closer to home. To peace. To the truest version of myself—the man I am in her eyes. A bit frayed and emotionally bruised. But strong and steadfast.

Unbroken. Like her.

As I reach the bottom of the stairs, Dylan steps into my way with a nod. "Congratulations on handing that reporter his ass."

My eyes narrow. "The only ass I want my hands on is the one you're blocking me from."

He smirks. "Classy."

"Dylan, if you get out of my sight right now, I'll pay for you and Sven to have a three-week vacation in Maui."

His eyes grow wider than I've ever seen them. He chokes on a breath. I pat his shoulder and skirt around him, striding past the pool and across the grass.

When I'm several feet away, Talia senses me and turns with a smile. I take a moment to soak in the sight of her: my brilliant, resilient, utterly bewitching goddess—who also happens to be a natural at Judo. Sven thinks she'll have a yellow belt in another week and is confident he can get her to a black belt in four years. He's already sending me links to islands, trying to call my bluff.

Only I wasn't bluffing. If he gives Talia the means to never again feel defenseless against a bigger adversary, he's getting his damn island.

I open my arms and Talia slips into my embrace, her head tucked beneath my chin. Sucking her scent into my lungs, I stroke her back, hips, and arms to cement what my sight couldn't fully convince me of: that she is real, safe, and mine.

When the sharpness inside me finally dulls, I kiss her head. "Thanks for letting me grope you."

She looks up, eyes teasing. "No complaints here."

I tuck a strand of hair behind her ear. "How was your day? How's Gabe?"

"The day was good," she says, smiling. "I wrote another chapter. It's really starting to flow."

"I can't wait to read it."

In addition to being my literal soulmate, I've discovered —to no surprise—that Talia is an incredible writer. She's going to destroy every bestseller list with her book, a mix of memoir, psychology, and kink education.

Her fingers play along my jaw. "As for Gabe, he's antsy and irritable as usual. The nurses will probably throw a party when he's released in a few days."

I chuckle. "No doubt."

Within hours of waking up from surgery to remove a thankfully small caliber bullet and sew up a hole in his lung, Gabe was asking when he'd be cleared to return to work.

When I broke the news that I was putting him on paid leave for five months of rehab, he looked like he wanted to take a swing at me. He changed his tune when Talia told him about the beachfront rental and private chef waiting for him. Now all he wants to do is get out of the hospital so he can sunbathe and sip smoothies while ogling bikini-clad women.

Talia tucks her head back against my chest, snuggling closer as the wind kicks up. "That press conference was insanity. I'm glad you convinced me not to go or I might have tested a few Judo moves on that reporter at the end."

Grinning, I lift the heavy mass of her hair and palm her neck, massaging it lightly. "I would have liked to see that, but full disclosure—he was a plant, albeit an ignorant one. Turns out his bosses aren't too fond of him."

Her head lifts, an eyebrow cocked.

I wink. "Chess, mo ghrá."

Her laugh is mostly a groan, but she sobers fast. "Sven told me about the call you got while you were prepping for the conference this morning. You don't have to talk about it if you don't want to, but I'm here for you. Always."

Her love burns through me, peeling off the final scraps of the mask I maintained all day.

With a heavy sigh, I bury my face in her hair. "I don't know how to feel about it. Part of me is relieved—so fucking relieved —but another part of me is having a hard time believing it. I'm so accustomed to the guilt, I'm not sure how to let it go."

This morning, the LAPD's chief of police personally

called me to relay that of all the charges Oliver and Lyle are facing, there's one crime they had nothing to do with.

Liz's murder.

There's absolutely nothing linking the men to her carjacking, which took place more than four months before Lyle approached Oliver for the first time. Liz's death was exactly what the cops always said it was: a tragic, random crime that had nothing to do with me.

"Breathe with me," murmurs Talia. "Feel the wind. Feel my arms. Hear the ocean. Breathe."

I do as she says and my heartbeat slows, the vice around my chest loosening a fraction. The past recedes, my feet sinking into the present with her.

"A tropical beach," I murmur. "You, me, warm sands, turquoise water. You can bring your laptop and work on your book. I'll feed you mangoes and orgasms."

Her laughter is the sweetest sound in the world.

A hard gust of wind brings the first raindrops to our heads. We look up at the same time the sky decides to open and dump an atmospheric river on us. We're soaked in seconds.

Talia laughs in delight, arching back in my hold and spreading her arms to embrace the storm. Trusting that I won't let her fall.

"Marry me, Talia." The rain carries away my soft words, so I yell them instead. "Marry me!"

She whips upright, her mouth ajar. A thick lock of wet

hair is plastered to her cheek. She blinks huge eyes. "What did you just say?"

I palm her beautiful face, pressing my forehead to hers. "Marry me." Rain mists from my lips to hers, still parted in shock. "I know who you are and where you belong—with me. You'll always belong with me. You're Birdie. My Birdie. Stay with me."

The nickname hits her like electricity. She rears back to scan my face, my eyes. "It was real," she says in disbelief. "I didn't—I convinced myself I imagined it. Why haven't you said anything? How long have you known?"

Before I can answer, her palm slaps over my mouth. I blink at her in bafflement. She laughs, the bell-like sound coating her words. "Sorry! I just—you can't tell me yet, okay?"

I have no idea what's happening, but her sparkling eyes at least reassure me that my heart isn't about to be tossed off the cliff.

"Okay," I mumble into her skin.

Her hand slides off my mouth, replaced a second later by her rain-slick lips. The kiss is warm and soft. An answer and a promise.

"I love you," she murmurs. "Let's go inside."

TALIA

Barefoot but still in our wet clothes, I guide Kieran by the hand through the warm, empty house and into the dojo. When he sees the flickering candles along the walls and the two cushions in the middle of the bare wood floor, he laughs.

He lifts my hand, warm lips pressing to my cold fingers. "Did I ruin the surprise, Birdie?"

My heart, still pounding from his question outside, leaps again. I don't answer, instead tugging him toward the pillows. We sit facing each other, our knees touching, hands clasped between us.

Kieran's eyes shine with amusement as they track over my face. "You're nervous," he whispers.

"Shut up."

His crooked grin widens even as his eyes sharpen. "Tell me."

The eloquent speech I've been working on for days evaporates. I blurt, "When I walked into that graveyard, I'd never felt more alone in my entire life. I'd also never been drunk before. When I first saw you, I thought there were two of you."

His rumbling laugh vibrates in my chest. "Two of me?"

"Two of the most beautiful, hungry-looking boys in the world," I confirm. "Obviously, my blurred vision corrected itself."

He nods, still grinning. "Obviously."

I groan, knocking my knees against his. "This is supposed to be a serious moment."

He bites his lips, eyes wide and shimmering with mirth. The urge to laugh is so intense I have to close my eyes and belly breathe to keep from losing it.

"Is that what tantric breathing sounds like?" he asks curiously.

"Kieran, I swear—"

"Sorry, sorry." He doesn't sound sorry at all. "I'll be serious."

I peer up at him, gratified to see he isn't laughing anymore but watching me with tenderness and warmth. Clearing my throat, I squeeze his hands. "Seventeen years ago, you took pity on an angry, lonely girl and listened to all her teenaged woes without judgment. In the darkest time of my life, you gave me hope when you said I would be okay, that someday the world would kneel to me."

"In my defense, I didn't realize you'd pursue the goal so

literal—*Oof*." He chuckles as he rubs his stomach where I punched him.

"Are you done?"

He winces. "Maybe?"

"Oh, for fuck's—" I yelp as he tackles me backward. His palm cups my head, preventing it from slamming into the wood.

"Birdie," he murmurs silkily, his nose running along mine. He leans back just enough for our eyes to connect in the candlelight. "My fragile hummingbird who grew into a lioness. My warrior queen. Fuck science—I know in my heart that we're magic. My gran brought us together that day and spoke her last prophecy through me. You took a piece of me with you, and now I'm whole again."

Tears roll from the corners of my eyes. Kieran catches them with his thumbs before they reach my hair.

"I'm so mad right now," I whisper through quivering lips. "You hijacked my romantic gesture."

His smile makes my toes curl. Lips grazing mine, he whispers, "Marry me, Talia."

I'm sure he can feel my heart thrashing against his chest, just like I can feel his. Elation and panic make me tremble.

My voice wavers. "We've been in a relationship for four weeks. And that's being generous. Impulsivity is also a well-known symptom of PTSD. You might feel differently in a few months."

"Is that so, Dr. Stirling?"

I choke on a breath as he rolls his hips against my center. Sparkling waves of heat spread through me.

"You know what I think?" he continues, his eyes sober and focused. "I think I've never been more sure of anything as I am of the fact you're mine and I'm yours. I'm putting babies in you. We're growing old together. The end."

More heat pulses through me, this time with my heart as the source. I wrap my legs around his hips.

"In that case, ask me again in a year."

A smile plays around his mouth. "I can do that."

I grin and pat his cheek. "Such a good boy."

He laughs, the unfettered, joyous sound rippling across my skin, stretching my grin even wider. When his mirth fades, he gazes down at me with carnal intent. My breathing turns choppy as he lifts his hips from mine. Sliding a hand between us, he cups me through soaked linen. The base of his palm moves in slow circles over my clit as his fingers stroke me through layers of fabric.

"I think I deserve a treat," he says huskily. "Since I'm such a good boy."

I'm panting now. "Yes, I think you do."

He observes my hips circling against his palm, his cock turning to steel against my thigh. When he licks his full lower lip, I'm surprised my clothes don't start steaming.

His eyes flash to mine. "Actually, a treat isn't going to fill me up. I deserve a feast."

I moan breathlessly. "Don't leave any crumbs."

"Like I'd ever waste a single morsel of you," he murmurs.

He peels off my wet clothes and his, then adjusts me so I'm propped on the cushions. Warm, strong hands grip the backs of my thighs, lifting and spreading my legs. Diving forward, he breathes me in, hot breath fanning my center.

"Mmm, delicious."

I try to lift myself to his mouth, but his grip keeps me pinned. "Kieran," I whine.

"Tell me a secret, Birdie." His breath and the vibration of his voice make my pussy clench. I'm embarrassingly close to orgasming from *air*.

I admit softly, "I fell in love with you when I was fourteen and a part of me never stopped loving you."

He flicks my clit with his tongue, sending electric currents zinging through my limbs. I gasp, my head arching back.

"Another."

"I was twenty-three when I saw your face on the cover of a magazine. I almost passed out in the grocery store checkout lane. I bought it and read the article a thousand times. I still have it in a box under my bed."

A rumble of pleasure in his throat, he drags his tongue up my slit. But the pressure is nonexistent and he avoids my clit.

"More."

Lifting my head, I glare at him. He offers me a grin. My resistance melts away, my head thudding back to the floor.

"I'd never felt sexual attraction before meeting you. My first orgasm was while thinking about you."

His tongue spears me without warning, a single penetration that makes me wail. When he retreats, I exhale shakily and close my eyes.

"Another."

"Every sexual partner I've had, I was initially attracted to because they reminded me of you at eighteen. But I didn't realize it until recently."

He dips two fingers inside me and pumps them lazily. My back bows, my eyes rolling up and closing in relief. It's short-lived—he pulls them out seconds later, and I open my eyes to see him licking me off his fingers.

I don't make him ask again.

"When I was fifteen, I made myself forget you. Consciously, at least. But when I saw you on that magazine cover, it all came roaring back. For weeks, I Googled you obsessively, learning everything I could about your life. I even drove by Lumitech a bunch of times, hoping to catch a glimpse of you."

"My little stalker," he whispers, rubbing his chin gently against the sensitive space above my clit. "I wish I'd seen you."

"I'm glad you didn't," I say dryly. "To say we wouldn't have been a good match back then is an understatement."

Kieran chuckles, his hands fanning over my thighs, spreading warm prickles of sensation across my skin. He strokes my belly, my arms. Grazes fingertips over my breasts and flicks my nipples until I'm rocking against the cushion. I close my eyes and submit to the sensual torment. The ache inside me crosses the line from pleasure to pain, becoming a sharp, insistent throb. Denying my nature, I don't fight it—him.

"Such a good girl," he whispers, squeezing my breasts before dragging his hands back down to my thighs. He spreads me open and blows onto my pussy. My raw moan echoes against the bare walls of the dojo.

"Where were we? Ah, that's right. At twenty-three, you made yourself forget me again?"

"Yes," I admit breathlessly. "It wasn't easy, seeing as you decided to become a famous billionaire in my damn hometown."

A puff of silent laughter hits me, then more kisses and soft licks—my inner thighs, my mound, every centimeter of my pussy *except* my clit.

Cupping my hot cheeks, I ramble, "I succeeded until two years ago. I was newly single, sexually confused, and wine-drunk. I found old pictures of you online from a vacation you took with your parents. You were coming out of the water on a beach."

I feel his smile against me. "Tahiti."

"You were so much bigger than any man I'd been with. More muscular. You were scowling. Angry and fierce and powerful. But I still saw the boy from the graveyard. My first fantasy." I look down to find his eyes on me. Lowering my hands to his head, I push my fingers through soft, wet hair. "That was the first time I imagined being dominated by you."

The tip of his tongue drags through me, making me

shudder. "Finish it," he whispers with a devious smirk, "if you can."

His mouth finally covers my clit, subjecting the over-sensitized bud to deep, pulsing suction as he simultaneously shoves two fingers inside me. They curl and pump hard, dragging over my G-spot with devastating precision. The air fills with decadent sounds: my wetness and thready moans, his guttural grunts of approval and pleasure.

My legs begin to shake.

My voice, too.

"When Gail called me and said you needed help, I thought... thought I could repay you for—*Oh God*—what you did for me in the graveyard. B-but if I'm honest with myself, I think... I think deep down I wanted to see if—*Ah!* If you could be what—what I always dreamed you were."

The rhythm of his hand never faltering, he lifts his head long enough to demand, "Tell me."

"Mine! I dreamed you were mine!"

He bites around my clit, then lashes it with the tip of his tongue. My bones tingle. The roots of my hair vibrate. My awareness of the room—the whole world—narrows to a dense, shining point situated somewhere near the base of my spine. Then it detonates. My climax tears through me with concussive force, waves upon waves, reducing me to atoms in its wake.

Kieran rises above me, thrusts inside me, and the sudden pressure and fullness makes every sensation so much *more*. His hips slam into mine over and over, setting off an unending chain reaction. I sob and cling to his shoulders. Our lips fuse together in a sloppy, consuming kiss.

"Yours, Talia. Always."

Just when I think I can't possibly experience any greater pleasure, he groans and stills inside me. In the candlelight, his eyes are my personal starry sky, his features fierce and wolfish.

Impossibly beautiful, like some forgotten dream.

Or a remembered one.

EPILOGUE

KIERAN

363 DAYS LATER

The forecast called for rain when I checked it last night, but the skies over Galway are a stunning cobalt. I'm not the least bit surprised. In fact, I wouldn't blink if a fairy popped out of a tree and said my gran had strong-armed a god into polishing the sky with his beard.

In the last year, I've given up on pretending I don't believe in magic—at least in private.

I do have a reputation as a scientific genius to maintain.

Despite the clear sky, the air is glacial. Talia is bundled up appropriately while I shiver in a peacoat. My dad's fault. When we left his house this morning, he gave Talia a kiss on the cheek and Mam's favorite wool hat and scarf. To me, he gave a ration of shit for allowing California to thin my Irish blood.

I'm paying the full price for my pride now.

Even our three shadows are in insulated jackets, heavy boots, and beanies. Probably having a nice big laugh at my expense, the fuckers.

"I don't remember it being this beautiful," says Talia with hushed awe. Her sharp gaze roams over the mortuary chapel, the sea of gray headstones, and lingers on stretches of grass that are an almost surreal bright green.

I squeeze her hand. "Might have something to do with the fact it was dusk, spitting rain, and you were plastered."

She smiles, throwing me a quick glance. A gust of wind sneaks under my collar. I flip it up, compressing my head like a turtle. I can't feel my fucking ears.

"Here, take this." Talia tugs me to a stop and unwraps her scarf.

"Nah, I'm good."

She rolls her eyes and loops the scarf around my neck, twisting it under my chin. "Don't be a brat."

I grin. "But you like it when I'm a brat."

Her cheeks, already rosy in the cold, flush darker. Instead of rising to the bait, though, she tugs my hand. "Come on, we'll walk faster. It's this way, right?"

Picking up our pace does help. Also helpful—thinking about waking up two days from now in tropical heat, as well as what I have planned for the day after that. And the little box stored in the bottom of my luggage.

By the time we reach Gran, I'm almost thawed. We come to a stop a few feet from the headstone we slumped against as teenagers. As strangers.

"What does it say?" she asks, her gaze on the Gaeilge inscription on the headstone.

My throat tightens, my voice emerging hoarse. "It's a line from a poem, *On Raglan Road* by Patrick Kavanagh. *'And I said,/ Let grief be a fallen leaf at the dawning of the day.'*"

Talia wraps her arm through mine. "That's lovely."

Reading the words again, a smile twitches my lips. "A few months before she died, she showed me the poem and told me she wanted the line for her epitaph. Even highlighted and underlined it and swore to haunt me if I let Dad put a generic or religious quote on her headstone." I shake my head ruefully. "I gave her shit because the poem itself is pretty depressing, about a failed relationship. But Gran said that's the whole point—finding light in the dark. We only appreciate the dawn because of the night that precedes it, and we only survive the night because of the moon and stars."

Talia's arm slips from mine. My thoughts on Gran, I don't notice she's not beside me until she says my name. I turn on my heel.

And freeze.

She kneels before me, looking up at me with hopeful eyes and a soft smile. Rosy cheeks and a red nose. My mam's hat askew on her head. A silver ring pinched between her fingers.

"I love you, Kieran. Will you marry me?"

I'm horrified.

Humbled to my core.

Ecstatic beyond belief.

From ten feet away, Sven rumbles, "Close your mouth, jackass."

Dylan and Gabe give me shooing gestures.

One stumbling step brings me to her. My weak knees deposit me on the ground. I grab her face and kiss her cold lips, sucking on her smile.

"Yes, Birdie. Of course I'll marry you."

Grinning, she grabs my hand and shoves the band on my ring finger. It fits perfectly.

Lifting my gaze to her face, I attempt a glare. "Did these assholes ruin my surprise?"

She blinks. "What surprise?"

"Idiot," hisses Gabe.

Talia glances at the men, then fills the crisp morning with her ringing laughter. Shaking her head, she says matter-of-factly, "They haven't said anything, but I figured you had something planned for two days from now. You're predictable like that. This was simple payback. You hijacked my romantic gesture last year, so I decided to hijack yours."

My laughter startles a flock of blackbirds from a nearby bush. Sven bats them away from his head, cursing, while Dylan and Gabe observe his dramatics with sadistic grins.

I haul Talia into my arms. "Tá grá agam duit, Talia."

"I love you, too," she whispers, rubbing her nose against mine, which is sadly too numb to feel a thing.

❧

2 DAYS LATER

DAWN LIGHT FLOWS like a sparkling river of ichor across the bedroom and Talia's naked body, turning her skin burnished gold. I kept her up most of the night and should let her sleep, but I can't fucking wait anymore.

Crawling onto the bed, I lie on my side facing her. She's on her stomach, head turned away. Her left hand is conveniently accessible, elegant fingers loosely curled on the ivory sheets. They twitch when I slip the ring on. I admire the custom, emerald cut black diamond as it glitters in the dawn.

Eventually she stirs, twisting toward me, eyelashes fluttering and parting. She smiles sleepily, then catches sight of the ring. Her eyes widen, jaw dropping as she lurches onto her elbows.

I trail a finger down her bare arm, delighting in the swift rise of goose bumps despite the sultry air.

"Surprise."

She sputters. "You didn't even ask me!"

I shrug. "I figured it was a done deal since you locked me down already. I told Sven and Dylan to enjoy the sunset yacht cruise on our behalf. You won't mind skipping my flowery speech, right?"

Her outrage is immediate and incandescent. "You *what*? No! I've been waiting a year for this!"

Unable to hold it in a second longer, I grin. "I'm kidding, sweetheart. Not about the ring but about the yacht. You still have to listen to my longwinded proposal. The boys have a bet going as to whether I'll make you cry."

Irritation drains from her eyes. Her lips dance and finally, she laughs. "Not so predictable after all, Mr. Hayes."

She yawns, stretching, all glorious skin and tangled dark hair. My mouth waters. I sneak my fingers toward the nearest rosy nipple, but she bats my hand away.

"In a minute, future husband. Look under your pillow first."

Frowning, I lift the pillow off the bed. A curled piece of paper pinwheels to the mattress. "What's this?" I ask, snatching and unrolling it.

I stare unblinking at what's revealed.

Talia sits up. "Remember how I told you my period was late, and that it was probably due to all the stress from my speaking schedule and the book release coming up?"

I nod, still staring at the tiny white bean in a sea of murky black.

A star in the night.

A light in the dark.

Talia grabs my arm. "Say something."

"We're having a baby?"

I don't recognize my own voice.

"Yes," she says crisply, "but I'm suddenly more concerned you're having a stroke."

"A baby," I whisper. "Our baby."

I finally look up. When she sees my awe and joy, tears fill her eyes. Her smile is brighter than the dawn.

Pulling her into my arms, I kiss every inch of her face until she's laughing and I'm laughing.

We cry, too.

Then we celebrate so enthusiastically the bed breaks. The thunderous crack brings a panicked Sven running into our bungalow with a knife in his hand. He skids to a stop at the sight of me, a brand-new expression on his face: unmitigated shock.

I wiggle my fingers in the restraints securing my wrists to the sagging headboard. "A little help, buddy?"

A bell-like giggle sounds from somewhere under a mountain of sheets and pillows.

Sven does an about-face and marches out the door.

BONUS EPILOGUE

EXCERPT FROM

MIND OF MAGIC:
A BIOGRAPHY OF KIERAN HAYES

BY ISLA HAYES

Kieran Hayes and Dr. Talia Stirling were married that summer in the backyard of their Malibu home. The intimate ceremony was officiated by the groom's father, Cian Hayes. Talia was escorted down a flower-strewn aisle by Sven Akerman and longtime friend, Dr. Leo Chastain.

No photographs of the event were released to the press, but for months afterward, rumors circulated about the wedding. Contrary to the tabloids, no orgy took place, nor did Talia lead Kieran down the aisle on a leash. Professional dominatrix Charlie Rhodes was later quoted saying the wedding and reception were, "dreadfully vanilla and exceedingly romantic."

The ceremony was a traditional Irish handfasting. The braid of ribbons used to bind the couple's hands and wrists is now a treasured heirloom of their four children.

For their vows, they knelt facing each other.

The couple both wore white.

THE END

Playlist

"Blur"—MØ, Foster the People

"Young & Unafraid"—The Moth & The Flame

"Game"—Mating Ritual

"Hummingbird"—Run River North

"Heat"—L.A. Rose

"Free Animal"—Foreign Air

"Fire Breather"—LAUREL

"Good Luck"—Broken Bells

"Dirty Mind"—Boy Epic

and more...

Listen on Spotify:

WHAT TO READ NEXT

The Dark Before Light is a crossover novel between my Vision Series and *The Fall Before Flight*. Some of the side characters mentioned have their own love stories.

The Fall Before Flight
Mia and Leo -
Patient/Therapist Romance

Double Vision
Liam, "the crazy Dubliner"
Romantic Suspense/BDSM

Perfect Vision
Dominic and London
Romantic Suspense/BDSM

The Illusions Duet
Deirdre, Nate's sister
Dark Romantic Suspense

Acknowledgments

Numerous people made this book possible. First and foremost, thank you to my beta readers: Heather, Paramita, Dawn, Amanda, Leti, and Danielle—and my illustrious editor, Emily Lawrence. You helped me turn a rough gemstone into a glittering black diamond.

Heather and Paramita, your professional backgrounds and experience were especially appreciated. Talia was one of the most rewarding and challenging FMCs I've ever written—I'm so grateful for your understanding of her neurodivergence/IQ/EQ and your help tweaking parts of the story to honor her unique personality.

To Maisie, Brit, Nichole, and Shan, thank you for lifting me up when I'm in the weeds and making me laugh on the daily.

Shan, you wanted butt-stuff—you got butt-stuff. Thank you (and you're welcome). ::wink:: On that note, special thanks to Ryan, who was kind enough to sensitivity-read the scene where Talia dominates Kieran.

To the usual suspects who keep my head above water:
Lacee, Lauren, Jessica, Sydney, Molly, Megan, Mom, and
Dave. To my beautiful daughter, Stella, thank you for being
proud of me. In nine more years, you can read my books.
Actually... better make it fifteen.

Last but not least, thank you to the readers and bloggers
who share and recommend my books. If not for you, I
might have given up years ago.

Xo,
    Laura

Also by L.M. Halloran

FORBIDDEN ROMANCE

The Dark Before Light

The Fall Before Flight

The Muse

ROCKSTAR ROMANCE

Breaking Giants

Breaking Silence

Loving Wild (2025)

SMALL TOWN

Room for Us

Time for Us

DARK ROMANTIC SUSPENSE

Double Vision

Perfect Vision

The Golden Hour

Art of Sin *(Illusions Duet #1)*

Sin of Love *(Illusions Duet #2)*

About the Author

When not writing or reading, the author can be found chasing her daughter. Some of her favorite things are puzzles, podcasts, and small dogs that resemble Ewoks.

Home is the Pacific Northwest.

lmhalloran.com

facebook.com/lmhalloran

instagram.com/lm.halloran

tiktok.com/@lmhalloran

pinterest.com/lmhalloranauthor

bookbub.com/authors/l-m-halloran

amazon.com/author/lmhalloran